I0627611

THE MOST UNLIKELY LADY

BARBARA DEVLIN

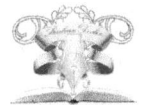

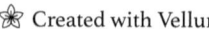 Created with Vellum

DEDICATION

This book is dedicated to my little sister Carla Castillo, who, much like the heroine of this story, always marches to the beat of her own drummer. Carla, you are fun and fearless, and you have a heart of gold.
To my father, Eddie. Thank you, Dad, for loving me unconditionally.

PROLOGUE

The Ascendants
England
The Year of Our Lord, 1313

"*J* have a daughter." The stars mocked Arucard as he gazed at the night sky, and his brother knights, the last surviving Templar mariners and first members of the Brethren of the Coast, a fledgling order formed by Edward II, remained conspicuously silent. Since his marriage, he had received one command from the King, to produce a suitable heir, and in that he had failed. Swallowing his disappointment, he scratched his head, kicked a small stone, and sighed.

"Commiserations, brother." Demetrius frowned and handed Arucard a flagon of ale. "How is Isolde taking it?"

"She must be devastated," added Morgan.

"Inconsolable, I imagine." Geoffrey poured two more tankards, passed one to Aristide, and set the pitcher on the bench.

"Well, her reaction has been quite curious." Propping

an elbow on his thigh, Arucard rested his chin in his palm. "She seems—"

"Hysterical?" Aristide shook his head. "Poor thing. Must be disconsolate."

"On the contrary, my wife is overjoyed." Arucard gazed at his fellow Nautionnier Knights and grimaced. "And I am at a loss to understand her response."

"Perhaps reality has yet to set in." Morgan offered a reassuring pat on the back. "I mean, she carried the babe in her womb for nine months, only to discover it was not a boy. It cannot be easy for her."

"All that labor for naught." Demetrius clucked his tongue. "But Isolde is still young. You have many opportunities to succeed."

"And a girl can be of some use," said Geoffrey, although he appeared pressed to explain his assertion.

"Oh, really?" Arucard arched a brow. "How so?"

Morgan snapped his fingers. "They cook."

"They clean," chimed Aristide.

Painful silence hung in the air.

Seconds ticked past.

His fellow knights shared discomfiting glances.

"They sew," offered Demetrius.

"Wonderful." Arucard slumped forward. "I have produced a future serving wench."

"Now, wait a minute." Aristide stood. "There are many benefits to be had in the fairer sex."

"Name one." Arucard narrowed his stare.

"They are quite lovely to admire," replied Aristide.

"As is green water when it washes over the rail, but it is never a good sign when you are at sea," countered Arucard.

"How can you compare your daughter to green water?" Geoffrey shrugged. "What harm can she do?"

"Precisely." Demetrius took a healthy swig of ale. "Now, boys, on the other hand, are a world of trouble."

"Exactly." Morgan slapped a palm to his thigh. "Boys are always more difficult than girls, because boys must be educated. You would have to teach him how to handle a sword."

"And any son of yours must learn to sail," said Aristide, to a chorus of agreement that rustled a bird from a nearby perch.

"He would have to know how to fish. Think of the demands on your time." Demetrius pointed in emphasis. "A daughter is Isolde's responsibility. What have you to share with a girl?"

"Brothers, you have eased the weight of my burden." Arucard emptied his tankard. "Because you are right, and a daughter can be a blessing in disguise. I mean, what trouble could she cause?"

CHAPTER ONE

The Descendants
London
April, 1812

For most young women, attracting a man was as simple as breathing. Inhale. Exhale. A reflex action executed with little or no effort.

Simple.

But Sabrina Douglas considered courting something more akin to having a tooth extracted. Necessary, if she wished to marry, but painful—downright agonizing.

Standing in the entranceway of Hawthorn Hall, she craned her neck and surveyed the crush. Her intended target Lord Everett Markham, dark, dangerous, and devastatingly handsome, stood amid a crowd of rakes. He glanced up, and she was certain he spied her.

"Sabrina, your wrap," her father prompted.

As she gave her cloak to the footman, she kept her eyes averted. Everett fast approached their group, and she fought the urge to assess his reaction when he saw her—the new Sabrina—for the first time.

Yes, that was the moment for which she had been waiting.

The reason she had allowed herself to be poked and prodded while she was fitted for new gowns. The reason she had passed the morning with a gooey beauty potion slathered over her cheeks. The reason she bit her tongue while that fussy Frenchman cut her hair. Did the tight curls framing her face seem as ridiculous as she thought they appeared? Cara, her older sister and Miss Perfect, assured Sabrina that she had never looked lovelier.

Indeed, that singular fragment of time was why she had spent the better part of winter walking up and down the stairs of their country manor, while balancing a book on her head. And with all that practice she still could not descend a flight of stairs without dropping the blasted old tome. As a soldier heading into battle, she had prepared herself for the start of the Season.

Everett shook hands with her father, Admiral Mark Douglas. He bowed before her mother, Lady Amanda, and Cara.

Sabrina was next.

What had Cara said? *Stare at your feet, and pretend not to notice him. Just stand there, looking like you do not care.*

That advice had been a mistake.

It reminded her of the daring, low-cut bodice of her gown, and telltale warmth flooded her cheeks. The dressmaker assured Sabrina the emerald silk contrasted nicely with her raven hair and cerulean eyes. She hoped the bloody woman was right.

"Miss Douglas." Everett swept her an elegant bow.

With feigned surprise, Sabrina smiled. "Lord

Markham." Was her voice too high pitched? "How wonderful it is to see you again." He quirked his brows at her greeting, and she suppressed a shiver as he took her gloved hand and raised it to his lips.

"May I compliment your sense of fashion?" His gaze scrutinized her from head to foot, and she wanted to run for the hills. "Daresay I almost did not recognize you."

Anticipation licked at her nerves, and she peered into the crowd, attempting to appear disinterested. "Perhaps I am not the woman you thought I was, my lord."

"Perhaps not." His voice was as thick as the beauty muck she had smeared on her face as he held out his arm. "Would you allow me the honor of escorting you?"

"I suppose you will do." Her heart beat wildly in her chest when he chuckled at her response, and she reconsidered her plan.

"You know, I expected no less than a saucy reply, and you did not disappoint me." Everett shot her a boyish grin. "I wondered if your outward transformation had an impact on your charming personality. But to my relief, you seem to be in fine form."

"I am not sure if you are complimenting or insulting me, Lord Markham." Sabrina lifted her chin and fixed her stare on the back of her sister's head. "And I know of no such transformation. I merely made additions to my wardrobe during the summer."

"And you have restyled your hair." He quirked his brows. "Oh, my, are you wearing rouge?"

"I have done nothing of the sort." She lied. "And my personal habits are none of your affair. If you do not cease your mindless prattle, I shall trounce your toes."

"Relax, my dear. I merely took note of the changes in your appearance. I thought all young ladies lived in hope of such praise," he teased. "And, if memory serves, you will trounce my toes regardless of intent."

"Now you are insulting me." In that instant, Sabrina quit the field. Her short-lived campaign to catch a husband at an end, she resolved to contract the plague and die at the first opportunity.

"Stating a fact, my dear. So you deny the renovations to your person?" The insufferable man had the nerve to wink. "If that is your story, Miss Douglas, you stay with it."

They navigated the throng until they came to an arched opening. Couples whirled on the polished marble floor, beneath elegant crystal chandeliers. Vases filled with a wild mix of hyacinths, tulips, and white roses stood on pedestals in every corner, and their subtle bouquet hung in the air. A musical ensemble occupied the center of the back wall of the luxurious mirrored ballroom.

Conscious of the multitude stares in their direction, Sabrina inhaled deeply. She had not anticipated the attention her unconventional campaign would attract and, given her less than stellar social performances in the past, she was unaccustomed to the limelight.

"Shall we dance?" he inquired, with a squeeze of her hand.

"O—I mean—yes. That is, it would be my honor, Lord Markham." It was hell being a lady.

Biting her lip and swallowing an unladylike curse, she followed his lead to the dance floor, sucking in a breath as his arm encircled her waist, pulling her close to his sinewy frame. Her ears pealed with excitement, as the bells in a Wren steeple, and fire coursed her veins, as every nerve charged.

What had happened to her?

As casual acquaintances, Sabrina had danced with

Everett on many occasions and had often teased him, as would a distant relative. For his part, he always seemed disinterested, so that time could be no different.

But it was different.

Deep down inside, where she was always brutally honest with herself, she had to admit there was something drastically unfamiliar and enticing in the way he held her. How his arm anchored her near as they twirled to the soft beat of the music, and the way his thighs brushed her skirts. And whereas before he would stare at the crowd from over her head, searching for a new ladybird, no doubt, his amber eyes now captured hers. Sabrina stumbled and stepped hard on his foot.

"Ouch." His brow creased.

"So sorry, Lord Markham." She was supposed to be charming, alluring, and seductive. At least, that was the advice Cara had given. But, true to form, she was a poor excuse for her sex, and Sabrina lowered her head in defeat.

"Tell me, my dear Miss Douglas, has anyone ever mistaken you for a lady?"

In an instant, she lifted her chin. "No more than have mistaken you for a gentleman."

"Well said, my dear." He laughed, and she realized he had deliberately baited her.

How many times had Everett taunted her with the same insult, and why could she not resist him? Because she had not wanted to resist—a fact of which she suspected he was well aware.

"You, sir, are a devil." She smiled and lost her footing once more.

"Oomph." Everett winced. "Tell me you are not doing that on purpose."

"Certainly not." She chucked his shoulder and focused on their dance. "I am clumsy by nature, as you well know."

When the music ended, Everett escorted Sabrina to her group of friends.

"What are you so smug about?" Cara whispered in her ear, moments later. "Having some success?"

Sabrina clenched her fists as Everett circled the dance floor with yet another beauty in his embrace. The man must have Herculean vigor, and again she wondered if she could compete in his league. Although she hated to admit it, she wanted to be the one for him—not the one of many.

"Well, we have danced twice." She frowned. "I suppose it would not be prudent to risk a third." In silence, she counted the Brethren of the Coast, her lifelong friends, as they made rotations with various partners. Then she realized she had not seen Everett go by, and in a second, she scoured the room.

Near the terrace doors, she spotted her connubial conquest as he reached into his waistcoat pocket and checked his timepiece. With a glance left and then right, he backed through the doors and slipped into the darkness beyond.

What was he about?

"It is dreadfully warm in here." Sabrina fanned herself with her hand, exaggerating her movements. "I believe I will step outside for a bit of fresh air."

"Do you want me to come with you?" Cara asked.

"No." She shook her head, as she required no additional witnesses to what could be grave humiliation. "I will only be a moment."

With a casual pace, though fighting the urge to charge forth, she strolled to the same exit through which Everett had disappeared. Sabrina stepped quietly onto the tiled floor, so as not to disturb the laconic rendezvous inhabiting the shadows. As she navigated the gardens, a wicked thought crossed her mind. Perhaps tonight she would kiss Everett. Or was the man supposed to initiate such behavior? On the thought, gooseflesh covered her from head to foot, and she wrapped her arms about herself.

A graveled path led to the opening of a meticulously groomed labyrinth. The lilting singsong of lovers mingled with the crunch of pebbles beneath her slippers, and she shivered, though she knew not why.

Oh, where could Everett have gone?

Was he not supposed to be chasing her? And then Sabrina homed in on his voice, smooth as well-churned butter, coming from the labyrinth. As she stood beneath the entrance to the maze, a pergola covered in pink climbing roses, she focused on his rich baritone, letting it guide her through the manicured hedges. Sabrina veered left, then right, and then left again.

To whom was he talking?

Another turn brought her to a small opening and what appeared to be a dead-end. A flirty feminine laugh brought her up short.

The silvery light of the moon cast the silhouettes of her prince charming and a mystery woman in a clearing. With arms entwined, there was no possibility theirs was a family reunion. And Everett had never hugged Sabrina like that.

"Darling, why so reticent?" The strange lady kissed Everett, and a familiar giggle tickled Sabrina's ears. "Surely you are not interested in that gawky Douglas girl? What you need is a real woman."

She flinched at the inference and at once recognized the voice. The enemy was none other than Lady Moreton, a petite young widow, who was everything Sabrina was not, and she drew his head to her again.

No.

She wanted to cry out, to rush in, to part the lovers and halt their play, but she could not, because Everett was not hers to claim.

He never had been hers.

Her brief but ill-fated campaign had been a lark, because Everett was truly out of her league. With a heavy heart, Sabrina took one last look at the man for which she had set her cap and tiptoed away.

IT WAS at that very moment Everett broke the kiss and gazed in horror as Sabrina fled. Setting the lovely widow aside, he cleared his throat and tugged at the lace trim of his sleeves.

"It would appear, my lady, that I have acquired a fond-ness for gawky women. You may consider this an end to our arrangement and feel free to plant your affections else-where," he said, offering a dutiful bow.

"Arrogant bastard." Lady Moreton snickered. "I can name ten men who would kill to have me—and they have titles."

The virago had pricked his Achilles heel, and Everett suddenly wondered what had attracted him to her in the first place. As she stormed off in a huff, he headed in the opposite direction.

For all of the last ten minutes he had tried to convince himself he could ignore the inimitable Miss Sabrina Douglas. His jaw had almost hit the floor when he first set eyes on her in the foyer. But when she removed her cloak, he was positive lightning had struck his gut. He could not get over the change in her appearance. Although they had done nothing more than dance, his blood still boiled after holding her in his arms.

They had not met since the last assembly of the Little Season. Thereafter, she had retired to the country for the holidays. The woman who had returned to London sounded like Sabrina, and acted like Sabrina, but had most definitely not looked like Sabrina. The jewel-toned dress encasing her body was a siren song of sensuous femininity, which was a drastic departure from the plain, immature, and unflattering styles she usually favored.

What man could resist her?

Certainly, not him—not that he ever could. Her frank honesty bordered on the improper and always delighted him, because with her there was no façade. Sabrina was genuine, and amid the various gems of society, he believed she was a diamond of the first water that he had grossly overlooked and neglected.

Winding his way through the complex network of greenery, Everett paused and subsequently apologized to the couples he disturbed. He veered left, then right, and then left again.

Where could Sabrina have gone?

Everett had not realized that he was searching for a wife when he arrived at the evening gala, but he was smart enough not to pass on a golden opportunity when it so readily pounced on his feet.

Sabrina Douglas wanted him.

The second son.

A man with a fortune but no title.

How many women had turned their noses to him and sneered, *I never dance with younger sons*. Of course, as the boy grew into the man, and the man amassed a treasure in the transatlantic timber trade, his prospects as a suitor suddenly seemed more appealing.

To everyone but Everett.

And then one witty, somewhat unconventional woman danced, or rather tripped, into his staid existence. She waltzed on his toes, swore like a sailor, and ate twice the amount of any man in the room. She laughed at his jokes, elbowed him in the ribs when his teasing grew illicit, but above all, she accepted him—just as he was, and her sincere appreciation had somehow escaped him.

Until now.

"Excuse me," said an obviously perturbed male from the shadows.

"I beg your pardon," Everett replied, as he interrupted another tryst. "Please, carry on."

How extensive was the bloody maze?

Just as he was about to abandon his search, a feminine sniffle caught his trained ear. Peering into a hedged rose garden, he found the object of his quest, sitting on a small stone bench.

"What were you thinking?" she asked, eyes looking to the heavens.

Perplexed by her query, Everett paused, glanced around, and discerned they were alone.

"To think I could ever attract a man like that." Sabrina shook her head and emitted a soft sob. "I must have been out of my mind."

So her transformation was for his benefit. Conscious of his surroundings, he compressed his lips and folded his arms with nary a sound so as not to disrupt her.

"Why, he is prettier than I am, and he could have any woman." She snorted. "I must have been daft to think he could ever want me."

A tremor of surprise shivered down his spine, and he bit his tongue against a ripple of laughter, because her unintended confession was a treasure not to be missed.

"Why would any man ever want to marry such a woman?" She sighed, and her shoulders drooped.

Her despair, her defeat, scored a direct hit, and Everett could take no more. "That is quite a compliment, my dear, but wholly inaccurate, I assure you."

She spun, shock evident in her features as he emerged from the shadows. "How did you find me, and why are you here?"

"Darling Sabrina," he purred as he strolled in a circle about the bench, eyes pinning hers.

Averting her stare, she wiped tears from her cheeks, and he cursed himself for making her cry. "It is Miss Douglas to you."

"Oh?" He chuckled at her haughty demeanor. "Since when have we become so formal?"

"We have never been informal, Lord Markham," she replied, cold and impersonal.

"And you wish to marry a man with whom you have never been informal?"

She snapped to attention. "Who said I wanted to marry you?"

Rounding the bench, Everett stalked Sabrina, as a lion would hunt its prey. "You did, my dear."

"I did no such thing." She humphed. "I made polite conversation."

"With yourself?" He wrinkled his nose.

"Indeed." She pouted and shrugged. "People talk to themselves all the time."

"I see." He lowered his chin, but he believed her not for a second. "So you do not want to marry me?"

"I did not say that."

"So you do want to marry me?"

Sabrina bit her lip. "I did not say that, either."

"Then what do you want to do with me?" Brows arched, he hinted at something more illicit than a betrothal and could only hope she took the bait.

"I do not...that is to say...oh, blast." She stared at her feet, which left her unguarded.

And Everett made his move.

Straddling the bench, he grasped her by the waist and hauled her against him.

Venting a plaintive cry, she pressed her palms to his chest. "Lord Markham, what are you doing?"

"I thought it obvious, my dear." He smiled as he prepared to conquer his prize. "I am going to kiss you."

Her eyes grew wide. "Everett, no—"

There was no time for protest as he enfolded her in his arms and set his mouth to hers. Their lips moved in concert, slowly at first, but quickly reached a fevered pace that could rival a Hungarian dance. Hands that were once pushing him away inched to his shoulders and squeezed, and Sabrina moaned low in her throat.

With gentleness and patience that should qualify him for sainthood, he prodded her with his tongue, begging a sultry dance with hers. After a few frustrating seconds, she twined her fingers in his hair, pulled him impossibly closer, arched into his embrace, parted her sumptuous flesh, and came at him with a hunger to match his own. The woman was temptation personified, and Everett shuddered.

God, she was sweet.

The next moan was his.

Fire raged in his loins, as had a rampant erection. How he wanted to let go the reins of lust and ride wild inside her, but he could not. He would do the honorable thing and marry her first, and then he would have his way with her— every morning, noon, and night for the rest of their lives.

After a few desperately heated, groping minutes, they separated.

Stunned by the power of their voracious kiss, Everett sat stone still as he struggled to maintain control of his desires and regain his composure. Hanging on by mere threads, he dared not move for fear he might topple Sabrina onto her back and take her in front of God and everyone.

An obvious innocent, with a countenance of unutterable shock and mouth agape, Sabrina simply stared at him. Her breath came in a rush of pants, as she balled her right hand into a fist. Everett saw the punch coming but had not paid it much heed because she was, after all, only a woman.

That was his last coherent thought as he fell, unconscious, on top of her.

"GET OFF ME, YOU OAFISH CLOD." Sabrina had not realized she was shouting as she squirmed beneath Everett's large frame. Nor had she given any regard to the multitude of whispers growing in number until it was too late.

Lady Cowper's shrill scream was the first hint of the audience that had amassed in the opening of the tiny rose garden.

Sabrina froze. "Bloody hell."

While everyone gathered was more than willing to watch her struggle with Everett's weight, no one stepped forward to aid her.

No one, that is, except her father.

"What in the devil is going on here?" Her sire stomped

into the garden and dragged Everett's limp form from atop her. "Lord Markham, I demand—" He blinked owlishly. "Great heavens, he's out cold." He trapped her gaze. "Sabrina Francis, why is this man unconscious?"

Oh, dear.

Was it too late to plead insanity?

Perhaps she could play the ignorant.

She was sitting in the maze, minding her own business, and had no idea how the man came to be on her. Or she could claim that he had dropped from the sky. Then, an even better story came to mind; one that she was positive would save her posterior.

"I tripped and fell beneath Lord Markham," she declared with gumption. "In the process, Everett swooned."

"Sabrina!"

"Well." She winced. "You have to admit it was one of my better excuses."

"Young lady, I am waiting." Her father tapped his foot in a telltale rhythm, which conveyed the depth of her predicament and portended a sound lashing.

"Well, all right." With nervous agitation, she shuffled her feet. "I hit him."

For a brief respite, her father glanced at the night sky before refocusing his ire on her. "Why did you do that?" He narrowed his stare. "Was Lord Markham making improper advances on your person?"

"Good gracious, no." She held a hand to her throat. "Lord Markham is a perfect gentleman."

In a flash, she grimaced, because the words were spoken as Sabrina realized she had left herself without a justifiable excuse for her behavior. Whatever was she going to do now? "Papa, I can explain."

He shifted his weight. "You had better, or I will kill this man."

Her mind raced in numerous directions in an effort to save Everett. After all, she could not marry a corpse. At that moment, her prize mumbled. His eyelids fluttered, and Everett rubbed his jaw as if she had hurt him.

"What happened?" He gazed, with an expression she would characterize as dazed and confused, into her sire's angry eyes.

To wit her father groaned. "Young man, that is precisely what I wish to know."

CHAPTER TWO

The following morning, as she stood before the door to her father's study, Sabrina took one last assessment of her attire. The pale blue sprig muslin dress was Cara's choice, not Sabrina's. She would have preferred to face her father and Everett in breeches and boots, with her trusty foil strapped to her side. Taking a deep breath, and uttering a last prayer for the health and welfare of her posterior, she knocked once and charged forth.

Her father perched behind his imposing desk, his hands folded and rested, neat and calm, in his lap. It was an illusion—one that did not fool Sabrina.

Her mother, the co-prosecutor, occupied a seat beside Sabrina's father.

So she was to face the inquisition—what else was new?

Everett sat in a high-back chair before the desk, with an empty mate that had been relocated for the occasion. Looking quite pale, he stood as she entered the room.

"Mama. Papa." Slowly, she curtseyed. "Lord Markham."

"Come in, my dear." Her sire rose. "Have a seat."

As she took her place, Sabrina reminded herself of her plan.

Her father was angry, and of that she had no doubt. He would insist Everett marry her, to wit she would refuse, not that she had not wanted to marry him; she just had not wanted to appear a charity case. No, she would let her father force the marriage and, by default, she would wed the man of her choosing. And though she was certain Everett loved her not, in time, she would win his heart.

"Sabrina!"

She flinched. "Yes, Papa?"

He sighed, a weighty affectation often associated with her visits to his study. "I asked you a question."

She shifted with wild anticipation of a glorious future. "Could you repeat it?"

Her father gazed at the ceiling and huffed a breath again. His shoulders seemed to ease when her mother placed her hand on his arm.

"As I stated, Lord Markham has made a gracious offer." Her father rubbed the back of his neck. "What say you, my dear? Do you wish to marry him?"

"While I am conscious of the scandal resulting from the events of last night, I cannot allow Lord Markham to sacrifice himself for my honor. I do not wish to marry him." With bold determination she lifted her chin and cleared her throat. "Indeed, I will not marry him."

The ensuing silence was deafening.

Aware of nothing save the beat of her own heart, Sabrina was very proud of herself. She had delivered her speech as she had prepared it. All she had to do was sit back as her father ranted and raved. He would insist she marry Everett and, as a dutiful daughter should, she would acquiesce, her pride intact.

"You cannot be serious." Everett stared at her, wide-eyed. "Think of the malicious rumors."

"Lord Markham." Her father leaned forward and rested his steepled hands on the blotter. "I love my daughter and value her happiness more than anyone's good opinion, so I stand by her decision. If Sabrina does not wish to marry you, I will not force her."

Sabrina thought she would faint from the shock.

She blinked several times and was afraid she might swoon. And Sabrina Francis Douglas would not swoon. But he had not made sense.

Was that her father?

Why was he not yelling?

Why was he not pounding his fist on the desk?

She knew the routine, had seen it many times for a wide variety of infractions. He was supposed to force her into a betrothal. Whatever was she going to do now?

"I beg your pardon." Everett tugged at his cravat as though he had tied it too tight. "Admiral Douglas, with your permission, I would like to court Sabrina. Perhaps, with gentle persuasion, she would see fit to accept my offer. I am entirely to blame for the situation. Had I not kissed her—"

Oh, dear.

"You kissed her?" Her father bounded out of his seat, and his icy gaze pinned Sabrina to her chair.

She had been hoping that particular piece of information would not present itself. In the face of her sire's fury, she traced the pattern on the fabric-covered armrest.

"Sabrina Francis!"

"Yes, sir?"

His hands settled on his hips, and she knew she was in serious trouble. "Why the devil did you not tell me Lord Markham accosted you?"

"You did not tell him?" She was certain Everett's amber orbs were going to pop out of his skull at any moment. "Why ever not?"

"I forgot." She shrugged. "And he did not accost me. We kissed—that is—he kissed me, and I kissed him."

Her father closed his eyes, pressed a hand to his temple, and shook his head in disbelief. Her mother appeared to be staving off tears, or possibly laughter, she was not sure which. Everett continued to stare at her as if she had sprouted horns. Bother that. A good pair of antlers might be just the thing to keep her halo atop her head.

"Sabrina, are you sure you will not consider Lord Markham's proposal?" her father asked in an uncharacteristically gentle fashion, which frightened her a vast deal more than his shouts in anger.

She bit her bottom lip. If she would not change her tack, she could lose Everett, forever. What mattered more, a measure of pride or the man for which she had set her cap? Faced with such dire circumstances, the solution, when it came to her, was obvious.

"I believe Lord Markham asked permission to court me, and I would be amenable to such a proposition, Papa." She peered at Everett. Was that relief in his countenance?

Her father studied her as if she was a priceless portrait, and for some reason she could not fathom, she wanted to cry. "Are you certain, my dear?"

"Yes, Papa." For good or ill, she nodded once. "Lord Markham may court me."

Two days later, with a large bouquet of roses in hand, Everett bounded up the entrance stairs to 24 Upper Brook

Street. After gaining admittance to the home of his lady, he waited with baited breath in the fashionable drawing room.

Ever since the night in the maze, when he had stolen a kiss from Sabrina, his life had been a whirlwind of emotions. He still could not believe Admiral Douglas had not insisted Everett marry Sabrina.

He had ventured to her residence, expecting her father to hurl a slew of curses on his head, and the admiral had not disappointed Everett, in that respect. Afterward, he was fully prepared to offer for her. The admiral would then threaten Everett with death if he would not marry the awkward debutante. He could spare his dignity and spend the rest of his days with the woman, laughing all the way.

That had not happened.

Instead, the man supported his daughter's refusal of his proposal.

Who would have thought it?

He supposed a gentleman would have accepted her rejection. And prior to that night, he might have. But Everett could not, would not. Not now.

Not after that amazing kiss.

So, faced with the prospect of losing her, he had done the only thing possible. He had requested permission to court his most unlikely lady. Of course, he had not doubted his ability to win her. Attracting the fairer sex had never been a problem. But one single fact nagged his conscience.

Sabrina had refused his proposal.

Prior to the meeting in the admiral's study, Everett would have sworn she was indifferent to his lack of title. The quirky Miss Douglas seemed unconcerned with social status and rank among the *ton*. Could he have been wrong? Was her new hairstyle and flattering attire an attempt to ensnare a better prospect?

For that reason, Everett had never felt more uncertain—or unworthy—in his life.

The previous day had been spent purchasing various objects of affection, all intended to declare his suit. Today was only the beginning. To mark the special occasion, he had chosen red roses, the bloom of love, for the commencement of their courtship. As would any other female, Sabrina would fuss and preen, and perhaps express her gratitude in the currency he cherished most. At the thought, he smiled.

"Lord Markham." She curtseyed.

Ah, there she stood. He held the bouquet behind his back. "Hello, my dear. As I have secured permission to court you, you must call me Everett. May I address you as Sabrina?"

"You may." She narrowed her stare. "What are you hiding from me?"

"I can see I will never be able to pull the wool over your eyes." He chuckled, straightened his back, and presented her with an offering to her beauty. "These are for you."

"Oh?" Sabrina studied the fragrant flowers. "It is not my birthday."

"My dear, they are a gift." Waiting for acknowledgement, he shifted his weight, and his smug, self-satisfied confidence faltered. "Do I need an excuse to give you something which might bring a smile to your lovely face?"

"I suppose not." Turning the bouquet in her grasp, she looked at him as if he had spoken some long dead language she could not comprehend. "But whatever am I to do with them?"

As if on cue in a romantic comedy of errors, Cara, holding a cut-glass vase filled with water, entered the room. Without a word, she approached her younger sister, took the roses, placed them in the vase, and set them on a nearby table.

Everett remained stock still until the elder Douglas exited. Sabrina cleared her throat. He stared at her from the corner of his eye. She seemed to find the hem of her sleeve infinitely fascinating. He clasped his hands behind his back. She shuffled her feet.

Bloody hell, they were getting nowhere.

He searched his mind for an explanation to make sense of her reticence, but he thought his course reasonable and sound. "Sabrina?"

"Yes?" She peered at him through her lashes.

Everett inclined his head. "Do you like the flowers?"

"They are very nice." She rocked in place.

Yet she seemed displeased. "But—"

"They must have cost a fortune." She walked to the table and stroked a delicate bud. "And I do not require such frippery."

"What does that matter?" Thoroughly befuddled by her utter lack of response, he grasped at the slightest clue to decipher her demeanor and followed in her steps. "It is only money."

"Perhaps." She frowned. "But you could have purchased an armload of daisies for much less."

"Is this a discussion on economy?" With a finger, he tipped her chin, bringing her gaze to his. "Or are you trying to tell me you prefer daisies to roses?"

"I am sorry." Sabrina swallowed hard. "But I do so love daisies."

"Duly noted." With a roll of his shoulders, Everett relaxed. Her displeasure with his first gift had nothing to do with rejection and everything to do with personal preference. "From now on, I shall bring you daisies."

"I must sound rather churlish." Her brow a mass of furrows, she cast him a precious pout. "Are you angry with me?"

The urge to feast on her rosy lips was compelling, but he managed to stay his course and settled for a subtle trace of her cheek with his finger. "No."

"Why are you courting me?" Sabrina asked in a small voice and then closed her eyes.

Everett was positive he had just been punched in the gut. Letting his hand fall to his side, he turned and clenched his jaw.

Could he tell her the truth?

That their union would set his parents on end? Indeed, Sabrina was just the sort of woman his mother would reject as a suitable wife for her youngest son. And that fact, alone, made his chosen bride-to-be all the more irresistible.

But there was something else.

He had noted a mysterious, altogether unique quality in her, evoking fond memories he could not quite place, from when first they met. Although they had conspired to bring two friends together, it was he who had lost his wits. Unlike most women, she had never fallen at his feet or been an easy mark. No, she mocked him at every opportunity, and he adored her for it.

In short, she made him laugh.

But would she mock his admission of admiration?

Everett adopted what he hoped was a cocky grin and faced his most unlikely lady. "Because it is what I wish."

"Why?" Her beautiful features were invested with confusion and a mystical essence that defied recognition.

"Does it matter?" As he seized on the perfect rejoinder guaranteed to get their encounter back on track, he shrugged in an attempt to appear nonchalant. "Suffice it to

say you will, one day, be my wife. Get used to the idea, my
dear. I will be your lord and master."

"Lord and master?" Her eyes flared—just as he had
known they would. "You forget yourself, sir. I submit to no
man."

"You will submit to me." Everett smiled with devilish
delight. How he loved rankling her. "It will make the taking
of you all the sweeter, my saucy Sabrina."

"I am not your Sabrina." She pressed a palm to her
bosom. "I am my own person."

With a chuckle, he raised a hand and caught her other
fist, mid-air. "My dear, you really must curb your propensity
for violence."

"Ooh!" Sabrina wrenched free. "Get out!"

Everett strolled to the door, laughing all the way. "I will
be back," he said over his shoulder.

HER DRESS WAS the epitome of femininity, which left
Sabrina feeling quite naked. Gowned in crimson, with her
raven hair piled in loose curls atop her head, she chewed
her lower lip. It was a nervous habit her mother had long
bemoaned and one Sabrina could not break. But she could
not help herself, because she was certain her suitor would
think she had worn the dress for his benefit, a point of fact
she would deny until her last breath should anyone ask.

Determined to portray an air of unperturbed aloofness,
she could not help peering at Everett from the corner of her
eye. Had he found her attractive? Was that why he wanted
to marry her? His bold declaration in the drawing room had
both stunned and infuriated her—until that morning.

When the daisies arrived.

Every hour, on the hour, the bell sounded. An army of deliverymen, bearing armfuls of daisies in every conceivable color, appeared at her doorstep. By noon, the staff ran out of vases and had resorted to using pitchers from the kitchen, and her bedchamber resembled a hothouse.

The Netherton ball was the first major event of the Season, and the *ton* turned out *en masse* for the fete, as had the Brethren of the Coast. They were five men who served the Royal Navy in silence, and five women who stood by their side in greater secrecy, from five noble families. Long ago, on a moonlit night, they had gathered to pledge an oath of fellowship; and their childhood vow had stood the test of time.

Recently, two had married. Lady Caroline Elliott had wed Trevor Marshall, Earl of Lockwood. And last year, Dirk Randolph, Viscount Wainsbrough, married Lady Rebecca Wentworth, as was. If Sabrina had her way, she would be the third member of the Brethren to tie the knot. And she wondered who would next join the ranks of indentured servitude, as she considered the marital state.

She had been suspicious of Cara's friendship with Lance Prescott, but nothing had come of their liaison, so she discounted such beliefs. And as he was, for all intents and purposes, family, her idea seemed a ridiculous notion. His cousin, Elaine Prescott, had not appeared to set her cap for anyone, in particular. Neither had Damian Seymour or his younger sister Alexandra, Alex for short. Dalton Randolph and Blake Elliott seemed far too popular with the ladies to narrow the field to one.

"You are woolgathering, my *saucy* Sabrina." Everett carried out the 'S,' which gave her gooseflesh.

"I am not." Although she resolved not to look at her

tormentor, she flinched when he expelled his breath to her neck.

"Dance with me." He slipped his arm about her waist, and her knees buckled.

"No." Despite her refusal, he drove her to the dance floor. And then Everett pulled her close, and her skirts brushed his thighs. Together, they whirled.

"May I say you are very beautiful tonight." His voice was smooth as silk.

Sabrina gazed, uncaring, at the throng. "Thank you."

"Dare I ask if you donned this luscious ensemble for my benefit?" Again he teased her, and she ignored the bait.

Yet his question coiled in the pit of her belly, roiling her insides, and a sharp denial tickled the tip of her tongue. But since she doubted she possessed sufficient strength to deliver the rapier retort without embarrassing herself, she settled for silence.

"Will you not face me, my saucy Sabrina?" He chuckled. "Or are you still sulking?"

"I am not sulking." She would not meet his stare, though she felt it, as warm honey enveloped a hot scone. And she cursed herself, because her meek tone belied her conviction. What power had the man wielded to muddle her senses whenever he loomed in her presence?

The music stopped, but they continued to navigate the crowd, and before she knew it, Everett steered her through an opening in a pair of velvet drapes. The black of night enshrouded her, and she blinked. It was a small, private balcony, overlooking the gardens below. Her wicked lord cornered her against the railing and placed a hand on either side of her.

"You are absolutely succulent in that gown," he purred. "I could nibble on you all night."

"Might I suggest a turkey leg?" She glared at him through the darkness. "It would provide more sustenance."

"But I prefer your lips." The glint of his teeth betrayed his smile, and then he pounced.

Sabrina was going to protest, but his naughty mouth smothered her pitiful complaint. She was going to resist, but somehow her hands became entwined in his hair. She was going to retreat, but instead she charged her errant suitor.

Good heavens, the man could kiss.

"Everett."

Sitting in the reading room at White's, Everett dropped the copy of *The Times* he had perused and stood to welcome his childhood school chum, and the only man he had ever called friend. "Trevor, old boy, how are you?" They shared a vigorous handshake.

"Fine." Trevor Marshall, Earl of Lockwood, commandeered the opposite seat. "Life could not be better."

"You are disgusting." Since Trevor's wedding, he had become unutterably besotted with his wife and new son. In that instant, Everett imagined Sabrina carrying his child, and the mere thought warmed him to his toes. He envisioned her round as a pumpkin, sitting on his lap, as he pressed a palm to her belly and felt their babe moving within her for the first time. He would, no doubt, dote on her shamelessly. Indeed, she would make an excellent mother for his heirs, except he would teach them to dance.

"I do not know to what you refer." Grinning from ear to ear, Trevor propped an elbow on the armrest and rested his chin on his hand. "But my boy is already quite the rapscallion."

"You positively gush, but I am happy for you, really I am. And I was surprised to receive your missive." He considered the shine of his boots, as his feet still smarted from the previous night's foray on the dance floor with his bride-to-be. "Is everything all right? No trouble in connubial paradise, I hope."

"It is Caroline." Trevor frowned. "She asked me to speak with you."

"Oh?" Everett had not appreciated the sound of that singular declaration. "Whatever for?"

"Well, mind you, if it were anyone else, I would not dream of interfering. But I have an affinity for sleeping with my wife." He grimaced. "I do not care for being locked out of my own bedchamber. So here I am."

Arching a brow, Everett smiled. "Spill it, my friend."

"Well, not that it is any of my business." Trevor shifted in his seat. "But she wants to know if you are serious about Sabrina Douglas."

He thought of his most unlikely lady, of the sweet kisses they had shared on the balcony at Netherton House. He could still taste her luscious lips, which had tempted him beyond reason. In his mind, he revisited the shapely curves of her body, when she had pressed herself against him, as a wanton siren, how her unschooled hands reached and groped in desperation, and her sultry moans of pleasure, which had led him to make licentious use of four fingers and a thumb in the wee hours of the morning.

"I do not believe it." Trevor signaled a waiter. "And I need a drink."

"What?" Everett snapped to attention.

"I know that look." Trevor leaned forward and narrowed his stare. "You have it bad."

Beneath such disconcerting scrutiny, he reclined and crossed his legs. Just as fast, he uncrossed his legs and folded his arms. "I have—what?"

"And you deny it." With one finger Trevor pointed, as if preparing to make a grave accusation, and shook his head. "My God, you are taken with Sabrina Douglas. Wait till I tell Caroline."

"You will do no such thing," Everett hissed. "Do you want to ruin the rest of my life? You cannot give a woman that sort of ammunition, regardless of the facts in opposition. I do not care if she is your wife."

"Aha." Trevor grinned. "So you admit it?"

"I admit no such nonsense, but you are sworn to secrecy, in any case." He scowled. "You may tell your lovely, nosy wife I am in earnest. I intend to marry Sabrina, because she makes me laugh, if only I could get our courtship on calm seas."

"What do you mean?" Trevor smirked. "Is she being difficult?"

"I do not think the answer is that simple." Everett rubbed the back of his neck and frowned, because he was still uncertain of his intended's willingness to marry him and was losing sleep over his predicament. "I have sent her flowers, bundles of them, if you must know. I have bought her chocolates, monogrammed stationary, and a set of lace handkerchiefs. Yet none of my gifts have produced the usual reaction. I had to waylay her at the Netherton ball just to sneak a kiss." He slapped his thigh. "The woman is frustrating beyond belief."

"Wait a minute." Trevor stuck his tongue in his cheek. "Are we talking about Sabrina Douglas?"

"The very one." He sneered.

"Stationary and handkerchiefs?" Trevor snickered. "You are using the wrong bait, my friend."

"What?" Everett scooted to the edge of his seat. "I do not understand."

"If you wish to impress Sabrina, try buying her a fishing rod or, better yet, a new foil." Now Trevor had the audacity to laugh. "But beware, she parries like a bloody pirate."

~

"MY LORD, IT IS BEAUTIFUL." Sabrina squealed with delight. With the practiced expertise of a master swordsman, she challenged an imaginary opponent. "*En garde.*"

As his prospective bride executed a series of maneuvers, Everett surmised she could overcome any adversary. And although her reaction met his expectations for a courtship offering, it had not been brought about by the usual inducement. Then he reminded himself that Sabrina was a most unlikely lady.

"I thought, perhaps, I would join you in a light workout." He displayed his foil. "If you are so inclined."

"You wish to fence?" Her eyes sparkled, as if he had just gifted her a diamond necklace or another exceedingly expensive bauble, and she all but bounced with excitement. "With me?"

"Indeed." He nodded once and smiled in earnest. "I understand it is one of your favorite pastimes."

"I will have to change." With uncharacteristic timidity, she bit her lip and shuffled her feet. "But I shall hurry—I promise."

"No worries, love." He chuckled. "I shall await your return."

She turned to leave but, without warning, whirled and launched herself at him, and Everett barely had time to drop his foil. Winding her arms about his neck, Sabrina giggled and showered his face in kisses.

Now that is more like it, he thought.

CHAPTER THREE

*T*wo days later, Everett and Sabrina circled the floor in the drawing room of her home.

"One, two, three—ouch!" Everett closed his eyes and gritted his teeth against the pain. He was certain that crunching in his boot was another broken toe. After tripping through the ballrooms of the *ton* with her the past few nights, it had seemed a good idea to help his lady with her waltzing. Now, with another ache in his foot, he was not too sure of his plan.

"I am sorry, but it is your fault." Sabrina retreated a step and frowned.

"My fault?" He gazed in bewilderment at his bride-to-be. "How can you blame your preference for dancing on my feet on me?"

She rested hands on hips. "You hold me too tight."

He opened his mouth and then clamped it shut.

Was Sabrina so naïve she could not understand that proximity—particularly the closeness partners could achieve without offending those present—was the point in regard to waltzing?

"Why not just carry me?" She gestured, wild and ungraceful, and gave him her back.

"I thought you liked it when I held you tight." Regaining his composure, and feeling quite the devil, Everett smiled. He swaggered near, bent his head, and whispered in her ear, "Do you not enjoy having my arms about you?"

"You are shameless." In a flash, Sabrina whirled, and her forehead collided with his nose. She tamped her fingertips to her brow. "That hurt."

On a groan, he tugged a handkerchief from his waistcoat pocket and pressed it to his offended appendage, which bled profusely. "Are you injured?"

"No—oh, dear. Here, let me help you." Taking him by the elbow, she guided him to sit on the sofa. "Tilt your head back. Good heavens, you are a bleeder." Biting her bottom lip, she giggled.

"I am so glad I could provide you with a bit of entertainment, Miss Douglas." His words might have been terse had the cloth staunching the red flow not filtered them.

"Do not be cross, as I did not know you had come to stand behind me." She offered him a somewhat remorseful grin. "You should not have sneaked up on me." Standing between his outstretched legs, Sabrina leaned forward and set a palm to his cheek. "Are you feeling all right?"

When she brushed the insides of his thighs, sending flames shooting through his loins, Everett clenched his jaw. Before he could do or say anything, she unbuttoned his coat and pushed the wool aside. His future wife edged precariously within reach, and he swallowed hard. Could she not feel the searing heat in his groin?

"Sabrina, you should not tempt me." He summoned unimpassioned thoughts.

"Are you in pain?" Her innocent expression evidenced

she remained oblivious to his condition—and the threat to her own person. "Shall I loosen your cravat?" Bringing a knee within striking distance, she knelt into the cushion of the sofa, nudging the swell of his healthy erection. She jerked her head down and stared, blinking in unmasked fascination.

Everett glanced at the door. If her father were to walk in right then, their ridiculous courtship would cease, and their wedding would, no doubt, take place posthaste at the unfriendly end of a sword. As long as he survived the admiral's initial reaction, Jolly Roger intact.

"It looks awfully big." She appeared awestruck.

"Thank you." He was pleased with her assessment. "I will take that as a compliment."

She inclined her head, as she continued her study of his most male member, from the bulge in his breeches. "I thought they were all small and soft."

He winced, as that was every man's worst nightmare. "I beg your pardon?"

"I meant the ones I have seen—"

"The ones you have seen?" Given her declaration, he was horrified in an instant.

Sabrina retreated to a safe distance, though she proceeded to eye him with unveiled curiosity. "When Cara and I were young, we spied on the boys, with the rest of the girls. Our brothers swam naked in the pond near Pembroke, the Elliott ancestral home. We would sneak into the vicinity and hide in the bushes." Her inquisitive stare was riveted to his crotch. "But theirs were tiny and bounced when they ran."

"Oh, I say." Unable to help himself, Everett burst into laughter. "I would dearly love to tell Blake Elliott and Damian Seymour their manhood has been described as small, soft, and bouncy." In mere seconds, he succumbed to another fit of hilarity.

"Is it always so...angry?" Sabrina shuffled her feet.

Despite his good humor, her interest in the mysteries of his anatomy had not escaped him, and it was an enthusiasm he fully intended to indulge. "It is when I am around you." He pocketed the soiled handkerchief, stood, and walked to her.

Brave and unflinching, not that he expected any less, she faced him. "Does it hurt?"

"Not in the manner you suggest, because it is an ache of a different sort." And how he ached, but Everett smiled. "One I shall have to endure until we are properly wed."

"I have not agreed to marry you." She thrust her chin in an act of open defiance of his statement, but he allowed her a moment of rebellion.

"You will," he said matter-of-factly and caught her before she could flee.

"Let me go." Sabrina braced her hands against his chest and squirmed in his grasp, until she noted the resurging rise of his erection, and then she stilled and peered between their bodies. "Why does it do that?"

"Because I want you, my saucy Sabrina." He cupped her cheek and pinned her gaze. "So how long will you make me wait?"

"Why do you want to marry me?" she inquired in a small voice.

Though Everett should not have been surprised, her directness floored him. Given her propensity for unvarnished honesty, he had thought himself accustomed to her habit, but his ears rang a carillon of shock. To deflect her query and gain a measure of sanity, he pulled her close and rested his head atop hers. A subtle lavender fragrance teased his nostrils and calmed his frazzled nerves. "Does it matter?"

"It does to me." She buried her face in his chest.

"Why?" For a scarce second, he thought her afraid, yet his Sabrina feared nothing. When she wrestled free to meet his stare, he was prepared and tucked in his chin.

"I will not marry a man who does not love me." She grabbed the lapels of his coat. "Mama always says the only reason Papa puts up with her is because he loves her, and if ever a woman needed an indulgent husband, surely it is I."

"Point taken." Once again, as a result of her unique forthrightness, he surrendered to laughter. Never in his life could he recall enjoying such genial levity, and Everett thought such conviviality boded well for their union. Which brought to mind a question he had been longing to pose. "Tell me, my dear, do you love me?"

Atypical shyness encompassed her features, and she shrugged. "I am not sure."

Everett felt as if he had just been poleaxed.

As earlier, it appeared Sabrina remained oblivious to his tremulous state.

"My guts grumble fiercely whenever you are present, and I used to think it was poor digestion." She seemed so calm, as if declaring herself were an every day occurrence. "But I have since determined I would have been long dead for the number of times I have suffered such malady. There is no other explanation, so it must be you."

How he wanted to believe her, wanted to trust that she harbored such sentiment for him, but Sabrina was far too young to recognize real love. So Everett discounted her clumsy admission as a fancy, a girlish crush, and nothing more.

"My dear, yours is a dainty vernacular. We will get on

well, you and I." Propriety be damned, he pulled her impossibly close, and the unholy serpent in his breeches raged. It was unfortunate for him that Sabrina noticed his oh-so-jolly Roger. With nary a bit of reticence, she inched a hand between them. And before he could stop her, she touched him where he wanted it most.

Everett caught her wrist just as she squeezed. It was a dream come true, having her massaging him, her fingers loving him. Even through his buckskin breeches, her untutored attention was heaven—a heaven he had envisioned countless nights.

Intending to halt her exploration, he covered her hand with his but schooled her, instead. Showing her where to linger, where to stroke, and where to caress. Then he dropped his arm to his side and thrilled to her touch, alone. A groan came to him through the sultry haze of pleasure, and Everett realized it was his own.

"It is like stone," Sabrina whispered, with a countenance of inexpressible fascination.

Near to exploding, he halted her play. "You unman me, my dear."

"I apologize, my lord." With another charming pout, she gazed at him. "That was not my intent."

"Oh?" He marveled at her pluck. "What was your intent?"

"I want to know you," quick as a wink she replied. "I wish to make you happy."

"Marry me, and I will teach you more." In that promise Everett would not fail. "I will show you pleasures as you have never known."

"Do you love me?" Unfazed by his bold proclamation, she brought them full circle.

How could he tell her what he could not understand?

Call him a coward, but he sought refuge in an unsportsman-like counterattack. "Will you marry me?"

"I will if you tell me you love me." She fidgeted with the hem of her sleeve.

Everett sighed, because he could not lie to Sabrina, even if he thought her affection true. But since he doubted her ability to develop such depth of emotion at her tender age, he held fast to the defenses protecting his heart. Perhaps one day they would share a deep and abiding commitment, but now was not the time. "I will tell you when you accept my most gracious proposal."

It was a standoff, a test of wills between two people quite evenly matched.

Sabrina humphed and chewed her bottom lip.

He waited with patience that should qualify him for sainthood.

She opened her mouth and then closed it. His fiancée averted her stare and appeared to consider her response. After a moment, she beamed and stuck her tongue in her cheek. "Take me fishing."

"What?" His bride-to-be could not have known it, but she had just struck terror in his heart. Everett abhorred the sport, always had. "You must be joking."

"On the contrary." She rocked on her heels. "I am quite sincere."

~

"So, are you taking her fishing?" Trevor asked, with a touch of amusement in his voice.

"As must needs." Everett glared at his friend, as they shared a private room at White's. "Lord, help me."

"I take it from your reaction that you have never acquired a taste for the sport?" Trevor grinned.

"You know very well I have not." Everett swallowed a healthy gulp of brandy. "I am a hunter, a horseman. I prefer worthwhile endeavors. I have never understood the lure of standing by a cold stream for hours, waiting for some fish to swallow your worm." He grimaced. "Tell me, where is the pleasure in that?"

Of course, what Everett neglected to mention what that fishing had been his father's favorite hobby. And while his sire had been more than happy to take his heir on his afternoon jaunts, Everett had never been included in their trips. Therefore, he had never learned the skill. "Bloody hell, according to many of our set, most fish only nibble on the worm and elude capture entirely."

Trevor burst out laughing, and Everett sank in his chair.

"Double-entendres, old man." What began as a chuckle soon erupted into full-scale jollity, and Trevor slapped his thigh. And just when Lockwood quieted, he pressed a palm to his belly and succumbed to another gale of hilarity. "Oh, I say. There is something to be said for the sensation you get when your favorite fish nibbles your worm."

"Are we not the quick-witted one?" Everett frowned, as he knew only too well to what illicit act his chum referred. "And I am overjoyed to provide for your amusement."

Dirk Randolph entered the room. "Is this a private conversation, or may I join you?"

"Good evening, Wainsbrough." Trevor glanced at Everett, and he nodded his assent. "Will you have a drink?"

"Of course." Dirk unbuttoned his coat and weighed his anchor. "So, what is the topic of choice?"

"Fishing," Trevor interjected before Everett could intervene. "Tell us, do you enjoy the pastime?"

"Aye, indeed I do." Dirk signaled a waiter and then crossed his legs. "It is one of my favorite diversions, second only to my wife."

Trevor smiled, his body shook, and he fell victim to another howling fit.

"What is so funny?" Dirk inquired.

"W-worms," Trevor managed to say between guffaws.

"LORD MARKHAM, YOUR PROPERTY IS STUNNING." Lady Amanda's eyes sparkled, as she admired the landscape. "And so close to London—how fortunate for your future wife."

"Indeed, your daughter will be nearby." Everett smiled smugly, casting Sabrina a triumphant glare. "You may visit whenever you like."

It was a shame Admiral Douglas could not join them for the day. He had hoped to engage the man in a rousing discourse on sailing. Without his future father-in-law, he had no valid excuse to forego the much-dreaded fishing excursion.

Sitting opposite him, his sumptuous target swayed gently with the movement of the carriage, and Lady Amanda occupied the seat beside his intended. He thought Sabrina irresistible in her feminine sprig muslin dress, and a matching bonnet graced her head. Lace framed her ample bosom, a sight from which he struggled to keep his gaze. It was a lilac version of the pink one worn by her sister, who shared his bench. The elder Douglas had, no doubt, attempted to influence her younger sister, and it was an aim he could not dispute, given the outcome.

Daring his bride-to-be to gainsay him, and engage in

another spirited verbal duel, which he had so enjoyed, he added, "Of course, we will spend our summers at Beaumaris, my principal estate."

"I have not agreed to marry you." Sabrina pursed her lips and rolled her eyes in evident frustration.

How he loved ruffling her feathers, and she was an easy mark for his taunts. Summoning years of well-honed self-control, he resisted the urge to stick out his tongue because, knowing Sabrina, she would bite it off. Then again, considering his expertise in the physical realm, he would have her licking at him in no time.

"You will," he replied with an air of indifference. In his mind, he counted to three and braced for impact.

"You dare me to refuse you, my lord." She shifted her weight and stared daggers at him. "I ought to—"

"Sabrina, behave yourself." Lady Amanda sniffed and smoothed her skirts. "I apologize, Lord Markham. My daughter forgets her manners."

"No apologies necessary, Lady Amanda. After all, we are practically family." At that moment, Everett grinned at his now incensed bride-to-be. Oh, she was a veritable spitfire, which required careful handling, as he might get burned. "Come now, my dear Sabrina. Do not frown, as it spoils your lovely face."

After the short carriage ride from London, they took their afternoon repast on the terrace of his estate. It was not a sizable property, as his holdings in Northampton were considerably larger, but it was impressive for a man with no title, and he so wished to impress his prospective in-laws. At long last, he surrendered to Sabrina's wheedling and sent for his man to collect their rods and tackle.

"Are you sure you will not join us?" he asked Lady

Amanda and Cara, praying for any excuse to avoid what promised to be a misadventure of the worst sort.

"Oh, no." Lady Amanda pressed a hand to her throat. "Cara and I do not care for the sport. Sabrina is her father's daughter."

"Well, Sabrina and I do not have to indulge ourselves. If you would prefer, we can fish another time." Though he would deny it if anyone asked, he would prefer to stay there and talk about whatever women talked about than go fishing.

"Bother that." Lady Amanda dismissed him with a casual wave. "No need to stand on formalities. You two enjoy your recreation, and Cara and I shall wait here. Have a wonderful afternoon."

Everett valiantly suppressed a frown. Casting his bride-to-be a brittle smile, as she tapped her foot in an affectation of impatience, he steered her into the copse.

Pebbles crunched beneath their feet, as they strolled down a winding path, which led to the stream at the north end of his property. It was a lengthy walk, and he had expected Sabrina to complain and turn back about halfway through the jaunt. He had been wrong. She trudged forth, with no fuss or grouse, commenting on various trees and wildflowers, as she catalogued the area with lethal accuracy.

Surprising him with her knowledge of herbs and their myriad medicinal qualities, she bubbled with enthusiasm about a seemingly nondescript topic. While he tried to focus his attention on their conversation, he inevitably fell victim to her lush mouth and pink cheeks.

Dew kissed and flushed by the time they neared the stream, Sabrina reached to remove her bonnet, and the bodice of her gown pulled tight across her breasts. In a flash, the old Jolly Roger hoisted his mast with a vengeance. Why could he not resist her?

Salacious images materialized, and he rued the fact that he wanted her, right then and there. He could ease her onto the soft grass and take her alongside the stream. The gentle trickle of water would be the foundation for the sounds of love in a sensuous melody—

"Can I have the bucket of worms?" Sabrina inquired, breaking his reverie.

"Certainly." Everett blinked and swallowed hard. Worms. Would his torment never end? "Be my guest."

In unmitigated horror, he stood paralyzed, as she tugged off her gloves, tossed them to the ground, and plunged her dainty hand into the pail. When she captured a plump crawler and proceeded to bait the hook, he almost fainted.

Rod in tow, Sabrina perched at the edge of the stream and cast. In an elegant ballet, of sorts, she moved, graceful and poetic—so unlike her dancing.

Glancing over her shoulder, she asked, "Are you not going to fish?"

"Oh—er, yes. Yes, I am." For a long while, he scrutinized the bucket of worms, and his mouth went dry. Bile rose in his throat, and Everett was certain he was going to hurl his noon meal to the ground. He dug into the damp earth and winced when a slithery form slid over his skin. He jerked and closed his eyes. Bloody Hell.

"My lord, are you unwell?"

He opened his eyes and found Sabrina staring at him. "I am fine, my dear."

"Are you sure?" She inclined her head. "You are as white as a sheet."

"I am quite positive."

Sabrina set her rod on a nearby rock and walked to him.

"Here, let me do it for you." She took the end of his line and, after pulling another wiggling worm from the pail, baited his hook. "There, you are all set."

Together they approached the stream. Everett cast his hook as she retrieved her rod.

"It must be heaven to have this at your disposal." Sabrina surveyed the immediate surroundings. "I would be here every day if this were my property."

"Accept my proposal, and I will give it to you for a wedding present," Everett stated, hoping to tempt her.

"You cannot mean that." Her gaze widened, and her mouth fell open. She gulped and faced the stream. "Would you really?"

"For something far more precious, yes." Everett realized, in that moment, he was serious. He would give up everything he owned to possess Sabrina Douglas. To have her in his bed at the end of a long day. To wake with her every morning. To hold her in his arms in the hours between.

"I would never require it of you." Her chin hit dangerous heights, and her lovely features were rife with tension. "If I marry you, it will be because I want to be your wife, not for your holdings, however grand."

"I have offended you." Everett marked another blunder. "Why is it I can converse smoothly with every marriageable woman in the *ton*, yet you turn me into a blithering idiot?"

The ends of her mouth lifted. "Perhaps you are a blithering idiot."

From the corner of his eye, he studied her profile, and she smiled. She teased him, and he liked it.

"Oh." All of a sudden, she jumped. "I have a bite."

"Hold on. Do not let go of your rod," he shouted, as if he were some sort of master fisherman. He came up behind her, placed his arms about her waist, and covered her hands with his.

"Step back," Sabrina hissed and wrenched free. "I know what I am doing."

He had done as she bade and gasped in amazement as she hauled a rather large trout from the stream. The slimy looking creature fought and flopped as Sabrina caught hold of it, keeping it near, flicking water all over her dress without care. Gently, she removed the hook from the fish and, at the edge of the water, returned the trout from whence it came.

"What are you doing?"

"We were not going to eat it." She turned and shrugged. "So there was no point in keeping it."

"I do not understand." Everett plopped on the grass and stared, mouth agape, at her. "We are going to release everything we catch? What is the bloody use of fishing in the first place?"

Preparing to re-bait her hook, Sabrina paused, set down the pail, propped her rod on the rocks, and sat beside Everett.

"The thrill is in the catch," she explained. "It is the excitement of the sport, not the end result, that matters." She seemed to think for a moment, and then she added, "Well, unless you are hungry and relying on skill to provide dinner." She bent her knees and crossed her arms over her legs.

Everett could not suppress a smile. The thrill was definitely in the catch. But in his arena the end result, to make her his wife, was everything.

Slowly, so as not to frighten her, he leaned toward Sabrina and nudged her with his nose. She had not resisted as he set his lips to hers. Instead, she welcomed him to taste, sample, and explore. Aroused by her mere proximity, he was careful not to touch her. The only contact they shared was with their mouths. Moaning softly, she reached for his wrist.

Everett sensed her interest, her desire to know him, as he ached to know her. If she had determined to learn that sport, there was no one better to teach her the games men and women played. And he was a master in that particular skill.

Let the lessons commence.

He had thought to rouse her with a beckoning kiss, but as heat poured through his veins, inviting him to run wild, he answered the call.

Her call.

Because he sought not to scare her, he steeled himself with the knowledge that Sabrina was an innocent. He wanted to take his time, to show her measure for measure the passion they could enjoy, what he could give her, and all that she could give him. Envisioning her warm and inviting on their wedding night, an event he looked forward to with great anticipation, Everett decided he would gladly wait.

Until she scored her nails to the back of his neck, held him to her, and emitted a plaintive cry. Blood pooled in his loins, as an elemental warning, and he feared he might be erect until the New Year. He needed to pull back before he stripped her bare and took her like a navy man just returned from sea.

His fishing rod skittered on the ground, and they came up for air.

Sabrina leapt to the fore. "You have a bite."

"Hell and the Reaper." Everett took a long, deep breath before jumping to his feet. She was going to kill him.

"Hurry." She grabbed the wayward instrument,

laughing as she struck a battle-ready pose. "No worries, as I have it."

In a flash, he ran to her side, and she handed him the rod. Before he could lock his stance, the fish at the other end tugged hard. "Whoa."

"Pull back." Sabrina jolted his elbow. "You must be steadfast."

"I am." He gritted his teeth.

"Watch the line." She yanked his wrist. "Do not get it tangled on the rocks."

"Do you want to bring in this fish, or shall I?" Everett snapped, as another jerk brought him to the water's edge. "Bossy woman."

"Watch out!" Sabrina shouted an alarm. "Oh, he is a big one."

In her excitement, she stepped too close to the shoreline and slipped. In the heat of the sport, Everett caught her in his clutch, even as he held tightly to the rod, and Sabrina managed to stabilize herself. But he stumbled into the shallow, rocky bank of the stream, while chasing the resistant catch, and moss-covered stones were like a sheet of ice beneath his booted feet.

In an attempt to gain traction, Everett released the rod and flapped his arms, as he fought to gain his balance and avoid going into the drink. To his utter mortification, he was positive he headed for an unscheduled bath in front of his future wife, and she would never let him forget it. Suddenly, he grasped something solid, anchored himself, and stood upright.

Unfortunately, that something solid was Sabrina, just before she fell, face first, into the stream.

CHAPTER FOUR

"*Achoo!*"

Sabrina wiped her nose and huddled beneath a blanket as the carriage conveying her, Cara, their mother, and Everett turned onto Upper Brooke Street. In a state of nervous unrest, she chewed her lip, marveled that any of it remained intact, and peeked at the others.

Everyone stared out the windows, ignoring the fact that she closely resembled a drowned rat. Or perhaps they sought to avoid the not-too-subtle odor of *eau de trout* she currently sported.

She was thankful when the carriage halted in front of the Douglas townhouse before anyone was overcome by the smell. Ever quick to open the door, the footman wrinkled his nose when he caught wind of her, and Sabrina stepped down without accepting a hand.

"*Achoo!*"

Sabrina was not sure what was worse, enduring the silent trudge through the woods with Everett, the repeated squish of her slippers the only sounds to be heard, or facing her mother and Cara upon return to the main house.

Wiping at her runny nose, she felt awful, and a dark sense of foreboding settled in her chest.

If Everett quit his suit and ran, screaming mad, for the country, she would not blame him. And to compound her misery, she was sure no one else would blame him, either. Polite society, which was anything but polite, would think he had finally come to his senses.

"*Achoo!*"

"SABRINA, go straight upstairs and get out of those wet clothes. You need a hot bath." Lady Amanda turned to Everett. "Lord Markham, please forgive my daughter—"

"I assure you, Lady Amanda, it was entirely my fault." How unfair it was that his most unlikely lady bore the burden of his clumsy buffoonery, when she was an innocent victim. He frowned as Sabrina climbed the stairs, Cara in tow, without so much as a backward glance.

"Rubbish." Lady Amanda smiled and shook her head. "It is not the first time Sabrina has taken an impromptu splash. She is her father's daughter."

"Damn right she is." Admiral Douglas appeared in the hall to the left. He stepped forward and shook Everett's hand. "What is this about an impromptu splash?"

"Oh, you will favor this, though you will not be surprised." Lady Amanda tugged off her gloves. "Your youngest daughter decided to take a swim, fully clothed, while fishing with Lord Markham."

Everett held his breath, awaiting the explosion that was, no doubt, forthcoming, and it were no less than he deserved. Admiral Douglas stood stock still for a pregnant moment. Then, without warning, he burst into laughter.

"Please, sir, I am to blame," Everett explained. "I lost my footing, almost broke my neck, and Sabrina saved me."

"This is your fault." Lady Amanda folded her arms and cast a stern stare at her husband. "You encourage her without thought of the consequences."

"Enough, Amanda. As you so eloquently assert, on occasions too numerous to count, Sabrina is my daughter." With a palm pressed to his belly, Admiral Douglas chuckled and then arched a brow. "If Lord Markham is to marry our girl, he had best become accustomed to her...carefree nature."

"Humph." Lady Amanda whirled about and ascended the stairs. "Carefree, indeed."

How Everett's heart ached for his future wife. An afternoon of fun had turned into an exercise in humiliation, and never had he seen her so downcast. Despite his pleas to the contrary, her mother remained convinced of Sabrina's guilt, and she endured the scolding without once proclaiming the truth of the situation, and that had not sat well with him. For good or ill, he vowed it was the last time she shouldered the blame for his transgressions.

"WHAT ELSE CAN you tell me of this institution called marriage?" Everett swirled the amber liquid in his brandy balloon and shot Trevor a quick glance. With his old friend from Eton and Dirk, Everett once again commiserated their respective positions in a private room at White's.

Having always tried to be the best at any endeavor he had undertaken, he approached his nuptials in much the same manner, by formulating a strategy to ensure his ultimate success.

Had there been books written on the topic, he would have poured over each volume, as he would have studied for an exam. However, after a trip to the bookseller yielded no serviceable results, as no such subject matter existed, Everett resorted to seeking what he considered expert advice. He so wished to be a good husband to Sabrina and desperately wanted their union to be a triumph in cooperation.

"Ah, yes." Trevor snapped his fingers. "For some odd reason they will come to you with a litany of problems, with no expectation of a solution."

"He is right." Dirk concurred, with a dip of his chin. "If she brings you what appears to be an insurmountable quandary, and the answer stares you in the face, for heaven's sake do not tell her."

"Do not offer advice unless it is solicited." Trevor pointed in emphasis. "Else you will suffer the consequences."

"Oh, I say." Puzzled, Everett shook his head. "Then what the devil am I to do?"

"Listen," Dirk inserted.

"Exactly." Trevor nodded in agreement. "And keep your mouth shut."

"I am to do nothing?" Scooting to the edge of his seat, Everett narrowed his stare. "I do not understand."

"Neither did I, at first." Dirk shrugged. "But after having my head lopped off, despite my good intentions, I have learned to sit there, with my lips sealed, and endure my wife's complaints with a semblance of unimpaired aplomb."

"You can nod—sympathize, even." Trevor leaned forward, planted elbows to knees, and rested his chin in his palm. "But by all means do not solve her conundrum."

"Trust us." Dirk crossed his legs and sighed. "You will be much safer that way."

"Bloody hell." Everett downed the last of his brandy in a single gulp and frowned. "How am I to remember the rules of such shark-infested waters polite society has the audacity to call marriage? I should have stayed in the navy. If you ask me, war is much simpler than wives."

"Oh, do not fret, my friend, as you need only find your stride, and the first year should suffice. Plus, there is one benefit to the situation that trumps the pitfalls." Trevor smirked, reclined in his chair, and cast Dirk a side-glance. "All that pent up energy often lends itself to another arena, with which you will have no complaint."

Dirk's eyes widened, and recognition dawned in his expression. "Ah, Lockwood is correct. When my wife is in a state, one touch, the slightest caress, and I often find myself in another more appealing scenario."

"Really?" Everett snapped to attention. "Are we talking a few chaste kisses or a full scale seduction?"

"The latter, and my Becca actually bit me, once." Dirk gazed at the floor and smiled. "Rouses my roger just thinking of it, but if you ever mention it to her, I will kill you."

"Do I look like a chatty chit?" Everett snorted. "And are you serious?"

"Indubitably." Trevor waved for a refill. "Caroline fancies herself quite the Delilah, a regular temptress, if you get my meaning. Tore my best coat and took me on the floor of the drawing room, before the hearth, after a ripping row. But if you breathe a word of it to her, I will slit your gullet."

"Now I would never betray your confidence, but I will remember that the next time I join you for dinner." Everett winked and raised his glass in toast. "Gentlemen, I believe I am going to like being married."

IT WAS THE FASHIONABLE HOUR, and the *ton* turned out in force for the daily ritual known as the Promenade. Strolling behind Alex and Elaine, Sabrina and Cara smiled and nodded their acknowledgement to various acquaintances.

"I wonder where the men are this evening?" Cara scanned the crush. "The Brethren are curiously absent."

Sabrina smiled, a knowing smile. "They are preparing to sail."

In an instant, Alex and Elaine stopped and cornered Sabrina.

"The devil you say." Alex glanced left and then right. "Spill it, Brie."

"It is true." Sabrina nodded once. "The Brethren had a meeting this morning."

The Brethren of the Coast was a secret order of Nautionnier Knights whose members descended from the famed Templars, the warriors of the Crusades, and Sabrina's father led the group.

"Oh, little sister, shame on you." Cara arched a brow and frowned. "Were you listening outside papa's study again?"

"Do not scold her, Cara." Elaine elbowed the elder Douglas in the ribs. "She is our best and most reliable source of information. Without her, we would know nothing."

"Enough stalling." With unveiled determination, Alex folded her arms in front of her and lowered her chin. "Tell us what you heard."

"Well, since the brave assault at Badajoz, Wellington has pushed eastward, at great cost to our troops." Sabrina paused and chose her words carefully, as Alex harbored a wicked crush on the captain of the HMS *Intrepid*, Jason Collingwood, and Brie had not intended to worry her friend. "The Brethren are to assist the Royal Navy, namely the *Intrepid*, by delivering reinforcements and supplies."

"Oh, dear." Alex clasped her hands and bit her lip. "I do hope their mission will not be too dangerous."

"I suppose that is why mama told me that you two are coming to stay with us, and you should not fret for their safety." Cara gathered Alex and Elaine in a circle of comfort. "I am certain everything will be all right."

As Cara tended their friends, it amazed Sabrina how her older sister always knew the right thing to say. She wondered why Everett had not chosen someone more refined—someone like Cara—to marry.

In truth, Sabrina wondered why he had chosen her.

"Just think, we can enjoy the delights of the Season and stay up late, trading stories." Cara shot Sabrina a sly glance, and the hair at the nape of her neck stood on end. "I daresay the most promising entertainment is my sister's courtship."

"Ooh, I almost forgot." Elaine squealed and bounced. "Do tell, Brie. How goes it with the impossibly handsome Lord Markham?"

"Thank you, ever so much." Sabrina glared at her older sister, because she had been hoping to divert attention from her somewhat awkward situation with Everett by focusing the conversation on the Brethren's latest mission. "I do not know what you mean."

"You are most welcome, and do not play innocent, as you know what I reference." Cara grinned, the cat that ate the canary. "Does a headfirst dip in the stream while fishing ring any bells? Perhaps your ears are still filled with water?"

"What?"

"You took a swim with Lord Markham?"

"Were you clothed?"

"What was he wearing?"

Again Sabrina looked left, and then right, as she faced the rapid-fire questions from Alex and Elaine. How could she respond to their queries and save a measure of pride? "Well—"

"No, she did not take a swim with me. I accidentally knocked her in the drink when she tried to keep me from falling. And, yes, we were both clothed."

So engrossed in conversation, Sabrina had not noticed Lord Markham approached their group. And though she would not have thought it possible, she had managed to embarrass herself twice in front of her prospective groom in a sennight. Why on earth would the damn fool man not quit his suit? Uncharacteristic and unappreciated unease and self-doubt clawed at her nerves. She wanted to marry him, yet she wanted him not. Oh, where was a runaway carriage when she needed one?

Swallowing an unladylike curse, she faced her nemesis.

Everett smiled, a brilliant smile that melted her heart in a flash of teeth. Slowly, with what she was certain was a well-orchestrated flourish, he bowed.

Sabrina wanted to crawl beneath the nearest rock.

It was bad enough she had to share the folly and subsequent mortification of their fishing expedition, but to be caught by Everett while doing so was the height of humiliation. And yet she wondered why his approval was so important to her.

He trapped her gaze as he straightened. "May I escort you, Miss Douglas?"

She would have given anything to refuse him, but to do so would be tantamount to a cut and very bad form. And her form was bad enough, already. So Sabrina had done what she would normally do when faced with dire circumstances.

She persevered.

Accepting his proffered arm, she held her head high. "How very kind of you, Lord Markham." She took two steps —and tripped on the uneven pavement.

It was her good fortune that Everett was prepared for the awkward antics of his unconventional bride-to-be. He caught her by the forearms and discreetly righted her. One hand skimmed her fast rising gooseflesh and claimed her wrist, thereby depositing her hand in the crook of his elbow in one refined move.

Sabrina stood stock-still, expecting a chorus of laughter at any moment, which she hoped would drown the pounding of her heart. A quick scan of those nearby showed none the wiser. So Everett was her savior, in more ways than one.

"Thank you," she whispered.

To wit, he winked. "Always a pleasure, Miss Douglas."

EARLY THE FOLLOWING MORNING, sitting tall in the saddle of his chestnut hunter, Everett surveyed the park until his eyes fell upon the object of his desire. Admiral Douglas hinted the previous night at the Waddlington Ball that his youngest daughter had a particular fondness for morning rides.

Puzzled but grateful, he had the distinct impression the admiral aided Everett's suit.

Dressed in a teal wool riding habit, Sabrina painted a pretty picture of elegance atop her roan mare. He chuckled. Oh, how appearances could be deceiving. Her strength was in her abrasive underbelly, not a polished veneer. For her sake and his sanity, he hoped she was a better rider than dancer.

Heeling the flanks of his mount, Everett set a course for his lady. The admiral turned and waved a greeting, and then Sabrina peered in his direction. He knew the minute she recognized him, because she stiffened her back.

Everett smiled.

That a woman most men of the *ton* ignored had felled a rake of his caliber was rumored to be the supreme comeuppance. Their courtship was currently the favored *on-dit* by the gossipmongers, which had not bothered him a bit. Though most looked on him with sympathy, he considered it his ultimate good fortune. Now if he could only get Sabrina to accept his offer of marriage before the rest of his set warmed to her positive qualities.

He reined in, bringing his chestnut aside her mare, sandwiching her between himself and the admiral, and nodded once. "Admiral. Miss Douglas. A fine morning, is it not?"

"Lord Markham, fancy meeting you here." The admiral winked and grinned, all but declaring his part in the connubial conspiracy.

"Lord Markham." Sabrina faced forward, refusing to meet his gaze. "What a lovely surprise." The last was said with a measure of sarcasm, as if she knew full well her father had supported his campaign.

"Mind if I join you?" Though he addressed the admiral,

his eyes never left Sabrina. Since she continued to avoid his stare, Everett was afforded only a view of her charming profile.

"Oh, I say, I see Chomley over there, and I need to have a word with him." The admiral drew rein. "Lord Markham, would you be so kind as to accompany Sabrina on her ride?"

Why you sly old salt. Confidence surged to the fore, and Everett lowered his chin. "It would be my honor, Admiral."

SABRINA'S PULSE raced in direct proportion to the rapidly increasing distance between her and her father. Traitor. How could he leave her alone with Everett? Even in the park, the damn fool man was bound to make some illicit advance, and she knew she would not refuse him.

"Ouch!" A sharp pinch to her right buttock brought her to attention. As self-consciousness set in, swift and unsteadying, she searched the immediate area to check if anyone might have witnessed his affront. Lucky for her, the park was all but empty. Leashing her temper, Sabrina confronted the bane of her existence. "My lord, you are deliberately trying to compromise me."

"Actually, I desired only your consideration, and I believe my actions quite conservative—for me." Everett tilted his head and cast her an unrepentant grin. "But you have given me food for thought, so let us not abandon your idea."

"Scandalous." She rolled her eyes and groaned. "I assure you, Lord Markham, anything you do would pale in comparison to the embarrassments in which I have already landed, so I need no help, in that respect."

"Why so formal?" He frowned and shifted in the saddle.

"If memory serves, you have called me Everett, and a wide assortment of colorful alternatives, on a number of occasions."

"Because you addressed me as Miss Douglas." He had, and she had not appreciated it. She loved the way he said her name, because his voice always grew husky, which gave her delicious shivers from top to toe. She stared at him through her lashes. "You used to call me Brie, as do my friends. Are we not friends, anymore, Lord Markham?"

"We are, my lady." Everett reached for her hand and held it snug in his own. Slowly, he tugged at her calfskin glove, baring her flesh. "But we could be so much more, if you would only marry me."

"W-what are you doing?" She stuttered in nervous antic-ipation and then licked her lips. "Everett—no. Someone might see you."

To her surprise, he made no reply, just arched a brow, daring her to refuse him, as he traced delicious circles on her palm with his thumb.

"Everett, you mustn't." Though she protested, she made no attempt to break free from his grasp. Instead, Sabrina closed her eyes, clutched her throat, and savored his improper advances, as he thrust a finger between two of hers in a sensuous caress. The movement was repetitive, enticing, and maddeningly explicit, and his meaning was not lost on her.

Once, when she had been but a young and curious girl, she inadvertently discovered her parents engaged in marital relations, in the summerhouse at their country estate. While her father reclined on a daybed, her mother rode him, as she would a horse. Sabrina had not watched them for very long, but it had been an enlightening experience.

But that was an altogether different incident, because

now she was no spectator. Indeed, she was an active partici-
pant, as heat sang in her veins, soothing her frazzled nerves,
and she moaned her appreciation. Sabrina felt bold, wild,
and wanton. Without thought, she reached for him.

"Sabrina Francis, either you marry this man, or I will kill
him." Her father spoke in a familiar tone, which conveyed
the gravity of her infraction.

Irritating warmth pooled in her cheeks, and she came
alert in an instant, a mere second before Everett flinched. In
that moment, she realized he had been just as lost in their
exchange.

Was it possible?

Could Everett care for her?

Though he had made no formal declaration, he had
taken her fishing. Surely that was tantamount to the same?

"Admiral Douglas, sir. I am sorry if I have caused
offense." Everett released her and pulled at his cravat. "I
assure you, none was intended, as I hold your daughter in
the highest esteem."

Her sire stared at the sky before chuckling in his deep
baritone, and Sabrina breathed a sigh of relief, because her
father was not angry.

"Oh, I do believe you got it, Lord Markham." With a
dramatic flair, she waved her hand in the air but fidgeted
beneath her father's scrutiny. As she fumbled with her
glove, she swallowed hard. "There was a splinter in my
finger."

"Rubbish, my dear." Her father actually snorted. "I do
not claim to understand the arrangement between you, but I
will not indulge it much longer. Either you accept Lord
Markham, or I will forbid him to call on you."

"Papa, no." Accustomed to her sire's ire, as they were
well acquainted, Sabrina drew herself up with the hauteur

one would expect from the daughter of an admiral. "You mustn't blame Lord Markham for my shameful behavior."

Everett nudged his mare. "Sabrina—"

"It is true." And then she recalled a familiar phrase from the night in the maze and turned it to her advantage. Her father had bellowed it loud enough that she was certain she would never forget it. And, in a sense, it was an accurate depiction of what had occurred. She could have rejected Everett, but she had not wanted to do so. In any case, the declaration was for the greater good. "I made an improper advance on Lord Markham's person. If you wish to heat my posterior, I will be happy to accommodate you."

The outrageous statement was a means to an end—to spare Everett an appointment at dawn, on Paddington Green, with her father. Her sire opened his mouth and then closed it. Was it possible? Had she, at long last, stumped her father?

"All right, miss. But I want a word with you in the study, upon our return home." And then he heeled his stallion. "Be quick, as you do not want me to come for you."

"I shall be right behind you, Papa." She chewed her lip. "But I owe Lord Markham an apology."

"Sabrina, why did you tell your father you initiated our contact?" Everett snickered. "Spinning falsehoods is not your forte."

"Because he was going to forbid me to see you." She stared at her hands and summoned courage. "And I could not let that happen."

"Oh?" Sporting an arrogant countenance, Everett shifted his weight. "Are you finally admitting you welcome my suit?"

How she wished to evade the question or, better yet, ignore it. But Sabrina Francis Douglas was neither a coward nor a liar. Grudgingly, she met his amber gaze and was stunned by the intensity of his stare.

"I—" Her voice faltered, and she gulped. In a desperate effort to maintain what remained of her dignity, Sabrina nodded the affirmative.

Everett rewarded her with a radiant smile, boyish and sweet. Relief washed over her, as a gentle spring shower, and she returned his smile, measure for measure.

"*Sabrina!*"

"Holy mother." She started at her father's summons. "I-I must go."

But Everett stayed her, when he caught her hand and pressed his lips to her gloved knuckles. "Until tonight, lady mine."

THE BALLROOM at Richmond House filled to overflow, and dapper dandies and delightful debutantes engaged in a rollicking game of cat and mouse. Amid the crush, Everett focused on a cascade of raven locks piled in loose curls, and a sapphire silk gown encased the body he ached to know on a more intimate level.

Sabrina stood among her friends, a quirky group known throughout the *ton* for their close familial ties. To his advantage, the men were not present. After partaking an afternoon in the pugilist ring with Trevor, Everett had learned some mysterious endeavor for their shipping company had called the legendary mariners into action.

Since Trevor married Lady Caroline Elliott, as was, he declared he had paved the road for newcomers into the rather odd extended family. Given Sabrina's clumsy but sweet confession in the park, Everett was confident he would be the next member of the notoriously exclusive clique. In fact, he had entered the fray with that precise goal in mind, if only to claim the woman of his fancy. With patience growing thin, he had wasted enough time. She was going to be his wife, and it was past due she reconciled herself to that fate.

But he strolled at his leisure, steering left and then right, as a predatory hunger burgeoned in his belly. And each successive step only increased his appetite. Ah, he was sincerely looking forward to his wedding night, as his bride-to-be was a spirited woman.

When the crowd parted, Cara noticed him and alerted the other ladies present, as evidenced by Elaine and Alex, when they turned and faced him. But Sabrina kept her back to him—which was a wise move on her part.

He smiled his wolf's smile.

Oh, yes.

"Good evening, Lord Markham." The personification of feminine deportment, so unlike her younger sister, Cara held out her hand in welcome, and he placed a chaste kiss on her gloved knuckles, as would a refined gentleman, and greeted the remaining ladies in similar fashion, with one exception.

At last, when Sabrina rotated, he grasped her wrist, pulled her dangerously near, inched down her glove with his thumb, bent his head, and pressed his lips to her palm. When she gasped and shivered, raw lust pooled in his loins, and he chuckled. "Dance with me, my saucy Sabrina."

Much to his surprise, she made no protest, as he led her into a sea of couples. With his arm resting at her waist, he kept her close, and their embrace bordered on the indecent, but he cared not. Staring over the top of her head, Everett savored the flirty sashay of her skirts to his thighs, and formidable ardor seared him to the marrow.

At the ripe old age of one and thirty, women had long since ceased to command his senses, and his attachments had devolved into a series of practiced widows, superficial attractions, and base desires. His bed partners knew what he wanted from them, what they wanted from him, and he gave it to them. For a while, such relationships satisfied him—until he met Miss Sabrina Douglas. And that stolen kiss in the Hawthorn's maze, permanently forged in his memory, had carried him to the heights of passion, as he had never experienced.

And he had not even taken her—yet.

That knowledge worked on Everett in ways he could not have anticipated. As he whirled his future wife, she trounced his foot, a common occurrence to which he had become painfully accustomed. He peered at her face.

And he stumbled.

With her lower lip trembling, and an unmistakable plea in her blue eyes, he noted, for the first time, the heat of her gloved palm against his. When he exerted the slightest pressure at the small of her back, her breath hitched. But it was the raw, unconcealed passion investing her expression that held him captive and almost sent them tumbling to the floor.

Recognition dawned.

Hunger for hunger. Desire for desire.

Sabrina wanted him as he wanted her.

He cleared his throat. "My dear, are you all right?"

"Oh, Everett. I feel so...I do not know what I feel." With an exhalation of utter helplessness, she closed her eyes, shivered in his arms, swallowed hard, and licked her lips. "I fear I may have a fever."

"Bloody hell." He cursed under his breath and scanned the vicinity.

Yes, she had a fever, all right, and he had known Sabrina was not immune to his charms, but never had Everett expected her to reciprocate with such unrestrained fervor. As a man of the world, he knew how to hold tight the reins of desire. As an ingénue, Sabrina knew no such control, and heaven help him if she brought her honest, explorative nature into that realm.

As the music played, he navigated the throng, nudging her to the edge of the dance floor. To rouse no suspicion, he reversed course and then halted. Slow and methodical, he escorted his errant debutante to the back wall. Drawing from memory, he located the terrace doors, glanced over his shoulder to ensure their privacy, and handed Sabrina across the threshold.

Stepping onto the flagged surface, Everett welcomed the cool night air against his heated flesh. The gardens spread before them, welcoming and enticing, for a lover's tryst. Silvery moonlight peeked between the foliage of the large maples, casting a mosaic of intricate shadows on the grass. At a fork in the pebbled walkway, she paused and drew him up short.

"Where are you taking me?" Sabrina whispered.

"Shh." At that moment, he located what he required. "Perfect. Come with me." A mountainous oak, boasting thick, low-hanging foliage, which shrouded the trunk, provided fortuitous concealment.

With nary an objection, she followed in his wake, as Everett was a man on a mission. Sheltered beneath the tree, he turned on a heel, reclined against the bark, and hauled Sabrina against him. With something between a sob and a sigh, she lunged, twined her fingers in his hair, and bit his lip.

How he reveled in her jerky and unschooled, but wildly wanton, maneuvers. As an unpracticed but earnest seraph, she moved, frantic and rushed, as she engaged his tongue in a frisky little duel he could not resist.

Of one thing he was certain. What had happened in the Hawthorn's garden had not stayed in the Hawthorn's garden. That rendezvous had been no aberration. Somehow, some way, Sabrina touched him on a level he had not known existed, and he wanted more. The nagging doubts, the worries that his hopeful imagination had made something of nothing, which had plagued his consciousness, evaporated in an instant.

But when his most unlikely lady gave vent to a rather vigorous moan, he recognized the depth of her ardor and understood, too well, her affliction. And before she sounded the alarm, not to mention the admiral, Everett summoned years of finesse, focused on her needs, and soothed her frayed nerves the best way he knew how.

With one hand he kneaded her breast, while he trailed the pearl-like nodes of her spine to massage her lower back with his other. When she pressed her curvaceous body to his, teasing his Jolly Roger, which was dangerously jolly and only too ready to plow her field, he concentrated on not responding.

But how he ached, and how he burned.

It was a tender torment unlike any he had ever known, and he craved release. As his heart pounded a warning knell, pulse points blazed to life, and he could not breathe. Against his better judgment, he walked his fingers over her lush landscape, tracing every peak and valley, and the beast below his belly button raged.

The next moan was his.

In his mind, he grasped at the last vestiges of personal constraint, but he had inadvertently swept Sabrina off her feet, and she took him with her. He simply had to have her.

But could she trust him?

Would she marry him?

"Lord Markham, I must protest!"

Sabrina half-screamed as the admiral pulled her from Everett's arms, and a cacophony of panicked whispers echoed from the surrounding hiding places. Her father reared back, with his fist poised to strike, and she barely managed to catch it. Everett sighed in relief.

"Papa, no." Clutching the admiral's wrist, she held fast. "Please, stop."

"Sabrina, stay out of this." Her angry sire turned his steely gaze on his youngest daughter and tried but failed to shake free. "He has defiled you in full view of the guests."

"You misunderstand." Sabrina refused to yield, and Everett thanked her in silence. "We were celebrating."

"What?" Admiral Douglas snorted. "Your ruin?"

Why, he was not sure, but Everett braced for her rejection.

"No—our betrothal." She swallowed hard and stared Everett straight in the eye. "You are about to murder your future son-in-law."

CHAPTER FIVE

Standing before the long mirror in her bedchamber, Sabrina smoothed the skirts of her dusty blue jaconet dress and assessed her appearance. Downstairs, in the study, Everett conferred with her father regarding their marriage contract.

As she gazed at her reflection, she smiled and then laughed, as she recalled the open-mouthed stare she garnered from her arrogant lord when she accepted his proposal, somewhat belatedly. It was nice to set him on his heels, for a change.

For a scarce moment she had wondered if Everett would refute her declaration, but he had not. Instead, he masked his shock and offered his hand to her father, who teetered in an equally dumbfounded state. The men shared a congratulatory shake; complete with hearty backslaps, before her father embraced her, swelling with obvious pride.

Wrapping her arms about herself, Sabrina giggled. It had not happened as she had planned, but the important thing was it happened. She was to marry Lord Everett Markham. Self-doubt crept into her mind, but she quashed it as she would a bug. Like a giddy schoolgirl she twirled, around and around, in her room.

A knock at the door had her reaching for the rail of a chair for balance. "Come."

Her mother peeked around the edge of the oak panel. "My dear, your father is almost finished with Lord Markham. I thought perhaps you would enjoy a bit of privacy with him before he leaves." She inclined her head. "There will be little time to be alone until you are married. I can send him to the drawing room once he has concluded his business."

"That would be lovely, Mama." Clutching fistfuls of her skirts, Sabrina gazed at the floor as her stomach flip-flopped. Uttering a silent prayer that she had done the right thing, she nodded. "I shall be there in a moment."

"Very well, but do not keep Lord Markham waiting." Her mother arched a brow. "It is not polite."

"Yes, Mama." The creak of a hinge signaled her mother's departure, and she hugged herself and paced the floor.

What would Everett say?

Could he truly want to marry her?

Though he had offered for her, he had only done so because he thought he compromised her. The cold, gnawing hand of doubt traipsed her spine and shivered over her skin.

Staring at herself in the long mirror, she said, "Sabrina Francis Douglas, you march in there and face him this instant." With chin held high and shoulders squared, she heeded her own advice.

Until she reached the landing.

Worry nipped at her confidence, and her courage faltered. Downstairs, all was quiet, and the foyer remained vacant. On a sigh, she bit her lip and trailed her fingers along the oak balustrade. As a child, Sabrina often rode the rail and was forever getting her posterior heated as a result. The activity had survived her formative years because a ripping slide was the perfect remedy for nervous anxiety, but the tongue-lashings and spankings lessened, as she grew smart enough to choose more opportune moments.

Sabrina peered below. No doubt such behavior would be frowned upon were she marrying a titled gentleman. Thank heavens Everett was not of the noble set. There were no witnesses, so what could it hurt? Hiking her skirts, she swung a leg over the wooden rail.

WITH A SPRING IN HIS STEP, Everett exited the study.

What a difference a night made. The admiral was all smiles, the transgressions of the past forgotten. He, on the other hand, still was not sure what had happened. One thing was certain—Sabrina was his.

The contracts were drawn and signed.

Marriage negotiations were a new experience for him. He could hardly complain, however, since the admiral provided a substantial dowry for his daughter. Not that Everett needed her money.

It had been a surprisingly painless process, over before it had begun. The next thing he knew, the butler informed him his bride-to-be waited in the drawing room. With a polite farewell, he took his leave of Admiral Douglas and set off in search of his future wife.

What would Sabrina say?

Could she truly want to marry him?

As he entered the foyer, sudden movement caught his attention. He choked back laughter when his eyes lit upon a pair of shapely calves and froths of lace. Quick as a wink, he moved into position and braced for impact.

Sabrina landed right in his arms.

With a smile, Everett gazed into her stunned expression and declared, "There is a God."

WITHIN THE WELL-WORN walls of Almack's, Everett made his first formal appearance with the Douglas family. Enduring the pinching discomfort of knee breeches seemed a small price to pay for the honor of escorting his bride-to-be, or so he whispered in her ear, along with a few improper comments on her attire that made her cheeks burn.

Gowned in burgundy silk trimmed in old gold, her ebony locks piled atop her head, with a flirty curl dangling at her throat, Sabrina was unaccustomed to the wealth of attention she suffered from almost every male in the grand ballroom. But she had not bothered to look past the man at her side. There were pointed stares from women who, no doubt, had more in-depth knowledge of her fiancé, but she cared not.

He is marrying me.

The words sang in her head, again and again, a triumphant refrain. The little ditty served as an impenetrable defense shielding her from every upturned nose, cruel scoff, and cutting remark.

And there were many.

But as far as Sabrina was concerned, the gossipmongers could go to the devil. No, she was not the best example of a proper English gentlewoman. For that reason, had her intended stood to inherit, she never would have set her cap for him.

The screech of a violin announced the dancing was about to commence. Out of nowhere, a crowd of rakes appeared to vie for her hand.

"May I have this dance, Miss Douglas?" Lord Fells bowed with a dramatic flair she thought should be saved for a stage performance. With a sly expression, he made a point to ignore Everett. She decided the cad would have to pay for such an affront to her future husband. Or perhaps the stuffy aristocrat had simply forgotten his spectacles.

"But, I am Sabrina."

"Of course you are." He offered his escort.

"Would you not prefer to partner Cara?" She held tight to Everett.

"I have always appreciated your charming sense of humor, Miss Douglas." Lord Fells stepped closer. "Shall we?"

"Go." Everett inched from her side. "I will wait here for you, my dear."

"But no one ever wants to dance with me," she whispered.

"I am afraid the announcement of our betrothal will bring us both unwanted attention, my lady," Everett replied softly and then chuckled. "Have your dance, as I am not going anywhere." The last was said within earshot of Lord Fells.

As Lord Fells led her to the floor, Sabrina glanced over her shoulder at the man who would be her husband.

He winked. She tripped.

The music played, couples passed within arm's reach, hands touched briefly, fell away, and then touched again. If her partner ever looked at her, she knew not.

Because Sabrina only had eyes for Everett.

A wrong step here, a crushed toe there, and she was

positive that would be her first and last dance with Lord Fells. The poor man perspired when he returned her to Everett. Of course, she told herself she had not trounced his toes on purpose to ward off any future advances from the overbearing lord. She comforted herself in the knowledge she was clumsy by nature.

Everett claimed her waltzes—every one of them—casting a lethal stare in the direction of any man who might dare think of approaching her. She thought she might grow accustomed to being in his arms, but as each dance proved an affecting experience, her heart racing, her ears ringing, she decided to relax and enjoy the emotions whirling within her. And when she surrendered, her response grew even more intense.

By the time they sought a table for two in a well-hidden corner for supper, Sabrina felt as if she were floating. She cared not that her hair was arranged in a new style. She paid no attention to the low-cut bodice of her gown. With Everett, nothing else mattered.

"Can I get you another sweetmeat, sweet?" he asked as she shoved the last of three lemon tarts in her mouth.

Unable to form a coherent reply without embarrassing herself, she shook her head and smiled.

"Perhaps some more ratafia?" Her future husband arched a brow. "We could seek an alcove before the dancing resumes."

Still chewing, she nodded a vigorous affirmative.

"Wait here." Everett laughed and tapped a finger to her nose. "I shall be right back."

Moments later, he returned with two glasses of champagne.

She must have looked her surprise, because he inclined his head and clucked his tongue. "I smuggled it in. I thought we could share our own private toast to our eminent wedding."

A screened alcove on a balcony above the huge dance floor became their safe haven. The soft chink of their glasses was lost amid the noise of revelers.

"To our impending nuptials." Everett raised his glass and cast her a dimpled grin.

"And may we live happily ever after." Sabrina borrowed a line from many a childhood tale.

As they sipped the intoxicating bubbly, a nearby conversation caught their attention.

"Why do you suppose he is marrying her?" a male voice inquired.

"Probably because no one else will have him," an unknown female added. "He is, after all, a second son."

"But he has money to burn."

"He would have to in order to secure a more noble hand."

"Really, a man with no title cannot possibly hope for better," another person chimed. "But one would think he could secure a more refined candidate for a wife than that Douglas chit. She trips over her own shadow."

A chorus of laughter erupted.

EVERETT CURSED as the charming glow in Sabrina's countenance faded. Anger roared through him, and lust for revenge road hard in its wake. He stepped out, but she caught hold of his arm and stayed him. "I will not let—"

"Shh." She held a finger to her lips. Her gaze dropped to his mouth, then returned to look him in the eyes. "Kiss me, please. I need you desperately."

"They are right, you know." Turning into her, he took her glass and set it on a ledge beside his. With his hands at her waist, he pulled her near and kissed her forehead. "I have no title."

Sabrina framed his face. "What care I for titles when I have you?"

He pressed his lips to her palm. "You are not disappointed?"

"I could ask the same of you." Unbearable sadness invested her expression. "I am not the most graceful lady, but I am grateful you chose me, and I will endeavor to make you glad of it."

The slow burn of desire quenched his fury. If it were any other woman, he would have been skeptical. But the truth shining in her tear-filled blue eyes was undeniable. In that instant, he counted himself the most fortunate of men for having selected her as his bride. And, once again, she accepted him. She knew who he was, had seen what he was, and still she wanted him. Not for his money. Not for his land—but for him.

"Sabrina." He set his forehead to hers. "I do not deserve you."

"Are you sure you do not have it wrong?" She inhaled a shaky breath. "Are you trying to tell me I do not deserve you?"

"Let them talk." Everett scoffed. "They can all go to the devil." Slowly, he bent his head and suckled lightly on her lower lip, drawing her sumptuous flesh into his mouth. With a sob, she opened to him.

And he devoured her.

～

THE NEXT MORNING, Sabrina sat in the back parlor twiddling her thumbs. Over and over again the ugly comments from the previous night echoed in her head.

Accustomed to the harsh criticism, she had endured it as long as she could remember. As far as she was concerned, her detractors could hang from the nearest yardarm. But never had she heard anyone speak ill of Everett until he became connected with her. To her amazement, it hurt. It also scared her.

What affect would such carping have on him?

Would he regret choosing her for his bride?

"Sabrina, you have a visitor," her mother called out, as she opened the door and then waved a summons. "Cara is with Lord Markham in the drawing room. I am busy with the household accounts, so she will act as chaperone."

"All right." They had no scheduled appointment, so what could Everett want?

"Mind your manners." With a wag of her finger, her mother cautioned, "Do as your sister says and behave yourself."

"Yes, Mama." Self-doubt gnawing at her heels, Sabrina made her way to the drawing room. It was a new experience, one with which she was not comfortable.

Perhaps she should offer to quit their betrothal?

Or was he there to end it, himself?

The doors were open, and she had crossed the threshold before she realized it. Everett and Cara stood as she entered.

"My lord." Sabrina curtseyed.

Everett bowed. "My lady."

"May we have a moment in private?" She glanced at her older sister. "Please?"

"Mama is in the study." Cara gave Sabrina's fingers a

reassuring squeeze. "Papa is in Greenwich. I will be in the foyer and shall whistle if anyone nears."

"Thank you." Sabrina waited until they were alone to face her fiancé, as she desired no witnesses to her possible humiliation. "My lord—"

"Everett," he corrected her.

She huffed. "Everett, will you not be seated?"

Gowned in a simple pale pink morning dress, she felt a pauper when compared to his elegant attire. She wondered how anyone could look so grand so early in the day? Wearing fawn colored breeches tucked into gleaming Hessians, a crisp white shirt and starched cravat, a navy waistcoat and a chocolate brown coat, Everett was the epitome of a well-heeled English gentleman.

Drowning in self-consciousness, she smoothed her skirts before sitting beside him on the sofa.

"I wanted to—"

"I came to—"

She laughed nervously.

He dipped his chin. "Ladies first."

Sabrina inhaled and summoned every ounce of courage within her, then settled her hands in her lap. Despite what she wanted, she decided she had to put Everett's needs above her own. Let the *ton* say what they would about her, but she could not sit idly and let them disparage him.

"I was thinking about last night—the comments we overheard." She swallowed a sob. "I thought perhaps you might want to revisit our engagement."

"Are you reneging on our agreement?" With a curious countenance, Everett leaned forward. "Because I made an honorable offer, and the contracts are signed."

"No." She prayed for strength.

"You wish to end our betrothal?" Narrowing his stare, he

slapped a fist to an open palm and stood. "Well, I never would have figured you for a quitter, Miss Douglas, but I suppose even I can be mistaken."

"Blast!" Sabrina leapt to her feet. "Blast! Blast!"

"I beg your pardon?" He folded his arms and frowned. "Calm yourself, woman, and make your point."

"I am making a dreadful mess of our predicament." She gave vent to an unladylike snort, so what else was new. "I do not wish to end our engagement, but I thought, perhaps, you did, and I only wanted to make it easy for you."

"What on earth ever gave you that idea?" Everett shifted his weight, and his brows almost reached his hairline.

"I have exposed you to harsh criticism." Must she air their dirty laundry in such detail? If Sabrina were going to address the problem, she would not, in good conscience, omit any part of the distressing situation. "While I am quite accustomed to such nonsense, as I have suffered it for years, I was not sure how it affected you. This cannot be pleasant."

For a few seconds, Everett just stared at her, mouth agape. Then his shoulders trembled as he laughed hysterically. After a moment, he dragged the back of his hand across his forehead and rolled his eyes toward the heavens. "My dear Sabrina, I can assure you I am immune to such prattle. As it is, I am a second son. There will be no title if you marry me, you know?"

"Indeed, and I daresay I much prefer you that way." She grinned, feeling flirty and naughty, at once. "And I am not the most graceful lady. You do understand that you might have ensured yourself a lifetime of broken toes?"

"Of that I have no doubt, love." Everett chuckled. "But it is a pain I shall gladly bear."

"How generous of you." She stuck her tongue in her

cheek. "So, my lord, to what do I owe the pleasure of your company?"

"Ah, yes." He snapped his fingers and reached into his coat pocket. "As you are not planning to throw me over, I brought you a gift, which I hope meets with your approval."

When he produced a tiny box, Sabrina sucked in a breath. He lifted the lid, revealing a betrothal ring twinkling on a bed of white satin.

"Oh, Everett," she whispered. "It is lovely."

Without hesitation, he plucked the gold band adorned with a simple round diamond. He took her left hand in his and slipped the ring on her finger. "Well, do you like it?"

Her heart sang with joy as she launched herself at her future husband. In welcome, she parted her lips as their mouths met, engaging his tongue in a fiery dance. Delicious heat simmered in her veins, and a familiar flutter blossomed in the pit of her belly. His hands roamed her waist, her back, and her bottom—before a conspicuous cough interrupted their interlude.

Sabrina peered in the direction of the entryway and discerned that Cara, the soul of discretion, God bless her, had remained in the foyer. When she returned her attention to her fiancé, she discovered he had retreated behind a chair. "Everett? Is something wrong?"

"My dear, would it be rude to ask you to refrain from doing anything too encouraging—at least until we are wed?" He grimaced as though he were in pain. "Afterward, you may come at me to your heart's content."

Rocking on her heels, Sabrina giggled. "My lord, I make no promises."

CHAPTER SIX

a sennight later, Sabrina stared at the early morning sky. The first streams of pink and gold cut through the black of night, in a dazzling display of nature's omnipotence. With not a cloud visible, it was a beautiful day for a wedding.

That Everett insisted on a hasty ceremony had been quite a shock. Of course, the scandalmongers speculated on the necessity of a speedy wedding. The latest *on-dit* surmised she was pregnant. She laughed. Her future husband thrived on controversy, making no attempt to dispel the gossip.

Sabrina would have taken issue with his indifference had his conduct not been above reproach. But everything he had done during their whirlwind engagement bespoke his regard. And though he had not said he loved her, she hoped he might soon be inspired to make a declaration.

After a light meal of tea and dried toast to quell the cries of her empty belly, her lady's maid helped her dress for the momentous occasion. Her mother stopped by before departing for the church. Cara, Alex, and Elaine peeked in to wish her well. Caroline and Rebecca had done so last night, at their ritual pity party on the eve of her wedding.

It was a tradition, of sorts, for the ladies to gather and toast the future with wine and sweets. Caroline and Rebecca passed on the wine, explaining their odd behavior by announcing the impending arrival of two members of the next generation of the Brethren of the Coast. It was sad that their husbands, Trevor and Dirk, respectively, were at sea and remained unaware of the new additions to their families.

"Sabrina, it is time."

She shook her head and blinked. Rotating slowly, she faced her father. How resplendent he was in his formal regimental of rich navy blue adorned with gold epaulets. Sabrina shrugged her shoulders to ease the tension investing her.

Smiling, she curtseyed. "Papa."

"Oh, my girl." Her sire took her gloved hands in his and raised them to his lips. "You are so beautiful, dearest."

"I would not say that." She basked in his praise. "But I do feel quite splendid."

"It is true." Her father sighed and trailed a finger down her cheek. "You are a very lovely young lady, my dear. You have a unique quality, a charm all your own, and Lord Markham is a fortunate man. While I could not be prouder of you, I shall miss our mornings together. I shall miss the pitter-patter of your feet in the hall. But I shall miss your delightful smile most."

"Papa." Tears welled in her eyes, and Sabrina swallowed a sob. "I shall miss you always."

"None of that, now." He chucked her playfully on the

chin, something he had done for as long as she could remember. "My Sabrina never cries." With precision and grace, he lifted her veil and placed a chaste kiss on her forehead. "I loved you before you were born, and no doubt I shall love you even after I am gone from this life."

Wrapping her arms about his waist, as far as she could reach, Sabrina hugged her father. His hand cradled the back of her head, and the sunlight filtering through the windows bathed them in comforting warmth.

THE BALLROOM at Everett's posh Park Lane mansion filled to capacity. He could not believe how many members of the *ton* had turned out to see him wed Sabrina.

Bloody hypocrites.

Casting a side-glance at his wife, who sat beside him, pretty as a picture, devouring the second course of their wedding breakfast with her customary gusto, he chuckled. If he were lucky, her healthy appetite might extend beyond a mere zest for food. How Everett longed to whisk her upstairs and relieve her of the lacy confection that was the stuff of many a man's fantasy.

It had taken all his concentration to focus on the ceremony. Twice, Admiral Douglas had to nudge Everett when it was his turn to speak. With Trevor at sea, Everett had asked the admiral to stand with him. Hoping his parents and older brother might see fit to attend his wedding, he had written to them as a common courtesy. There had been no response, no sought after condemnation. They merely ignored him.

Some things never changed.

But should it matter? Everett had his own family now.

He had Sabrina. They would have a pack of children, and he would love them all with equal fervor, never favoring one over the other. They would take trips together. They would celebrate the holidays, and he would do them up grand.

Never again would he be alone.

From where he stood, the future looked rosy, indeed. And he had everything planned to the smallest detail. Life was good.

And what he had once borne as a ball and chain, his lack of a title, was actually a blessing in disguise. Because of his status, or lack thereof, he could marry a woman of his choosing. There were no agreements to be honored between two noble houses, no longstanding alliances to be fortified. A union would gain nothing with him. He could not be more grateful, more content.

As though sensing his perusal, Sabrina turned to him and smiled. Her blue eyes sparkled and her cheeks flushed. Without care for the audience, Everett cupped her chin, leaned forward, and kissed her passionately.

He had not thought it possible to be so happy.

A commotion in the crowd brought him up for air.

"Make way! Make way!"

The revelers parted, and a grey-haired couple neared the bridal table. Their expressions were harsh, severe, and forbidding. But it was their attire that brought the throng to attention.

They were dressed in the somber black garb of full mourning.

Everett stood, wondering if the shock encompassing his being was evident in his countenance.

"What is it?" His bride stared at him. "Who are they?"

"My parents."

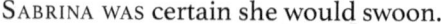

SABRINA WAS certain she would swoon.

In a rush of confusion, the celebration ended and the guests were hustled out the door. At last, after the final felicitation was offered, Sabrina, Everett, and their respective parents gathered in the study.

"Charles was thrown from his horse," Lady Elizabeth, the marchioness of Talbot, said in a sterile tone. "His neck snapped, and there was nothing we could do to save him."

"The boy was foxed, Lizzy." The marquess snorted and perched on the edge of Everett's desk. "It was a miracle he was able to get in the saddle."

Still wearing her wedding gown, Sabrina fiddled with the lace sleeve in an effort to disguise her dismay in regard to her callous in-laws. How could they be so indifferent to their heir's passing?

"John," the marchioness snapped, "Please refrain from addressing me so informally in front of strangers."

"As of today, they are family." Everett reclined in his chair and steepled his hands. "You need not worry about appearances, Lady Elizabeth."

Sitting on a daybed and hugging the wall, Sabrina stifled a gasp at her husband's sharp retort. Never had it occurred to her that her heretofore-charming spouse could have such a barbed tongue.

"Lord and Lady Talbot." Her father bowed in deference to their rank. "Please accept our sincerest condolences on the loss of your son."

"Thank you, Admiral." Lady Elizabeth compressed her lips, and Sabrina wondered if she was plagued with a digestive ailment. "We had intended to arrive in time to delay the nuptials. Since Charles was unwed, Everett stands to inherit. There were agreements made that he will have to honor in his brother's stead."

A tremor of unease shuddered through Sabrina's not so petite frame.

"I see no problem with that." Her husband seemed none too pleased, as he shifted in his seat. "Rest assured I would do as must needs."

"Excellent." The marchioness stared down her nose at Sabrina. "I am sure Miss Douglas will understand. Now that you are an earl, she cannot hope to hold you to this union."

Sabrina just managed to keep herself from fainting—or swearing. Or punching the marchioness in her face. She had not married Everett to gain a title anymore than she had married him for money. What objection could his mother have to the daughter of a respected naval officer?

"I beg your pardon." His face as red as a tomato, her father appeared on the verge of an apoplectic fit. "What the devil are you insinuating, Madam?"

"Easy, Admiral." With a tug at his cravat, Everett loosened his neck cloth, tossed the linen to the blotter and adopted an almost predatory demeanor. "Mother, Sabrina is my wife. And it would seem she is now the countess of Woverton. If Charles made an arrangement on that account, then it will go unfulfilled."

"But, Everett—"

"It will go unfulfilled." Everett stood, crossed the room, and took Sabrina's hand. She rose, and he positioned her at his side. "This woman is my wife, and in that there will be no argument."

"But you were recently wed." Raising her chin to imperious heights, the marchioness said, "Unless the vows have been consummated, there is still time to obtain an annulment." She reached into her reticule and produced a bundle of documents. "I have taken the liberty of having our solicitor draw up the necessary papers. He assures me everything can be handled with the utmost discretion and expedience."

The world tilted beneath her feet, and Sabrina clutched her husband's arm. Afraid she might spill the contents of her belly on Everett's fine rug, she bit the fleshy side of her hand.

"Lady Talbot, I have never struck a woman in my life, but you stretch the limits of feminine deportment to dangerous depths." Her formidable father glowered as he came to her defense. "I suggest you guard your tongue."

"Well." Elizabeth's eyes grew wide with shock. "I have never—"

"Indeed! I am bound by no such constraints." Her mother, who thus far had remained silent, stepped into the fray. "How dare you insult my daughter? I ought to—"

"Pray, a moment." Everett accepted the offensive documents from his mother, made a show of perusing them, walked to the fireplace, and tossed them into the flames.

It was then that Sabrina realized she had been holding her breath. Had she swooned in front of her mother-in-law, she would have killed herself.

"What are you doing?" the marchioness asked.

"I am fully prepared to undertake the responsibilities of the title." Slowly, deliberately, Everett turned and pinned his mother with a harsh stare. "As to the matter of my wife, there will be no annulment. End of discussion."

MUCH LATER, Everett escorted Sabrina to her chambers. Her parents had gone home, her mother having promised to send a suitable dress for mourning. Her reluctant in-laws had been ensconced in a guestroom for the night. They were to journey to Oxfordshire at first light.

It had not occurred to Sabrina that her wedding night loomed until they entered her sitting room. Despite the sad revelation of the day, and the fact that her new relations wanted nothing to do with her, nervous excitement burned beneath her skin. Desire licked at her senses, and she suppressed a quiver of anticipation.

Everett closed the door and leaned against the oak panel. "Are you all right?"

"I am fine." She mustered her best smile. "And I was going to ask you the same."

Cool and casual, he strolled to her. Was there something she was supposed to do, as his wife? When he snaked his arms about her waist, she skimmed her palms over his shoulders and twined her fingers in his hair.

And waited for the kiss that never came.

Instead, he nuzzled her temple. "This is not how I had planned to spend our wedding night."

"I am sure we can survive it." She pressed her lips to the warm flesh of his neck. "We will have enough nights for two lifetimes, I imagine."

Everett pulled back, brought up her hands, tugged off her gloves, and tossed them to a chair. Her pulse raced out of control and her heartbeat sounded in her ears as he paused to nip each fingertip and then licked her palms.

The apprehension that gripped her at the mention of an annulment vanished. In its place, the flame of desire flickered, commanding her senses. Pleasure danced a wicked waltz over her skin, and lust burned in her loins. And for the first time, Sabrina understood the pain Everett had spoken of that day in her parent's drawing room.

Because she ached with a powerful hunger.

With boldness she never knew she possessed, she set her mouth to his and a sensuous duel ensued. A desperate need bloomed in the pit of her belly, and she was frightened and undaunted, at once. But when she slid her hands beneath his coat, he broke their kiss.

"You should rest." He escorted her to the entrance of her bedchamber. "Try to forget about today."

Sabrina recalled the fascinating conversation with her mother concerning the event that would take place tonight. No doubt her thoughtful husband would allow her the customary opportunity to prepare herself. It would not be proper for her to appear too interested. So, despite the inclination to topple him to the floor, she deferred to his judgment.

"All right." Should she inform him she could be naked in a matter of seconds? A countess would probably not be so hasty. "I shall ready myself for bed."

FIGHTING every urge to claim his bride in the most elemental fashion possible, Everett turned on his heel and had not stopped until he gained the safety and sanity of his study. Staring into the flames in the hearth, a balloon of brandy sat, untouched, in his hand.

"Charles, you must have needed this every day of your life." He toasted his older brother and downed the contents in one gulp.

Everett revisited the loneliness of his childhood and the years spent in confinement with only his nanny for company. While his brother was included in all the family gatherings, and was often the center of attention, Everett had been left to watch from afar—as an outsider. And though no one had ever said as much, he knew what he was, nothing more than a spare. He was the extra, the second son.

But as Charles achieved adulthood with nary a scratch, it became painfully evident no one had much use for Everett. While Charles cried like a pathetic milquetoast when he left home for Eton, Everett had welcomed the move. At least at school, he expected to be alone.

How ironic was it that Eton was where he had discovered true friendship in the form of Trevor Marshall. With similar parental relationships, he and Trevor shared their despair. Years of solitude made them a perfect pair. When other boys went home for the holidays, he and Trevor stayed behind, often taking dinner with their schoolmaster and his family. At night, they ran the cavernous halls of their dorms, playing hide and seek or telling scary stories until they grew tired and finally slept.

They never talked about their relations.

As they grew into men, they entered Oxford. The family pinned their hopes on Charles, only to be disappointed as he failed his exams, time and again. To his abiding delight, Everett graduated at the top of his class. Afterward, he entered the Royal Navy and fought under Nelson. He served his commission with honor, while his elder sibling had done nothing more than bear the societal rank.

Having survived the infamous Battle of Trafalgar, he opted to go into business for himself, rather than recommission in the navy. He purchased shares in an American timber company and made a fortune. Shortly thereafter, he acquired property, while his brother had done nothing but squander money by gambling and drinking.

Strange, he had spent his entire life envying his elder sibling, his title, and the love and affection he garnered from their parents. Now that he had it—all of it—Everett realized he did not want it.

The future he had planned seemed impossible, because he was now the earl of Woverton. There were strictures to observe, estates to manage, and tenants to oversee. The weight of the title and its accompanying duties were an anchor about his neck.

The only positive aspect was he needed to get himself an heir. At the moment, there was nothing he would rather do than tumble his wife. But Sabrina had married Lord Everett Markham, second son and ordinary man.

What if she preferred not to be a countess?

While he could not walk away from his family, she could. When he declared there would be no annulment, he had spoken on his behalf. He had not considered what she wanted. If he took her now, if he consummated their vows, there would be no escape. Regardless of how much he desired her, he could not make love to his wife.

At least, not yet.

He needed to give her time, even if it killed him— and it might. Tomorrow, they would journey to Tantallon Hall, the Talbot ancestral pile, and Everett despised the place. It held no happy memories for him, because he had never felt welcome there. His brother would be buried in the family plot, amid a sea of Markham's past.

Once the unpleasant business concluded, he and Sabrina would do as he had originally intended. They would journey to his home, Beaumaris. Then, should she express such a wish, he would grant her an annulment.

"God, help me if it comes to that."

Resting elbows to knees, Everett buried his face in his hands.

SABRINA WOKE SLOWLY the following morning, stared at the ceiling, stretched her arms above her head, and frowned. Something was amiss. Seconds later, she bolted upright.

She was not in bed.

She was not naked.

She was not curled beside her equally naked husband.

According to her mother, that was to be expected.

Her heart beat, wild and rapid, in her chest, and she winced with shock. It was morning, and she had spent her wedding night, alone, on the *chaise*, where she had adopted a seductive pose to wait for Everett to return.

Standing, she paused to rub the small of her back before crossing the room to tug on the bell pull. After dressing in a high-neck, black bombazine contraption she might have read about in a book on torture, she descended the grand staircase, her mood as morose as her attire.

Nodding an acknowledgement, Everett said nothing when she entered the dining room. At the table, Sabrina sipped some tea and shuffled her eggs from one side of the plate to the other. It was remarkable that she was too upset to eat. But food was not on her mind. A single question claimed her attention to the detriment of all else.

Why had Everett not come to her last night?

She was a married woman and still a virgin. Surely there was something wrong with that.

After his numerous promises.

After the subtle innuendoes and naughty whispers.

After the illicit caresses.

He had done nothing? It made no sense. Unless...Everett had not intended to consummate their vows, given the change in his circumstances.

There was one reason she could think of for not relieving her of her maidenhead. Despite what he had said in the study, her husband considered an annulment. Perhaps, now that he was an earl, he no longer found her an acceptable wife.

And she could not blame him.

Because Sabrina knew not the first thing about being a countess. There were so many rules to follow—and she had never been good with rules. Her experience was in breaking them. But she knew the expectations were high, and there would be many among the *ton* hoping to see her fail, if only for a good chuckle.

In a blur of activity, their trunks were packed, and Sabrina soon found herself sitting beside her silent spouse in the sumptuous traveling coach belonging to his parents. Occupying the seat opposite them, the marquess and marchioness gazed out the windows. Without warning, Everett's father inclined his head and caught her studying him. He appeared a friendly sort when he smiled, which he had done just then. Sabrina returned the gesture. Her father-in-law stretched his legs and shuffled in his seat before settling once more.

"Tell me a bit about yourself, my dear," the marquess asked, unaware of the hazard into which he had entered.

It was his misfortune, and probably that of the others present, not to know that when Sabrina Francis Douglas Markham was nervous, she chatted incessantly at the slightest prompt.

"Well, my mother always says I am my father's daughter, and I suppose she would know. I have always preferred fishing to embroidery." Sabrina grimaced. "Never have taken a liking to such drudgery. I ask you, what good can come of it?"

The marquess chuckled.

The marchioness humphed and turned up her nose.

Everett reclined in the corner, folded his arms, and closed his eyes.

Two hours later...

"When I was ten, I could climb a tree better than most boys, though my mother thought it highly improper. But she had Cara, and my older sister is the feminine ideal. I call her Miss Perfect, and I cannot fathom why she is not married. You know, I never thought much of getting married, as it seemed quite unfair to be subjected to the whims of a man."

The marquess laughed, hearty and boisterous, and slapped a hand to a thigh.

The marchioness snorted and rolled her eyes.

Everett still propped in the corner, the hint of a smile on his lips.

Four hours later...

"And then when I was sixteen, I slid down the balustrade in our townhouse and fell flat on my bottom. I could not sit comfortably for a sennight. It was dreadful and reminded me of the time I was thrown from my horse." Sabrina groaned. "I tried to jump a hedge, and a rather large one at that, and the mare had the good sense not to follow my lead. Unfortunately, I sailed through the air like a sparrow. However, as I do not have wings, my landing was awfully rough."

The marquess held a hand to his belly, as his guffaws reverberated through the coach.

The marchioness sat, spine straight, and made a point to ignore her daughter-in-law.

Enjoying the retelling of her existence, Sabrina showed her mother-in-law the same courtesy. But how she wished for some sign of approval from her husband.

Everett remained still as deadwood in the squabs—but all of a sudden, he offered her a whisper of a wink.

CHAPTER SEVEN

*T*antallon Hall was a dreary estate built entirely of beige Barnack stone. It boasted no embellishments, no ornamentation, and not even a crenellated tower. The flowerbeds contained no colorful blooms, only severe, boxed shrubbery. It was, Sabrina thought, the perfect venue for a funeral.

The family viewing was a small affair. She took her place beside her husband, who sported a black armband like his father. As she gazed on a portrait of the brother-in-law she never knew, she noted the similarities he shared with Everett.

Both siblings had the same unruly brown locks. An austere, patrician nose sat as a prominent feature between chiseled cheeks, and his chin was squared and proud in an uncanny replica of his younger sibling. And though Charles had possessed the same amber-colored eyes, his had not danced with fiery sparks, as her husband's.

The service and subsequent graveside ceremony were an equally solemn affair. While there were those who shed tears, Sabrina noted neither Everett nor his mother cried. The marquess, however, looked to be a man of broken spirit.

The wake was an ocean of Markhams and their connections, and the great hall filled to overflow. Soon, she was lost amid the many names and titles. Somewhere in the middle of the gathering, it dawned on her that as the future marchioness, it was her duty to assume the role of matriarch to the sizable dynasty.

With that thought in mind, she sought her father-in-law and found him sitting alone in the library. "My lord, you seem so sad. Is there anything I can do?"

"Do not frown, my dear." Mustering a lopsided grin, he chucked her chin. "I will be all right. But while I have lost my eldest born, I feel as if I have no connection with my second son, either."

Unprepared for his frank revelation, Sabrina flinched. "My lord, you mustn't say such things."

"But it is true." His shoulders drooped, and the marquess lowered his gaze. "I fear I have made a dreadful mistake, and Everett will never forgive me."

"Rubbish." Clenching fistfuls of her skirts to conceal her unsteady hands, she realized she might not be ready to assume the roll of matriarch. "Everett is an exceedingly forgiving and indulgent man. I daresay he never would have married me were he otherwise." Of course, she prayed her husband intended to keep her for his wife.

The marquess smiled, an affectation she found genuine, and chuckled in a deep rumble that quaked his chest. He cleared his throat and in a hushed voice said, "My dear, you are a ray of sunshine peeking through the darkest of clouds. I am pleased my son married you, as you are exactly what he needs."

"Thank you, my lord." How nice it was to hear kind

words from her in-law. "I hope he shares your opinion." And in that she had not lied, because Everett had yet to come to her bed.

Perhaps he had forgotten the necessity.

Perhaps it was time she reminded him.

She left the marquess to search for her errant husband.

They had spent little time together since arriving at Tantallon Hall. Of course, Everett had been busy meeting with solicitors and land agents. And she had been tasked with managing the guests and aiding the marchioness with preparations for the funeral.

While Sabrina thought it the height of impropriety, and surely the greatest insult to the dead, she could not erase the matter foremost on her mind. It was an obsession that kept her waking hours occupied with no relief in sight.

Why would Everett not make her his?

Was the man not supposed to be nipping at her skirts? Although she could hardly blame him—the marchioness had installed them in separate rooms. But what bothered her most was Everett had not complained. She had expected her new spouse to raise the rooftops, because Sabrina had surely wanted to say something, but he had not uttered a word, merely accepted the situation with impassivity. With each passing day, her heretofore-unfailing confidence flagged to perilous depths.

For what was he waiting?

They were married.

They were supposed to make love.

She tried not to wonder at his motive for leaving their union unconsummated, tried to push it into the farthest reaches of her mind. But somehow, lingering doubts taunted her at every turn. When she located her other half on the terrace, he was engaged in conversation with a young lady. As she considered whether or not to intrude, Everett spied her.

"Ah, here is my lady." He flicked his wrist in entreaty. "Darling, this is Lady Celia Devane. She was to marry my brother." Everett slipped his arm about Sabrina's waist. "Lady Celia, this is my wife, Sabrina, countess of Woverton."

Petite, blonde, and green-eyed, Lady Celia had a waist to rival a wasp's. She was the definition of femininity, beautiful, and elegant—everything Sabrina was not. In short, she was perfect. If Sabrina could ever hate anyone on sight, she thought that woman an excellent candidate. But she had never cared for the ugly emotion, so she settled for fierce dislike.

"Countess." With poise and refinement, Lady Celia curtseyed. "So pleased to make your acquaintance."

Bloody hell, even her voice was dainty.

So that was the woman the marchioness preferred to her current daughter-in-law. Sabrina would have loved to tip her challenger on her backside, but she resisted the urge. Let it never be said she was a poor sport. "It is lovely to meet you, as well, Lady Celia."

"I believe I see my father." Lady Celia dipped her chin. "If you will excuse me." Grace personified, the young woman glided onto the terrace, giving Sabrina another reason to feel less than perfect.

"Walk with me," Everett whispered in her ear.

Gooseflesh covered Sabrina's arms, and she was grateful for the long sleeves of her black gown. "I should like that very much, my lord," she managed to reply calmly. Inside, she danced a merry jig, as it was the first time since their wedding that her new husband expressed any desire to spend a moment alone with her.

Together they coursed the pebbled path through the

rose bushes to the topiary gardens. The winding trail led beyond a tall hedge and forked. Everett steered her to the right. There, tucked amid the oaks, stood a tiny gazebo.

Sabrina blinked when they entered the small structure. As her vision adjusted to the dimness, she spied two small stone benches on either side of the gazebo. She sat on one and was disappointed when Everett perched opposite her. Grasping the edge of the bench, she stared at her slippered feet.

"How are you faring?" she inquired, to mask her dismay.

"As well as can be expected." Everett sighed. "This is not how I foresaw the beginning of our marriage."

Sabrina glanced at her husband. With a downcast expression, he seemed so melancholy, and she desperately wanted to comfort him but was unsure of her welcome. And right now, she could take no rejection. "Do not worry. This will pass, and everything will be as it was."

"I wish I could believe that." He met her gaze. "But I fear our lives will never be as I had planned."

She frowned.

What had he meant? Had he thought her incapable, inadequate, or both? Was he trying to tell her they had no future? Had he truly wanted an annulment? How could she let her husband know she was up to the task, that she could be a good and dutiful countess?

"We will get through this and, I daresay, many a storm in the coming years." She inhaled a shivery breath and hoped she had swayed him. "We have to be strong and persevere."

"Forever the optimist." Everett unfolded his arms, uncrossed his legs, and appeared to relax. "Have I told you how proud I am of you? I have watched you this week, and my mother would never have been able to arrange this affair without your help."

"It is my duty, as your wife, to be of service." Bloody hell, Sabrina would rub her mother-in-law's feet if it would convince his family of her competence. "Of course I would offer assistance, and I shall continue to do so for however long we are here."

"That's my girl." For a few seconds, Everett said nothing, though he stared at her with unveiled interest. "We will not stay here forever, I promise. There is business to which I must tend, then we shall set off for Beaumaris, as I originally intended."

Shuffling her weight to conceal her nervous trembling, Sabrina decided she would have been much more comfortable if her husband were sitting beside her. "Just the two of us?"

"Aye." He chuckled. "Just the two of us."

For several minutes, Sabrina waited for him to do something—anything. How she wanted him to kiss her, to touch her, to love her. Was there any rule of etiquette that barred her from making the first move? Bother that. They were married, and propriety was never one of her strong suits.

She stood, crossed the floor, turned aside, and plopped herself in his lap. Everett looked his surprise, and before he could protest—if he was going to protest—she wound her arms about his neck and pressed her mouth to his.

Everett rewarded her with a lustful kiss she felt all the way to her toes. His hands groped and kneaded, caressing her body through the forbidding restriction of her gown. A familiar heat burned in her belly, and delicious shivers danced along her spine. His was not the response of a man wishing to end their marriage, and neither was it a rejection.

Sabrina could have jumped for joy.

A callused palm grazed her ankle and captured her attention. Gasping in surprise, she opened her eyes and discovered Everett watching her. Had his gaze held any hint of danger she might have retreated from the shock. But what she saw was indescribable. There was no threat, only unshakeable reassurance and something more—something mysterious and enticing.

Focusing on the movement of his hand, she squirmed as he traced circles on the under side of her knee and urged her legs apart. But when his fingers touched the sensitive flesh at the apex of her thighs, Sabrina broke their kiss and buried her face against his neck. If she were not so fascinated, she might have been embarrassed by the intimate invasion.

WITH HIS FINGERS bathed in the fire and honey essence of her desire, Everett rested his head against the wall of the gazebo. Maintaining an illicit rhythm, he imagined how it would feel when his lady took him deep within her for the first time.

Wafts of breath rushed over his skin as she panted and moaned in a sultry summons. How he wanted to make love to his spirited bride, but he had promised himself he would give her the opportunity to decide if she wanted to remain his wife. However, there were other ways to pleasure her without the deflowering. With maddening deliberation, he stroked her swollen flesh, and her hips wriggled in a naughty dance on his lap, taunting the turgid crest of his arousal.

Faster and faster he moved, flagrantly inciting. With her hands fisted in his hair, she stretched her legs, and the tension grew. When her head fell back, Sabrina inhaled sharply, and Everett knew what would happen next. Virgin completion beckoned as her body went rigid. In a flash, he covered her lips with his, and she gave her scream into his mouth. Never had he witnessed anything so erotic in his life.

Indeed, Everett had thought he orchestrated their liaison, until her achingly sweet contractions lured him into an earth-shattering climax, and the warmth of his seed oozed over his skin beneath his clothes.

He had not expected that.

Twenty minutes later they strolled at a relaxed pace to the main house. Her skirts had been righted and a faint blush colored Sabrina's cheeks. And although it was almost summer, Everett had buttoned his coat to conceal the evidence, a telltale stain on his breeches, of his afternoon delight.

And how delightful it had been.

THROUGHOUT THE FOLLOWING WEEK, elegant equipages of all makes and models rolled up the graveled drive in a steady procession of condolence calls. Each stopped before the entranceway and deposited another matron of the local community. Sabrina assisted her mother-in-law by supervising the refreshments and wondered why she had been allowed anywhere near the drawing room during the visits.

While she and Everett remained at Tantallon Hall, the marchioness had made it clear she approved not of her daughter-in-law and had done everything in her power to make Sabrina feel unwelcome. Though she had done her best to be strong, she grew weary of the constant criticism.

"Would you care for more tea, Lady Celia?" Sabrina

smiled at the young woman the marchioness had been fawning over ever since she had arrived.

"Yes, thank you." Lady Celia held her cup steady while Sabrina refilled it.

"Sabrina!" The marchioness stood and folded her arms rigidly in front of her. "How many times have I told you, take the empty cup to the trolley and replenish it. Do not carry the teapot around like a common servant."

"I am sorry, my lady." Sabrina flinched and almost spilt the hot liquid on Celia. "I forgot."

She had tried everything she could think of to earn Lady Elizabeth's approval. While Sabrina had given her new relation use of her name, the marchioness of Talbot insisted Sabrina address her in-law formally.

"Stop dawdling and return the pot to the trolley, at once," the marchioness snapped.

Although the majority of guests snickered and eyed Sabrina with disdain, Lady Celia cast a sympathetic expression. Was there nothing she could do right? Holding the porcelain to her chest, Sabrina crossed the room—and tripped.

The teapot launched from her grasp, and its hot contents sprayed her dress as she fell, face down, on the Aubusson rug.

"Clumsy girl." The marchioness shrieked. "Look what you have done."

Propping on her elbows, Sabrina tucked her legs and sat on her heels. Her flesh burned from the scalding tea, but it hurt nowhere near as much as the injury to her pride, and the pot scattered in pieces about the floor.

"Are you all right, Lady Sabrina? May I be of assistance?" Lady Celia offered unfailing support. "Do you require a doctor?"

"No." Painfully conscious of the disapproving stares from the other ladies present, Sabrina crossed her arms in front of herself. "But I need to change my dress."

Lady Celia inclined her head. "Please, let me help you."

As they neared the doorway, the marquess and Everett appeared.

"What is going on here?" The marquess looked at Sabrina, then his wife. "What on earth are you screaming about, Lizzy?"

"That wretched girl broke my teapot. She did it on purpose to spite me." In a performance Sabrina thought worthy of the stage, the marchioness bent and made a show of retrieving the shards. "This was from my grandmother's service."

"What?" Sabrina froze in her tracks. "I did no such thing. It was an accident." She faced her husband. "I tripped and fell. It was unintentional, I swear."

"Go to your room." Everett patted her shoulder and kissed her temple. "Let me handle this."

"I shall accompany you." Lady Celia gave Sabrina a gentle nudge. "Perhaps you need a nap."

Sabrina exited the drawing room with nary a sound, but she halted and would have returned to defend herself, had Celia not stopped her, when Everett replied, "I assume full responsibility and will compensate you for the damages."

As though she had been ordered to the Tower, Sabrina trudged up the stairs, Lady Celia in tow. Once they gained the relative privacy of her bedchamber, the young woman helped Sabrina change from one dour black dress to another. Because some of the pins in her hair had loosened during the commotion, Sabrina sat at her vanity to reset the tight knot atop her head.

"Here." Lady Celia retrieved a silver-backed brush and

smoothed Sabrina's tangled curls. "Allow me to be of assistance."

Sabrina scrutinized her reflection in the mirror and sniffed. "Why are you being so nice to me?"

"You have been nice to me." Lady Celia shrugged. "Since I do not have many friends, I had hoped to claim you as such."

"That may not be possible." Sabrina stared at her shaking hands and wondered about the conversation currently taking place in the drawing room. "I am not sure how much longer I will be welcome here."

"Do not worry about the marchioness." The incomparable Lady Celia smiled, set the brush aside, and placed her hands on Sabrina's shoulders. "Lady Elizabeth is angry because she cannot control you. You are your own woman, Lady Sabrina, and I envy your fortitude."

"You are in the minority." Sabrina snorted. "And I think your envy is seriously misplaced."

"Well, I disagree." Lady Celia fixed a pin and then reset another curl. "And may I call you Sabrina?"

"Of course." She chuckled. "But only if I can call you Celia."

Celia gasped. "Please, do so."

"Perfect." She turned. "Then let us shake on it."

"Oh." A wide-eyed Celia declared, "I feel so powerful."

"What is this?" Everett stood in the doorway to her sitting room. "Are you conspiring, as I am not certain I can survive your combined efforts?"

"Fie on you, sir. We were simply trading pleasantries, Lord Woverton." She peered at Sabrina and winked. "May I call on you, Lady Sabrina?"

Holding herself with regal hauteur, which consumed her last scrap of dignity, Sabrina borrowed a response from her newfound friend's repertoire and dipped her chin. "Please, do so."

With a marginal rally, she recovered some of her customary derring-do, until her delicate collaborator paused, perched on tiptoes, and whispered something in Everett's ear. For the second time in as many minutes, Sabrina feared she might swoon. When he furrowed his brow and pinned Sabrina with a troubled gaze, she teetered on the brink of unconsciousness.

Uh, oh.

Perhaps Sabrina had been wrong to take Celia into confidence, given the title that hung in the balance. A dark sense of foreboding traipsed her spine and settled in her gut. Alone with her husband, she wanted to confront him about his mother, their marriage, and the maidenhead she seemed destined to maintain. But her knees buckled, as she trembled. To her chagrin, she was scared.

And Sabrina Francis Douglas Markham was unaccustomed to fear.

Had Everett, at last, decided she was unfit to be his countess? Would he commit her to an asylum? Past powerful peers had resorted to such distasteful tactics to rid themselves of objectionable wives. Perhaps, if she were lucky, he would have her personal effects packed and return her to her parents, in humiliation and scandal.

She would rather promenade naked through Hyde Park.

"Sabrina, are you all right?" Everett knelt before her. "What is it, love? You are white as a sheet."

"My lord, I swear I did not drop your mother's teapot, on purpose. It was an accident." For good or ill, it was time to accept her fate. Was ever a man known to divorce a wife over a bit of broken porcelain? "You may take a lash to my bottom if it would make you feel better, but I am guilty only of being clumsy, because I stumbled. If Lady Talbot requires an apology, know she will have my most humble regrets. But I say again, it was unintentional."

Everett tapped the tip of her nose. "I know."

"You do?" She opened and then closed her mouth. "But—how?"

"Darling Sabrina." With his arms at her waist, he stood and carried her with him. "You are trembling. What is wrong?"

"I thought you angry with me," she blurted and inhaled a shaky breath. "And I did not know how you would react."

"My lady, I would never hurt you." His expression softened as he set her on her feet. And then he cupped her chin. "I would never hurt you. As to the incident with the teapot, Mother tripped you and caused the whole ugly affair."

"What?" A wave of nausea left her reeling. "How can you be sure, as you were not in the room when it happened."

"Lady Celia witnessed the entire incident," he explained with a frown. "As you returned to the trolley, Mother stuck out her foot and sent you for a tumble."

"But—why?" How she wanted to cry, but she was no water pot.

"Why else?" Everett scowled as he tucked a wayward curl behind her ear. "To discredit you. To embarrass you in front of her friends."

"Oh, Everett. Can we leave this place?" Sabrina shuddered. While insults were nothing new, malicious disruption was entirely unfamiliar. "Your mother hates me."

"What is this?" With a demeanor of concern mixed with a tinge of humor, he caressed her cheek. "Is my saucy Sabrina afraid of a miserable old woman?"

"Yes." Could he not see the urgency, the danger? She wrenched his wrist. "I am afraid of anyone and anything that threatens to drive us apart."

"Nothing will ever come between us, but we must remain here, for the time being." With a finger to her lips he silenced her impending protest. "Give me a sennight, Sabrina. There are tasks I must complete, but I promise, a week at most, and we will journey to Beaumaris."

Against instincts to the contrary, she acquiesced with a nod.

"But in the meantime, I see no reason we cannot pass the afternoon in private." In a single swift move, Everett swept her off her feet, whisked her to the bed, and eased her to the down mattress. "And I know well my lady's pleasure."

Because her hopes had been dashed too many times, Sabrina had not wanted to believe Everett would finally stake his claim and make her his in the most elemental but irrefutable fashion. To her infinite disappointment, he had not touched her since the spectacular interlude in the gazebo, when she had tasted heretofore-unimaginable bliss. And though she would deny it should anyone ask, she had waited for him that night, until the first light of dawn. Since then, she had resigned to become the oldest living married virgin.

Or, dare she think it, suffer an annulment.

Everett shrugged off his coat and waistcoat and tossed them to the foot of the bed. Then the mattress dipped, he stretched beside her, and she rolled against him with a half-shriek. In an instant, she reached for him.

And he reached for her.

Their lips met, tongues tangled in a playful dance, and she speared her fingers through his hair. Certain that her bones had turned to mush; Sabrina feared she might never walk again. But when Everett moved to rest atop her, and she bore his delicious weight for the first time, she summoned the strength to arch into him.

Salacious shivers coursed her skin, a hedonistic hunger burgeoned in her belly, and she wanted nothing more than to rid herself of her clothes and slide naked against his mysterious male frame, which she ached to know on a more intimate level. With his knee, he nudged her legs apart and settled his hips to hers. And the ridge of his impressive erection rode hard against her, his wool breeches and the thin silk of her gown no real barrier, as he pumped methodically.

Ravenous lust licked at her nerves, and passion followed in its wake. With a cry of desperation, she untied his cravat, drew the yard of linen from his neck, and then unfastened his shirt, which proved tricky with shaking fingers. When she brushed aside the fine lawn, and discovered the heated flesh of his chest, she moaned her appreciation, and Everett rewarded her efforts with a husky groan.

But just as their impromptu but prayed for assignation gained traction, he eased to her side. Bereft of his warmth, Sabrina prepared to protest, but her complaint died in her throat when he tickled her calf and then hiked her skirts. Clutching her wrist, he pressed her palm to the bulge in his breeches, and she longed to touch him, as she recalled his tantalizing tutelage in the drawing room. At her husband's prompt, she spread wide her thighs in unmistakable welcome—then her foot struck his boot.

And an ugly realization dawned.

Much to her dissatisfaction, Everett remained fully clothed, as had she. According to her mother, he should have stripped her bare to make love. Nagging suspicion clawed at her nerves, and she deduced his intent to perform the same enjoyable but altogether insufficient act he had executed in the gazebo. After all, he could not claim the proof of her virtue and consummate their vows with his fingers.

"Everett—no." How well she remembered the pain and the emptiness that had haunted her waking hours, for days, after their seemingly harmless tryst. Even now, revisiting that memory buoyed a cold chill in her breast. In stark panic, she closed her legs, locked her knees, and denied him entry. "I cannot do this."

"Why?" He lifted his head. "What is wrong?"

"Stop." She pushed down the hem of her gown, as if doing so might staunch the relentless shame of his rejection. "Please, I can take no more."

"I beg your pardon, my lady." For what seemed an eternity, her husband had not moved. Without a word, he inched from her side, tossed his legs over the edge of the bed, and stood. After retrieving his clothes, he glanced over his shoulder. "I apologize, madam. It will not happen again."

As Everett exited her chamber, Sabrina felt as if he were walking out of her life.

It will not happen again.

Inside, she wanted to die.

For a long while, she studied the canopy of her four-poster, appraising and second-guessing her courtship. Had she misinterpreted the depth of his ardor? Had she overestimated the profundity of his attachment? Had she spun unsubstantiated conclusions from whole cloth?

Preferring the solitude of her quarters, she refused to join her husband and his family for dinner and had a tray delivered to her chambers, but she consumed not a bite. And though it was late when she climbed between the sheets, it was hours before she slept, because an oppressive pain nestled in her chest, and she struggled to breathe. Inexorable agony dammed her throat, and she succumbed to inestimable grief.

And then the tears flowed.

It was a new experience for her, one she would not relish.

For the first time in her life, Sabrina Francis Douglas Markham cried herself to sleep.

CHAPTER EIGHT

*T*o Sabrina's abiding gratitude, Lady Celia called the very next day. Call her a coward, but Sabrina had her friend shown to a sitting room, because she had spoken to no one, other than her lady's maid, since the unfortunate incident with Everett the previous afternoon.

"Sabrina, forgive me for saying so, but you look dreadful." Dressed in pale yellow muslin, Celia portrayed, as always, the enviable picture of elegance.

Assessing her own gloomy mourning togs, Sabrina sighed. How odd it was that she had never given much thought to the clothes she wore or her coiffure, but now she tangled with an overwhelming desire to slip into a dress of vibrant blue or pink and muss her hair. Of course, she would have marched stark naked through the drawing room if it would encourage her husband to make love to her.

"I am afraid I am not a successful countess." But was it her fault? Could any man find appealing a woman wrapped in black, especially when her demeanor matched her dour togs? That morning, sitting at her vanity, she had not recognized her reflection in the mirror. Dark circles beneath her eyes contrasted sharply with her pale face, and sadness was evident in her visage.

"Nonsense." Celia crossed her legs. "You are a marvelous countess."

"And, by the by, thank you for setting the record straight, in the matter of the broken teapot." Sabrina shook her head. "I knew I did not trip, at least, not on my own. I was so careful."

"The marchioness has you in her sights." Celia frowned, cast a quick glance at the door, and then leaned close as if to impart a secret of utmost importance. "And she wants me to marry Lord Woverton."

"I already guessed that." Sabrina wrinkled her nose and bit her lip. Should she ask the question foremost on her mind? "Do you wish to marry Everett?"

"Heavens, no." With an expression of unutterable horror, the young woman smoothed her skirts. "And I did not want to marry Charles. He always smelled quite foul—like my father's study, after one of his late-night card games."

Relieved but confused, Sabrina considered her predicament. "Then why did you agree to the marriage?"

"Duty, I suppose." Celia shrugged. "And the marriage was arranged before I was born, and I have always obeyed my parents, without complaint, which is why I have an ulterior motive for befriending you."

"Oh?" Sabrina picked a speck of lint from her sleeve. "Do tell."

"I want to be more like you, if you would consent to teach me. You are so dramatic—so vibrant. You married a man of your choosing, and I want to do the same." With a bounce of enthusiasm, Celia clasped her hands to her bodice. "Can you do it, Sabrina? Can you help me be more assertive?"

"I am not sure." Just as Sabrina was about to point out that she was not the best role model, a brilliant plan dawned in her brain, and she snapped her fingers. "But I will do it on one condition."

"And that would be—what?" Celia furrowed her brow.

"You teach me to be a lady," she blurted.

With a pact sealed by an oath of eternal damnation in recompense for breaking the bond of secrecy, and the necessary equipment procured from the butler, she led her unconventional student to the requisite environment, and the initiation of Lady Celia Devane to the world of independent thought commenced.

"Pull on the line, now ease up a bit," Sabrina instructed her pupil. "The goal is to tease the fish."

"Like this?" Barefooted, Celia followed the directive and made her first cast, holding tight to the rod, but the line snagged a patch of grass. "Oh, dear."

"Free the hook, take your time, and try again." Tutoring from an awkward vantage, Sabrina commenced training, of a different sort, and traversed a fallen log, while balancing a book on her head. After two successful steps, she lost her balance, waved her arms, wild and unsteady, and stumbled for the umpteenth time. "Bloody hell."

Theirs was an awkward alliance.

"Concentrate." Celia glanced over her shoulder and laughed. "You must focus."

"It is hopeless." Sabrina rolled her eyes and emitted an unladylike groan. "I failed this portion of finishing school, and even Cara could not teach me to be graceful."

"Get back up there, this instant." The young woman set aside her rod, approached, and placed her hands on Sabrina's hips. "Stand straight. If this were a new fishing technique, I daresay you would have mastered it long before now." Celia checked Sabrina's posture and then nodded her approval. "All right. Imagine a fishing line is tied from your nose to your toes. Now, when you take a step, pretend there is an egg between your slipper and the log and tread lightly."

Placing one foot in front of the other, Sabrina traveled the distance without once dropping the book. "I did it." In her excitement, she bent her head, and the heavy tome fell to the ground. "Oh, blast!"

With an expression of awe, Celia covered her mouth. "My, but you swear magnificently." In an elegant sweep Sabrina could never hope to imitate, Celia retrieved the book. "Again."

As before, Sabrina successfully navigated the fallen tree. "Hell's bells, I did it."

The fishing rod skittered on the rocks, and Celia shrieked with joy. "I have a bite."

"Hurry." Sabrina scrambled for the fleeting rod, but Celia caught the end and stood upright.

"What do I do?" She tripped. "Help me."

"Do not panic." Sabrina suffered a vague sense of déjà vu, which transported her to the past and another day, another place, and another stream. Mindful of the moss-covered rocks, she anchored herself. "Pull back, easy. You are doing fine."

Celia engaged the would-be-catch in a tug of war that was anything but fluid. After a wicked yank, she stumbled forward and wrenched hard on the rod. Without warning, the line snapped, and she fell on her bottom.

"Bloody hell!" With eyes as wide as saucers, Celia gasped. "I did it. I used foul language."

"Yes, but I would not tell your mother, if I were you." Sabrina chuckled, pulled her friend off the ground, and dusted her skirts. "She may not share your enthusiasm."

After gathering the rod, the tackle, and the book, they wound their way through the woods toward the main house.

"Sabrina, why are you sad?" Celia slowed her gait. "You seemed so happy when you arrived at Tantallon Hall."

She shrugged. "I fear my husband may regret marrying me."

Celia stopped in her tracks, and Sabrina bumped into her. "Your honesty shocks and humbles me." She held a fist to her chest. "I vow I shall always offer you the same."

"You know, you have a natural dramatic flair all your own." Resituating her fishing gear, Sabrina gave her a nudge. "I doubt you need tutoring in that respect."

"Do you mean it?" Celia looked as if she had just been paid the most spectacular compliment of her life. "Tell me truly."

Sabrina nodded. "Indubitably."

"I have always wanted to be thought of as dramatic." With a whimsical countenance, Celia stared at the sky. "Like an actress on the stage, you know?"

"You have a good start." Sabrina grinned and trudged forth. When she entered the rose garden, she glanced at the gazebo and flinched, because it hurt to recall the afternoon tryst.

"Do you really think Lord Woverton is having second thoughts? I mean he did marry you, after all. There was no arrangement. He must have wanted to take you to wife." Celia compressed her lips. "Think, Sabrina. How did you land him?"

"I do not know." Again she shrugged. "I was just myself."

"Well, you are still you." Celia clucked her tongue. "Right?"

Sabrina stopped so suddenly that she tripped poor Celia. Dropping the pail and the rods, she whirled and hugged her conspirator. "Lady Celia Devane, you are a bloody genius."

THE DINNER BELL PEALED, and Sabrina trod softly, recalling her afternoon lessons, as she descended the stairs. In obeisance of the hastily sketched plan, which she hatched with Celia's aid, Sabrina had lingered in her bedchamber, waiting with forced patience and hoping to be the last one down. As she entered the foyer, Everett, the marquess, and the marchioness strolled from the drawing room.

"So kind of you to see fit to join us," her mother-in-law snapped.

Sabrina refused to take the bait and ignored the miserable crow. "Good evening, Lady Elizabeth."

"Darling Sabrina." Everett's heated gaze traveled her from top to toe, and then he offered his arm. "You are a vision."

"Hello, my lord." Remembering some of the techniques Celia had shown Sabrina, she inclined her head in regal repose, licked her lips, and looked him in the eyes. Then, just before she spoke, she averted her stare and smiled. "I trust you enjoyed a pleasant day."

"On the contrary, it was rather ordinary, love." The flex of his muscles beneath her palm conveyed she had scored a direct hit. Perhaps her husband was not as indifferent as she thought. "At least, until this moment."

Bless you, Lady Celia.

After showing Sabrina to her chair, Everett claimed the opposite seat at the long table, and the marquess and marchioness perched at either end. What her husband had not known was she had deliberately skipped the noon meal, so her usually healthy appetite, absent of late, was in rare form.

In little more than half an hour, Sabrina polished off two bowls of vermicelli soup, a large portion of boiled salmon, a filet of trout, a roasted quarter of lamb, a serving of lobster curry, a modest allowance of prawns, and had set her sights on the Neapolitan cakes.

"Never have I seen such gluttony," the marchioness declared with unmasked disgust.

"Let her alone, Lizzy." The marquess winked. "It is rather refreshing to see a young lady enjoy a meal, instead of picking at her food like a bird."

"May I refill your wine glass, darling?" Everett asked in a low, husky voice, and his entire demeanor bespoke an open challenge she was only too happy to meet. To her delight, his amber depths twinkled with amusement and something mysterious she could not place. "Perhaps you favor a sweet-meat, sweet?"

Sabrina met his gaze, held it, counted to ten as Celia advised, and lowered her stare. She scooted her plate aside as he played footman. "If it is not too much trouble."

"On the contrary, I am most definitely at your service."

Though she resisted the urge to look at him, she had a hunch Everett's service referred to more than dessert, and she could not suppress a delicious shiver of excitement.

～

Burdened with the most stubborn, most painful erection in the history of man, Everett wondered how he would survive dinner without tumbling his wife on the dining room table. Still smarting from her rejection, he had not seen or spoken to her since that awful confrontation in her bedchamber. Because Sabrina had never refused him, he had viewed the incident as a death knell for their marriage and was all but ready to surrender his cause.

Not so anymore.

Perhaps he had rushed her. Had his forceful passion frightened her in the gazebo? They'd had scarcely a moment's peace since their wedding, so her reticence was understandable. And, to his abiding regret, she remained a virgin. But if he claimed her virtue, she would have no choice but to remain his bride.

The death of his brother had turned his world upside down. But it was not only his life, he reminded himself. He was married. Yet he had not considered the effect his newfound status would have on Sabrina.

She had wed Lord Everett Markham—not an earl.

But an earl she now had.

Everett recalled a conversation with Sabrina, from their whirlwind courtship. She had made it very clear that she preferred him without the benefit of rank. It would be just his luck to lose his bride because he had gained a title.

In that instant, Everett realized he needed to rethink his strategy.

"Care to join me for a drink, my boy?" his father inquired.

Everett snapped to attention. "Certainly, sir."

"Well, I believe I shall adjourn to the drawing room." His mother stood and fixed Sabrina with a narrow-eyed stare. "Are you coming, Sabrina?"

"If it is not too much trouble, I should like to withdraw to the library." Casting him a shy glance, his wife set her napkin on her plate. "I need to catch up on my reading."

It was either wishful thinking or an arousal-induced hallucination, but Everett was certain her expression intimated an invitation—one he was inclined to accept. "Bring on the brandy."

The usual English male bonding that occurred after dinner consisted of an intoxicant of some sort, expensive cigars, and ribald discussions involving horseflesh, politics, and mistresses. The ritual typically lasted at least an hour and a half.

Everett managed to escape his sire's company in fifteen minutes.

Fortified with two glasses of his father's finest stock, which he had all but gulped down, Everett stood before the library door. The knob was cool against his damp palm, as flagging confidence had him uttering a prayer for mercy and success. With a last check of his appearance, he buttoned his coat to conceal his aroused state, because he had not wanted to risk frightening Sabrina.

In quiet, he opened the door, peeked inside, and discovered the room was dimly lit. A single candle sat on the table beside a winged back chair, the light insufficient to read. Standing before one of the tall windows, his wife gazed at the night sky beyond the glass.

Careful not to make a sound, he closed the door behind him. For a while, he studied the inexpressible beauty of his most unlikely lady. Her raven hair was piled in a knot atop her head; loose wisps teased the back of her neck. Gowned in black silk, the dark material emphasized the creaminess of her skin, and he imagined the rest of her flesh was just as enticing. And he had to imagine, because although they had been married for three weeks, he had yet to see her naked.

In his mind, he revisited her soft moans and cries as he had pleasured her in the gazebo. The way she had melted in his arms as she experienced completion for the first time. Her expression of innocent fascination had visited his dreams, and he wanted to see it again as she held him within her. As he brought her to sweet release with his body.

Sabrina turned and gasped when she spied him. "My lord, I did not know you were there."

As a hunter, he stalked her. As his prey, she skittered away.

Everett halted and took a minute to calm himself. He had promised himself he would not rush her. They would consummate their marriage soon enough. "I forgot to tell you. It seems my business will be concluded earlier than I had thought."

Strolling along the sidewall, her fingers trailing the bindings of shelved volumes, Sabrina peered over her shoulder. "Oh?"

"Yes." He followed in her wake but slowly closed the distance between them. "We will journey to Beaumaris on Friday, instead of Sunday."

"I shall give instructions to have our things packed."

Everett wished she would face him so he could read her mood. "I trust you are pleased?"

They coursed the interior wall, and Sabrina kept a relaxed pace. "I wish whatever you wish, my lord."

Her apparent indifference portended doom. After enduring his mother, he would have thought she would fly into his arms at the prospect of their departure. Disappointment bloomed as a weight in his chest, and Everett frowned at the back of her head. She reached the corner and continued along the sidewall. In a game of cat and mouse, they had come full circle and were nearing the table bearing the candle.

Though the light was faint, he had not missed the goose-flesh bared by her short-sleeved gown. As it was almost summer, and the room was warm, she could not be chilled. That meant...

Everett grasped her wrist and whirled her around. With something between a sob and a sigh Sabrina flew at him. Lips met, fused. Her arms twined about his neck, she held him to her. The minutes ticked past on the mantel clock as he stood there, gently loving her with his mouth. It was so good to taste her again.

Despite his promises of self-restraint, Everett touched her everywhere, learning her feminine landscape anew. Soon—very soon—he would trace her bare curves with his hands, lips, and tongue. But at that moment, he sipped her slowly, like a fine wine, savoring the warm softness of her body.

Everything inside him ached to take. To claim. But that house was not his home, and he wanted their first time to be on his territory, in his chamber, in his bed. He wanted to make her scream with pleasure and hear her cries reverberating off his walls. Wanted her to lose herself on his silken sheets.

But not tonight.

In one swift move, Everett swept his wife into his arms and settled them into the cozy chair next to the table on which the candle burned. He cradled Sabrina on his lap, one hand resting possessively on her hip. She made no move to resist him, not that he thought she would, so he breathed a sigh of relief and grinned like a randy fop.

"Are you comfortable?"   Everett rubbed his cheek against her hair.

"Infinitely."

"I am sorry I have not had much time for you. I promise that will change once we reach Beaumaris."

"Promise?" She shifted her leg and wiggled her bottom in what he felt sure was an unintended caress of his aching erection.

Everett closed his eyes and bit back a groan. Could she know how she affected him? "You shall enjoy my undivided attention, Lady Woverton."

"I preferred Lady Markham."

In an instant, his overheated body chilled. She had just given voice to his worst nightmare. "My dear, I would gladly return to my untitled state, but I have no choice in the matter."

Sabrina pulled back and stared into his eyes. With a smile and a shrug, she said, "Then we will do as would a Douglas and persevere."

How anyone could make something so complicated sound so simple was beyond him. But at that moment, Everett was not about to correct her. As he let his gaze fall on her rosy lips, she trailed her little pink tongue across her flesh.

"Yes, we will," he murmured against her mouth.

"*Bloody hell!*"

The cry echoed in the air, sending birds scattering from the trees. It was Wednesday, and Sabrina and Celia sat, side by side, on the log near the stream, trading valuable lessons in decorum. One was graceful, polite, and charming.

The other—well, less so.

"Once more." Sabrina leaned forward and placed her hand on Celia's belly. "From your gut."

With steely determination, Celia lifted her chin and inhaled a deep breath. "Bloody hell!"

"Perfect." Sabrina was so proud. "Try again, this time stand with fists on hips."

The young woman assumed the proper stance. "Like this?"

Sabrina nodded. "Let it rip."

Her expression grew serious, and her brow furrowed. "Blast it all!" Celia roared.

"Wonderful." Sabrina could not help but gush over her protégé's progress.

"Was I forceful enough?" Celia inquired with the eagerness of a puppy wanting to please its master.

"Oh, yes," Sabrina assured her.

"If you were my husband, would you take me seriously?"

"Without doubt." Sabrina nodded. "Were I a man, I would be quaking in my boots."

"Really?" Celia clasped her hands to her chest.

"Truly." Sabrina wrinkled her nose. "One more thing. Try not to smile when you swear."

With a huff, Celia pouted. "Did I smile?"

"Afraid so, and it is difficult to garner respect when you smile and swear at the same time." She tapped her slippered foot as her mind searched for a solution. Sabrina snapped her fingers. "I have it. Pretend you have just entered the kitchen and smelled boiling cabbage."

With an expression worthy of the marchioness, Celia grimaced. "Eeewww."

"That is it!" Sabrina hooted. "If we were not fast chums I would fear for my life."

"It was nothing." Celia plopped next to her on the log and frowned. "You are going away so soon. What will I do without you, dearest Sabrina?"

"What you will do is come for a visit." Adopting the most regal pose she had recently learned, Sabrina said, "As the countess of Woverton, I hereby issue a standing invitation to one Lady Celia Devane. You must come, because I want you to meet my friends."

"After all you have told me, I can almost picture them in my head." Celia dusted off her skirts. "Well, enough swearing. We need to prepare you for dinner tonight."

Sabrina would rather walk the plank on the most onerous pirate ship than discuss the impending gathering the marchioness hosted that evening.

"But...I had thought we could begin your fencing lessons."

"Oh, dear." Celia twiddled her thumbs. "I am afraid of sharp objects."

"We can use a stick."

"You are attempting to delay the inevitable." Celia elbowed her in the ribs. "And I want you on your best behavior when you meet my parents."

"Are you coming?"

"Yes, my parents and I will dine with you this evening, so you had better be ready. All right, fold your hands in your lap just so." Celia demonstrated, before reaching out and resituating Sabrina's hands, herself. "Now, keep your chin down and tilt your head ever so slightly."

For the sake of her friend and her husband, Sabrina focused on every morsel of information. She wanted Everett to be proud of his chosen bride, even if he had not wanted to make love to her. As the tears threatened to spill forth, she swallowed hard and committed to memory the finer points of feminine deportment.

Unfortunately, in her zest for etiquette, she lost track of time, and it was late when Sabrina showed Celia to the door. After running up the grand staircase, she rushed through her bath and had to dress for dinner as her hair was pinned into a topknot. When she took her place at her husband's side to greet their arriving guests, her heart pounded in her chest, her palms were damp, and Sabrina was as nervous as a bride on her wedding night—or so she supposed.

Celia was the daughter of the earl and countess of Sherbourne. They were a friendly sort, all warm smiles and twinkling eyes, and Sabrina took to them in an instant. She hoped to make a good impression, because they were the parents of her new friend, and she was thrilled when they asked her to address them informally. Dinner passed without a hitch, and soon the women filed into the drawing room, to be joined shortly thereafter by the men.

"Would you care for more tea, Celia?" Sabrina inclined her head as her dear friend had instructed.

"I would love some," Celia replied.

Sabrina shot a side-glance at the marchioness. She accepted Celia's empty teacup and crossed the room in one elegant sweep, grinning from ear to ear.

The marchioness shrieked, which she had done with annoying frequency. "Ouch!"

"Was that your foot, Lady Talbot?" With an air of cherubic innocence, Sabrina managed to suppress her pleasure at evading another not-so-accidental-fall. "Oh, I am so sorry, how clumsy of me."

Her mother-in-law seemed at a loss for words, which was a miracle.

Celia snickered, and Sabrina bit her tongue to keep from doing the same.

Standing near the tea trolley, Everett caught her stare and arched a brow. "May I be of assistance, my lady?" He lifted the teapot and filled the cups. Quietly, he whispered, "That was inspiring."

She looked at everything but her husband. "I beg your pardon?"

"Join me in the library tonight?" The subtle deepening of his voice told her he had not intended for them to read. "After our guests take their leave?"

Was he asking her to...in the library? Although her mother said the act most often occurred in bed, Sabrina supposed it could be done in alternative locations. Her hands shook, and the tea sloshed in the delicate china. Sabrina closed her eyes, then opened them and focused on his amber depths. "You may depend upon it."

Strange, she had never known it was possible to be hot and cold at once.

The festivities continued late into the night, and Sabrina remained in the drawing room after their dinner guests departed. She cleared the tables of empty glasses, returning everything to the trolley. When she heard her in-laws climbing the stairs, she stepped into the foyer and tiptoed down the hall.

Nervous anticipation licked at her nerves, at her senses, and desire beckoned.

The library door was ajar, and pale gold light shone through the opening. Sabrina looked left, then right, and slipped inside. An iron-like grip encircled her waist, and her feet lost contact with the floor.

"What—"

The words died in her throat as Everett's mouth covered

hers. He kicked the door shut, leaned against the oak panels, and let her body rest against his full length. They had been there before—in a heated clinch, and always she walked away with her virginity intact. A familiar ache gnawed at her belly, and the weight of disappointment settled in her bosom. Sabrina told herself to remain unaffected, to lower her expectations.

She had speared her fingers through his hair and pulled him closer when she realized she had moved.

Sensuous heat melted the chill of frustration as his tongue darted and flicked, inciting her to respond in kind. Everett groaned his appreciation, and she rode a tide of wicked wantonness, pressing her hips to his, mimicking his every movement. A telltale bulge declared his desire, and passion simmered in her veins.

"Oh, Everett."

When he pushed away from the door and delivered her to the comfortable chair in which they had shared a previous pleasurable evening, Sabrina was certain tonight was the night. Whether it happened on the floor, in the chair, against the wall, or atop a pile of books, she cared not, so long as her husband claimed her body.

Settled in his lap, she moaned unabashedly when he slipped his hand inside her bodice and cupped her breast. Desire shivered over her flesh, raw lust licked at her senses. She sighed and squirmed as he pinched a pebbled nipple, but no matter how lovely that felt, he made no move toward the place she wanted—craved—his attention most.

As familiar tension built, panic and frustration beckoned, and she sobbed without restraint.

Everett lifted his head. "What is it, my saucy Sabrina?"

How could she tell him?

She wanted him to touch her in that mysterious place at

the apex of her thighs. Wanted him to wreak sweet havoc on her as he had in the gazebo, culminating in that indescribable bliss. She needed him to do that for her, but she was too embarrassed to ask.

"I want—" She could not say it.

The pain in the pit of her belly grew in epic proportions. Her breath came hard and fast, and she cried his name as Everett bent his head, fastened his lips over her nipple, and drew her into his mouth. The library walls seemed to fall away, and Sabrina floated near the precipice of her sensuous goal. But release eluded her, remaining one step beyond her reach. Drowning in desire, she wiggled her hips in a restless entreaty, all but begging for the rippling contractions that would ease her hurt. But Everett made no move to touch her where she needed it most.

Finally, in blinding desperation, she grasped his wrist and pressed his hand to her belly. Burying her face in his neck, she slid his hand down. "Please."

A SHUDDER of recognition trembled through him, and Everett knew without doubt that Sabrina wanted him. Perhaps, if he played his cards right, she would accept the life mired in social strictures that came with the title he possessed. But now was not the time to broach the subject.

Not when she lay, soft and feminine, in his lap.

His patience had paid off, and victory was near. He had only to wait a little while longer, and he would claim her. When they arrived at Beaumaris, he would give her a few days to adjust—well, perhaps a day—and woo her. Then he would pounce on her.

Sabrina moaned again.

"Shhh, love." He kissed her bare shoulder. "I know what you need."

Very slowly, he trailed his hand along the sumptuous curve of her leg. Reaching for the hem of her gown, he slipped his hand beneath the black silk and skimmed his palm over her heated flesh in the opposite direction.

An hour later, with the rest of the house abed, Everett carried Sabrina, asleep in his arms, to her chamber. He entered her room and closed the door with a nudge of his hip. Over and over her sweet cry of surrender played in his head. As he rid her of her gown. As he forced himself not to remove her chemise—he would have made love to her if he had. But they had only one night left in that house.

Then they would journey to Beaumaris.

They would begin the life he had carefully planned, starting with the consummation of their vows. They would start a family, and he would get the earldom in order. It was going to happen. He would live his dream.

And his most unlikely lady would be right there with him.

After looking his fill, at least for that night, he pulled the covers over her, tucking them securely under her chin. Everett bent and kissed her, careful not to wake her.

"Soon, Sabrina."

CHAPTER NINE

The next morning, Sabrina steered her mount toward the downs, wanting to put as much distance between herself and Tantallon Hall as possible. Disappointment hung like a storm cloud on the horizon, and her mood was just as tempestuous. Woe the poor soul who ventured into her path.

She cursed herself for falling asleep last night but reserved her most inventive expletives for her husband. His insult was a bitter pill to swallow.

How dare he not make love to her again?

It was enough to make a woman scream. Waking to nothing more than a cold pillow was becoming a habit she wished to forswear till the end of her days. But it was apparent Everett shared neither her enthusiasm nor her desire.

And that hurt.

Before their marriage, he had flirted with her at every opportunity. An illicit caress here, a lurid comment there, and the man would boil her blood at every turn. But they were promises it was obvious he had not intended to keep, because once Everett put his ring on her finger, his much-professed ardor waned. Was it not the woman who was supposed to lose interest in that respect?

"Blasted cold fish," she mumbled in disgust.

According to the Brethren, save Dirk and Trevor, who regularly bemoaned the marital state, the wedding vows often rendered the wife useless from the waist down.

Why had she enjoyed no such luck?

If anything, that magical spot below her belly button had come roaring to life of its own accord. How she rued the enlightening discussion with her mother. The one that detailed the heights of passion a husband and wife could share. Her expectations had not been raised; they had flown through the roof. In her situation, ignorance would no doubt be bliss. Had she the choice, Sabrina would have rather been naïve than rejected.

And she was rejected.

But she was not going to cry about it. She had done that already and decided weeping was not for her. She was angry. She was incensed.

"Blast it all!" She shook her fist in the air. "I am bloody well furious!"

At her terse bellow, the horse started and shifted beneath her. Leaning forward, Sabrina patted the chestnut hunter on its muscled neck. "Sorry, old boy, I am not upset with you. It is that rake of a husband I have married. Rake, humph. He will not even seduce his own wife."

Of course, if he were seeking a divorce, there was no reason to consummate the vows.

Approaching hoofbeats brought her up short. Twisting in the saddle, she spied the interloper. Sitting high atop a black stallion, Everett fast approached. When he saw her, he smiled and waved a greeting.

"What the deuce does he want?" She snorted. "Well, I know what he does not want." Sabrina held tight to the reins, heeled hard, and set the chestnut into a full gallop.

At the edge of the field, she caught a trail and urged her mount faster. Thunder rumbled behind her, as Everett gained ground. She rode, reckless and rash, darting from one side of the path to the other, determined to keep him in her wake.

"I hope you choke on my dust," she muttered under her breath.

The trail disappeared into the woods, winding perilously between the trees. Ducking her head to avoid the occasional drooping branch, Sabrina had reined in her horse not the slightest, even though the danger had increased.

"Sabrina, slow down!" The warning came from behind.

"Go to the devil!" She kicked the hunter's flanks.

Ahead, the path veered to the right. In front of her, a low-lying hedge threatened to cut her off. A rush of derring-do traversed her spine, and she set her chin firm. Without care, Sabrina steered the chestnut straight for the natural hurdle.

"Sabrina, no!" Everett shouted.

With her leg hugging the saddlebow, she urged her mount faster. Her husband continued to protest, but his remonstrance only spurred her forth.

In one graceful movement, horse and rider rose, soared into the air. For a brief moment, time stood still. Glancing down, the earth passed beneath her, and she felt weightless, as though she had separated from her mortal shell. Her heart pounded in her chest and beat a wild rhythm in her ears. Everett screamed her name; it came to her as a faint whisper, as if from afar.

And then, in a flash, the world caught up with her.

She landed hard, jostling rough and unsteady in the sidesaddle. Sabrina set the chestnut in a wide arc, riding full circle to face her husband. As she had suspected, he had not jumped the hedge behind her. It lay, like her maidenhead, as a very real barrier between them.

"What the devil are you about!" Everett raked a hand through his hair, and his handsome features were mottled with undisguised anger. "You could have broken your neck. Worse, you could have been killed!"

"What do you care?" Her voice was pure acid, and although they were married and social strictures demanded she acquiesce to his authority, she averted her stare in a brazen display of defiance. If he preferred not his chosen bride, he could bloody well call a solicitor. "I will do as I please." Heeling the chestnut, she turned her mount and bounded into the meadows amid a hailstorm of creative curses.

As HIS WIFE rode hell bent for leather through the tall grass, a cloud of dust trailing her, Everett scratched the back of his head and exhaled for the first time since Sabrina had reconnected with terra firma. The hedge he had not expected her to jump seemed an insurmountable obstacle in more ways than one. Sabrina was angry—no, she was furious —with him.

But, why?

Searching his mind, he replayed the events of the day. If something were amiss, it would have happened since their tryst in the library the previous night.

He frowned.

Had he done something different? Closing his eyes, he revisited the memory and swore under his breath. As usual, his body reacted in an instant. And because he wore a hacking jacket, which was too short to conceal the evidence of his aroused state, he would have to draw out his ride.

And then it hit him.

Could it be that Sabrina thought what he had thus far done to her body constituted a consummation of their vows, and an annulment was no longer possible? In a flash, he quashed the idea.

For a scarce second, Everett considering leaping the hedge and chasing after her, but it was obvious she cared not for his company. Dinner would bring them together again, and because his parents were dining with friends, he would have Sabrina to himself. Then he would find out what had put her in a state.

After all, he had done nothing unseemly in the library— or anywhere else. She was still a virgin.

THEY POSTURED at either end of the imposing dining room table, squaring off like two enemies drawing battle lines. Everett downed his third glass of wine and signaled the footman for a refill. His usually ebullient wife sat, wrapped in a deafening silence, devouring the meal in her own unique fashion. The only sounds heard were the clangs of a knife blade as she dissected a portion of braised beef with frightful precision, and he had the uneasy suspicion she imagined he was on her plate.

Thus far, Sabrina had thwarted his attempts to take her to task for putting her life, and their future, at risk. Everywhere she went she took a maid. And he thought it a rather curious miracle that she had the good fortune to appear in the drawing room just before the butler had announced dinner.

Unwilling to enact a scene in front of the footmen, he tried to make polite conversation with her while they dined, but she responded quite coldly with one-word answers at his every prompting. As a consequence, by the time the meal concluded and they prepared to adjourn to the library, he was wound so tight he was afraid he would strangle her.

"Shall we, my dear?" He tossed his napkin to his plate, pushed away from the table, and stood.

"My lord, I fear I have a headache." Sabrina eyed him with unmasked trepidation and cast him a brittle smile. "I believe I shall retire early, if you do not mind."

"Not at all." So much for apologies and a compensatory interlude. "Allow me to walk you to your room."

"No, thank you." Retreating a step, she sniffed. "I would not intrude on the remainder of your evening."

"Very well." Everett lowered his arm and fisted his hands at his sides. A dark sense of foreboding swept over him, and he wondered if she considered an annulment. "As you wish."

"I bid you goodnight, my lord." Sabrina had half turned when he reached for her hand.

"And the same to you, my dear." Resolved not to go down without a fight for the woman he married, he brought her fingers to his lips and was surprised when she gasped. "Remember, we journey to Beaumaris in the morning."

As Sabrina made for her bedchamber, Everett stood in the foyer and enjoyed the gentle sway of her hips as she ascended the stairs. Cursing himself for saying nothing when his mother had installed them in rooms far enough apart that Napoleon could march an army in between without disturbing either of them, he headed for the study and comfort in a bottle of brandy.

But the intoxicant had done nothing to calm his nerves, and after imbibing half a decanter of the amber liquid, he navigated the halls of his ancestral home, stomped into his quarters, stripped, and slid between cold sheets. Punching a pillow, he rolled on his side and stared at nothing.

"Was I mistaken?" he asked no one. "Had her interest been no more than a girlish crush?"

Of course, Sabrina's reticence of late could be due to his recent acquisition of a title. For as long as he could recall, Everett had always considered himself unworthy of love and devotion because he had not stood to inherit. While the women of the *ton* were more than willing to enter into a liaison with him, none had been agreeable to marriage until he had earned his fortune. And even then, only those with families embroiled in scandal, in questionable financial straits, or in both had expressed tepid desire. But bartered brides had never suited his tastes. How ironic it would be to lose the one woman who had ever accepted him for himself because of his rank and not his lack thereof.

STREAKS of pale yellow and pink encroached on the indigo of night when they set out for Beaumaris the following morning. The first hour of their trip passed in tense, awkward silence. The second hour saw Everett once again attempting to engage Sabrina in conversation. And she had done as she had last night during dinner, responding in clipped, one-word replies. Everett wondered how they would fare for the remaining two hours.

Gowned in a dyed black traveling dress, his beautiful,

albeit stubborn, wife sat in the center of the seat opposite him. She had taken her place in such a manner as to force him to the other side of the carriage. With her head turned and jaw clenched, he was certain she pretended to find the countryside infinitely fascinating.

Everett was also positive she was still angry.

And he had not discerned why.

The sun set in the west when the traveling coach traversed a rough spot on the road. Splaying both arms wide, he barely managed to maintain his seat. Sabrina attempted the same, but because she had been napping, she was startled and thrown to the floor.

He reached out to give assistance, and she slapped his hands.

"Let me be." She gathered her skirts. "I can take care of myself."

"I know you can take care of yourself." Her obvious ire stung like a bee. "I was trying to be a gentleman."

"Trust me, my lord, you have never failed on that account," she replied, her voice laced with sarcasm.

Despite his confusion at her response, Everett lifted her to the seat and resettled himself in the squabs. "Just what do you imply, madam?"

Sabrina folded her arms and pouted. "I state a fact, nothing more."

A shiver of unease danced a jig down his spine.

Had she somehow perceived his behavior as nefarious? Perhaps he had offended her with his overt advances. Or— dare he think it—could hers be a prelude to an annulment? It chilled him to the bone to think he might have been wrong about her.

"Sabrina, let me assure you, what transpired between us in the gazebo and the library is perfectly acceptable behavior for a husband and wife." Gripping the edge of the bench, Everett bit back the bile rising in his throat. "There was nothing wrong with what we did."

"Well, I am delighted to hear it." Her nose rose to impressive heights. "We would not want to do anything unacceptable."

"That is why you are angry with me." Disappointment was an anchor about his neck. "Is it not?"

Her eyes narrowed. "Who says I am angry?"

"All right, you are not angry, you are furious." Everett raked his fingers through his hair. "I must confess, I have not the faintest notion why."

"I am not angry." Sabrina unfolded her arms and dug her hands into her skirts. "I am happy. Perfectly, splendidly happy."

He could not believe it. His fears sprang to life before his eyes. But before he jumped to unsupportable conclusions, anymore than he already had, Everett wanted to hear the words from her own mouth. "My dear, telling false-hoods is not part of your character. I know you are not *perfectly splendidly happy*. You are upset with me, and I would like to know why."

She remained stubborn and silent, with no evidence of changing her tack. It was clear he had to do something to break her from the icy shell in which she had encased herself.

In a flash, Everett made for her seat.

He reached for her, but Sabrina was just as fast. She shot to the spot he had occupied. They faced each other, positions reversed, fixed with unveiled determination on a specific objective.

His to claim her.

Hers to avoid him.

He lunged, and she evaded once again.

They ended up right where they began.

The coach rocked as they completed two more rotations. Fierce opposition visible in her expression, Sabrina's eyes flared. Everett could only imagine what his driver must think was going on between the newlyweds inside the elegant equipage.

"My lord, this is ridiculous," she said, as she gasped for air.

"You are deuced right it is." Everett pulled a handkerchief from his coat pocket and wiped the perspiration from his face. "We could enjoy this ride much more were we to share a seat. And there would be nothing unseemly about it."

"By that you mean more of the same endeavors you have undertaken thus far?"

"Sabrina, despite what we have done, you remain a virgin. Your virtue is intact." Her gaze filled with an emotion he had not recognized, and he decided then and there to contact his solicitor upon arriving at Beaumaris. "I have not disturbed the proof of your maidenhood."

In a hairsbreadth, she impaled him with an icy stare. "You do not say?"

"That is your concern, is it not?"

Sabrina humphed. "Why would I be concerned with the fact that I have been married almost a month, and *I am still a deuced virgin!*" Her tone rose as she bit off each word until she had worked herself into a roar.

"My dear, might I suggest you keep your voice down?" Everett blinked in confusion. "We do not want the coachman and escort to know of our delicate situation."

"What are you worried about? I should think you would want everyone to know you have not deflowered your bride.

I cannot, for the life of me, fathom why you continue the charade. It is obvious you do not want me." Though she shrugged, he thought he spied tears welling in her blue depths. "Why introduce me as your wife? Why take me to Beaumaris? Why not just hie me back to London and be done with it?"

In shock, he opened his mouth, and then closed it.

Then the meaning of her tirade dawned.

Everett realized his wife was angry with him not for what he had done but because of what he had not done.

To be specific, he had not taken her to his bed.

Relief washed over him, and what began as a chuckle grew into a fit of hilarity.

"I am so happy I could provide for your amusement, my lord." Sabrina sniffed with apparent indifference.

"My dear, I am not laughing at you but at the absurdity of our situation."

"Humph."

Freed from the worry of the past few days, Everett studied his wife with renewed zest. The predator within emerged, and passion followed in its wake.

Everett launched himself at his bride.

Sabrina was not fast enough that time, as he caught her by the waist and hauled her into his lap. Bracing her arms to his chest, she tried to push him away, but he covered her mouth with his in an attempt to entice. To arouse.

But she broke their kiss.

"Let me go. You do not want me." She gasped as he trailed his lips along her jawline and nibbled at her neck. "Oh, no. Not that. I cannot think straight when you kiss me there."

At her breathless admission he could not help but chuckle.

And Sabrina went rigid in his embrace. "Let go of me this instant."

Everett lifted his head and looked her straight in the eyes. "Hush, wife."

As the thrill of the hunt pervaded his senses and a hunger that had nothing to do with food gnawed at his belly and charged his nerves, he let her scramble to what she no doubt considered safety in the opposite seat. "Allow me to tell you what will happen upon our arrival at Beaumaris."

Inclining her head, Sabrina averted her gaze. "I am sure I am not interested."

"The staff will gather in the foyer to meet their new mistress. I will give you five minutes to greet as many as possible. Shortly thereafter, I will take you to my bed where I will relieve you of the affliction that has you in such a state."

Sabrina snapped to attention. "The devil you say."

Everett lowered his chin. "Five minutes."

Her eyes grew wide. "You cannot be serious."

"Five minutes."

The heat of his stare must have convinced her he meant business, because her hand flew to her mouth and a charming shade of pink colored her cheeks. "You do not want me."

"Five minutes."

"Do not dare pity me."

At that precise moment, they passed through the gates of Beaumaris. The lamps had been lit, although the sun had not yet set on the horizon. They would arrive at the main house shortly, and he gazed at his wife and charted the divestiture of her gown and anything else she might be wearing. Like a conqueror preparing to invade to a much-desired prize, he surveyed her. And in a voice invested with a wealth of resolution and raw lust, he said, "Five minutes."

THOUGH SHE WAS NOT COLD, Sabrina hugged herself and shivered. Her husband looked to be on the verge of eating her alive. Worse, she was not so sure she would object. But no matter what he said, no matter his countenance, she had not believed him. He could not want her. In making love to her, he would only placate her. Though she had wanted to be deflowered, prayed for it, expected it to happen, that was not how she envisioned the momentous occasion. Not like that.

Not in anger.

Not as a sense of duty.

She wanted Everett to want her—as she desperately wanted him.

Beyond the window, the grand residence loomed as a fortress of doom. She had to do something. Drowning in nervous agitation, she bit her lip and searched for an escape. If she was going to make her move, now was as good a time as any.

Grasping the brass handle before her, she cranked down the lever, threw open the door, and leapt from the moving coach.

"*Sabrina!*"

As soon as she hit the grass, she hiked her skirts and ran as fast as her feet would carry her. She had not bothered looking over her shoulder as Everett shouted her name, but she hastened her pace when he ordered the coachman to hurry.

Using the front lawn as a short cut, she ascended the

entry stairs before the coach turned into the forecourt. As she gained the foyer, she skidded across the polished marble floor in her kid half boots. Splaying both arms wide for balance, she managed to remain on her feet.

As Everett had predicted, the staff had assembled in two rows, shock evident on their faces. No doubt, Sabrina was not what they had expected.

So what else was new?

A somewhat stodgy character neared and bowed with a precision and grace she could only envy. "Lady Woverton, I presume?"

"Y-yes." She stuttered as Everett hollered her name, that time from much closer proximity.

"I am Mr. Ware—"

"The butler?"

"Indeed." He smiled when she reached for his hand and gave it a vigorous shake.

Then she recalled that was a decidedly male greeting and cursed herself in silence.

"I am so pleased to meet you. I am sure we will have time tomorrow to become better a-acquainted." She stammered as her spouse shouted once more, and she spied Everett fast approaching.

"Sabrina."

With fistfuls of her skirts, she scampered up the grand staircase but paused halfway. "Mr. Ware, my chambers?"

Either amused or dumbfounded, the butler gazed at her. "At the top of the stairs, turn left. At the end of the hallway, turn right. Yours are the apartments at the end of the hall, your ladyship."

Her thanks were shouted over her shoulder as Everett charged the foyer. In his Hessians, he slid across the floor in much the same fashion, as had she. Sabrina halted on the landing.

Their eyes met, held.

Pinning her with a lethal glare, Everett said, "Ware, dismiss the servants. Have dinner served in my reception room in two hours."

They stood there, her on the landing, him in the foyer, breathing heavily, eyeing each other with unfettered interest.

He the wolf, and she his prey.

She gulped.

He smiled, his hunter's smile.

With a half-smothered shriek, Sabrina fled down the hall. Behind her, the thunderous rap of his boots bespoke a furious chase.

Slamming each and every door in her path after she had passed through, she finally found sanctuary in her apartments. With a definite twist, she engaged the key in the lock and set the bolt. In a rush, she whirled about and assessed her compound. Two additional doors presented a threat.

She crossed the floor; discovered one led to her sitting room, and wasted no time in securing it. The other had no lock and opened to reveal a small corridor. The portal at the end led to another chamber. Before stepping into the passageway, she peered over her shoulder and was both surprised and disappointed that her husband had not pummeled the oak panels. Aside from her pounding heart, the house seemed eerily quiet.

Sabrina sprinted through the tiny hall and found herself in a magnificent bedchamber. That one was much bigger than hers and boasted the largest bed she had ever seen. The counterpane and drapes were of burgundy, and the air smelled of sandalwood. They were masculine quarters. And then it dawned on her.

It was the master suite.

At the center of the opposite wall situated a double-door entry. She ran for the breach in her security, reached for the key in the lock, and grasped—nothing.

There was no key.

She turned the knob and tugged hard, but neither door budged. Because they were already secure.

The hair rose on the back of her neck.

Swallowing a sob, Sabrina rotated slowly. Hugging the wall, she scanned the room, searching for what she could not explain. Nothing was amiss, and no one was there. The room was silent save the ticking of the mantel clock. Gooseflesh prickled her arms, and she regretted ever leaving her quarters. Hiking her skirts and digging in her heels, she made for the corridor leading to her chamber. As she neared, the door began to swing shut.

Unable to halt her flight, she ran straight into Everett's arms.

CHAPTER TEN

"*S*o good of you to come to me, my saucy Sabrina," Everett murmured against her mouth. "Your five minutes are at an end."

She struggled in vain as his hand twined in her hair, and he changed the angle of their kiss. But she kept her lips compressed and denied him entry. If she could keep his naughty tongue out of her mouth, she could keep her wits.

Until he relented and licked the crest of her ear.

"Oh, no. Not the ear." She inclined her head to give him better access. "Anything but the ear."

Sabrina wrapped her arms about his shoulders as her knees buckled. Resistance waved a fond farewell, and she welcomed the now familiar stirrings in her belly. "My, but that feels heavenly."

Laughter rumbled in his chest. "I am glad you like it."

How amazing it was that surrendering to an amorous assault was nowhere near as bitter a pill as pride. So she was not going to be strong. So she was not going to be firm. So she was not going to reject him.

But Sabrina Francis Douglas Markham was bloody well going to have a good time.

At her urging, Everett lifted his head, and she came at him with all she had and for all she was worth. As if she had just hooked a large catch, she focused her attention on her husband, pressed her body to his, and nipped his chin. Scoring her nails at his nape, her reward was the utterance of her name on a husky growl.

To her dismay, he set her on her feet. "What is wrong?"

"I want to see you naked." With a tug at his cravat, he drew the linen from his neck and tossed it to the floor. His coat and waistcoat soon followed.

For Sabrina, it was some performance. And if a proper lady was supposed to avert her gaze, she was about to make another break from polite decorum. When he stripped the shirt from his back, she thought she might swoon. "My heavens, but you are lovely."

"I am pleased you think so," he said with a chuckle. After doffing his Hessians, Everett faced her, shoulders squared. "Now, Lady Woverton. It is your turn."

"But—what about your breeches?" She gulped.

"Darling, without some sort of restraint, I fear this will be over before we get started." He shuffled his feet.

"I do not understand." Kicking off her slippers, she reached behind and pulled at her laces.

"You will soon enough." Setting his hands to her waist, Everett turned her back to him. "Allow me."

In mere seconds, he rid her of the heavy carriage dress and dropped it in a pool at her ankles. A moment later, he whisked the chemise over her head, and it seemed to float as a gentle whisper on the air as he cast it aside. But the removal of her garters and stockings was a heretofore-unmatched marvel of salacious excitement.

Kneeling, Everett unhooked her garters and rolled down her stockings, laving and suckling every inch of newly bared skin. Pleasure rippled through her body whenever he touched her, and through half open eyes, she stared in fascination just waiting to see what he would do next.

When she stood as God fashioned her, her husband sat on his heels and studied her from top to toe. "My dear, you are more beautiful than I had imagined. Are you afraid?"

That was a curious question. For a moment, she pondered her reply and decided the truth was the best response.

"No." But doubt crept into her mind, burned in her cheeks, and she crossed her arms in front of her. "Should I be?"

"Never." With a boyish smile, he rose from the floor and placed a chaste kiss to her forehead. Quick as a wink, he swept her into his arms and conveyed her to the bed.

Sabrina held on for the ride of her life.

Prowling on all fours above her, Everett launched a full-scale assault on her faculties, and his naughty mouth seemed to be everywhere at once. She moaned as he suckled her tongue, giggled as he nibbled her ear—which earned her a curious glance, and wiggled as he nipped her belly. The sensations shimmering in her veins left her giddy. Until he moved between her legs, gripped her hips, and shouldered her thighs wide.

"Everett?" She focused on the ceiling, as an anchor to her mortal shell, as, in that moment, she lacked the courage to meet his gaze.

"Shh." He expelled his warm breath over her triangle of black curls. "I promise I will not hurt you, but I ache to taste you."

"Yes, but—oh." Her protest died as he licked her most intimate flesh.

It had not seemed possible—to kiss her there. But as she endured, or rather enjoyed, the results, Sabrina would not complain. Again and again Everett pressed on her illicit caresses, and again and again, she let him. Fire burned in her veins, and she felt as though she had melted in the inferno. Had she likened marital relations to fishing? How wrong she had been, because nothing compared to the experience. Tossing her head from side to side, she teetered on the brink of reality and fantasy. The world seemed to collapse around her, and she feared she would suffocate.

But when he fastened his mouth over her nether lips and hummed, sending a wicked vibration spiraling into her loins, Sabrina realized she needed neither air to breathe, nor sustenance to survive. She needed nothing but her man.

And the sweet pinnacle fast approached. It was the magical place where she existed outside herself, where her body soared to unimaginable heights on waves of blissful oblivion. It was the pleasure dome, where sight and sound bowed to touch, to feel. A paradise to which only Everett had taken her.

The wondrous tide of ecstasy beckoned, bathing her in unadulterated rapture. Finally, she exhaled.

"Holy Mother!"

HER VOICE CAME to him through a lusty haze. When he comprehended what his wife had shouted, Everett chuckled. Resting his forehead against the inner side of her quivering thigh, he succumbed to gales of laughter.

"Everett?" Sabrina patted his head. "Did I do something wrong?"

"No, darling. You have done everything right." He scooted to the foot of the bed, stood, and unfastened his breeches. As he was about to remove his last vestige of clothing, he noticed his bride propped on her elbows and gazing on him with unfettered interest. "What is it?"

"Pray, continue." Her attention focused on the area south of his navel.

He held tight to his waistband lest she swoon. "Are you frightened?"

"Good heavens, no." She bit her lip. "But that is the part I have been waiting to see."

Once again, uncontrollable mirth plagued Everett. In a single swift movement, he dragged his breeches to his ankles and then stepped out of them. He knew the exact moment Sabrina lit upon his most protuberant part.

Her jaw dropped, her eyes grew wide as saucers, and the age-old question blossomed in her expression. "Oh, I say, you are going to kill me with that."

That time, he bit his lip and tried in vain not to laugh. He laughed anyway. "Sabrina, you say the damnedest things."

"Is that bad?" She pouted.

Crawling atop the mattress, he settled himself over her and gave her his weight. "No." Everett nipped her nose. "I think—for us—a little levity is a good thing."

She said nothing, merely nodded, which seemed odd in light of her usual forthrightness.

And then it struck him.

He rested chest to breast, hip-to-hip, and skin-to-skin with his wife.

Despite years of experience and countless encounters

with some of London's most notorious courtesans, Everett was suddenly nervous as a green lad with his first whore. Yet his bride was no lightskirt teasing his senses; she was a lady, albeit, a most unlikely lady. And if ever a soul could love him, he believed Sabrina up to the task.

"Are you comfortable?" He framed her face with his hands and caressed her cheeks with his thumbs. "Am I too heavy?"

She shook her head.

Was it possible? Had he managed to render his chatty wife speechless? A telltale shiver coursed her body, and he recognized the blush of desire coloring her flesh. Erratic gasps and nails digging into his shoulders provided clues of the passion investing her, and Everett knew the time had come for him to claim his prize. With his knee he nudged her legs apart, and she set her thighs wide in a bold, wanton move that left him reeling.

"Sabrina, I will try to be gentle." Over and over he kept repeating the statement in his mind, and he was not sure whom he tried to comfort, the guileless virgin or himself.

"Just do it." She favored him with a shaky smile that was trusting and naïve. "Please, before I die of wanting you."

He shifted and brought himself to her moist passage. Pressing forward, he moved slowly, entering her inch by glorious inch. He groaned as her warm wetness surrounded him. Trapping her gaze, he delighted as her blue eyes filled with wonder, amazement, and only a hint of fear. As he butted against the filmy barrier of her maidenhood, her forehead creased, and she inhaled sharply.

And Everett thought he might faint.

Sucking in a breath, he pushed, swift and hard. Though she tensed and tears welled, Sabrina had not blinked. In his arms, innocence died and a sultry seraph was born.

It was as though he had fired the shot at Ascot, because the horses bolted and the race commenced.

With his flesh encased deep in hers, she heeled his flanks, and Everett thrust. Yes, a gentleman would have allowed her a reprieve to adjust to his invasion. And yes, a gentleman would have tempered his penetration. But for him, with her, gentlemanly behavior was not going to happen.

Setting a blistering rhythm, he drove himself to the brink of insanity and just managed to remain coherent. His lusty bride wound her arms about his neck, pulled him close, bit his lower lip, and then trailed her tongue along his chin. The finesse of a lifetime abandoned him.

Everett was undone.

A soul-scorching passion burned in his chest, and he plundered her mouth as a ravenous beast. No woman had ever touched him, as had she. When he slowed to savor the sensuous slip and slide of their tempestuous coupling, Sabrina grabbed his backside and fire poured into his loins, renewing his frantic tempo. And he made love to his wife with a force he never knew he possessed.

Everett whispered encouragement, and she moaned in response. Like an accomplished seductress, she wrapped her legs higher around his waist and tilted her hips, and he sailed even further into the depths of her honey sheath.

As a man on a mission, he moved faster still. Riding her hard as he would an unbroken horse, their union grew desperate, almost panicked. Delicious tension coiled tight as a clock spring. Beneath him, Sabrina went rigid, and he knew that release had come for her. On the next thrust of his hips, she surrendered. "Everett!"

The feminine cry, achingly sweet, coupled with the provocative enticement of her contractions, drew forth his

seed in a rushing climax. And his growl of appreciation
sounded nowhere near human.

When Everett found the strength to lift his head some-
time later, it took a few minutes to gather his wits. As the
knowledge dawned that he was still sprawled atop his wife,
his limbs still weighted with sated languor, his now re-
aroused flesh still buried deep within hers, he smiled.

All was right with his world.

How he would love to take Sabrina again, but to do so
would be the height of neglectfulness. She was untried and
would most definitely be sore in the morning. A good
husband would withdraw from her and ring for a soothing
bath. But a feathery tracing of circles on his shoulder
brought him up on his elbows.

"Did I wake you?" Sabrina stared, sparkling and capti-
vating, at him.

"No." Everett carefully shifted his hips.

With her eyes closed, she bit her lip. "Oh."

He froze. "Did I hurt you?" Bracing himself, he rose in
an effort to relieve her of his weight. "Here, let me get off of
you—"

"Stay, my lord." With her legs coiled tight about him,
she pulled him near, kissed his throat, and nibbled the edge
of his jaw. "I was wondering if we might do it again."

"Sabrina—"

"Please."

"It is too soon," he cautioned. "You will be dreadfully
sore tomorrow."

"So I will be sore." She averted her stare. "You could
soothe it with a kiss."

At her suggestion, Everett choked. "Enjoyed yourself,
did you?"

"Immensely," she replied with a definite nod. "You

know, Mama likened it to riding a horse. But, I daresay, I have never enjoyed my mare half so much."

Once again, unrestrained mirth rumbled in his chest—until Sabrina grasped his bare buttocks and squeezed. He thrust, and she moaned. The room filled with a sensuous symphony of her feminine sighs and his husky praise. That is, until the air was pierced by a primal groan and her lusty, "Holy Mother!"

∼

"CANNOT SAY as I recall ever having been so hungry." Sabrina dabbed the corners of her mouth with her napkin and leaned back in her chair. "Must be the country air."

"I would wager our evening exercise has something to do with your appetite." Wearing matching burgundy silk robes, Everett dined with his bride in his reception room. Gazing at her over the rim of his glass, he smiled when he spied the subtle shading in her cheeks. "Promise me something?"

She regarded him with guileless affection that made his heart skip a beat. "Anything, my lord."

"Never change." Pondering his empty plate, he lifted the lid on the serving platter and served himself another portion of braised beef. "No matter what the future brings, as the years pass and we have children, however many disagreements we suffer, promise you will always be my saucy Sabrina."

"That is an easy request to fulfill, because I know not how to be anyone else." She tucked a wayward lock of hair behind her ear. "Though I imagine you will on many occasions regret having made such a request."

"I daresay you are probably right." As she struggled

with her black mane, still wet from a bath, he set down his fork and pushed away from the table. "My dear, fetch your brush, and I will see if I can work those tangles from your hair."

"You should." Sabrina rose from her chair. "You put them there."

He cast her an unrepentant grin and swatted her lovely derrière as she passed. While he waited for his wife to return, he tried not to consider what tomorrow would bring.

Were he nothing more than Lord Everett Markham, second son, the future would be relatively simple. His accounts were settled, and he had money to burn. Solicitors engaged years ago managed his estates. But things were much more complicated thanks to his new title.

In his study, awaiting his perusal, loomed a trunk filled with account books and land contracts his brother, God rest him, had woefully neglected. It was a safe wager the properties were in similar disrepair. Soon, he would journey to each estate and personally survey the conditions.

Though his father had tried to educate him in governing such vast holdings, Everett could not escape the feeling that he was singularly inadequate to the task. The life of a second son had afforded him a rather carefree existence, and he had been beholden to none. He could come and go as he pleased.

Not so anymore.

Now he was lord to many, and his responsibilities boundless. When he married Sabrina, he prepared himself for commitments expected of a husband and father. That, coupled with the burdens of the title and a campaign to win her declaration, presented a daunting prospect. And if he were honest with himself, his top priority was winning his wife's heart.

But if he failed as an earl, would she think him worthy of her love?

"Here it is." Sabrina stood before him, offering a silver-backed brush.

"Ah, yes." Masking his concern, he spread his legs wide, smoothed his robe over the chair cushion, and patted the surface. "Have a seat."

Arching a brow, she planted hands on hips. "You said you were going to brush my hair."

"Do you not trust me?" He grinned.

"Oh, indeed." With a finger to her chin, she wrinkled her nose. "I am just not sure I trust myself."

"My dear, you say the damnedest things." Laughing, something he had done with greater frequency since his marriage, he again patted the space between his legs. "Come now, of what are you afraid?"

It was a challenge.

And he knew his wife would rise to the occasion as swift and sure as the erection currently roaring to life in his loins.

"All right." Sabrina whirled about and, oblivious of his state, plopped herself down in perilous proximity to his arousal. "But I warn you, birds will nest on my head if you do not get the tangles out of my hair."

Everett accepted the brush and stroked her raven locks in long, drawn-out movements. When she wiggled her bottom and resituated herself, she seduced him without knowing it, and he clenched his jaw against a groan.

But the randy beast within emerged.

Amid sweeps, he planted his lips behind each ear, and she rewarded him with a sigh of contentment. At that precise moment, an idea sparked in the functioning part of his brain not focused on lovemaking. If he could tether his lady with restraints of a sensuous nature, she might be inspired to love him. Lifting her luscious locks, he trailed butterfly kisses along her nape.

"Oh, my." Through his robe, she grasped his thighs and squeezed. "You make me want to be so bad."

"But you like it." Everett chuckled, set the brush aside, untied her belt, parted the silk, and bared her shoulders. Shifting her in his lap, he slipped the garment from her succulent body. "Do you not?"

"Yes," she whispered in reply.

Indeed, a sumptuous web might be the answer to his prayers. With time and tenderness, he could weave a voluptuous net and make her his sweet captive. Of course, he would not force Sabrina to do anything beyond her wishes, but there was nothing wrong with providing a bit of salacious persuasion.

Cupping her breasts, Everett pressed on her caresses meant to entice and arouse. And his charming wife moaned and squirmed as a sensuous seraph in his lap. After a few maddening minutes, he discovered his intended target was not the only one vulnerable to his tack. Yet nothing about the revelation made sense.

He was a rake.

He should be impervious to such simple pleasures.

To test the limits of his fraying self-control, he pinched her nipples, to wit she cried out, and his thighs went up in flames.

"Spread your legs," he said against her neck.

Sabrina mumbled an incoherent response and let her knees drop at either side of his. When he teased the nest of curls at the apex of her thighs, she rested her head on his shoulder and exhaled a shivery breath. As his fingers walked a naughty path, he nuzzled her temple. Slipping his fingers inside her passage, he thrilled to the evidence of her desire. Drawing on his well-honed finesse, Everett brought her warm wetness to the little pink gem he loved to suckle and in a licentious massage stoked her fire to impressive heights.

She wanted him, but could she love him?

She was his wife, but would she honor their vows?

For her sake and his sanity, he hoped so.

Sabrina shifted with restless abandon, yet with catlike grace in his embrace. Was there anything more erotic than his wife in the throes of passion? Each sultry song she sang was a priceless treasure he hoarded as a miser of love. And Everett had to have her.

"My lord, please." She grasped his wrist, pulled his hand away, and he could have cried—until she added, "I want you there."

In regard to her request, he required no explanation. "Stand up."

Stand up?

Sabrina obeyed but prepared to make her preferences known, when Everett opened the folds of his robe and flicked an entreaty. "Come back."

Well, perhaps he understood, after all.

For a moment, she studied his most male member. Protruding proud, flagrant, and angry, it was intimidating. Staring at her with its one good eye, it reminded her of a pirate. And though an hour ago it had been inside her, she still was not convinced it would fit. "How—"

"Just sit," he said as he guided her down.

Excited by the prospect of learning something new, she followed his direction and straddled his lap. "Like this?"

"Perfect."

Peering between them, Sabrina gasped. Positioned, as they were, the Jolly Roger, as the Brethren often referred to that particular aspect of their anatomy, looked as though it could be attached to her instead of Everett, which was a disconcerting development, to say the least.

"Scoot closer," her husband said as he shimmied beneath her.

"Are you sure this will work?" Instinctively, she tensed when the plum-shaped tip of his miracle of flesh slipped inside her. And nagging doubt lingered yet subsided, when he cupped her cheek and smiled.

"Trust me." Grasping her hips, he pressed further still.

It was a humbling experience, and more beautiful than anything she had ever known, to have part of him encased in her body. And as she was his, he was hers. Despite his mother's wishes, there would be no annulment, so Sabrina opened her heart and let it sing. With something between a sob and a sigh, she bent her head and set her lips to his.

How she loved the way Everett kissed her. How he nipped at her nose and tickled her tongue. How he held her so tight she almost could not breathe. Never had she felt so special. Never had she felt...passion, desire.

For good or ill, she was now a woman in every sense of the word. And no one—not even the marchioness—could take that from Sabrina. On the thought, hunger and need welled anew. And she wanted more.

Sabrina broke their kiss and asked, "What now?"

"Pretend I am your favorite mare." He cast her a lazy grin.

Confused, she stiffened her back. "I beg your pardon?

Everett buried his face in her breasts. "Ride, lady mine."

Shocked and curious at once, she rocked her hips. And she was rocked. "Holy Mother!"

Her scandalous husband chuckled, reclined in the chair and peered at her with the devil in his eyes. For the briefest moment, she wondered what he found so amusing about their lovemaking. But as she continued to move over him, and on him, she no longer cared.

With each thrust of her hips, a wicked wantonness simmered beneath her skin. She was emboldened, undaunted. No longer a spectator, she found power and strength in the intimate dance.

"You are so beautiful." Everett sighed. Murmuring suggestions and praise, he caressed her everywhere, setting her alight in places she never knew existed.

But when he massaged the place just above their joining, her world turned on end. The now familiar tensing of her thighs commanded her attention and her senses. As heaven on earth claimed her, she stared into his amber depths, her soul as naked as she, hiding nothing, and daring him to accept her. All of her.

And Everett was with her.

When he fisted his hands in her hair, she framed his cheeks. They were together. Face to face. Scaling the heights of passion, then soaring even higher.

There was tenderness.

There was devotion.

And finally, there was unimaginable release.

CHAPTER ELEVEN

A fortnight later, Everett rode through the meadow at the north end of his estate, and he paused for a moment to survey the land. Nothing more than a thin band of shimmering gold, the summer sun had just peeked over the horizon. Straightening in his saddle, he gave vent to a rather profuse yawn.

Though he had gone to bed at his usual hour the previous night, he had not slept much. It seemed his charming wife had taken quite a fancy to a particular aspect of marital duty.

To put it simply, the countess of Woverton enjoyed making love.

And in true Sabrina fashion, she had taken to her responsibilities with her characteristic vigor, dedication, and unbridled enthusiasm. And she drew him like a lodestone. The end result? He ravished her at every opportunity. But since she had not complained, neither would he.

Everett succumbed to another yawn.

Their marriage had progressed beyond his wildest expectations—as had his wife. His staff adored her, and to his amazement, even his normally stuffy butler had the audacity to blush whenever she fussed over something he had done for her. As a man, he was embarrassed for the poor chap. And once her fondness for Cook's lemon tarts had been discovered, the flaky dessert pastry made its way to their dinner table five times in a sennight. Yes, everyone loved Sabrina.

If only he had succeeded half so well.

The estates he had inherited from his late brother were in shambles. There was much to be done, and as the damage had occurred slowly, during years of neglect, nothing would be achieved or repaired overnight.

And during the wee hours when he was not making love to his wife, he would frequently lie awake, wondering if he was adequate to the task at hand. A good portion of his days were spent locked in his study, pouring over agricultural reports, purchase orders, and much needed improvements to a wide array of properties, all of which he had yet to examine in person.

To make matters worse, his myriad responsibilities consumed his attention to the detriment of his new wife. While he knew it was not fashionable for a couple to live in each other's pockets, he truly regretted he had not more time to dedicate to Sabrina. He wanted to nurture their union, to strengthen their bond, to entice her to declare her love, so she would not leave him.

Soon, the peerage required he survey his holdings, one at a time. But Sabrina had arranged a *fête-champêtre* to introduce herself to the local community, and he decided to delay his business a few more days. Given they were in mourning, there would be no dance, but polite decorum dictated she host the affair, and he would not venture and leave her to face the masses alone.

Especially since the invited guests included his parents.

His mother made no secret of her disdain for his chosen bride, and, as dastardly as it sounded, he found some sort of twisted pleasure in his mother's objection. While he did not give a damn about his mother's discomfit, Sabrina did, and he would not abandon her. He yawned again and smiled.

Last night had been a memorable experience. They sneaked into the rose garden and made love in the moonlight. There had been a minor mishap involving a few thorns—his posterior still smarted, but it had been a singular triumph, and his resourceful countess soothed his aches with a few well-placed kisses. Actually, since that first fiery evening when they consummated their marriage, each joining had been a celebrated attainment of pleasure, unlike any he had ever known.

Her inquisitive nature and inherent derring-do was a perfect match for his voluptuous appetite. Whatever he asked of her, she charged forth, headlong into the breach, without question. His wife was so in tune with his body, she seemed to know the precise moment to grasp his buttocks and squeeze—something no woman had ever done for him. Never had completion been so forceful, almost violent.

A sick feeling swept over him.

How could Sabrina, a novice in their marital bed, know when he neared climax with such unfailing accuracy?

She had been an innocent when first he took her—of that he had no doubt. Whereas women tensed just before they reached fulfillment, men signaled no such response. While Everett had enjoyed the skills of mistresses conversant in the sexual arts, and incomparable in their cultivation, none could read him half so well.

How had she become so learned, gaining impossibly intimate knowledge of his body, in so short a time?

Dare he think it?

Could someone else have tutored his bride?

Cursing himself a fool, but unable to quash the question foremost on his mind, Everett made his way back to the stables. It was early yet, and although a few of the hands were up and about, he stabled his horse himself. Just as he exited the stall, he spied his lovely wife, with a riding crop tucked under one arm, skipping in his direction and tugging on her gloves.

Quick as a flash, he ducked into the nearest stall. As she passed, he caught her by the waist and hugged her against him.

She started. "What—"

He smothered her shriek with his lips and before things got out of hand, and with his wife that was a near certainty, he lifted his head. "Where were you going?"

Though it was evident she mustered a pout, and it was an adorable attempt, she only managed a lopsided grin. "You did not wake me for our ride."

"Yes I did." He nipped the tip of her cute little nose.

"My lord." Sabrina averted her gaze, and a blush stained her cheeks. "You know what I mean."

"You were sleeping so peacefully I did not want to disturb you." He gave her a squeeze.

Her gaze fell to his lips, and she splayed her fingers over his chest. "But I do so look forward to our morning exercise."

Good God, she tempted him even then. "Darling, I believe I exercised you quite thoroughly this morning."

"Everett." Although she swatted him, it was a playful gesture. "You are shameless."

Rocking on his heels, he clucked his tongue. "You knew that when you married me."

"I did." She giggled. "And I like it."

Oh, yes. Sabrina wanted him, and he rested his hands on the sumptuous curves of her bottom. "Do you?"

Her breath hitched as he kneaded her pliant flesh, and he thrust his hips in a suggestive rhythm. "What else do you like?"

Closing her eyes, she nuzzled him. "The way you make me feel."

"Tell me."

"All warm inside." Her brow furrowed. "It is similar to the first time I drank brandy, but without the choking."

Though Everett was not in a comedic mood, he could not suppress a chuckle. "Sabrina, you say the damnedest things."

"You knew that when you married me." She snuggled close.

"I did." He waggled his brows. "And I like it."

"What else do you like?" she asked in the throaty tone that told him she was primed for passion.

"The way you make me feel." Was there not something about which he needed to speak with her?

Sabrina pressed herself to him, and rational thought escaped him. "Tell me."

"As if I could conquer the world." He uttered the words before he realized what he had said. "If only to deposit the spoils at your feet."

His beguiling bride cast him the misty-eyed expression that declared he had managed to touch her without actually touching her. "But I do not want the world."

How he loved her. "What do you want?"

"You." Perched on her tiptoes, she whispered against his lips, "Only you."

The kiss he bestowed on her that time was hard and

tinged with urgency impossible to deny. When next Everett lifted his head, they both breathed erratically.

"I want you." He glanced left then right. "Now."

"Here?" Was he mistaken or had she looked interested?

"No. Though the stalls are clean, I do not relish the idea of someone interrupting us." Everett peered skyward. "How about the loft?"

"Oh, my lord." Sabrina giggled her naughty giggle. "Last one there is a rotten egg."

Offering his escort, he led her to the wooden ladder access to the hayloft. "After you, my dear."

With a mischievous grin, she draped the skirts of her riding habit over one arm, clutched a rung, and began her ascent.

He waited until she was half way up to follow. When he checked her progress, he was treated with a spectacular view of her bare bottom. Whistling a frisky little ditty, he hastened his pursuit.

Approximately twenty minutes later, Everett recalled what had plagued his morning ride and spurred his quick return to the stables. As had become her post-coital custom, Sabrina drew imaginary circles on his naked backside. With a frown, he propped himself on his elbows.

"Darling, there is something I have been meaning to ask you." For a few seconds, he searched for the proper words with which to frame his delicate query. "When I near a certain point in our lovemaking, you put your hands on my posterior and squeeze rather roughly."

"Have I displeased you?" Sabrina appeared crestfallen. "Do you not like it?"

"On the c-contrary," he stammered. Bloody hell, his cheeks burned—and he referred not to the ones on which he sat. "I like it very much. But how do you know when to do it?"

She wrinkled her nose. "You mean just before you howl?"

"I beg your pardon?" That was his worst nightmare. "I do not howl."

Whistling in monotone, she rolled her eyes. "Oh, yes you do."

"Madame wife, I assure you I do no such thing." The gentleman in him would not allow it. "I merely groan my pleasure."

"What is this?" She pinched his arse. "Is my shameless lord embarrassed?"

"Do you not want to know my secret?" When Everett tried to disengage, she wrapped her legs about him. "What signals that you are about to howl?"

"Do tell." His male ancestors must be rolling in their graves, as Markham men were known for their talent with ladies.

"You get gooseflesh." It was apparent Sabrina tried to keep a straight face, but in the end she succumbed to another flirty giggle. She settled her palms on his backside, and her fingers sank into his flesh. "Right here. When I feel it, I squeeze, and then you howl."

"I do not howl," he reiterated through gritted teeth. Of course, he might have argued the fact more had she not, at that instant, kneaded his bottom.

Bloody hell, it felt good.

In less than two seconds, he was aroused. So, there was only one thing to do. However, another twenty minutes later, Everett admitted, albeit in silence, she had been right.

He howled.

IN THE FOLLOWING DAYS, Sabrina busied herself with preparations for the celebration. She prepared the menus for the refreshments, arranged for an orchestra to entertain their guests, and planned a series of games to amuse the children. After checking and rechecking the guest list, she assigned the multitude of guestrooms in the grand home by rank.

But no matter how hard she worked, she could not elude the doubts plaguing her. When she married Everett, she had fully prepared to be his wife and mother of his children.

Not his countess.

How she wished she had paid more attention to her mother when she had the chance. Though nothing had been said, or even implied, she could not help but feel inadequate to the task. A countess was supposed to be a regal lady. A beauty. Graceful. Charming. All knowing.

Sabrina was none of those things.

As a child, she and Cara had often played lady of the manor. Dressed in their mother's clothes, they held tea parties, complete with the King as an imaginary guest. Cara's affairs were elegant events that never failed to go off without a hitch. Hers, however, almost always digressed into something more akin to a food fight, with shortbread and scones sailing through the air. Recalling the time she tripped over the toes of her mother's slippers and broke her arm, she stared at herself and sighed.

Though the mourning clothes she wore were made expressly for her, the jewel on her finger signified the husband was hers, and the ring of keys in her pocket declared her chatelaine of Beaumaris, she could not escape the uneasy feeling that something had not fit.

Sabrina was not certain she belonged amid such elegant surroundings.

She feared that if she inquired, she would discover it had been a horrid mistake. That some years long ago, Parliament had passed an edict declaring any woman found to be failing in her wifely duties should be packed up and exiled to the Americas.

And she could not agree more.

While she stumbled and tripped through household management, Everett had governed his estates—and succeeded brilliantly. He had already ordered new roofs for several tenant homes. And after an in-depth study of agricultural reports, he reorganized the planting schedules and purchased additional livestock.

Though the situation was still muddled, things were getting better. Her husband was a marvel, and everyone loved him. The staff and tenants sang his praise. And she heard it all, because she dealt with them every day, and not a one passed without someone telling her that the Earl of Woverton was a wonderful lord.

Everett was kind, generous, thoughtful, and held in high esteem. And he deserved a wife just as accomplished.

Instead, he had her.

Sabrina had determined not to let him down, had resolved to try harder. She spent every afternoon in her sitting room, pouring over her book of etiquette; the one Celia had given her before departing Tantallon Hall. Having met with the cook and the housekeeper, she discerned that everything was well ordered and efficiently run. Why fix what was not broken?

So she was content to let things remain as they had before she married Everett, only making changes where she was certain improvement was possible. She paid attention to the duties of each servant, gleaning every last drop of information about the home. In her spare time, she helped stock the stillroom, assisted in making preserves, and began to oversee the purchase of household supplies.

And yet Sabrina felt incompetent.

Perhaps it had something to do with the fact that wherever she was, and whatever she had done, she perceived the ever-present gaze of her husband. Everett watched her constantly. Had she done something wrong?

Could he not trust her?

But that was not the only thing bothering her. She tried not to dwell on the fact that her husband had not declared his love. She was positive his mother's criticism would not gnaw at her half so much if she had Everett's heart as a shield.

While all was well in their bedchamber, and in the alternate locales they had shared illicit trysts, their time spent together in other endeavors had dwindled to almost nothing. And she was not so naïve as to think that marital relations alone could sustain a marriage. At least, not the kind of partnership for which she hoped.

As a result, on the eve of the *fête-champêtre*, Sabrina tossed, restless and impatient, in bed. Beside her, Everett snored softly, sleeping the sleep of the sated after a vigorous round of lovemaking. Fraught with worry, wondering if there was anything she had missed, her mind raced.

At the rate she was going, she would never get any rest. And if she continued on her present course, she might wake him, and they would both be exhausted for their special occasion. Finally, with great care not to disturb her husband, she slid from the bed, pulled on her silk nightgown, and shrugged into the matching robe.

The thick carpets of the master suite muted her footsteps as she crossed the room to the door. She hesitated, then tiptoed to the tallboy and retrieved the candlestick Everett left atop it just before they had ripped each other's clothes off and jumped into bed.

Once in the hall, she held the candlestick high and made for her intended target. Since rolling in the sheets with her husband had not quieted her mind, there was one other activity that all but guaranteed to dispense with her pent up energy.

Before she knew it, she stood at the top of the grand staircase. Glancing from left to right, she determined no one would witness her christening of the banister. Sabrina chuckled.

Yes, it was childish.

No, it wasn't appropriate behavior for a countess.

But, at the moment, she cared not.

Tomorrow was a big day, and she needed sleep. A ripping ride down the banister at home, her childhood home, she corrected herself, had always done the trick.

She was sure it would work.

Setting the candlestick on a nearby table, she noted the faint light it afforded in the cavernous entryway of the elegant estate house. Reminding herself to be careful of the newel post at the end, she perched atop the polished oak and let go of the rail. Accustomed to the cotton of her old nightgowns and day dresses, she had not prepared for the slippery slide of silk against the polished banister, as she all but flew down the staircase and barely managed to stifle a squeal of delight. The ride was exhilarating.

Until Everett shouted her name. "*Sabrina!*"

Startled, she lost her balance and waved her arms in the air in an effort to regain control. "Whoa."

THE SUN SHONE brilliantly in a clear, azure sky. The orchestra played on the terrace, and music filled the air. Manicured lawns of emerald showcased clusters of geraniums and red-hot poker. Hedges trimmed in precise shapes opened into rose gardens overflowing with blooms in every conceivable color. Stately oaks, nature's guardsmen, lined the graveled drive, and elegant carriages coursed beneath, conveying well-dressed gentlemen and women.

The staff had been well prepared and seemed to anticipate every necessity. Overnight guests were shown to their quarters. The food had been served, and refreshing beverages flowed.

At the end of the receiving line, Everett and Sabrina stood, side-by-side, welcoming their guests.

Dressed in an impeccable coat of charcoal grey Bath superfine and matching breeches, a crisp white cravat, woven in a meticulous knot, sat at his throat, secured by a twinkling diamond pin. Mirror-shined Hessians completed the ensemble, and she thought him the epitome of an English country nobleman.

So why had he fought a frown?

At his right, Sabrina prayed she cut the picture of a refined lady. Dressed in one of her best mourning gowns, her raven hair piled in carefree curls atop her head, she smiled and offered her hand to everyone who came through their door. On occasion, she bit her lip, and for a fleeting moment she doubted not that a pained expression crossed her face.

Something troubled her.

But it had nothing to do with the *fête*. It had nothing to

do with the refreshments, the lawns, the gardens, the staff, or the entertainment. It had nothing to do with her attire.

It had everything to do with the curious stares and none-too-silent whispers of their invitees.

Which had nothing to do with the *fête*. And had nothing to do with the refreshments, the lawns, the gardens, the staff, or the entertainment. And had nothing to do with her attire.

Perhaps the disquietude stemmed from the dark, hideously black bruise circling her right eye.

As luck would have it, everyone had been polite enough not to comment on her injury. Everyone, that is, until the marquess and marchioness of Talbot arrived.

"Good God, what happened to your face?" her mother-in-law squalled, and Sabrina would have loved to give the harpy a matching bruise.

Biting her lip, Sabrina peered at Everett and wondered if he would notice if she dug a hole in the lawn and buried her head.

He cleared his throat and tugged at his collar. "My wife had a minor mishap."

"Are you all right, my dear?" the marquess inquired, with wrinkles appearing at the corners of his eyes. He had, no doubt, fought laughter.

"Oh, indeed," Sabrina assured him with an enthusiastic nod. "I am fine. Just a tad bruised, nothing more."

"There's a girl." The marquess winked and patted her cheek, taking care to avoid her wounded eye.

The marchioness merely frowned as they turned away.

Sabrina might have been disconcerted had it not been for the next person in line. "*Celia!*"

Lady Celia's smile fell to an open-mouthed stare when she spied her friend. "C-countess?"

"It is nothing." In that instant, she wrestled with shame.

"How—" Celia reached but pulled back just shy of touching Sabrina.

"An accident." Aware of her husband's heated stare, Sabrina ushered her friend along. "We will talk more, later."

She would swear—although it was unladylike to swear but the situation merited it, that her ears still rang from the stern lecture she had received as soon as Everett revived her last night.

Damn fool man.

It was not her fault she hit the newel post. He should not have hollered at her. In her confusion, she had forgotten about the large knob at the end of the banister. Sabrina was thankful she could not recall the impact. Such ignorance was welcomed bliss as she stood and greeted her callers.

It was not to be borne.

But she must. She had to persevere. After all her hard work, and all her careful planning, she had to remain firm beneath her humiliation while she assembled the district as the new, albeit marred, countess of Woverton.

"Where is my girl?"

Sabrina blinked. "Papa!" As she had on countless occasions, she flew at her father, arms outstretched to embrace him.

"What the deuce?" Her sire caught her at length and held fast. Anger mottled his features. "I am going to kill him."

"No." Sabrina clutched her father tight. "It was not his fault. I slid down the banister and hit the newel post."

For a pregnant moment, the foyer was quiet. Then, without warning, he burst out laughing. Behind him, her mother rolled her eyes, while Cara covered her mouth and giggled.

FEELING FAINT, Everett realized he had been holding his breath. He exhaled just as Admiral Douglas hugged Sabrina and winked at Everett over her head. When the admiral extended his hand, he took it in a firm shake.

"I suppose you can live, son." His father-in-law dabbed at his eyes before trembling from another fit of chuckles. "Some things never change."

Everett tried, but failed, not to grimace. "Admiral, I am afraid she will one day break her neck."

"Nonsense." The admiral chucked his shoulder. "She is a resilient one, that Sabrina. She can survive anything."

"Of that I have little doubt." Everett dipped his chin. "But can my sanity survive her?"

CHAPTER TWELVE

*T*he event passed as quick as it began. The meal had been a singular success, and everyone loved the orchestra. The games kept the children occupied, and there was only one casualty, a scraped knee. Before long, the guests dwindled to those staying the night.

The Brethren of the Coast were in full attendance, and with the constant complaints of the marchioness, Sabrina was grateful for their support. Rebecca, Dirk's new wife, had brought her younger brother Lucien, sixth earl of Calvert and a lieutenant in the Royal Navy. Sabrina thought him a perfect match for Celia, but there had been little she could do to further a liaison between the two. In a gross miscarriage of fortune, duty called him to London in the morning, because his ship, the *Intrepid*, would sail the following evening.

After a celebratory dinner, the women withdrew to the dining room, leaving the men to take their brandy and cigars.

"Sabrina, you must speak to the cook. The turbot was tough and the sauce too thin. And this tea is weak. Mind you, servants need a firm hand, or they will put forth only half an effort." With an imperious expression, the marchioness returned her cup to the trolley. "I seem to have misplaced my handkerchief. Must have left it in the dining room."

A tense silence held the room prisoner like an iron shackle, until the harbinger that was her mother-in-law disappeared down the hall. Sabrina gazed at her lifelong friends, her sister, her mother, and Celia. Shame, incompetence, and defeat loomed as a storm cloud. And her embarrassment compounded when she considered how her ineptitude reflected on Everett. "I apologize if the meal was unsavory."

"Nonsense," her mother snapped. "There was nothing wrong with dinner, my dear."

"Everything was perfect, Brie." Caroline crossed the room and sat beside her.

"She is right," Alex chimed. "You are quite the countess."

Despite their praise, she had her doubts. "Do you really think so?"

"My little sister has become a true lady. And I heard Blake and Damian make similar remarks." The picture of perfect feminine deportment, Cara clasped her hands in her lap and smiled. "I am so proud of you."

The pall lifted from her heart, and Sabrina enjoyed a modicum of vindication. "I could not have done it without Celia."

"Oh, stuff." The lady of the moment basked in the compliment. "I did nothing, because Sabrina is a marvelous countess, and I admire her courage."

"You are too modest." Sabrina snorted. "She taught me

how to walk after comparing it to fishing. I tell you, she is a bloody genius."

"Well, it was the least I could do." The picture of innocence, Celia inclined her head and blinked. "After all, you taught me how to swear."

The room filled with a chorus of gasps, which mutated into giggles, before erupting into riotous laughter.

THE HARMONIOUS OUTBURST from the other gathering brought Everett alert.

"My heavens, it sounds as if someone sneaked rum into the teapot," his father bellowed as he lit another cigar.

Ensconced in the dining room with the men, and enduring another lecture on livestock bidding in full view of his guests, he decided he would rather join the women. At least then he could flirt with Sabrina.

"I beg your pardon." His mother stood in the doorway. "But I need a word with the earl."

The earl?

What was wrong with her? Could she not call him son?

But since Everett would jump from the nearest cliff to escape the sheer boredom of his sire's tutelage, he stood. "Now?"

"If it is not too much trouble." She smiled, a gesture that made the hair stand on the back of his neck. "Your study, perhaps?"

"Very well." He was curious and suspicious at once. When she ignored his proffered escort, he dropped his arm to his side. "After you."

"What is it now, Lizzy?" his father inquired.

"Nothing you need concern yourself with. Perhaps you

should adjourn to the drawing room," she said over her shoulder. "We shall only be a minute."

In complete silence, they walked down the hall, crossed the foyer, and slipped into his study. As his mother sank into the chair before his desk, Everett closed the door. Once he rounded the hand-tooled antique his wife had recently acquired, which he dearly favored, he took his seat, leaned forward, and steepled his hands. "All right, Mother, what are you about?"

"I have been giving some thought to the state of your affairs." She wrinkled her nose. "In particular, your residence."

"Oh?" A chill of dread settled deep in his chest. "I had not thought it any of your concern."

"As your mother, it is of paramount importance." That had to be the first time she ever referred to herself as such, and the moment was not lost on him. "And as the heir apparent, what you do reflects on your father and I. Therefore, all appearances must be considered."

"Make your point," Everett said, though he was certain down which path she headed.

"The household staff is poorly trained. The residence needs a thorough remodeling. The grounds are unkempt and an embarrassment." His mother huffed. "I could go on, but I believe I have made my case."

As usual, she found him lacking. So what else was new? "You suggest there is room for improvement?"

"Precisely." She scowled.

Even in that instant, she treated him as a bastard step-son. "Where do you recommend I start?"

"Your marriage." With palpable disdain, she compressed her lips.

"I knew it." He slapped a fist to his open palm. "If you

seek to assess fault, then put the blame at my feet. You see, I had the house remodeled prior to my marriage. As for the staff, I hired them—including the gardener. If there are deficiencies, I alone am responsible."

"But a well-bred wife would have already corrected the situation." He should have known she would pose an additional argument. "Management of the manor is the responsibility of the chatelaine."

"Marchioness, if you hope to talk me into an annulment, let me assure you, my marriage has been consummated, many times, in fact." And he reveled in it.

"Of that I have no doubt, and you need not burden me with the details." The marchioness frowned. "But I have another solution to your unfortunate pairing, one I urge you not to ignore."

She rose from her chair, neared the desk, lifted the leather blotter, and retrieved a crisp set of papers.

"What is that?" Everett snatched the documents from her grasp and scanned them. "You cannot be serious. A divorce? On the grounds that Sabrina is mentally unfit? I would never agree to it." He turned to toss the lot in the hearth and recalled he had ordered no fire because it was a warm evening.

"But Lady Celia—"

"Will make another match."

"Everett, be reasonable—"

"*Me* be reasonable?" White-hot rage trembled in his hands as he gathered the offensive parcel of parchment, opened a side drawer, and shoved the bundle inside. "Listen to me, and listen carefully. Sabrina is my wife, and I will have no other. Do you understand?"

His mother said nothing, only nodded.

"We are done here." Everett pushed from his desk and

stood. He stormed to the door and set it wide. "I suggest we rejoin the party."

With an icy expression, she paused before him. "If you will not listen to reason, then perhaps your wife will."

"Hear me well, Marchioness." Everett gripped her elbow and summoned his vaunted self-control in an effort to suppress the anger ripping at his insides. "Continue on this course, and you will no longer be welcome in my home or my life."

His mother gasped. "You would not dare."

He bared his teeth. "Yes, I would."

Without so much as a backward glance, the woman who birthed him stomped to the drawing room. In the off chance his mother made good on her threat and hurt his bride, he hugged his wife's heels for the remainder of the evening. And in true Sabrina fashion, she flirted with him at every opportunity. By the time he climbed into bed, his ire had yielded to desire.

"Everett?"

"Yes?" He resituated a pillow, reached for her in the dark, and grasped only air.

"Have I done something wrong?" she asked in a small voice.

"No." From the sounds, he surmised she fumbled with the fastenings of her robe. "Why do you ask?"

"You were brooding when you entered the drawing room."

The black mood returned, and he was grateful Sabrina could not see his face. "Was I?"

"Yes." The mattress dipped as she climbed beside him. "And I think I know why."

Impossible. He had remained fixed as a sentry on guard. His mother never got anywhere near Sabrina. "Oh?"

"You are upset because Trevor and Caroline are staying for an extended visit." She snuggled close and set her palm to his chest.

"Not likely, my dear." Slipping an arm beneath her head, he pressed his lips to her temple. "Because my parents and Lady Celia are doing the same."

Sabrina flinched. "Oh, no."

"Darling, much as we both dislike it, you must learn to deal with my mother." Should he tell her of the confrontation in the study?

"I know, but she is always complaining about nothing. And she is unkind to the staff." After a quiet moment she added: "Why does she not like me?"

The pain was evident in her query, and he cursed himself for subjecting her to such abuse. "My dear, it has nothing to do with you. Mother treated Charles as a marionette on her personal stage and even negotiated his marriage. Old habits die hard."

"She wants you to wed Celia." His wife draped her leg across his thigh.

"I know."

"Well?"

Everett had avoided that conversation. He would rather be the lone male at a coming out ball at Almack's. Rolling on his side, he grumbled when a silk barrier halted his amorous assault. "I want my saucy Sabrina."

"And I want my shameless lord." She caressed his cheek.

His fingers tangled in the material, and Everett struggled to break free. "Why do you always come to bed wearing a nightgown?"

She giggled and shifted, loosening the snare. "Because it is proper?"

Finally, he trailed his palm along the curve of her bare hip. "Since when are you proper?"

Sabrina shoved him back to the mattress, straddled his hips, pulled the nightgown over her head, and tossed it to the floor. "I do not suppose I am, my lord."

∾

"I ASKED FOR A BOILED EGG, and the yolk is runny." The marchioness tossed her napkin to her plate. "This food is deplorable. Really, Sabrina, you should fire your chef."

"A thousand apologies, your ladyship." As chatelaine of Beaumaris, she smothered her agitation and forced a smile. "Ware, please have Cook prepare another egg."

"As you wish, my lady." The butler bowed and removed the offensive item.

At the other end of the table, Everett winked. Would he mind terribly if she dispatched her mother-in-law to the devil?

"And one more thing."

Sabrina braced for another complaint.

"My room was not adequately aired." The marchioness thrust her nose to new heights.

Sabrina was certain that if it rained in the right direction, her mother-in-law would drown. She could almost imagine those flared nostrils filling with water, the sputtering and choking. Perhaps she should caution the Royal Pain of Talbot.

"If you cannot manage the household staff, I would be happy to speak to the housekeeper." The marchioness sniffed.

That was it, she was going to—

"Really?" Blake interjected. "I daresay it is an aberration, because my accommodations are impeccable." He stuffed a large bit of kedgeree in his mouth.

"As are mine," Damian added. "Cannot recall when I have ever enjoyed such pleasant guest quarters."

Sabrina averted her gaze and stuck her tongue in her cheek. How she would love to see the marchioness gainsay not one, but two dukes. Especially when those dukes were Blake Elliott and Damian Seymour.

The marchioness glanced at the marquess, devouring a plate of meat pie and toast, as if expecting him to come to her defense. "Perhaps it was a simple oversight?"

Setting her fork on the table, Sabrina reclined in her chair. Were she the finest statue and the marchioness armed with a chisel, she was positive there would be nothing left but an empty pedestal and a mountain of dust for the constant assault on her confidence. "Again, I offer my regrets, your ladyship. After breakfast, I shall speak with Mrs. Formby. Rest assured, the situation will be corrected, posthaste."

"Well." The marchioness sneered. "See that it is done."

Good God, could the woman not let her have the last word? Staring out the window, Sabrina noted the clear blue sky and prayed for rain.

AFTER THE MORNING MEAL, the trunks were packed and farewells traded as their guests departed. The last carriage to roll down the gravel drive belonged to her parents. Sabrina stood, with Everett at her side and his arm about her waist, in the forecourt and waved until they were out of sight.

"Wish you were leaving with them?" he asked, with a chuckle.

"Only if you were with me." She twined her fingers in his. "Think anyone would notice if we ran away?"

"*Everett!*"

He winced at his father's summons, and they turned toward the house.

In the doorway, the marquess puffed on a cigar. "Come to the study. We need to discuss the Eppingham property. A bridge has washed out and requires your immediate attention."

"All right." Everett sighed. "I shall be there momentarily."

"Do not dawdle." His father hurried down the hall.

"It would appear it is your turn in the fire." Sabrina grinned.

He rolled his eyes. "Help."

"It cannot be that bad." She giggled and placed a chaste peck on his cheek.

"I beg your pardon. My saucy Sabrina can do better than that." He enveloped her in a tight embrace and bent his head. In an instant, their kiss turned hungry, fevered—

"*Everett!*"

On a groan, he retreated. "See you at dinner?"

"And later." Together, they ascended the entrance stairs. "In our room."

"Mmm." In the foyer, he sneaked another kiss. "I like the sound of that."

"*Everett!*" the marquess called. "Where the devil are you?"

As heat simmered in his veins and desire wove a sultry summons, he chastised himself for using his wife to avoid his father and his duty. Ravishing his bride was a treat he was reluctant to end, but there was no escape from the reality of their situation.

Sabrina broke their kiss. "My lord, your father—"

"Can wait." After several delicious minutes, Everett favored her with one last hug and a naughty pinch of her bottom. "Until tonight, lady mine."

"I have a date with a mountain of supply ledgers." She sketched a mock salute and retreated toward the parlor. "And if your father shouts one more time the roof may cave about us."

Marked by the pitter-patter of her feet, Sabrina all but ran down the hall. How Everett loved the playful bounce of her curls, and the carefree manner in which she took to her chores. With a light heart, he entered his study and soon regretted forgoing a tumble with his countess to discuss business with his father.

"What have you done about the Eppingham property?" The marquess reclined on the daybed and scratched his ear.

Sitting behind his desk, Everett peered at Trevor, who had been invited into the conversation, to his great misfortune, when he sought a riding companion for the afternoon. "I understand there is a damaged bridge and shall arrange for the necessary repairs."

"What?" His sire choked and flicked his ashes to the carpet. "You must address it yourself. Have you even been to the property? You cannot delegate everything to your solicitors. That is how the estates came to be in such bad condition. Your brother, God rest him, was a poor land manager."

"I suppose I could ride there and see to it personally." Everett frowned. "But I hate to abandon Sabrina right now."

"Are you afraid she cannot handle herself?" the marquess asked. "She seems a bright, independent girl."

"On the contrary, my wife has exceeded my expectations. She has ordered the estate and assumed supervision of the staff. In short, she is an accomplished chatelaine." If only Everett had succeeded half so well. "I could not be more pleased."

"Then there is nothing to keep you from journeying to Eppingham." The marquess narrowed his eyes. "Is there some other reason you do not wish to leave your wife? Might it have something to do with your mother?"

How could he put it? "Would Sabrina go to the gallows for strangling an in-law?"

"Perhaps." The marquess chuckled. "But it is a fight I would very much like to see."

"It does not concern you?" The shock in his voice was palpable, and Everett spied Trevor attempting to conceal a smirk.

"Of course, it does." His father's expression sobered. "Your mother has always been a difficult woman. But I wager Sabrina will outlast her. She is a strong one, that girl of yours."

"Do you believe it safe to leave them alone?" How could his sire be so obtuse?

"Good heavens, you do not think I intend to travel to Eppingham with you? I am not a bloody nursemaid to hold your hand." His father snickered. "Tried that with your brother and look at the mess it got me. Deuced if I will do it again. Be a man and handle it. I shall keep company with the women."

Everett bristled under his father's criticism. No matter how hard he tried, nothing pleased his sire. How he managed to hold his tongue he neither knew nor cared.

"Believe I shall catch a few winks before dinner." The

marquess stretched, yawned with a flair for the dramatic, and quit the room.

"I can accompany you." Trevor perched on the corner of the desk. "I have not toured this part of the country."

"If it is not too much trouble." Closing a ledger, Everett stacked the papers on the blotter. "It will be like old times. How I miss those carefree days when I was nothing more than Lord Markham."

"Buck up, old boy. Do not get maudlin on me. You are not your brother, and the title will take some getting used to." Trevor wrinkled his nose. "And it is no trouble at all. Caroline and little Welton can remain here until our return."

The mention of Trevor's heir reminded him of another duty he had yet to fulfill. "I understand Caroline is increasing again?"

"She is." Trevor waggled his brows.

"Not wasting any time, I see." How Everett yearned to build a family with his most unlikely lady.

"Why should I? Caroline's young and healthy, and we want several children." His friend from Eton shrugged. "Besides, the work is good."

Resting his chin in his hand, Everett envisioned Sabrina plump with his child. Once he had tended the Eppingham property, he would devote himself to his wife.

Surely that was an endeavor in which he could not fail?

"Where are the men?" Caroline sipped her lemonade and reclined in a cushioned chair on the terrace.

"They are in the study." Sabrina fingered a hot scone

and drew swirls in the jam on her plate. "Discussing a bridge."

"A bridge?" Celia asked.

"Indeed." Sabrina nodded. "On the Eppingham estate. It is one of the properties Everett inherited."

"How is he adjusting to the responsibilities of the earldom?" Caroline claimed a square of shortbread from a nearby tray.

"Stupendously." Sabrina wished the same could be said of her turn as chatelaine. "He was born to lead and has already commissioned several improvements to other holdings."

"So why the long face?" Caroline replied, quick as a wink.

Resorting to a familiar nervous habit, Sabrina worried her lower lip and wondered how long it would take to chew through her chin. "Bloody hell. Is it that obvious?"

"You never could fool me, Brie." Caroline dusted crumbs from her skirts. "We are one in the same."

"All right." Licking the strawberry goo from her finger, she set her plate aside. "The problem is Everett has done so well as an earl, he deserves a countess his equal in every way."

"And you do not believe you are that person?" Caroline inquired with unnerving accuracy.

A cold weight settled in her chest. "I know I am not."

"Why?" Caroline propped her elbow on the armrest and rested her chin in her hand. "What makes you say that?"

Celia leaned forward in her chair. "Is it because of the marchioness?"

Had her friends noted her failure? Had they shared her mother-in-law's opinion? "Nothing I do pleases her."

"You make too much of her grousing," Celia stated with

an air of authority. "You are a wonderful countess, and Lord Woverton adores you."

"He does not." She cursed herself for countering so fast.

"He does so," Celia insisted with a nod. "I see it whenever he looks at you. He goes all soft and fuzzy and, take it from me, Everett has never been soft and fuzzy."

How she prayed Celia was right, but her instincts told her differently. While her husband enjoyed making love to her, their relationship had progressed no further, much to her displeasure. She could go along with the assumption and allow her friends to believe everything was peaches and cream in the Woverton household, but that would be a lie.

And Sabrina Francis Douglas Markham, black-eyed Countess of Woverton, could not lie.

"You are wrong." She inhaled a shaky breath. "Everett may be fond of me, but I cannot see it going any further than that."

"How can you be sure?" Caroline arched a brow, and Sabrina steeled herself for the question she knew was forthcoming. "Has something happened between you two?"

Studying the lace of her morose black mourning dress, Sabrina tried but failed to form a response. A lump in her throat heralded the impending arrival of tears. When Caroline placed a hand on Sabrina's arm, she flinched. "He would not consummate our marriage." The words were spoken before she realized what she had said.

Caroline and Celia gasped in unison, and Sabrina searched for a rock to crawl beneath. They glanced at each other, then pinned her with inquisitive stares.

"Blast!" Sabrina thumped herself on the forehead with her fist. "I said that aloud, did I not? I just told you Everett and I did not have relations until we arrived at Beaumaris."

And she had said it again. She was going to march straight to the kitchen and cut out her tongue.

Someone snorted, and someone else gurgled.

For Sabrina, it was too much. "You think this is funny?"

With red faces and tears welling in their eyes, Caroline and Celia gave vent to gales of hilarity.

All she could do was sit there and suffer the indignation. After a few short minutes, Sabrina reached her breaking point and stood.

Caroline caught her by the wrist. "Brie, do not go away angry."

"Who says I am angry?" She pouted.

With the noble hauteur of a daughter of a duke, Caroline said, "Sit down."

Sabrina humphed and ungracefully plopped in her seat.

"Now then," Caroline continued. "I cannot believe you are the same fearless female with whom I grew up. You are not afraid of anything. And since when do you give a whit what anyone thinks? The Brie I know would tell the marchioness to go to the devil."

Sabrina stared at her hands clasped in her lap to conceal their trembling. "But I cannot."

"Why not?" Caroline asked.

Considering the fact that she had just admitted her marriage vows were not consummated until long after the wedding, Sabrina thought it a little late to worry about propriety. "Because—because she is Everett's mother."

"And as a marchioness, she has rank," Celia pointed out.

"Ah, yes." Caroline snapped her fingers. "I had forgotten that."

"This is dreadful. I feel like such a failure when she is about, as nothing I do pleases her." Sabrina whined and hated herself for it. "The linens are too rough. Her eggs are not cooked to her taste. The light is insufficient in the drawing room. Her room smelled stale. I could go on and on."

A shrill scream rent the air, and the women bounded to their feet.

"What now?" Sabrina threw up her hands in frustration.

They ran in the general direction of the ruckus and found the marchioness standing, with an imperious expression and her arms folded, amid the lush green hedges of the topiary garden.

Dreading the answer, but knowing full well it would be offered whether or not she inquired, Sabrina asked, "What happened?"

Before Her Supreme Pain in the Posterior could reply, the men came rushing from behind.

"What on earth is all the shouting about?" Everett demanded.

The marchioness stepped back and motioned to the ground. As Lady Elizabeth's nose rose in epic proportions, Sabrina's heart sank in her chest. "There is a root that almost sent me for a tumble. It is a hazard requiring immediate attention." The Devil in a Black Dress narrowed her stare as she gazed at Sabrina. "It is the duty of the mistress of the manor to ensure the grounds are safe and free of impediments while entertaining guests. I could have been seriously injured."

I should be so lucky, Sabrina thought.

"Nonsense." Everett squatted and assessed the offending protrusion. "It is barely visible, and there is ample soil on either side to prevent one from stumbling over it."

"But you can see the knot." The marchioness stomped in emphasis. "Someone could catch a toe and fall."

"Not if you pick your feet up when you walk," Everett replied.

The marchioness humphed. "I suppose there is no danger if one tromps about like an elephant."

Sabrina winced at the unmistakable inference but held her tongue. A slew of rapier retorts died in her throat.

"Oh, come now." Everett rolled his eyes. "You make too much of the situation."

"Well." The Queen of Complaining sniffed. "I see you persist in making excuses for her negligence."

Everett stood and placed both hands on his hips. "Negligence—"

With an elbow to his ribs, Sabrina silenced him. That her husband felt the need to defend her only intensified her humiliation. "My lady, I will speak to the gardener, at once, and ensure the root is dug up. Thank you for bringing it to my attention. Now, if you will excuse me, I must supervise the dinner menu."

With a leash on her temper, she balled her hands into fists, gritted her teeth, and tried not to stomp away. But, deep down inside, Sabrina wondered how much more she could take.

CHAPTER THIRTEEN

*B*y the time she gained her room that night, Sabrina was near to exploding. Nothing at dinner pleased Everett's mother. The beef was overcooked, the vegetables too raw, and the lemon tarts too tart.

Before she frightened her maid and embarrassed herself further, Sabrina dismissed Millie and undressed herself. Stripped of her black gown, which matched her temperament, she sat at her vanity, rolled her stockings to her ankles and slipped them from her feet. She tugged the pins from her hair and let her ebony locks fall in a cascade down her back.

For a moment, she studied her reflection in the mirror. Marriage was not what she had expected. Her mother-in-law hated her. Her husband loved her not. And she was not sure how to correct either situation. With her brush, she stroked twice, before lashing out in a wide arc.

"How am I ever to please her?" Sabrina cried aloud. "No matter what I do, or how hard I try, it is never enough. I do so want to be a good countess." Angry, hurt, she raked the brush through her hair. "And why will Everett not love me?"

She stopped mid-stroke.

There was one area of her marriage where she always succeeded. One aspect in which triumph was certain.

And she needed it—or rather him, right then.

Without care, she tossed the brush atop the vanity.

She crossed the room to her armoire and flung the doors wide. A gauzy nightgown and matching robe caught her eye, and Sabrina retrieved the set and spread them at the foot of her bed. After doffing her garters and chemise, she picked up the nightgown and paused. Everett had not favored them. So Sabrina set it aside, grabbed the robe, and thrust an arm into each delicate sleeve. Fastening the three mother-of-pearl buttons at the throat, she checked herself in the long mirror.

The ivory robe made her raven hair appear all the more dark. The sumptuous garment was a transparent creation that left nothing to the imagination. With enclosures only at the top of the opening, the robe parted to reveal her belly button and the triangle of black curls at the juncture of her thighs.

She touched the tips of her breasts and gasped when her nipples hardened. As she skimmed her hands over her belly, gooseflesh prickled her skin. Closing her eyes, she dropped her hands and touched her most intimate flesh. A wicked shiver coursed her spine and marked a fiery path to the secret place between her thighs in which Everett loved to play. Sabrina was shocked by her ability to arouse herself.

How powerful she felt.

With one last check of her appearance, she clutched the folds of filmy silk. Perhaps she should don a nightgown? Bloody hell, what good would it do? Everett would whisk the unwanted item from her body in seconds. A rumble of voices made her pause. Her husband had dismissed his valet.

It was time to strike.

With shoulders squared, she marched to the entrance, grasped the knob, and hauled open the door.

IT HAD BEEN A MISERABLE NIGHT.

Everett had done nothing right—according to his father.

The estate expenses soared, he had paid too high a price for the cattle, and he should have personally inspected the new roofs installed on the tenant homes. Everett rubbed his weary eyes. In the mirror, he settled his gaze on the reflection of the tiny door to the corridor connecting his suite to his wife's.

There was one venue in which he never failed. One arena in which he was never defeated. Success was guaranteed in Sabrina's arms. With her, he felt invincible.

And right then, Everett needed a win.

"I shall finish the rest, Pitton." He speared his fingers through his hair. "You are dismissed."

"As you wish, your lordship." The valet made a hasty exit.

In one minute, he shrugged out of his shirt, tugged off his boots, slipped out of his breeches, and walked to his dressing room.

When Everett emerged, he wore a sapphire silk robe, a smile, and nothing else. Seconds later, he yanked open the door leading to his personal slice of heaven. Gold light from her quarters signaled Sabrina's presence at the other end. With steely determination, he strode forward, arms outstretched, reaching for her.

And she reached for him.

They met in the middle, hands fisting in each other's robes, groping and embracing.

They were two like souls desperately seeking validation.

Acceptance.

"I want you," he murmured into her hair.

"And I you," she said as she nipped his chin.

So they sought the same prize. Thankfully, it was one they could share. And in sharing, achieve greater reward.

Everett lifted her in his arms and carried her into his chamber. Setting Sabrina on her feet, he divested her of the robe. She tugged on his belt and pushed the silk from his shoulders.

Naked, aroused, he moved toward her.

She moved toward him.

They erupted as soon as they touched.

Her hands skimmed his ribcage and moved up, fisting in his hair. With caresses meant to incite, he fanned the flames of lust. But Everett wanted more. Wanted her to want him. To desire him as he desired her.

It was a grudging admission, albeit, a silent one. A declaration he had not shared. To need her. To have her and wonder, in the next second, when he would have her again. To revel in her company. To listen for the pitter-patter of her feet on the marble floors. To look for her when she was not present and wonder where she was and what she was doing.

Had she felt the same tug? That powerful pull?

Would she ever love him?

As if she had heard his thoughts, Sabrina framed his face with her hands and stared into his eyes. "Everett, I need you, so much."

Well, it was not the declaration he yearned to hear. But, at that moment, he would settle for less.

On a groan, he took her mouth.

It should have been a fierce possession.

But it wasn't.

It should have been urgent, savage.

But it wasn't.

It should have been hungry, desperate.

But it wasn't.

Instead, it was a tender union. Gentle. A stealthy capture. And capture her, he had.

Sabrina stretched long, pressing herself against him. Was it acceptable for a wife to desire her husband? He hoped so, or he was about to err again. When she wriggled her hips in unmistakable invitation, he could only encourage her.

Everett cupped her bottom and lifted her. And though he had not asked, she wrapped her legs about him. With a fluid flex of his spine, he thrust, and the two became one. Blissful relief washed over him, erasing the tension of the day. She closed her eyes and let her head fall back. He feasted on her throat, stopping to lave his tongue over the pulse at the base. He set an achingly slow rhythm, his hips rocking back and forth, his flesh held deep within hers.

When Sabrina moved in unison, drawing out the delicious slip and slide, he walked them to the bed and sat on the edge of the mattress. For a change, he reclined and gave her the reins.

With a shy grin, she grasped his hands and brought them to her breasts. "I love it when you touch me."

"I love touching you." She squeezed his wrists and moaned her appreciation as he massaged her.

His brazen bride rode him hard and fast—just the way

he liked it. Through a sensuous haze, her tempestuous beauty seduced him. And just when Everett thought he would explode inside her, she stopped. Slowly, Sabrina rose, then slid down, enfolding him once again in wet heat. Someone groaned, he thought it might have been him. She repeated the intimate caress until her body went rigid with completion, and her soft sobs of pleasure inflamed the warrior within.

And as the conqueror preparing to lay siege to his spoils, he was patient. With infinite gentleness, he kissed her forehead, her closed eyelids, and both her cheeks. She whimpered, and he nibbled on the tip of her nose. The telltale flutter of her lids signaled she had returned to the mortal plane.

And she was ready for round two.

"Mmm, that was wonderful." Sabrina smiled, a feminine smile.

"I am glad you enjoyed it." He gripped her hips and shifted.

Her eyes grew wide. "Did you not—"

Quick as a wink, Everett flipped her onto her back.

With elbows locked, feeling every inch the predator, he looked down on her and licked his lips. And thrust. Again and again, in a repetitive rhythm, he claimed her. The hitch in her breath as their hips met spurred him into frenzy, drove him with an urgency he could not comprehend. But he counted each gasp, each moan a sweet victory.

And he wanted more.

Setting a relaxed pace, Everett thrilled to the subtle bounce of her breasts as he pumped within her. Sabrina attempted to pull him down, but he resisted. The sight of her taking him, his body, was enthralling, and he was not ready to surrender—at least, not yet.

He had married a strong woman. And her strength, her indomitable spirit empowered him, anew. Made him feel as though no matter what else he had or had not achieved in life, he had succeeded because he married her. She was his foundation. If he were a ship, she would be his anchor.

Tomorrow, he would journey to the Eppingham property. Though it was only a business trip, somehow it meant more because he knew Sabrina would be home, awaiting his return.

On the thought, he let her draw him close. He settled over her, giving her his weight. Resting on his elbows, with both hands cradling her head, Everett kissed his wife with a passion he had never known he possessed.

The mere taste of Sabrina was erotic.

The sensuous tension built like the winding of a clock spring. Until the spring snapped and release surged through him, robbing him of his breath, shaking him to his core. Their moans of fulfillment were given simultaneously.

His to her. Hers to him.

When sleep came for him, Everett drifted into dreamland, with limbs entwined with his wife's, content that in his marital bed he was always right.

EVERETT AND TREVOR departed after breakfast the following morning. As the two men rode down the graveled drive, Sabrina felt like the only survivor aboard a sinking ship, as the lifeboats sailed without her. She wondered how long it would take her mother-in-law to find another deficiency in her household management.

"*Sabrina!*"

At least the woman was consistent.

Staring at the cloudless sky, she prayed, "God, give me strength."

With one last wave to her husband, she turned and entered the house. It was only her mother-in-law, but she trembled as though she faced an executioner.

The first day Everett was gone passed much as she expected. Though Sabrina had girded herself for the worst, she could not have foreseen the catastrophes that would plague her at every turn.

Lunch had been a disaster—according to the marchioness, of course. Because someone left the compote of cherries uncovered, a mouse had found its way into the container, and orange water ice had been substituted for dessert at the last minute. How strange it was that the marchioness declared a sudden fondness for cherries, and the spoiled compote became a singular tragedy of monumental proportions.

Afterward, the entire household rocked, and the walls of the home reverberated, as a piercing scream echoed through the house. Sabrina took the stairs two at a time as she ran. She followed the howls to the guest wing and, more specifically, the room the marchioness occupied.

"What is it?" Out of breath and gasping for air, Sabrina held a hand to her bosom. "What has happened?"

"Someone put a burr in my bed." With a pitiable countenance, the marchioness pointed to the mattress. "I came upstairs to take a nap and discovered it."

"A burr?" Sabrina walked to the bed and prepared to deny the accusation but, there, in the center of the mattress, rested a gnarly looking seedpod.

"Good heavens, how did that get there?" She freed the burr from the sheets.

"I could have been cruelly wounded."

You still might be, Sabrina thought.

"What are you fussing about now, Lizzie?" The marquess strolled in unaffected, as if he was used to his wife's dramatics.

"Someone conspired to cause me injury." Pressing a palm to her brow, the marchioness appeared as if she would swoon at any moment. "I fear I am bleeding."

Sabrina shook her head. Her mother-in-law had missed her calling, because she belonged on a stage at Drury Lane. "Your ladyship, I am sure this is nothing more than an unfortunate mishap. As the linens were just cleaned, perhaps the burr was accidentally picked up in the wash. If you please, you may rest in my suite, and I shall have Mrs. Formby put fresh linens on your bed."

"Humph." The marchioness folded her arms. "I knew the minute my son departed you would try something like this."

Shocked by the conjecture and implication of her words, Sabrina swallowed hard. "Surely you do not think I had anything to do with the unfortunate mishap?"

"Lizzie, what are you inferring?" The marquess placed both hands on his hips and arched a brow.

"I infer nothing, as I state a fact," the marchioness snapped. "I believe she put the burr there in a deliberate attempt to cause me pain. The dreadful girl hates me."

"Oh, come now." His jaw dropped. "You cannot mean that."

"My lady, I assure you, I did no such thing. I swear it." Her heart pounded in her ears, and Sabrina stood fast. "Why would I seek to harm you?"

"Because I see you for what you are, and I call attention to your shortcomings. You never should have married my son." The marchioness stared down her nose. "You are not in his class, nor will you ever be his equal."

"Lizzie!" the marquess barked. "That is enough."

"It is true and you know it." Lady Elizabeth sneered. "Were she half the lady she pretends to be, she would vacate this marriage, at once, and spare us further humiliation."

Sabrina bit her lip to keep it from trembling. She would not cry in front of that woman, even though her harsh words cut sharp as a knife. "I am sorry you find me so lacking, my lady." Sabrina strode from the room—and almost ran smack into Caroline.

Her lifelong friend said nothing, merely looked into her eyes and no doubt saw the pain etched there. It was obvious she had overheard the conversation, because she grasped Sabrina's wrist and said, "My room."

When they reached the guest quarters Trevor and Caroline shared, she led Sabrina to the *chaise* near the window. "Sit."

Sabrina acquiesced without a reply.

Caroline plopped down next to her. Unable to speak, Sabrina covered her face with her hands. Stunned by the ache burning in her chest, she slumped forward and let the tears rush forth.

It was hours before she returned to her room.

Sabrina contemplated a mad dash to the coast when the dinner bell sounded. It was too late to escape, so she resolved to meet her nemesis over what she hoped would be a civil meal.

Reminding herself she was no coward, she stared at her reflection in the long mirror. Sabrina would give anything to be struck with a serious illness and thereby have a justifiable excuse for foregoing her obligation as hostess.

"You are the countess of Woverton," she said to her image.

Dressed in one of her best black gowns, she had Millie arrange her hair in a charming coiffeur. Turning to the side, she studied her profile and decided she looked every inch the lady of the manor. With a final nod, she headed for the drawing room.

To her relief, Caroline was the first to join her. "Feeling better?"

Sabrina smiled. "Yes, thank you."

"It is times like these I am grateful I have no in-laws." Caroline referred to the fact that Trevor's mother had run off with her lover when Trevor was just a child, and his father had long since passed away.

"Would that I were as fortunate." Sabrina reached and squeezed her friend's fingers. "Thank you for sitting with me this afternoon. I am not normally a water pot."

"I know you are not." Caroline patted her cheek. "Dearest Brie, if there is anything you ever need, know you can always count on me."

"Thank you." Sabrina covered Caroline's hand with her own. "But everything is going to be fine."

Footsteps in the hall caught her attention.

Sabrina braced herself for the next confrontation with the marchioness. But to her surprise, the marquess entered with Celia on his arm.

"Where is the marchioness?" Caroline asked.

"She suffers a headache and will take a tray in her room." The marquess wiggled his brows. "Looks like you ladies have me all to yourselves this evening."

Sabrina exhaled her relief and managed not to dance on her heels.

~

"I WILL NOT STRANGLE MY MOTHER-IN-LAW." Wringing her hands in front of her, Sabrina paced the drawing room floor and repeated the words like an ancient mantra for personal restraint.

"What has she done now?"

Sabrina started as Caroline entered the room.

"I will tell you what she has done. The marchioness took it upon herself to meet with my housekeeper and fired two of the upstairs maids. Of course, I have already rescinded those orders." Sabrina lashed out in anger. "But who does she think she is, coming into my home and usurping my authority as chatelaine?"

"Oh, my." Caroline perched on the edge of the sofa.

"And that is not all." Sabrina resumed pacing. "Thank goodness the gardener checked with me before digging up the rose bushes near the fountain."

"Why would he do that?" Caroline blinked.

"Because the marchioness told him they were going to seed, and she would rather have shrubbery in their place." Halting, with both hands firm on her hips, Sabrina stomped a foot on the carpeted floor. "How dare she!"

"Calm down." Caroline shook her head. "You will work yourself into a state."

"I am already in a state." With pulsing fists at her sides, Sabrina emitted an unladylike growl. "What am I going to do? Everett will be home tomorrow, and I cannot guarantee his mother will live to see him again."

"Come now." Caroline chuckled and patted the green damask sofa cushion. "Sit with me."

"This is a disaster." Sabrina trudged to the sofa and plunked down. With both elbows resting on her knees, she cupped her chin in her hands. "I do not want my husband to come home to a family at war, but how can it be helped? His mother hates me."

"There now, Brie." Her lifelong friend slipped an arm about Sabrina's shoulders. "The marchioness does not hate you."

"Then why does she thwart me at every turn?" Sabrina could take the witch in a fight, so why could she not manage the marchioness?

"Because, I surmise, she cannot snap her fingers and have you jump on command." Caroline tapped a finger to the tip of her nose. "And you, my dear friend, have never followed any dictates other than your own. Have you tried joining her in any common pursuits? Does she ride?"

"No." Sabrina scratched her temple. "She knits, and you know how I am with a ball of thread and needles. I would end up mummifying myself—or her. I know it is unsporting of me, but I wish Everett's parents would go home."

"Am I included in that wish?" Celia stood in the doorway, a pout on her face.

"Good heavens, no." Sabrina rose from the sofa and splayed her arms in welcome. "You and Caroline are the only ones keeping me from the hangman's noose."

Celia hugged her. "I gather you and the marchioness are at odds again?"

"She has interfered in my management of the household," Sabrina explained.

"Oh, my." Celia's eyes grew wide. "What will you do?"

"I am not sure." Sabrina searched in vain for a solution to her quandary.

"Everett will be aghast when he hears of his mother's behavior." Caroline reclined on the sofa. "He may ask her to apologize."

"Oh, no. That will only make things worse." Sabrina pondered the situation. "Perhaps I should not tell him what has occurred in his absence."

Celia claimed an overstuffed chair. "I do not think that is wise."

"He needs to know." Caroline compressed her lips. "You cannot keep this from him. His mother may be a marchioness, but that does not excuse poor manners. An apology is in order."

"I disagree." Sabrina paced again and fretted she might wear holes in the carpet. "I do not want him to think I cannot manage the household. I have failed him enough as it is."

"Brie—"

"No." Sabrina stopped before the window and gazed at the lush green lawns. She was not the perfect wife or count-ess, and she knew it. But she would not give Everett one more reason to regret marrying her. "Caroline, do not ask me to tell him. I simply cannot."

CHAPTER FOURTEEN

*E*verett and Trevor rode through the gates early in the evening, cantering down the graveled drive lined with grand oaks, which stood tall as sentries welcoming them home. Everett inhaled the familiar smell of fresh-cut grass, and then he held his breath as the trees thinned.

Beaumaris rose in the distance.

It was a warm structure built in the Renaissance style of red brick with Portland stone trim. Jacobean tracery framed the mullioned windows across the face. On a sparsely clouded day, as the white puffs reflected in the glass, it gave the illusion the building winked.

That was his home.

He smiled. It was the first property he had ever purchased with his own money. There was always smug satisfaction knowing he had bought it from a ne'er-do-well nobleman in dire financial straits.

The man had neglected the estate, and the gardens had been in ruins. As soon as the sale was complete, Everett engaged the services of an architect to restore the grounds and manor house to their original splendor. He could not believe several prospective buyers had passed on the parcel of land. It seemed no one had seen through the age and wear to the potential and quiet beauty of the old home. No one had noted the refined elegance, the classic lines, or the understated charm.

Much like the new lady of the manor.

Sabrina, his wife.

If he closed his eyes, he could taste her lips. His palms itched as he recalled the silky softness of her skin, and the warmth of her body beneath him. Mentally, he replayed her feminine sighs and murmurs as he drove his flesh into hers.

Emotions welled, crashing over him, wave after wave as the evening tide. For a scarce second he felt as if he could not expand his lungs. And he realized, in that moment, she had become as vital to him as the air he breathed.

Without her, he had no future. She was everything to him. And were he to suddenly find himself without her, there would be no laughter, no life, no love.

Ah, love.

Now there was a tricky emotion.

Being in love, helpless, enslaved, and enthralled by it, he was ecstatic. Yet, at the same time, he feared losing his treasure, losing Sabrina. It was exciting and terrifying at once.

He had not told her—yet. It was not fashionable to be hopelessly in love with one's wife.

But why should he care?

He knew what he feared, what had kept him silent—that she would dismiss his feelings.

Sabrina had told him early in their courtship that she felt something for him. She had likened her emotions to indigestion, and he had discounted her declaration as nothing more than the fancy of an innocent young woman too unschooled in the ways of love to recognize said emotion.

She had not mentioned it again.

And now he was truly sorry he had brushed her aside without care. He wanted to help her explore her feelings, wanted to foster what could be a deep and abiding ardor. He wanted to hear her say it, wanted her to utter those three simple but precious words.

"I love you."

"I beg your pardon?"

Everett had forgot Trevor rode beside him. And, at present, his old friend grinned ridiculously at him.

He blushed, he knew it, and he wished he could cut off his head. "Er, I did not intend to say that aloud."

"I did not think so." Trevor laughed. "I take it you were not declaring yourself to me?"

"Bloody hell." Everett rolled his eyes and shook his head. "I was just considering a situation and got carried away."

"I see." Trevor smiled and cast him a knowing glance. "Being married is nice, is it not?"

"Am I that transparent?" He blanched.

"Yes," Trevor replied without hesitation.

"Am I as bad as you?" He stiffened his back.

"Indubitably." Trevor snickered.

Everett groaned.

Trevor burst out laughing.

Perhaps he should avail himself of the opportunity to seek his friend's guidance. "And yet it is altogether unsettling."

"Ah, you have not told her." Trevor arched a brow.

Everett gulped, as his chum hit his target with unerring accuracy. "How could you possibly know?"

"I have been on the other side of that face." Trevor grimaced. "I do not envy you, as the first time is the most excruciating experience you will endure. But, as my wife correctly assured me, it gets easier."

"Does it?" Everett fumbled with the reins.

"Yes."

"And how often do you—"

"Every day and more than once." Trevor shifted in his saddle. "But my motives are purely selfish."

Again, the unfailing precision of his pal from Eton rendered Everett flummoxed. "I do not follow."

"I make my declaration because my wife never fails to respond in kind." Trevor averted his gaze and smiled. "And nothing compares to what Caroline does for me. She is, quite simply, my world."

"That I understand." Everett envisioned Sabrina. "You are most fortunate in that your affection is returned."

Trevor's mouth fell agape. "And you believe yours is not?"

"You sound surprised." Blast his honest hide and loose tongue.

Yet Trevor cast an expression of pure skepticism. "If I do, it is because I have seen how Sabrina admires you, when she thinks you unaware."

Again hope bloomed. "And how is that?"

"The same way my wife looks at me, and I would give you some unsolicited but well-intended advice." Trevor rocked with the motion of his horse. "Do not delay, as that is the mistake I made, and it almost cost me everything I hold dear."

For a few minutes, they rode in silence.

Everett pondered Trevor's counsel. On the surface, it seemed so pedestrian, yet his familial history resurfaced with a vengeance, the accompanying agony swamped him in despair, and he flinched. "Do you recall the Christmas I wrote and asked my parents to bring us to Tantallon Hall for the holidays?"

"If memory serves, it was the year Charles received a pony, and you remained at school, with me." Trevor frowned. "You shared my bunk and cried yourself to sleep for three nights."

"Never have I felt so alone. Even now, all these years later, their rejection still hurts, and I hate myself for it." Everett winced, as images from the past flooded his brain. "If not for you, I might have done something—"

"No." Trevor met Everett's stare. "You were a strong lad then, and you are a better man than you realize, old friend. As children, we were caught in the same noose, but it was not of our own making, and we have survived to enjoy far greener pastures."

How he wished that were so. "Were you afraid when you told Caroline?"

"Terrified, but she had declared herself twice and then begged me to love h-her." Trevor's voice cracked, and Everett studied his confidant's profile. "In my ignorance, I hurt her. I am ashamed that I reduced her to such desperation, and I wake every morning determined to deserve her heart."

"I sympathize." Everett chortled. "Did you ever think we would find two such extraordinary women?"

"Never." Trevor bowed his head. "But, given what we endured early in our lives, I would argue we have earned our good fortune. And I am most grateful for my wife and son, so I will not question what fate has sought to bestow."

"You make it sound so simple." Everett recalled Sabrina's plea, I am afraid of anyone and anything that threatens to drive us apart.

"You refer, of course, to your parents."

"Your ability to read my thoughts is altogether discomposing."

"I suppose turnabout is fair play." Trevor smirked. "Do you not recall the two nights I spent on the sofa in your study, as a newlywed nincompoop?"

"When you suspected your wife had involved herself with Darwith." And Everett had postulated Trevor's dilemma with equal fidelity. "I get your meaning."

"You know, my wife told me something once, and it took me some time to discern the truth in her statement." Trevor peered at the sky. "She said that love is a gift, not an obligation. And truer words were never spoken, because love holds no purse strings. You need only accept it."

"I understand." As they entered the forecourt and approached the main entrance, Everett was thankful for the conversation. The respite from his inner musings kept him from heeling the flanks of his horse and galloping full speed into Sabrina's arms.

"And on that note, I believe I shall search out my wife and make love to her until dinner." Trevor winked. "If you hear a scream, do not raise the alarm."

"Brother, you may not see me until breakfast, as my most unlikely lady boasts an appetite that could rival that of any man." Now Everett laughed in earnest.

"Ah, it is good to be a husband." Trevor slapped a thigh.

The undergrooms scurried to provide assistance just as Trevor and Everett dismounted. He turned to the double doors, his heart heavy with anticipation as he awaited his wife's appearance.

Everett wondered in what unconventional fashion his

bride would welcome him home. Would she charge forth from her chamber, hair still wet from a bath, gown clinging like a second skin, and jump him in the hall? Would she upend a table laden with dishes from afternoon tea, sending cups and saucers flying, in an effort to greet him? He chuckled as he pictured the last.

The doors opened as they ascended the stairs.

To his infinite disappointment, Ware loomed at the threshold. "Good evening, my lord. Welcome home."

Everett doffed his hat and tugged at his gloves, surreptitiously glancing at the stairs as he freed a hand. The one person he most wanted to see remained absent. He peered down the empty hall, and the deafening quiet disappointed him. At his side, Trevor passed his cloak to the butler.

"Where is—" The pitter-patter of familiar footfalls silenced him.

In that instant, Sabrina sprinted into the foyer, with her skirts hiked, affording a scandalous display of her calves, and her slippered feet sliding on the polished marble floor. "You are home!"

She cast him a radiant smile before leaping at him. In Sabrina's wake, Caroline mimicked the charming maneuvers and likewise flung herself at Trevor.

Tossing his gloves at Ware, Everett caught his wife, mid-air, in a bear of a hug, laughing in delight as she showered his face in kisses. When her lips found his, the laughter ceased.

Before things got out of hand, and with his wife that was a certainty, he headed for the stairs. Taking each step slowly, the toes of her slippers tapping against the shins of his boots, he suckled her little pink tongue.

"Dinner in your reception room, my lord?" Ware asked from the foot of the stairs.

The question barely registered. "Mmm hmm." Everett doubted he could take his mouth off his wife, even had he wanted to, and he wanted otherwise.

"Seven, my lord?"

Much to his displeasure, Sabrina broke their kiss. He stopped on the landing, with her secured in his embrace, and stared into her eyes.

A flirty grin blossomed. "Eight," she replied with confidence.

"Very good, my lady. I will make excuses to your guests."

Everett blinked. Was that amusement in his stodgy butler's voice? He shuddered when she scored her fingernails over the sensitive skin at the nape of his neck, commanding every inch of him. And currently his inches were at full sail.

His heartbeat and pace quickened. "Now, where were we?" he murmured against her lips.

～

"RINSE."

Everett slid beneath the surface of the water as not-so-dainty fingers scrubbed his hair. When he rose, Sabrina slipped between his legs, splayed her hands over his ribs, skimmed his shoulders, and wrapped her arms about his neck. Water splashed over the rim of the oversized bath, and he wiped moisture from his eyes before closing his arms about her.

She pressed her cheek to his chest and snuggled close. "I missed you so much."

"I missed you, too, love." He cradled her head. "Did everything go all right while I was away? Where there any problems?"

Sabrina bit her lip and tried not to flinch.

Should she tell him the truth and admit her failure?

Desperate to confide in him, she wanted to share the hurtful things his mother had said but was unsure of his response.

If only Everett loved her.

Sabrina could share everything; safe in the knowledge her husband would not reject her. She would be assured of his allegiance, of his support. But as much as it pained her to admit it, she would not lie to herself.

Everett had not loved her.

It was as though she skated on thin ice. At any moment, the hazardous ground upon which she had trod could collapse, leaving her to founder and cause him further embarrassment. And in her opinion, she had embarrassed him enough already.

Sabrina closed her eyes. "Everything is fine." She lied, hoping in secret it would be so.

"Mother did not give you any trouble?"

Her mind raced as she searched for a suitable answer. It was bad enough to be untruthful. She had not wanted to compound her dilemma. When no comfortable explanation came to her, she sought another escape.

A distraction.

There was one safe wager.

Shifting suggestively against him, Sabrina lifted her head and set her mouth to his. "Everything is fine," she whispered against his lips.

They were the last coherent words spoken that night.

~

"WELL, I am so happy you two could find your way out of your apartments and see fit to join us for dinner this evening." The marchioness sniffed at her soup and dipped her spoon in the liquid.

Preparing to sample the first course, Everett sighed and rolled his eyes. "Mother, it was a long journey, and I needed my rest."

"Lord Lockwood managed to dine with us." She cast Trevor a sickeningly sweet smile, which had him shifting in his seat. "I believe he made the same trip."

"Perhaps he is fortunate to possess more stamina than I." Everett lifted his napkin, dabbed the corners of his mouth, and signaled the servants to serve the next course.

At the opposite end of the table, Sabrina chewed her bottom lip and vowed in silence to forswear her nervous habit if she survived the meal without any trouble. Her mother-in-law was up to something. She could see it in the expression, supreme and confident, the marchioness wore. In an instant, Sabrina blamed herself for the impending danger.

After cajoling her husband into taking breakfast and lunch in their chamber, she had thought only of the immediate benefit—having Everett to herself. She had not considered the reaction she would incite in his mother, and she knew without doubt a confrontation loomed on the horizon.

What if her mother-in-law complained of the burr in her bed? Or worse, the marchioness could repeat the horrible things she had said afterward, for the delectation of all those present. Sabrina's humiliation would be complete.

On the thought, Sabrina almost fainted. Quick as a flash, she snapped to attention. Now was not the time for dramatics. Her mind raced in search of a distraction and every nerve stretched with tension. She latched on to the one thing she could think of to avoid a disaster.

"My lord, will you not share your success with everyone?" she suggested, and prayed she had done the right thing.

"Ah, yes." Everett smiled at her from across the table. "The bridge."

"Do tell," the marquess added, as he accepted a portion of roast duck from the footman. "Have you seen to the repairs?"

"Actually, I have issued orders to have the remains torn down and a new bridge built in its place—"

"Are you mad?" The marquess erupted into a violent coughing fit. He gulped his dinner wine and wiped his mouth on the sleeve of his coat. "It will cost a small fortune to rebuild that bridge."

Everett halted the tirade with an upraised hand. "Father, what remains of the bridge, which looks to have been built a century ago, is not stable enough to repair. I daresay I would be repairing it again before the year is out." He shook his head and caressed the stem of his glass. "No, it was not worth fixing. It is better to spend the money and rebuild it right, than to try and patch an unstable structure."

"I agree." Trevor rose to her husband's defense, and Sabrina could have kissed him. "The trusses had deteriorated and needed to be replaced. Best to tear down the lot of it and begin anew."

"Hmm." The marquess rubbed his chin in thought. "I suppose you secured the opinion of an expert?"

Everett frowned. "It did not take an expert to see the structure was completely unsound. I would not let my best hound cross that bridge."

"And what if you are wrong?" The marquess pounded

his fist on the table. "You will have squandered money on a useless endeavor."

"It is not a useless endeavor," Everett insisted. "That bridge is used by tenants who work the farmland on the other side of the river. It must be strong enough to support the carts and equipment necessary to farm the fields."

"You are just like your brother." The marquess tossed his napkin on the table. "And you will drive that estate into ruin."

"That is not fair," Everett responded through gritted teeth.

"You are quite right, my lord." The marchioness patted her husband on the hand. "Do not bother with him. He is as bad, if not worse, than Charles. How we managed to raise such ungrateful sons is beyond me."

Blasted old grouch. Wondering how she had managed to hold her tongue for so long, Sabrina shot out of her chair. "How dare you say such a thing, you miserable harpy?"

A chorus of gasps filled the air.

Everett stood. "Sabrina."

With the words of her in-laws ringing in her ears, and Lady Elizabeth's harsh treatment fueling her fury, Sabrina set both hands on the table and leaned forward. Anger colored her senses, and rational thought abandoned her. "Everett has done more for his tenants in a month than the previous earl did in his lifetime."

"Sabrina." Everett tried, but failed, to silence her, because she would not be denied retribution.

"He is thoughtful, kind, and generous." Mustering what she hoped was a lethal stare, Sabrina centered her ire on the marchioness. "And you? You are one to talk. You do nothing but complain. My staff has worked their fingers to the bone seeing to your comfort, but do you appreciate their efforts?" She lashed out with an arm. "Hah. You have not uttered the slightest bit of praise. You should be ashamed of yourself—"

"*Sabrina, that is enough!*"

In a state of confusion, with her chest heaving and pulse pounding, Sabrina glanced about the room. Save her very angry husband, and why he was upset she knew not, no one made eye contact with her, and she was not sure that was a good thing.

Trevor and Caroline stared at their plates. Celia seemed to find the hem of her sleeve quite curious. The marquess sat with an owlish gaze and his mouth agape. The marchioness blinked several times, as if she could not believe her ears.

Sabrina sensed it would not be long before reality dawned.

And it was not.

"Well." The marchioness huffed and thrust her nose in the air. "How dare you—"

"How dare you?" Sabrina countered.

"I have never been so insulted in my life—"

"Shut up, Lizzie," the marquess snapped.

The room grew quiet.

Sabrina had the uneasy suspicion she had just committed some egregious offense, but she was not sure what she had done. Was it possible that defending her husband had been so shocking as to merit such a response?

With both hands on his hips, Everett pinned her with an icy glare. "Sabrina, apologize."

Positive she heard wrong, she opened her mouth and then closed it. "W-what?"

"Apologize, at once." Everett furrowed his brow and bared his teeth.

Shuddering with fear, she clenched her jaw. "You cannot mean that."

"I mean precisely that." His icy tone bespoke some heinous transgression and portended doom. "Polite decorum demands an apology, this instant."

Still, Sabrina refused to believe she had erred. "But Lady Elizabeth is wrong. You are not—"

"You are mistaken." He inclined his head and lowered his chin, and she knew she was in trouble. "You must apologize."

She clung to denial, refusing to accept she was at odds with her staunchest ally. "You do not want me to apologize for what I said." It was a statement, not a question.

"I insist upon it." He gave her no quarter.

"But—"

"Now."

"My lord, how can you ask that of me?" Sabrina held her arms wide in supplication. "I am not the one who spoke ill of you."

"It does not matter what was said." Everett shifted his weight. "You have to apologize."

The world tilted on end, and Sabrina swayed. "Do you agree with her?"

Everett raked a hand through his hair. "Sabrina, are you or are you not going to apologize?"

For what offense? she asked herself. Stubborn and fortified with a wealth of pride, she shook her head. "I will not."

Everett threw his napkin to the floor. "Then go to your chambers—"

"What?" She stiffened her back. "But—why?"

He folded his arms. "Either apologize now or retire, at once."

She would rather eat her best bonnet. Sabrina swallowed the sharp retort she had prepared and, with head held high, inched from the table.

As she neared the door, Everett said, "You will remain in your chambers, without visitors, until such time as you are prepared to render a sufficient apology for your behavior this evening."

"I warned you that girl was unsuitable." The hateful woman got the last word again.

In the hall, she paused and waited for a response, for Everett to defend her from his mother's nasty remark. When none came, and the dining room remained quiet, she trudged forth. Despite the threatening tears, she navigated the grand staircase, anxiety mounting with each successive step, and turned left at the landing. The hall leading to their apartments suddenly seemed miles long.

Sabrina managed to maintain her stubborn façade until she closed the door to her bedchamber. Once ensconced in her safe haven, she slumped her shoulders in defeat.

If she were the dramatic sort, she would run across the room and fling herself on the bed.

If she were the dramatic sort.

She supposed she could open a window and toss herself to the ground below. No doubt Everett would regret his treatment of her then. Of course, she would probably regret it more.

But how could her husband betray her when she had acted on his behalf?

And it was a betrayal.

He had sided with his mother against his wife, and Sabrina was not sure she could ever forgive him.

Restless, she paced her room. With high dudgeon, she strode to the window, threw open the drapes, and stared at the sky. "He wants me to apologize?" she spat. "When hell freezes."

After a few hours passed, she undressed herself, refusing to ring for her lady's maid. As she tied the ribbon at the throat of her robe, she glanced at the connecting door to Everett's chamber. His deep baritone penetrated the walls of her suite as he conversed with his valet. When he dismissed his manservant, she approached the corridor.

Though she was angry with her husband, she still wanted him. All the pent up emotion roiling within her belly spurred a familiar reaction. And her favored method of venting had called to her. She stared at the door.

Should she go to him?

Would he want her after what happened?

Everett had banished Sabrina to her room, but had that meant she was barred from his bed, too? Ever since they had arrived at Beaumaris, they slept together. In fact, she had not given it a second thought. Every night, she donned her nightclothes and headed for his suite. It had never occurred to her to do otherwise.

And if she dawdled, her husband came looking for her. She smiled as she recalled the time Everett had charged the corridor, burst into her room wearing nothing but a robe, and sent Millie fleeing from the bedchamber in scandalized fright. Without ceremony, he had tossed Sabrina over his shoulder and stomped back to his suite, whereupon he ripped the clothes from her body. He had made love to her as a ravenous wolf—and she had loved every minute of it.

Perhaps she should wait until he came to her.

With a giggle, she walked to the *chaise* and plopped herself down. Adopting a seductive pose, she waited for the beast to invade.

As the minutes ticked by, Sabrina grew more and more

apprehensive. She chewed her bottom lip and, after the events of the night, she was surprised she had not chewed all the way to her chin.

What if Everett would not come to her?

She marched to the adjoining door and placed her hand on the knob. The metal was cool against her heated palm and provided sufficient impetus to halt her in her tracks. With flagging confidence, Sabrina set her forehead to the oak panel.

"Everett."

If her husband wanted her, he would have come for her. And he had not.

She tried to convince herself he might be tired, tried to ignore the blatant implication. It would not be unheard of for a man to sleep alone. Most married couples slept apart. There was nothing wrong with it. There was no shame.

Except Everett had always made it very clear, he liked his bed with her in it.

She suspected he further communicated his displeasure, and she could have told him that was not necessary. Closing her eyes in a failed attempt to shut out the pain, Sabrina let her hand fall to her side. Slowly, with one last mournful glance at the door, she withdrew and went to bed.

Alone.

EVERETT WAITED until his valet had exited his chamber before crossing the room to the door that led to his wife's suite. He listened for some sound; anything to indicate Sabrina was still awake.

Every fiber of his existence screamed at him to go to her, to hold her in his arms and soothe her injured pride, to make love to her and reassure her everything would be all right.

But for the first time since they had consummated their marriage, Everett was unsure of his welcome.

And he would not force her.

But neither had he thought he could take her rejection.

How he hated sending Sabrina to her chambers after the confrontation in the dining room, but she had left him no alternative.

To reprimand a peer of higher rank, regardless of the connection, was an egregious infraction of societal dictates. His wife had to know she could not commit such a breach of etiquette.

Sabrina was a countess.

There were standards to uphold.

She had to apologize.

As an earl, he had foundered in so many respects. According to his father, his agricultural skills lacked, he had spent too much money on improvements, and his supervision of the tenants insufficient. Managing his few personal estates had been nothing compared to the mountainous challenge of the earldom.

Everett was determined not to fail his wife.

And if he allowed her transgression to go unchecked, he would let her down. But no one had told him how much it would hurt to discipline his well-intentioned bride.

The haunting expression on her face when he ordered her to her room had scored a direct hit to his heart. How he ached.

Everett pressed his forehead to the oak-paneled door.

"Sabrina."

He was the man; he had to be strong for both of them, even if it killed him.

And it might.

For a minute, he held his breath, hoping to hear some indication his wife was coming to him, just as she always had. But there was nothing, not a sound.

He wondered if Sabrina was angry with him. Though he agreed with what she had said, and was more than a little pleased with her awkward exhibition of loyalty, he was convinced he had acted in her best interest. The remedy for her offense was an apology. She had to set it right, else suffer social censure.

And she had to do so of her own free will.

But would she see it that way? Would she hold his actions in the dining room against him? Had she thought him unfair or cruel? He was concerned about the effects of their disagreement. Had she cried herself to sleep? Perhaps he should look in on her, but he held himself in check. If she were asleep, he would only disturb her.

Everett turned his head and set his ear to the wood, but it was silent save the pounding of his heart. A dull pain settled in his chest, and a cold chill shivered down his spine.

Shoving away from the door, he went to bed.

Alone.

CHAPTER FIFTEEN

$\mathscr{J}$ t had been two days since her unplanned exile, and Sabrina again replayed the events of that ill-fated night in the dining room. As hard as she tried, she could not understand the fuss and was certain her husband had made too much of what happened. Surely her actions had not merited being treated like a recalcitrant child. If so, why had he not spanked her?

She paced the floor, an all too familiar occurrence of late, before the window overlooking the lawns, and marveled that there was any carpet left to cushion her footfalls.

Other than her lady's maid, she had spoken to no one. Everett had made it clear she was to have no visitors, and he remained true to his word. Of course, she could have spoken to him, but the one time her husband came to her door, fury colored her senses, and she refused to grant him an audience.

How she wished she could speak to her friends. Perhaps Caroline or Celia could make sense of her situation. But that was a poorly disguised excuse for the simple fact that she was lonely. And since it was well known Sabrina could converse with a potted plant, solitude compounded her misery to an unimaginable degree.

Now she was angry.

Below, Everett walked the topiary garden with Celia and his parents. Strange, they had never invited her for a morning stroll. She hated herself for resenting the young woman his mother doted on without shame, when Celia had been nothing less than a true friend. Yet, even from Sabrina's vantage, it was obvious the marchioness was still trying to convince her son that Celia would be a much better countess.

And Sabrina was no longer sure she disagreed.

Behind her, on a table near the *chaise*, a breakfast tray laden with covered dishes sat untouched. Her usually healthy appetite had dwindled with each passing day until it was non-existent.

She thought it a shame she could not eat herself into the size of an ox. With no one to gainsay her, she could gorge herself into oblivion. That would teach her ungrateful husband a lesson. But since she was positive she would revisit whatever she consumed, she passed on the opportunity.

It was small comfort when Millie confided that everyone on the household staff had heard of the incident and were firmly entrenched in her camp. It seemed Sabrina was lauded for coming to their defense and stood somewhere between sainthood and martyrdom in their opinion. Cook had even made a special batch of lemon tarts, her favorite. They, too, remained undisturbed on a plate.

She rubbed her tired eyes and turned away from the window. Though she had done nothing more than relax in her bedchamber, she had slept little and was exhausted. A glance in the vanity mirror reflected a woman with pale, almost ashen, skin. So she stopped looking in the mirror. She resumed pacing and thought she would have legs like a Thoroughbred when the to-do ended.

A creak had her facing the door. "Who goes there?"

Caroline peered around the edge. "Is it safe to enter?"

Sabrina nodded.

After closing the door, Caroline smiled. "I have missed talking to you, and so has Celia. By the by, she sends her regards. We worked together so I could sneak in here. Your husband has a footman guarding your chambers." With arms outstretched, she met Sabrina in the middle of the room and embraced her. "How are you bearing up?"

Biting her tongue, Sabrina resisted the urge to cry. "Fine, I suppose."

As Caroline set her back and stared at her face, her smile faded into a frown. She spied the *chaise* and led Sabrina to it.

"Brie, you look terrible."

Sabrina glanced at their clasped hands. "Well, thanks so very much."

"I mean it." With a grave expression, Caroline said, "You do not seem at all yourself."

"I am fine, truly." Though Sabrina mustered her best smile, inside she wanted to scream at the unfairness of her situation.

"I came to tell you we are leaving."

"No." Sabrina shook her head. "You cannot. You are the only ones on my side. Please, do not leave me alone."

"Unfortunately, your mother-in-law wears on my husband. We depart for London this afternoon." Caroline patted her cheek. "But I could not go without saying goodbye and dispensing some unsolicited advice."

Sabrina shifted in her seat and gooseflesh shivered over her arms. "Something tells me I am not going to like this."

"You may not." Caroline chuckled. "But it has to be said, and I would not count myself a friend if I did not encourage you to apologize to your in-laws."

"What?" Her gut clenched. "*Et tu, Brutus?*"

"Brie, I am always on your side but, in this instance, you were wrong." Caroline smoothed her skirts. "Hear me out."

Folding her arms, Sabrina nodded her assent.

"As I was born the daughter of a duke, I have had to live within the boundaries of society far longer than have you. I have had to fulfill certain expectations you have only experienced on the fringe. Whether or not you welcome it, your status has changed, and you are a member of the peerage. There are higher standards, and you must adhere to the strictures governing our set. To fly in the face of that would reflect not only on yourself, but also Everett." As if to underscore the importance of her lecture, Caroline clutched Sabrina's hand. "It pains me to do this, but it must be said. Celia was right; the marchioness outranks you. It is not your place to correct her, neither in public nor in private."

"Do you agree with what she did?" Sabrina asked as dread danced a jig down her spine.

It never occurred to her that her dearest friend would find fault in Sabrina's actions. Yet she knew Caroline would not do so lightly. Nor would she lead Sabrina astray. She felt an uneasy quiver in her belly, a sneaking suspicion she might have been wrong that night in the dining room.

"No. She is ill mannered, and her behavior is deplorable. You need not call attention to her. Doing so was very bad form." Caroline furrowed her brow. "But I have watched her goad you since we arrived, and never have you responded in anything but an exemplary fashion as suits a lady of your station. I have been so proud of you. Why on earth did you change your tack? She is, even now, berating your husband without mercy for his decision to marry, and remain married, to you. And she is using your outburst to justify her position."

Rebellion at the unfairness of it all echoed in her ears. Sabrina pointed a finger for emphasis as she prepared to make her argument.

And then it struck her.

Caroline was right—as was Everett.

The marchioness had made no secret of her disdain for her daughter-in-law. And she had been careful not to give the shrew any support. She had resisted every attempt by the harridan to lure her into an argument—except one. And it galled her to think it. The marchioness had attacked her own son to bring Sabrina down.

Blinded by fury, driven by an urge to protect her husband, she knew without doubt she had tripped—again. She had committed a horrible break from etiquette and prayed it was not unforgivable. But, worst of all, Everett suffered as a result of her infraction, which was the last thing she wanted.

"Oh, Caroline. I was wrong." Closing her eyes, Sabrina could almost envision her mother-in-law gloating over her victory. Her mind raced as she searched for a way to undo her blunder. Everett's words came to her amid the swirl of shame. "Is there any chance you could persuade Trevor to stay one more night? I would like to apologize at dinner, this evening."

"No." Caroline shook her head. "Our trunks are packed, and he is adamant about leaving. As it is, he is probably wonders where I am hiding."

"It seems so unfair." Sabrina blanched.

Caroline averted her stare. "Society is rarely fair, Brie."

They stood and clasped hands.

"But you do not require my presence to do what must needs." Caroline leaned forward and placed a sisterly kiss on Sabrina's cheek. "Remember, you are the countess of Woverton. No one, not even the marchioness, can take that from you."

Sabrina stood silent, choking back tears, as Caroline walked to the door. At the last minute, her friend peered back and said, "If you require a shoulder, we will be in London until the holidays."

Then she was gone.

And Sabrina had never felt more alone in her life.

TRAILING her gloved hand down the polished wood banister, Sabrina descended the grand staircase. Gowned in the familiar black silk of mourning trimmed in grey, and her hair arranged in a severe knot, she took each step one at a time. Though it was early in September, and the house was quite warm, she was chilled to the bone and kept her jaw clenched to keep her teeth from chattering. A lull of voices filtered through the foyer, and she knew everyone had been seated for dinner. At the foot of the stairs, she turned right and navigated the hall leading to the elegant formal dining room. When Sabrina reached the arched entry, she stopped.

The conversation ceased.

At the head of the table, Everett stood.

Though some would call her a coward, she focused on the black armband he wore to honor his brother's memory, because she lacked the strength to meet his gaze.

As a death knell played in her ears, Sabrina faced the marchioness. "My lady, I sincerely apologize for my behavior of two nights past and regret any embarrassment I may have caused. Please know it is nothing compared to the shame I have brought upon myself." She was almost finished, just one more concession. "I humbly ask your forgiveness."

"Well done, my dear," the marquess stated with warmth for which she would be forever grateful. "Your charming apology is accepted, and there will be no further mention of the unfortunate incident."

When Sabrina peered in his direction, her father-in-law winked and smiled. Celia cast her a sympathetic grin, and Sabrina prayed for composure. But when Everett neared and settled a hand at the small of her back, she could not stop herself from flinching. A subtle tensing of his fingers told her he sensed her fragile state.

He pressed his lips to her temple. "Will you join us for dinner?"

Inside, her nerves were a jumbled mass, and the mere thought of food was enough to make her ill. "I beg your pardon, my lord, but I should prefer to return to my chambers."

"Are you not hungry?" His voice was tinged with amusement—until Sabrina met his stare.

Light from the candles cast a halo over his head in her tear-filled eyes. She was going to cry, was powerless to halt the impending deluge, and hated herself for it. "No," was all she could say.

His brow a mass of furrows, Everett compressed his lips. "Sabrina, you must be—"

"Please, let me go," she whispered.

"I shall escort Sabrina to her suite." Slipping an arm

about her waist, he turned her from the table. "You may commence dinner without me."

"No." With a side step, she retreated. "I do not want to interrupt the meal anymore than I have already." Before he could object, she scurried down the hall. When she was positive she was out of sight, Sabrina lifted her skirts and broke into a full run, heading for the safe harbor of her suite.

IN THE HALLWAY, Everett frowned as his wife sprinted around the corner. While part of him swelled with pride because she had done the right thing, another part of him was anxious. Somehow, when Sabrina mended fences with his mother, he felt as if he had burned a bridge in their marriage.

With a wave to the footmen, he rushed through the meal. His appetite a mere memory, he operated on instinct, shoving in bites of food without tasting the fare. It seemed an eternity before dessert was served.

When Lady Celia and his mother rose from the table, his father claimed a decanter. "Port?"

"Actually, I am rather done for." Everett faked a yawn. "I believe I shall retire early this evening."

"Go on." His sire grinned and chucked him on the shoulder. "She is a dear girl, that wife of yours."

As the others filed into the drawing room, he took the stairs two at a time. Turning left, he strode down the hall, veered left again and walked into his receiving room.

Pitton, his valet, waited just inside the bedchamber. "Good evening, my lord."

Everett shrugged out of his coat and tossed it over the

back of a chair. "Pitton, I will not be needing you tonight." He stripped his cravat from his neck. "You are dismissed."

Everett was in the little corridor leading to his wife's room before his valet had exited the master suite. Of course, propriety demanded he wait until his servant was no longer present to declare his intent to seduce his wife. Never had he understood the necessity for such ridiculous airs. Sabrina was his wife, so it was safe to assume Pitton knew they made love on occasion. Bloody hell, considering the enthusiastic moans of pleasure his wife emitted during coitus, the entire household had to be cognizant of their marital relations by now.

At the other end of the corridor, Everett threw open the door and walked into total darkness. Muttering a terse expletive, he retraced his steps, crossed his room, and grasped a candelabrum from the tallboy. Once again he stomped through the adjoining passage.

The pale yellow light cast shadows on the walls. In quiet, he approached the canopied bed at the center of the rear wall. Beneath the covers, Sabrina lay motionless. On purpose, he took heavy steps, hoping she might stir. Yes, only a cad would rouse her after what she had been through.

But Everett wanted Sabrina awake and alert when he told her that he loved her and was proud of her. There were so many demands on his time; he wanted her to know she often occupied his thoughts, even if he had not an hour or so to dedicate solely to her.

He set the candelabrum on the side table and sat on the edge of the bed. His wife reclined on her side, her back to him. Placing a hand on her shoulder, he leaned over and pressed a gentle kiss to the crest of her ear.

"Sabrina, are you awake?"

Raking his fingers through her hair, he fanned the raven locks over her pillow. To his disappointment, she had not stirred. For a long time, Everett sat with his wife, listening to the steady sound of her breathing. Just being near her comforted him.

THE SUN HAD YET to peek over the horizon when Sabrina broke her fast the following morning. Dressed in a grey twill riding habit, which she chose to match her mood, not to mention the blasted mourning that seemed never-ending, she slipped into the stables, saddled a large black hunter, and headed for the meadow.

The impromptu confinement to her chambers the past few mornings had deprived her of her regular rides, and she was intent on getting an early start. As she picked the trail that would take her through the fields, along the southern edge of the woods, to the tiny chalk stream she often fished, Sabrina refused to admit she was determined to avoid her husband and his parents. She had feigned sleep when Everett entered her room the previous night. As he sifted his fingers through her hair, occasionally rubbing her scalp, she had drifted off in earnest.

And was spared further humiliation.

The first streaks of gold cut wide swaths in the black of night as she steered the hunter into the copse of oaks. The air was crisp and cool and hinted that fall was just around the corner. That meant they would soon journey to London for the Little Season, and Sabrina prayed she would be up to the task. If she were lucky, she would do nothing to bring more shame upon her husband.

But could she rely on fate?

What if she committed an error without realizing she had done so, as was the case with her unfortunate oratory in the dining room? And if she cut someone she knew not, but could not afford to insult, her husband would be ruined. She had to do something drastic else risk embarrassing Everett again.

Which Sabrina resolved not to repeat.

Reigning alongside the stream, she brought the horse to a halt and dismounted. Leaving the hunter to graze, she plunked down on a rock and stared into the water.

Spying a few pebbles, she grabbed a fistful and flicked them into the stream with tiny splashes. Eventually, she pulled her knees close to her chest, wrapped her arms about her shins, and rested her chin on her knees.

It was time to swallow some difficult truths with that lump of pride still stuck in her throat. It was time to face facts. Last night had been a difficult lesson in more ways than one.

While Sabrina wanted to blame her disastrous turn as chatelaine on the marchioness, she knew the fault was her own. She had erred and could either learn from her mistake or doom herself to repeat it. And though she was no authority on etiquette, she considered herself a sensible sort.

As a child, Sabrina had been indulged and encouraged in her shameless ways by her well-intentioned father—she could see that now. But she was no longer a child. What her sire found charming, and Everett professed drove him to distraction, namely her wild streak, would be her downfall if she could not control herself.

But where should she start?

Hours passed, and the sun rose high in the sky. Glimmering blades of dewy grass turned a vibrant green as the moisture dried. The air grew warm, and Sabrina regretted choosing the heavy twill habit.

Suddenly, she snapped her fingers. "That is it."

Having discovered an answer to her problem, she should have been relieved, should have been happy. But there was no triumph in which to revel. With renewed sense of purpose mixed with sadness, Sabrina mounted the great hunter and set a course for home.

"Is the tea to your liking, my lady?"

"Uh, yes." Confusion evident in her expression, the marchioness blinked. "It is quite acceptable, Sabrina."

Standing in the back corner of the drawing room, Everett studied his wife. It had been three nights since she made her apology and three nights since he had seen Sabrina.

His Sabrina.

Once before, she had transformed herself, the night he kissed her in the maze and decided to make her his bride. Then, the metamorphosis had been one of delightful surprise. The gawky girl who never failed to make him laugh had blossomed into an enchanting young lady.

The recent change, however, was most unwelcome.

Everett had first noticed the new Sabrina when he offered to take her fishing. He had almost fallen over backward when she informed him, in a polite and restrained manner, that she preferred to work on her embroidery.

Sabrina? Embroider?

When pigs fly.

And though she wore gloves that evening, he could not

miss her wince when he took her hand to escort her to dinner. Pain from a thousand pinpricks, no doubt.

At first, he had thought her odd behavior an aberration, until he asked her to accompany him on a survey of the fields. Normally, such request would garner him a squeal of delight, a lusty smack on the lips, and the joyous sight of Sabrina, not to mention her shapely calves, running at breakneck speed up the stairs to change into her habit.

Not so that time.

While the barest hint of enthusiasm peeked through the polished façade, she quickly masked her innate response behind a proper nod and a polite, "No, thank you, my lord. Lady Celia recites poetry, and I have promised an audience."

Everett wrinkled his nose.

Poetry?

It was too much to bear.

Worse, it was apparent the new version of his wife deemed it unacceptable to come to his bed. He waited with profuse tolerance every evening, his eyes trained on the little door to the corridor adjoining their rooms. And every night he slept alone.

Well, he was all out of patience.

Tonight he would not sleep alone.

Tonight he would go to her. He would tear from her body whatever polite and proper nightgown she wore and make very impolite, very improper love to his bride.

Lifting a brandy balloon to his lips, Everett sipped the amber liquid and stared at his delectable countess over the rim of the glass. Sabrina had donned a low-cut gown with a tight, form-fitting bodice. He imagined himself peeling it from her athletic frame and smiled.

Perhaps he would not wait until she undressed.

THE DRAWING ROOM WAS EMPTY, at last.

Sabrina cleared the cups, depositing them on the tea trolley before retiring. The marchioness and Celia had already withdrawn to their chambers. Everett and the marquess had adjourned to the study to discuss farming techniques. So she climbed the stairs in silence, as the long-case clock in the hall ticked the passage of time. She entered her sitting room and shut the door behind her. Holding her hands to her temples, she rubbed in circles. Her head ached wretchedly.

It was hell being a lady.

After much consideration of her situation, she had put her plan into action, and she had begun to wonder if it might have been simpler, and she was certain less painful, to kill herself.

Thus far, she had endured poetry readings, lecture upon lecture from the marchioness on household management, and three embroidery lessons.

Was it was possible to bleed to death from pinpricks?

However, her efforts were not in vain. She had to admit she enjoyed a measurable amount of success with her mother-in-law. While the marchioness still complained, she had done so with less frequency. And only tonight, she had commented on the tenderness of the roast.

But at what cost?

In her efforts to win Lady Elizabeth's approval, Sabrina had suppressed all her natural reactions, all her instincts, in favor of what she believed were appropriate ones. She had turned away from the activities that brought her joy, such as fishing, fencing, and riding astride. She had even foresworn swearing—well, at least she tried.

But Sabrina was no longer certain where she began and the social façade ended. It was as though she had lost her sense of self. Before long, the person she had always been might very well cease to exist. Yet the knowledge that she sacrificed herself for the sake of her marriage—for Everett, offered a modicum of comfort.

She wanted him to be proud of her. Wanted him to rejoice in his chosen bride. Wanted to be worthy of her position as his countess. A single kind word, an approving nod, an encouraging smile would make her trials worthwhile.

Yet her husband remained steadfastly silent.

Worse, they no longer shared a bed.

She pushed from the door and walked into her bedchamber. After tugging on the bellpull, she kicked off her slippers and sat at her vanity. Sabrina reached for one of the many pins in her coiffure and froze.

The woman in the mirror stared back at her.

Bringing her hands to her face, she traced the outline of her cheeks and the arch of her brows. She skimmed the wide expanse of her forehead and the gentle slope of her nose. Finally, she drew an imaginary line around the edge of her lips.

The reflection in the mirror may have been hers, yet she knew not the identity.

What had she become?

With her elbows on the vanity top, Sabrina slumped forward and covered her face with her hands. No longer certain of her persona, she drowned in a miasma of misery and shame. And there appeared to be no relief in sight, because when they traveled to London, accepted invitations, and attended the various social functions required of their set, she would have to be doubly careful. What scared her most was the thought of tripping and reverting to her old self. The one that fished, slid down banisters, and swore like a sailor.

Those days were gone.

Tears welled, and Sabrina cursed herself. Never had she cried so much in her life. Why was she suddenly so weak?

The door to her chamber opened and then closed.

Propriety demanded she hide her tears from Millie, so she wiped her eyes. It was bad enough to cry, but she would not be caught blubbering like a baby.

Fingers speared through her hair, rough and wild, and pins flew in all directions. Sabrina lifted her head and prepared to reprimand Millie.

"*Everett.*"

CHAPTER SIXTEEN

*E*verett smiled, his conqueror's smile. "Hello, my darling wife."

Dressed in nothing more than loose silk trousers and a haphazardly belted robe, gaping wide to reveal an impressive bare chest, her husband looked ready for...bed.

She gulped. "W-what are you doing here?"

He squeezed her shoulders with his hands, before roaming over her chest to cup her breasts. With his thumbs he circled her nipples through the constrictive fabric of her dress. A brow arched in unveiled arrogance. "Is it not obvious?"

Sabrina glanced at the door.

"Millie is not coming. I gave orders for her to disregard your summons." He abandoned her breasts, leaving her aching for his touch, and moved to the back of her gown. "Tonight, I shall undress you, my saucy Sabrina."

A shiver traipsed her spine as Everett unhooked her dress. The bodice loosened, and he slipped his fingers beneath the edge of the eau de nil silk and eased the gown from her shoulders.

She closed her eyes and licked her dry lips. "But, it is not proper."

"Perhaps not, but we are not going to let that stop us, are we?" With a tug at the ribbon of her chemise, he released the filmy gauze and inched it to her waist. As she made to reply, he bent his head and kissed her temple. "Stand up, love."

Conscious of her nudity, she bit her tongue and obeyed. The gown and chemise sagged to her hips, until Everett pushed the fabric, and the garments fell to the floor.

Clad only in her garters and stockings, with her back to him, Sabrina stared at their images in the long mirror and wondered how to make love like a lady. Since they had consummated their vows, she always acted on instinct. Wanton, unbridled instinct. But of late, she had suppressed those desires in order to be a proper wife.

The raw lust in Everett's eyes told her she would be bad tonight.

With his hands he roamed her body, visiting every peak and curve. His questing fingertips claimed her, branding her flesh. Molten heat simmered in her veins, warming her from head to feet, and curling her toes. The familiar hunger bloomed—the improper one. Desire licked at her senses, and passion rode hard in its wake.

Sabrina scored her nails across the skin at the nape of his neck and delighted in his appreciative groan. Pushing the silk robe from his shoulders, she reached for the belt, untied it, and sighed as the sumptuous garment fell to the floor with a whispery whoosh.

To hell with propriety.

A single step brought her in striking distance, and she framed his face and covered his lips with hers. With a flick of her tongue, she lured her earl and suckled his flesh.

God, she felt alive.

With a subtle shift, he whisked her into his arms and carried her to the bed. None too gently, he flung her atop the mattress—and paused.

What could Everett want?

In that instant, realization dawned. Flirty mischief charged her nerves, her heart sang with joy, and Sabrina smiled. She shimmied to the middle of the mattress, lifted her arms, and flicked her hands in entreaty. "Come to me."

And Everett obeyed.

He covered her in a clumsy swoop, but it mattered not. Seconds later, they were a tangled mass of limbs, groping, hugging, and rolling amid the pillows.

As if compelled by an urgent need too powerful to deny, Everett merely lowered his trousers before driving into her, and their joining was hard and fast. He rode her as a savage, completely out of control.

Sabrina sank her teeth into his shoulder. "Oh, yes, my lord."

And she spurred him, digging her heels into his flanks, inciting him with a sultry plea for more at every thrust. She clung to him as a drowning woman and he her only lifeline.

In truth, for her, Everett was a lifeline, of sorts. He was the last connection to the shadow of her former self. With him, in that arena, she could be Sabrina.

Naked, in bed, there were no titles.

They were nothing more than man and woman.

So she let go the reins and ran wild with her man.

GOLDEN RAYS PEEKED through the drawn drapes when Sabrina woke the next morning. As memories of the night flooded her mind and her senses, telltale warmth pervaded her cheeks.

Everett curled protectively around her, his chest to her back, an arm over her waist, and his hand cupped her breast.

After their initial tumultuous coupling, they had made love twice more during the night. Once, when she roused him. Again, when they simultaneously turned to each other in the dark. It was as though they needed to join their bodies. As if they reaffirmed their marital vows, ensuring each other that they were still committed, still solid, despite his mother's disapproval.

And Sabrina wanted more affirming, in that instant.

Though her husband slept, his body was definitely alert, and the hot hard proof nestled in the cleft of her bottom. She rocked her hips, and the friction resulted in a naughty caress. His hand twitched at her breast twitched, so she repeated the movement and pressed her derrière against him.

"Mmm." His breath was warm against her temple.

"Are you up?"

"You have to ask?"

She laughed. "Not really—" She gasped as his fingers walked a wicked path to the magic place between her legs and slipped inside her.

"What have we here?" He licked the crest of her ear. "You are awake, too."

"Oh, do not tease me, please." She shuffled her hips back and forth.

"All right." Everett chuckled softly. "Lean forward."

Uncontrollable excitement and curiosity drew her as a bee to honey, as he posited something new, and Sabrina was not about to waste the moment.

"Like this?" she asked with unfeigned eagerness as his questing strokes wreaked havoc on her most intimate flesh.

"Yesss." He probed her gently, sliding the swollen tip of his erection into her softness before withdrawing again.

As she moved to take him fully into her body, he pulled back. "Everett."

"What is your rush?" He repeated the sensuous torture. "We will get where we are going soon enough."

"Where we are going?" She sighed as he slipped inside once more. "What are you talking about?

He nipped her neck. "Pure unadulterated pleasure, my darling wife."

Without warning, he lifted her leg, draped it over his hip, and thrust.

Sabrina cried out and fisted her hands in the sheets. As heat blossomed from the point of their joining, coursed her veins, permeated every muscle, and ignited countless pulse points, she surrendered. Ruthless passion summoned, and she answered the call.

EVERETT SET A RELAXED PACE, as he had not wanted to pummel his wife, yet she tempted him beyond reason. Would he ever get enough of her? Would the mere sight of her never cease to stir a primitive lust that had him wanting to throw her to the ground and bury himself deep inside her?

Not anytime soon.

As his rhythm grew fervent, he snaked an arm about her waist and held her in place as he moved behind her. She sank her nails into his thigh and met his thrusts. In time with the delicate dance, she emitted a single, perfectly pitched sigh, a sensuous song that summoned the predator.

Finesse, skill, experience fled.

As had patience.

He found the little nub of her desire and massaged with bold intent, flagrantly inciting, deliberately arousing, setting her ablaze. Operating on instinct, Everett hugged her tight and pumped without restraint.

Sabrina shattered in his arms, and her cry of release reverberated throughout the room. Limp in his embrace, she inclined her head and licked his chin. The virile explosion that tore through him stole his breath and left him shuddering as spasm after spasm rocked him to his core. Vaguely, he thought he heard himself groan.

At long last, he rolled onto his back, and Sabrina snuggled to his side.

"You missed your morning ride."

"On the contrary, I just had a devil of a ride on a spirited Thoroughbred." Everett kissed her shoulder.

With a furious blush staining her cheeks, she tugged the covers to her chin and wiped a stray lock of hair from her face. "I have ached for our mornings together."

"And I have yearned for our mornings and our nights, my saucy Sabrina." He nuzzled her and sighed. "And before I forget, thank you for defending me, against my mother's charge, but never do so again. Society judges women far more harshly than men, and I would not have you jeopardize your standing, when I am immune to her accusations. I am sorry if I was terse with you, but do you understand why I was so strict?"

"As much as I hate to admit it, I do, and you were right. It just took me a little longer to discover my error. Of course, had I granted you entry to my chambers when you knocked at my door, the mystery would have been solved sooner. But in my anger, I was rather put out, and I am sorry." Sabrina frowned. "And although my marks for deportment were terrible in finishing school, I know better than to behave as I did and should never have let myself be baited into an argument with Lady Elizabeth."

"It was my hope that you would discover your infraction on your own. The earldom demands much of my time, and I will not always be here to referee between you and my mother. Though I must admit your outburst was quite a surprise." He resituated his pillow. "She had come at you with much worse, and yet you resisted admirably."

"After she attacked you, I could not help myself." Sabrina kissed his nipple and cast him a mischievous grin. "But as she has made it no secret she thinks me beneath you, she should not expect proper decorum."

"Really?" He retreated. "Did she tell you something to that effect?"

"Yes." His bride nodded. "According to your mother, you and I are not in the same class, and you never should have married me."

"How odd." He searched his memory. "I do not remember that conversation. When was this?"

At his query, she flinched. "Oh, I do not recall. But it does not signify."

"Like bloody hell." Everett sat upright so he could see her eyes. "Sabrina, when did this happen?"

Her face paled, and she chewed her lip. In that moment, he knew his wife had revealed a secret she had not meant to share.

When Sabrina maintained telltale silence, which spoke volumes, he grasped her shoulders. "Answer me."

"While you were away," she blurted.

Everett flung back the covers and leapt from the bed. Before he said something he would regret, he needed to calm himself. But in his current state of undress, he doubted his authority would impress his difficult other half. After a quick search, he snatched his robe from the floor and shoved an arm into each sleeve before securing the belt.

His guilty bride clutched the sheet to her breasts. "Everett—"

"Upon my return, you told me nothing untoward occurred." He raked a hand through his hair and stomped to the bed. "Did you not?"

"Yes." She nodded. "I did."

Her duplicity danced as a specter of doom, and something inside him fractured. "You lied to me?"

"No." She sobbed.

"You lied." Smacking a fist to his palm, he gave vent to an inhuman grunt. "What else would you call your omission?"

"My lord, it was a harmless oversight on my part." Sabrina scooted to the edge of the mattress and stood. "I did not want you to think I could not manage the household without you."

"So you deceived me?" He snickered. "I would rather you could not manage without me."

"It was my intent to make you proud." With a charming pout that threatened to dissolve his ire, she approached. "Have you no clue? Have you no inkling of the power you wield over me?"

"Do I appear pleased?" He shuffled his feet.

"No." Her chin quivered.

"I thought you incapable of deceit." What hurt worse, her untruthfulness or the fact that he had been fooled, Everett knew not. "It is obvious I was mistaken."

"Please, forgive me." As though embarrassed by her nudity, she slipped into the sheer creation that shielded little from his stare. "It will not happen again, I promise."

"I consider myself a tolerant man, Sabrina. But I will brook no deceit in our marriage." Through a haze of anger and betrayal, Everett clutched her arms. "Do I make myself clear?"

Fear permeated her expression, and he cursed himself.

"Yes." She bent her head. "I am sorry you find me so lacking."

Regardless of an overwhelming desire to comfort his wife, he stormed from the room. Once he gained his chambers, he stood stock still in the middle of the master suite. Clenching and unclenching his fists, he inhaled deeply.

And then it dawned on him.

The words sank in, penetrating his thick skull.

I am sorry you find me so lacking.

As a cruel refrain, her statement replayed a rapid salvo, haunting and taunting. In that instant, the room spun out of control, and he broke into a sweat. His ears rang, and he doubled over in pain. Then he ran to the basin, where he retched. After a few minutes, Everett wiped his face with a towel and sank to the floor.

How many times had he uttered the same apology?

Cradling his head in his hands, he inhaled a shaky breath. He would not hurt her as his parents hurt him, and yet he struck a lethal blow. His displeasure with Sabrina's omission blinded him to the content of his mother's verbal abuse. After the unfortunate incident in the dining room, could he blame his countess for concealing further shame?

Resolved to make amends and declare himself, he shot to his feet and retraced his steps. In the little corridor, he paused at her door when he overheard his wife conversing with her lady's maid. Closing his eyes, he faltered and lost his courage.

"Bloody hell." Again, he failed.

~

"S<small>ABRINA</small>?" The marchioness waved to a footman and requested an additional portion of eggs.

In the process of sipping her coffee, Sabrina flinched at the mention of her name in the all-too-familiar clipped tone and nearly spilt the hot liquid in her lap. What on earth could her mother-in-law want now? "Yes, my lady?"

"Celia and I are calling on some friends who live nearby." Spreading marmalade on a slice of toast, she stared down her nose. "You are welcome to join us, if you like."

She hesitated to answer, as her suspicions roused in an instant. Was it a trick? Another attempt to humiliate her? Sabrina frowned. Her mother-in-law need not expend much effort in that endeavor. She had stumbled all by herself, and she may have alienated her greatest ally.

"Oh, do come, Sabrina," Celia exclaimed. "It would be such fun."

A dark figure loomed at the opposite end of the table. Even in silence, her husband's presence, palpable as London fog, had cocooned her in misery. After their argument in her bedchamber, she was grateful for the distance, but the separation offered little shelter.

She could feel his gaze, dark, angry, and disapproving, as a weight in her chest. Perhaps a day trip would benefit her.

"Thank you, Lady Elizabeth." Sabrina managed a brittle smile. "I should be honored to accompany you."

"Perfect. We shall leave directly." The marchioness

dabbed the corners of her mouth and set her napkin on the table. "Come, Celia, we must dress for calling."

With a silent prayer that she had not made a horrible mistake, Sabrina pushed from her chair.

At the same time, Everett and the marquess stood.

"What say I give you a hand with the accounts?" her father-in-law suggested. "We can tally the totals for the month."

"All right." Everett nodded. "And if you would care to take a ride, I need to check on some of the tenants."

Although her relationship with her husband had taken a turn for the worse, Sabrina was glad to see Everett carrying on a civil conversation with his father. The marquess followed his wife and Celia out of the dining room, which left her alone with her angry earl.

Unwilling to enact another scene, intent on exiting as swift and sure as possible, Sabrina sidestepped her spouse. But he caught her by the wrist, and she was forced to halt. As he turned her to face him, she focused on the intricate folds of his cravat.

"You wish to speak with me, my lord?" She cursed herself when her voice quivered.

"I take it you are going out today?"

"I am." That was better. Sabrina vanquished the frightened little girl but kept her gaze averted, knowing she could maintain her composure as long as she avoided looking Everett in the eyes.

He trailed her jawline with his finger, and then tipped her chin, which forced her to meet his inquisitive stare. "Will you be all right?"

"I assure you, I am quite capable of behaving myself." Could he not trust her to make a simple house call without causing him further embarrassment? Bloody hell, she pouted, she knew it, and she seemed powerless to stop it.

With a frown she felt to her toes, Everett inclined his head. "That is not what I meant."

"Is it not?" Blast her hide, she whined.

"No." He cupped her cheek. "I wish I would not keep putting myself in the position of owing you an apology, but it appears inevitable. I am sorry I was short with you this morning."

"It is forgotten." She tried to escape, but he held her fast.

"I do not think it is." Everett sighed, as he studied her with his too-knowing amber gaze, bent his head, and pressed his lips to the corner of her mouth. "In any case, I sincerely regret spoiling an otherwise memorable morning. Have patience with me, darling. This is my first marriage and my first earldom. I am bound to make mistakes."

Although he extended an olive branch, she found no joy in his kiss or his overture, because she feared she had done irreparable damage to their union. Little by little, one blunder after another, she had eroded his heretofore-unshakeable support, and she had no one to blame but herself.

"So you are making calls today?" Her shameless lord adjusted his cravat.

"Indeed." Drowning in a pit of remorse, she accepted his escort, and they strolled into the hall. "And I am truly sorry I did not tell you of the confrontation with your mother. Rest assured, that is an oversight I will not repeat."

"Somehow, I know you will not." Everett cast her a boyish smile. "And if it helps, my father has spoken to her concerning her treatment of you." He nipped her nose in a playful gesture, as was his habit, which she loved. "I believe she understands you and I are married, for better or worse."

"So I am forgiven, at last?" She held her breath.

"Perhaps." He glanced at the ceiling, as if pondering his answer. "For another kiss?"

Sabrina exhaled in relief. As their mouths met, she caught his lower lip between her teeth and tickled it with her tongue. Then she angled her head and lured him into a searing kiss that made their last one seem chaste.

In seconds, six feet of aroused male cornered her against a wall. "How long before you depart?"

"Everett, please." She squirmed from his embrace. "Your mother awaits, and I am loathe to inconvenience her."

"All right." He groaned. "Then I suppose I shall mark the minutes until tonight to sate my senses in you."

"And that reminds me." She snapped her fingers. "I must leave word for the cook to defer dinner an extra hour, as I am not sure when I shall return. But I will have cook prepare a light snack for you and your father. Perhaps some Bath buns, black butter, and gooseberry cheese?"

"My favorite treat." He nudged her with his hips. "Second only to my wife."

"My lord, that is lovely, but I must change." She ignored the fluttering in the pit of her belly. "Your mother will be furious if I delay her appointments."

"Then I should help you, and you will be ready twice as fast." He smacked her bottom, in play.

"You only want to undress me." She skipped beyond his reach. "I will see you tonight."

"Sabrina—wait." Everett caught her wrist. "There is something I would say."

"Yes." She paused, as he cleared his throat. "What is wrong?"

"Nothing...it is just...I wanted you to know...oh, damn." Spearing his fingers through his hair, he shuffled his feet. Then, without warning, he yanked her into his arms. Caressing her cheek with his thumb, he sighed. "I am truly sorry for this morning, darling."

How she needed his kindness just then. "But it was my fault—"

"No. I understand your motivation more than you know, and you are blameless." He rested his forehead to hers. "My dear, in future there may be breakers, but we will survive if we navigate them, together."

"Oh, Everett. I am happy to hear you say it." Sabrina swallowed hard. "And I do so wish to make you proud."

"Darling Sabrina." He closed his eyes and pressed on her an inexpressibly sweet kiss—and kept kissing her.

Yes, she would be late.

CHAPTER SEVENTEEN

$\mathcal{A}$s the carriage lurched forward, a stubborn blush plagued Sabrina. Images of the brief tryst with her husband, only minutes ago in her sitting room, flooded her thoughts.

Once she and Everett had gained her apartments and thrown the bolt on the door, he pushed her to her knees on the *chaise*. After advising her to grab hold of the back, he flicked her skirts to her waist. Fully clothed, he knelt between her bent legs, freed his erection, and took her from behind.

It had been quick but effective.

"What are you grinning about?" From the opposite seat, the marchioness glared.

"Oh, nothing." Sabrina cleared her throat, shifted in the squabs, and gave her attention to the passing landscape. "Perhaps it is the thought of making new acquaintances."

At her side, Celia sat in silence, and though she could not see the younger woman's expression, Sabrina knew her friend smiled.

They called on Lady DeWinter first.

To her surprise, Sabrina discovered a genuine fondness for the elderly woman. Lady DeWinter, with her kind face and gentle manners, had laughed without restraint during their conversation.

Exactly what Sabrina said to cause such a response, she knew not. One thing was certain, the marchioness was displeased with her daughter-in-law when their visit concluded.

Enclosed in their coach, her mother-in-law made her discomfit known. "I have never been so humiliated in my life."

Sabrina said nothing and, God bless her, neither had Celia.

The marchioness caught her in a narrow-eyed stare. "Really, Sabrina, how could you behave so recklessly, without any regard for Everett and his title?"

Sabrina held her tongue, biting down on the tip. Mentally replaying the social call, she could think of nothing she had said or done to merit such censure. Since her mother-in-law needed no prodding to criticize Sabrina, she remained quiet.

But the marchioness would not be deterred. "You consumed half a pot of tea and six pieces of shortbread. A lady is known by the delicacy of her appetite."

And that was Sabrina's fault?

Her shameless, insatiable husband was responsible for her hunger, because lovemaking always left her famished. Had the marchioness not been so insistent they leave directly, Sabrina would have headed for the kitchens in search of another meal.

In the interest of keeping the peace, she sighed. "I apologize, my lady. In the future, I shall pay more attention to my habits."

"See that you do," the marchioness snapped.

The coach stopped before another grand estate, the second appointment of their outing. Sabrina accepted a hand from the footman as she stepped down behind the marchioness, who greeted another acquaintance.

As she made to follow, Celia grasped her elbow.

"What is it?" Sabrina inquired.

Celia glanced at the marchioness, then leaned close to whisper, "Do exactly what I do, and we shall survive the day with nary a complaint."

Sabrina could not help but smile. "What would I do without you?"

The remainder of the visits passed uneventfully, and soon the three women were nestled in the coach for the return journey to Beaumaris.

Having followed Celia's suggestion, Sabrina feared she would faint from hunger before she ever got home. She was positive the young woman had a stomach the size of a sparrow's. How else could Celia exist on such meager fare? As her belly protested, she made a mental note to have dinner moved up a half-hour.

And she wondered what it was about being a proper lady that was so exhaustive? Could it be that she was forced to scrutinize her every move and carefully consider her words before she uttered a single sentence? In dire need of a nap, she could barely keep her eyes open. After a while, she settled in the squabs and let her heavy lids fall.

Some time later, she awakened to the sound of gunfire.

"What is happening?" The marchioness screamed, and her hands flew to her throat.

"Sabrina." Celia shook her hard.

She sat up and peered outside.

Three masked horsemen waved pistols in the air.

Sabrina shrugged. "It appears we are about to be robbed."

"Oh, dear." The marchioness grabbed Celia and hugged her close.

"What will we do?" Celia's eyes grew wide and watery. "Will they hurt us?"

The coach lurched as the driver spurred the team in what was no doubt an attempt to outrun the highwaymen. Though his efforts were commendable, Sabrina knew his actions were futile. If the highwaymen wanted to rob them —they would.

"Robberies are a common occurrence when venturing to and from London," Sabrina explained. "I daresay it is the same in the country. There is no cause for alarm."

Celia and the marchioness kept a death grip on each other, and Sabrina tried to reassure them by patting their white-knuckled fists. "It will be all right as long as we cooperate. They want our valuables, nothing more."

Outside, the bandits managed to head off the team and eventually brought the coach to a grinding halt. The driver and footmen were ordered down at gunpoint. Sabrina gulped as they were forced to the roadside, their hands in the air. On command, their escort knelt in the grass.

She had been robbed while in the company of her family. Then, there had been no weapons displayed, and a threat was implied to gain compliance.

One of the highwaymen opened the door to their coach. "Awright, lovies, step lively now." With a jerk of his pistol, he motioned for the ladies to disembark.

"Certainly." With palms splayed, Sabrina nodded. She exited first, and then turned to help the marchioness and Celia disembark. Glancing to the side, she spied a third highwayman holding the team in check.

"There is no need for violence. We will give you no trouble," she stated in a calm fashion. "Please take what you want and leave us on our way."

"Well now, look who thinks she's the queen o' this gang." The highwayman at the reins dropped the leader and approached. His leering smile bared horribly crooked teeth. "We will take what we want." He eyed her from head to foot. "Whatever we want."

Celia shrieked and drew his interest.

"My, what a pretty thing you are." He reached out and caught Celia's chin. "Bet you are unbroken."

Pulling Celia close, he fondled her breast. Her face paled, and Celia sobbed.

"Take your hands off her," Sabrina barked.

He jerked his head and he leered at Sabrina. "And if I do not?"

Sabrina bit her lip. She could not endanger her friend and her mother-in-law, so she reconsidered her tack. "We have jewelry." She slipped her wedding ring from her finger. "Take it and go."

"I will." The blackguard sneered. "But I believe I'll pluck this bauble first." The highwayman snaked an arm about Celia and hugged her to him.

"Sabrina," Celia cried and stretched out her arms.

Lady Elizabeth screamed and cowered, covering her eyes with her hands.

"No." Sabrina stepped forward. "You cannot do this."

"I can do whatever I want." The highway summoned his partners in crime. "Watch these ladies while I sample a bit o' fluff."

"Wait." Sabrina put herself in his path. The world stood still for a scarce moment, and her breath came in a rush of pants. Her stomach was a ball of nerves, and her heart beat a rapid salvo in her chest.

She knew what the bastard intended, what he would do to Celia. She recalled the first time Everett made love to her. The tender caresses. The intimacy. The desire. She could not let Celia be taken in fear, in terror, in infinite cruelty.

"Take me, instead. I will come willingly." To further her offer, she added, "I am a married woman, and I know how to pleasure a man. I can make you howl like a wolf baying at the moon in under three minutes."

The last was a subtle reference to her husband. The mere thought of Everett gave her strength. She resolved to think of him if her hastily sketched plan went awry, and she ended up seducing the villain. That was how she would think of it.

Seduction.

She could not bear to consider the reality.

The highwayman hesitated. He glanced at Celia, who blubbered as a child, then eyed Sabrina. He licked his lips and shrugged. "Makes me no difference, my bloods up." He shoved Celia to the ground.

Rough and unrelenting, he clutched Sabrina by the arm and opened the door of the coach. "In you go."

"Not here." For her plot to work, she required an alternate location. A small grove on the other side of the coach fit her needs perfectly. "How about the trees? We will be more comfortable there."

He motioned with the pistol. "Right here's fine with me."

Sabrina gulped. "If I am to service you, the least you could do is allow me a measure of privacy."

"*My lady*," he replied, his tone dripping sarcasm, and bowed. "After you."

Memorizing the positions of the other highwaymen, Sabrina rounded the black coach. Visions of her life with Everett swirled in her mind, and she prayed she would see him again as she stepped from the road and into the field. The tall grass shushed against her skirts, and she fisted, released, and fisted her hands again. She walked slowly, drawing out the moment. Shadows danced among the trees as the sun dipped on the horizon.

"That's far enough," the highwayman called from behind.

With her pulse beating in her ears, she turned around. She was afraid, genuinely terrified. Her mouth was dry, and she tensed as she set her hands to her bodice.

"I do not wish to soil my dress." Her voice quavered, and her fingers trembled as she slipped a button free.

Although he was masked, she could see his gaze, focused and intent, on her movements. His grip on the pistol faltered, and the barrel dipped.

Sabrina knew she had to act fast because she would have only one chance to strike. Uttering another prayer in silence, she lashed out with her fist.

And caught him right under the chin.

The highwayman swayed, and his eyes widened with shock. He stood, suspended, with his arms limp at his sides. The gun fell from his grasp, hitting the grass with a muted thud. Then he stumbled forward and dropped face first to the ground.

Sabrina scrambled for the pistol.

After making certain the highwayman no longer presented a threat, she set her sights on the others. As she tiptoed through the grass, perspiration coursed her temples. She wiped her face with her sleeve and trudged forth. Careful not to make a sound, she peeked around the rear end of the coach.

The situation remained as she had left it.

To her good fortune, the highwayman guarding the driver and footmen had his back to her, as had the black-guard standing watch over Celia and the marchioness. She waved frantically and knew the moment one of the footmen spied her. He coughed loud and covered his mouth. Before long, the other escort made contact, as had the coachman.

Sabrina nodded, then stepped from behind the equipage. Leveling the pistol, she took careful aim. "You there, hold hard."

The highwaymen stared straight at her.

At that precise instant, the footmen and driver moved, swift and sure, and overpowered the robber guarding them. Once he assumed control, one of the footmen came to her aid.

"I have him, my lady." He disarmed the criminal she held at gunpoint. "What of the other villain?"

"I hit him." Sabrina ran to the marchioness and Celia and threw an arm about each frightened woman. She glanced over her shoulder. "He is unconscious, in the trees."

Celia lifted her tear-stained face, mottled with fear. "Are you all right, Sabrina? Did he hurt you?"

Sabrina shrugged and managed a lopsided grin. "My knuckles will bruise but, other than that, I am fine." She gazed at her mother-in-law. "My lady, are you injured?"

The marchioness, her eyes round as saucers, merely whimpered and cradled her head in her hands.

The footmen returned, dragging the highwayman Sabrina had knocked unconscious in the trees. And though she was not cold, she shivered and rubbed her arms.

"My lady, someone should alert the watch." The coachman approached. "And I need to see you safely home."

Sabrina shuffled the marchioness and Celia into the coach. "I will not leave one person here to stand guard over three dangerous highwaymen." She frowned. "We will remain here until such time as one of the footmen returns with the watch. Afterward, we shall journey to Beaumaris."

"My lady, if I may, I fear that is most unwise." The coachman appeared skeptical of her plan. "His lordship will wring our necks if we do not return with you, posthaste."

"His lordship will do no such thing." She planted hands on hips, winced when pain shot from her injured knuckles, and brought her chin to new heights. "I will explain that you acted on my orders."

"Yes, my lady." The coachman acquiesced with obvious reluctance. "But his lordship will not be happy."

Staring at her swollen appendage, Sabrina tried not to think about His Lordship.

THE SUN HAD long since dropped below the yardarm.

Everett reached into his waistcoat pocket and withdrew his timepiece. Dinner should have been served an hour ago. He descended the main staircase and crossed the foyer to the front entry. Turning the knob, he opened the door and stepped outside.

As he stared at nothing, he shrugged his shoulders in an effort to release some of the tension gripping him, but his efforts were for naught.

"I am sure everything is all right." His father puffed on a

cigar. "Your mother probably got to talking and lost track of time."

"I do not like it." Everett rubbed the back of his neck. "They should have been home before dusk."

"But...what do you suppose could have happened?"

Everett faced his father and frowned. "I do not know, but I am not going to remain here doing nothing any longer." He hailed his butler. "Ware, have my horse saddled and brought around this instant."

Ware bowed. "Yes, my lord."

"You do not think you can find them?" the marquess cautioned. "It is pitch black out there. You will end up just as lost as they are."

Everett snapped to attention. "You think they are lost?"

With an upraised hand, the marquess shook his head. "Poor choice of words, my boy."

"But you think something is wrong." It was a statement, not a question.

The marquess shrugged. "Who knows with your mother?"

"And my wife." Everett rolled his eyes. "I need to change." He retraced his earlier steps and headed up the stairs.

"Everett," the marquess called. "It appears the mystery is solved."

Rejoining his father on the front steps, Everett peered into the darkness and spied the glowing yellow orbs of coach lanterns in the distance.

As they entered the forecourt, Sabrina spied her husband running from the steps to meet them. Why had she agreed when the captain of the watch insisted on escorting them home?

"Are you all right?" Everett shoved aside the footmen and opened the door of the coach. "What happened?"

The concern in his voice made her gut clench. She had tried to think of some way to soften the blow, to color the truth in the best possible light.

Though the marchioness had said nothing since the ordeal with the highwaymen, she had whimpered and moaned plenty. Something she resumed with great frequency just then.

Celia stepped down and, with Everett's help, assisted Lady Elizabeth as she descended the coach. After passing them to his father's care, Everett stared inside and offered Sabrina his escort.

One glance at his face, and for the first time since the attempted robbery, the apprehension she had kept in check threatened to overwhelm her.

Sabrina wanted to cry.

Deep lines of stress extended from the corners of his eyes. His brow was furrowed, his jaw firmly set. But his amber eyes were filled with worry and fear, and he reached for her with both hands.

Without thinking, Sabrina set her palm to his—and winced.

Even in the dim lamplight, the swelling and dark bruises on the knuckles with which she had hit the highwayman were evident.

"Good God!" Everett froze. "What happened?"

"It is a long story." Sabrina scooted to the edge of the seat and kissed his cheek. "Let us go inside, and I will tell you everything."

They gathered in the drawing room. The marchioness

and Celia were given brandy to calm their nerves. Over Sabrina's protests, Everett sent for a doctor. To her frustration, the captain of the watch insisted on providing a detailed account of the whole affair, including how Sabrina sacrificed herself in Celia's place.

And she was forced to stand helplessly as her husband's expression went from one of worry, to shocked disbelief, to blank acceptance, and finally settled into a black anger she knew all too well. When it looked as if the captain would depart, Sabrina found herself grasping for excuses to extend his stay. She tempted him with dinner, a drink, a cigar, and a room for the night. But, alas, the captain departed.

Leaving Sabrina to face her husband.

And his wrath.

Not to mention her mother-in-law, who had yet to share her thoughts on the whole affair. And Sabrina was certain that whenever Lady Elizabeth found her tongue, her words would be anything but kind.

Everett closed the drawing room doors, and she braced for the storm. When he faced her, his heated stare left her in no doubt she was in trouble.

But how could it be helped?

In a meager attempt to spike his guns, and with shoulders squared, Sabrina inhaled deeply. "My lord, we were caught unaware, and the highwaymen were armed. Our escort and driver were taken prisoner. They threatened Celia, and I did what I thought best to protect her."

Everett had paced throughout her little speech, and though he appeared calm, Sabrina was not fooled. Danger lurked beneath that placid façade. When his footfalls brought him before her, toe-to-toe, anger emanated from him like heat from a fire. And while she resisted the urge to cower, she shook violently.

"And who, may I ask, protected you?" he inquired softly. Too softly.

Sabrina would have preferred a good old-fashioned tongue-lashing. Having imperiled her posterior on many occasions, she knew very well that his seemingly sedate inquiry was a trap. She proceeded with caution, taking great care not to incite him any more than she had already. "I beg your pardon?"

"My question was simple." His eyes flared, and his answering smile was anything but friendly. "I asked who protected you?"

She opened her mouth, considered the question, and then clamped shut her lips. "I do not understand."

"Everett," the marquess interceded. "The women have had a trying day. What say we have dinner, and let them retire early?"

"We will dine soon enough." Everett rested hands on hips. "I would like to know what on earth my wife was thinking *when she confronted an armed criminal with nothing more than her fist!*"

With arms spread wide in supplication, Sabrina tilted her head. "I had to do it."

"You could have been killed."

"And so might have been Celia."

"She would not have been foolish enough to try such a stunt."

"I could not let him take her."

"And why not?"

"Because he was going to...violate her."

"So you went with him in her stead?" Everett impaled her with an angry stare. "Knowing full well what he wanted?"

"Yes."

Emitting a beastly growl, he turned on his heel and stomped to the fireplace. Resting a hand on the mantel, he shifted his weight. Just as fast, he whirled around. "You had no right."

"What do you mean?" How she hated arguing with her husband.

"You are my wife." He stalked her, till his nose hovered mere inches from hers. "You belong to me. I did not give you leave to tender what is mine."

Now Sabrina had heard enough. "I am not your property to be placed under such restraints."

"You are exactly that, madam wife. And I will set such precepts as I deem necessary."

"How dare you—"

"*Just a minute!*" The marchioness was on her feet, and it was clear she was not happy.

Closing her eyes for a brief moment, Sabrina steeled herself for the onslaught. That was it, the final straw. Everett's mother would declare her daughter-in-law a lunatic and have her packed off to an asylum. And as angry as her husband was, he would probably allow it.

Those were her thoughts as a protective arm closed about her shoulders. Peeking against her better judgment, Sabrina almost swooned when she realized Lady Elizabeth loomed at her side.

Her mother-in-law inhaled and, on a blustery exhale shouted, "How dare you speak to my daughter-in-law like that!"

A collective of jaws dropped.

Sabrina blinked wide as an owl and tried to pull away, but the marchioness held her tight. She was not sure what scared her more, the look on her husband's face? Or her newfound favor with Lady Elizabeth?

"She saved our lives and this is her reward, you ungrateful man?"

The marchioness held out her other arm and beckoned Celia. She hugged both young women in a motherly embrace. "Come along, my dears." She shuffled them through the doorway and into the foyer. "We will leave the men to consider what horrible tragedy might have befallen us today had our dear Sabrina not acted with such courage."

Ware stood at the foot of the stairs.

The marchioness stopped. "Send for our maids. We shall need baths. And inform his lordship the countess will take dinner in her room before retiring. That will be all."

Sabrina submitted, as the mysterious creature once known as the wicked mother-in-law ushered her upstairs. She stared, she knew it, but she was afraid to drop her guard lest the woman eat her alive.

As they reached the landing, their lady's maids appeared.

The marchioness surrendered Celia, with strict instructions she be bathed, fed, and put to bed—in that order.

With Millie on one side and Lady Elizabeth on the other, Sabrina rushed to her apartments. By the time she gained her room, her ears rang and her head swam in a dark vortex of confusion.

That woman could not be the same person who had berated and reproved Sabrina at every turn. The interloper who had come to her wedding with annulment papers tucked in her reticule. The shrew that had declared Sabrina an unfit countess. Now, the marchioness appeared Sabrina's greatest ally.

Finally, Sabrina gazed at Lady Elizabeth and asked, "Who are you, and what have you done with my mother-in-law?"

"Poor dear." The marchioness smiled and patted her cheek. "She is overwrought."

Millie shook her head.

Dear?

She was sure that, at any minute, the marchioness would mutate into a hideous, fire-breathing dragon and reduce Sabrina to a pile of ashes.

It was too much to digest.

Sabrina collapsed in their arms.

CHAPTER EIGHTEEN

$\mathcal{I}$t was as though she floated on a fluffy white cloud. She was warm, safe, and content. Someone massaged her feet and slowly worked their way to her calves. It felt good, and Sabrina moaned her appreciation.

"She appears to be all right." A strange voice penetrated the blissful haze. "It was probably nothing more than a delayed reaction to the events of this evening."

"Poor girl," said Lady Elizabeth. "Is there anything I can do?"

Through the fog obscuring her senses, bits and pieces of the epochal day flashed in her mind. The robbery. The argument with Everett. The sudden transformation of the woman who, for all appearances hated Sabrina, into...her champion?

She shuddered.

"Sabrina, can you hear me?" Everett loomed, and she cringed.

"Let her rest. The amount of laudanum I administered will help her sleep, and that is what her ladyship needs," the stranger dressed as a doctor stated. "I will bandage her hand and be on my way."

A maelstrom of confusion colored her thoughts, and Sabrina fought to say something—anything. But it seemed there was no escape from the milky haze, so she surrendered to the sweet oblivion.

As HIS NAME fell repeatedly on a whisper from his wife's lips, Everett stood at her bedside and frowned. His mouth was dry as desert sand, and he was hot and cold at once. At her utterance, the anger investing his body washed away in seconds, but he could not relax. A strange force held him prisoner, kept him on edge.

"I will show you to the door, doctor." He turned from his countess. "Thank you for responding so quickly."

"Should her ladyship suffer a fit of hysteria, send for me at once," the physician said as they stepped into the hall. "Otherwise, I shall check her progress in the morning."

The butler stopped Everett on the landing. "I beg your pardon, your lordship. But the marquess requests your presence in the study."

What now? He stifled a groan of impatience and dipped his chin. "Ware, see to Dr. Howell."

"Yes, your lordship." Ware bowed and addressed the physician. "This way, sir."

Everett descended the stairs and in the foyer, veered left. The first door to the right led to his study. He found his father sitting behind his desk, his booted feet atop the blotter. "You wished to speak with me?"

"There you are." The marquess swallowed the last of his brandy and stood. "I am famished, what say we eat?"

"I am not hungry." Raking a hand through his hair, Everett shifted his weight. "Perhaps you should dine without me."

"Where is your mother?" After refilling his balloon, his sire neared.

"She is, at present, guarding my wife."

"So Lizzie has finally warmed to your chosen bride?" To Everett's surprise, his father chuckled. "I cannot believe your countess felled a highwayman with her fist. She is a resourceful one, that Sabrina Douglas."

"You mean Sabrina *Markham*."

"Indeed." With a grin Everett never thought his father capable of, the marquess said, "Do not be so hard on that charming girl. What she did may have been reckless, but her heart was in the right place."

Such praise from his sire was a rarity, and the significance was not lost on Everett. "You like Sabrina?"

"I adore her." Venting another chuckle, his father set a hand on Everett's shoulder. "Marrying that spirited young woman was the smartest move you have ever made. Now, do not tarry too long. You must rest, because I suspect you will need all the energy you can muster to keep pace with that darling wife of yours."

A gregarious laugh reverberated off the walls, as his perplexing parent headed for the dining room. Everett remained fixed at the center of his study. He had earned a kind word from his father. It was a feat he had not thought possible.

At the side table, he lifted a decanter and poured himself a drink. After consuming the contents of his glass in one gulp, he served himself another shot of the amber liquor and nestled in a high-back chair before the fireplace. The hours ticked past, marked by the mantel clock, as he studied the flames in the hearth.

Despite the approval he had gained from his father, Everett was cold and empty inside. A painful vise locked about his chest, and his heart raced, sounding a steady drumbeat in his ears. It was difficult to breathe, and never in his adult years had he been so crippled by the urge to cry. Without doubt, his torment revolved around one undeniable truth.

Sabrina had almost been killed.

At the mere thought, his gut clenched.

If that were what it meant to love, he would settle for intense like. Yet he knew the minute he pondered it, he lied to himself. He also realized he had no choice in the matter.

Fate and a fist landed him a wife.

And he would have it no other way.

Everett needed to manage Sabrina and his emotions. Of course, he still mastered supervision of the earldom. But had he not always said he loved a challenge? His willful wife was challenge incarnate. After downing the last of the brandy, he stared into the empty glass.

What had happened to the man who thrived on defying the odds?

It was an irrefutable fact; Lord Everett Markham and the earl of Woverton were now one in the same.

So where had he lost control?

Of his life?

Of his destiny?

Of his heart?

The mantel clock chimed three times. Night was fast slipping away, and dawn encroached.

After setting his glass aside, Everett stood. He lit a candle and steered for his suite. As he strolled the halls of his home, he considered the questions swirling in his ears. He was the same person who had collected myriad accomplishments. The title meant, more or less, nothing. There were no logical reasons he could not have the future he had planned— Sabrina, a family, and the unexpected addition of the peerage.

He could have it all.

In his chamber, he set the candle on the tallboy and pulled a gold pin from the folds of his cravat. Because he had long ago dismissed Pitton, he disrobed himself.

After donning a sapphire silk robe and matching trousers, he crossed to the tallboy and poured himself another brandy, which he carried to his bed. Given the night's events, he needed liquid fortification by the barrel. As he perched on the edge of the mattress, he stared at the empty space his wife normally occupied.

Everett hated sleeping without her.

His gaze rested on the door that led to her room. No doubt Sabrina lingered deep in slumber, but could he not share her four-poster? He had navigated the little corridor before he knew he had moved and stepped into her chamber.

The last thing he expected to find was his wife, fully *compos mentis*, standing in front of a window, bathed in silver moonlight.

She stared at the sky, with her arms wrapped about her. Raven locks cascaded down her back, contrasting sharply with the sheer confection she wore. The garment itself was a mesmerizing fantasy, more an afterthought, which had done nothing to disguise her ripe curves, and clung to her lush figure in a tantalizing tease he could not resist.

Oh, yes.

Without a sound, he closed the door behind him and

stalked her. As he stood within striking distance, she turned. A feminine gasp summoned as he covered her mouth with his. He fisted a hand in her hair and ruthlessly devoured her supple flesh. First, he claimed her lips, then lay siege to her tongue.

Everett was so angry with his wife, and yet he loved her beyond reason. So he wanted to be rough and gentle, at once.

~

SABRINA KNEW WELL THE BEAST. Knew when he was hungry and just how to feed him. And tonight, her predator was ravenous. It was futile to resist the sensuous onslaught, because there was no escape.

So it was fortunate for her, he was the only escape she sought.

She grazed her fingernails across his chest before fisting her hands in his silk robe and ripping it from his body. He responded in kind, pulling without mercy at the opening of her robe and sending buttons flying in all directions. She skimmed his taut stomach with her palms, but Everett caught her arms and pressed them to her sides.

"I want you naked." He caught the straps of her nightgown and slid them down.

"Only if you intend to join me." She skimmed her palms over his heated flesh, spurring him, arousing him further. Reaching with her fingers, she located the tie at the waist of his trousers and tugged at the ends. The slippery silk dropped to his hips before getting hung up—on his rampant erection.

If his expression had shown any hint of humor, she could have laughed at the situation, but there was none.

Burgeoning desire and something else, something dark and mysterious she could not recognize, stared back at her.

With the supple fabric, she stroked him in a blatant, inciting massage. His grunted approval told her she played with fire. Sabrina courted danger, knew it, and reveled in it.

Desire roared to life in her veins, hunger welled in her belly, and she conveyed her need with bold caresses meant to entice her barbarian to pounce. Then she would ride her husband hell bent for leather into a lusty battle.

"Enough." Everett grasped her wrist, ending her salacious massage, and sent his trousers falling to the floor. In a whisper of a second, he swept her into his arms and carried her to the bed.

There were no tender kisses or words of encouragement, but Sabrina had not expected any. Their mating would be fast, furious, and primitive. She parted her legs, resting her thighs wide in unspoken welcome. Her surrender seemed to halt her conqueror in his tracks. With elbows locked, holding himself above her, Everett closed his eyes.

He set his hips to hers and took her in one powerful thrust. As he moved within her, over her, on her, he kissed her not, but his heated gaze locked on hers. And though he could not have known it, her husband touched a part of her he could not touch in the literal sense.

She would not reach for him. Somehow, she knew he would not want it, so she lay there as he plumbed her, with her legs wrapped around him and urging him faster. She was flagrantly provoking, almost defiant in need.

She settled her palms on his shoulders and dug her nails into his flesh, but she would express no remorse. Just as she knew he would not apologize for the bruises he, no doubt, pounded on the insides of her thighs. And she cared not, because it felt good. After the harrowing events of the day, she sought to purge the fear and anxiety she had harbored since returning home.

In an instant, the simple act of joining no longer sufficed.

With a sob, she wrenched Everett to her, but he resisted, so she fought him. For a moment, the relentless thrusts halted, and he searched her eyes.

"Please." She wound her arms about his neck. "I need you."

"Darling Sabrina." With a sigh, he gave her his weight, framed her face with his hands, and kissed her.

When next he moved within her, achingly gentle and lovingly sweet, she gave vent to a plaintive cry. And with her body, Sabrina told Everett what she lacked the courage to express in words, infusing each tender caress with the same simple sentiment.

I love you.

SABRINA WAS SURPRISED to find herself alone when she woke the following morning. Yawning, she stretched her arms above her head before sitting upright. The room spun in wild rotations, and she slumped on her side.

After a while, the walls stopped dancing before her eyes, and she wrinkled her nose. Perhaps she had risen too fast. She tossed her legs over the side of the bed, slid her bare feet to the carpeted floor, and tested the solid surface. The world teetered, and she swayed and attempted to steady herself.

"What in bloody hell is the matter with me?" she asked aloud.

The altogether unfamiliar morning malaise had started almost a fortnight ago, but it seemed of no consequence.

It was nothing more than dizziness in the early hours, along with a tempestuous stomach that left her blanching at the mere thought of food. Was she ill? She shook her head and clucked her tongue. That was all she needed.

Hoping a bath would revitalize her flagging energy; Sabrina was surprised to discover she felt worse as she dried herself. After donning a black morning dress, she sat at her vanity while Millie arranged her hair. Her eyes widened as a possible explanation dawned.

She had experienced so many emotional upheavals of late, and it was no small wonder she had not exhibited more effects. And her sporadic sleeping habits could not have helped either. She suffered from jittery nerves. Perhaps Dr. Howell could prescribe a tonic.

EVERETT STOOD in front of the window in his study and gazed at the woods beyond the far edge of the topiary garden. His father launched into another endless discourse on estate management.

They had never been close. Since his brother died, they had forged a new, albeit tenuous, bond. The kind words his sire had imparted concerning Sabrina left him wanting more. In some way, it was as if he had reverted to a little boy, begging for affection.

He gave the matter half his attention, because the other half of him focused on his wife and, more perplexingly, on his intense regard for her. A raw sense of vulnerability pricked his nerves.

Was it possible to care too much for a spouse?

For a man accustomed to complete command of his personal life, as well as his business affairs, his apparent loss of control in both arenas had left him reeling. He had failed on so many fronts. He needed to get away. Needed to think things through and restore some measure of order to his life, before he introduced more disorder by declaring himself.

"I see there is a downed windmill at the Osterly property."

Everett came alert. Had fate smiled upon him? The perfect opportunity to flee, clear his head, and get himself in hand had just landed at his feet.

"Really?" He started. "Perhaps I should ride there and supervise the repairs?"

"An excellent notion." The marquess scanned a directive, which had arrived by messenger that morning. "By the by, we are departing for Tantallon Hall at the end of the week. Lady Celia is a bit overset after yesterday's unfortunate circumstances."

"I am sorry to hear that."

A brow arched, the marquess grinned. "Sorry we are leaving, or that Lady Celia is overset?"

"Both, of course." With a shrug, Everett sat on the edge of his desk.

"Balderdash." His sire chuckled. "You will be glad to be rid of us. It will provide you ample opportunity to pursue that spitfire you have married, and get yourself an heir."

"I do not have to pursue Sabrina." Everett snorted. "As you pointed out, we are married."

"Then why is her belly not rounding?"

Not for lack of trying, Everett wanted to say. "These things take time."

"Be that as it may," the marquess said as he stood, "It is

your duty to continue the line. Should you fail to fulfill your obligation, and some misfortune befall you, the title would pass to your cousin, Fredrick." He rolled his eyes. "God help us if that lack-wit inherits the marquessate."

He bit his tongue until his father quit the room, and then vented a violent series of expletives.

His seed could now be counted among his many short-comings. How Everett wanted to ask his all-knowing sire just how he should go about impregnating Sabrina. Was there a particular time of day coital activity proved more successful? Was one position favored over another? Perhaps he should stand his countess on her head immedi-ately after spilling himself inside her?

He laughed as he pictured the last.

Knowing his wife, and her adventurous spirit, she would probably oblige him.

With the departure of his parents and Lady Celia, he and Sabrina would finally be alone. He would have the opportunity to devote himself to his wife and marriage.

And Everett would declare himself.

He considered his situation and decided on a definite course of action. It seemed simple. Once his parents jour-neyed to Tantallon Hall, he would travel to Osterly. It was the perfect occasion to set himself right. When he returned to Beaumaris, he would tell Sabrina of his love and help her explore her feelings for him.

It would be a new beginning for them.

A warm sense of accomplishment swelled in his chest. Below his waist, something else swelled. Everett smiled and clucked his tongue. He had not made love to Sabrina in the afternoon in quite some time. How neglectful of him. So he went in search of his wife to rectify his deficiency.

THREE DAYS LATER, Sabrina sat in the drawing room with the marchioness and Celia. As they worked on their embroidery, she pretended to read a book. While her relationship with her mother-in-law had much improved, her relationship with her husband seemed to deteriorate just as fast.

And she had no idea why.

Since the attempted robbery, Everett hardly spoke to her. He avoided her during the day and spent most of his hours in the study with his father. At least, that was the excuse he provided for his continued absence.

They no longer indulged in their morning rides, rarely breakfasted together, and he was never at lunch. She saw him at dinner, from the far end of the dining room table, but they did not converse. She supposed she should not complain. He was an earl, and his holdings commanded his attention. If he could, she was certain he would spend more time with her.

Because he had certainly devoted himself to another aspect of their marriage.

At all hours of the day and night, Everett came to her. Yes, she was disappointed they no longer slept together in the literal sense, but it was difficult to find fault with him when he made love to her constantly. In fact, the marriage bed was all they shared, of late.

His odd behavior started the night after the robbery.

Thereafter, her husband sought her company at the most unpredictable of times, always with an expression of utter helplessness, vulnerability in his eyes, and an outstretched hand. And she would set her palm to his and go without comment.

But Sabrina worried.

Ideas danced in her head, providing ample excuses for his treatment. She had seized on one explanation, in particular. Though she hesitated to think it, could not dare speak it, inside, she was giddy.

Was it possible? Had Everett fallen in love with her?

She had spent an hour before the vanity mirror staring at her reflection, memorizing the dreamy yet urgent look. Was it the same for him? Hope overwhelmed her, especially in light of recent revelations.

To the best of her knowledge, she suspected she carried Everett's child. Her unstable stomach had become downright fragile, and though she slept well most nights, she often woke feeling fatigued. It had not occurred to her that she might be increasing until she received a letter from Caroline, bemoaning the same maladies.

Sabrina smiled as she recalled how she had counted the weeks on her fingers and realized it was a definite possibility. She was going to tell Everett, at once, but remembered their guests were leaving in three days. She wanted to wait until they were alone to deliver the joyous news. Absently, she placed a hand on her belly.

"My dear, fetch the ledger detailing the stillroom supplies, and we will compose a list of necessary purchases." The marchioness smiled and secured the needle in her embroidery. "Since winter is coming, you will need to procure additional quantities of certain items should severe weather linger."

Sabrina blinked. Would she ever become accustomed to her mother-in-law? The one who liked her, the one who had suddenly taken her under her tutelage and imparted sage advice on running a large household?

"Oh? Are you sure it is not too much trouble?" She closed the book she had not been reading and set it on a side table. "I do not wish to be a burden when you have so little left of your stay."

"Nonsense." Lady Elizabeth inclined her head. "As I have no daughter of my own, I consider it an honor to share what knowledge I possess with you."

"All right." Sabrina nodded and stood. "I believe Everett has the ledger. If you will excuse me, I shall be right back."

She met her husband in the foyer.

"My lord, I require the journal detailing the stillroom account." She noted he wore his hacking jacket and tugged on gloves. "Are you going for a ride?"

"Aye." Everett kept his gaze averted. "The book is in my desk. I believe it is in the second drawer on the left between some other accounts. Help yourself."

"Of course, I do not have to go over the books right now." Sabrina bit her lip and shuffled her feet. "If you would prefer, I could accompany you on your ride. It will take only a moment for me to change, I promise."

"That is not necessary, because I will be on my way before you gain your room," he replied with uncharacteristic aloofness. With a side step, he walked to the front door. "See you at dinner."

Swallowing her disappointment, Sabrina dragged her feet to his study. Standing behind his desk, she opened the drawer he had indicated would yield the ledger she needed and discovered a litany of account books.

"Great heavens, no wonder he is in here all day." She pulled a pile of journals from the drawer and sorted through them until she found the item she sought.

She was just about to return the volumes to their home in the desk, when her printed name captured her attention. Curious, she reached into the drawer. Upon realizing the parchment was caught, she worked it free, taking great care not to tear the paper. After a few tedious seconds, she withdrew an official looking document from the rear of the drawer.

Her name appeared beneath a signature line at the bottom of the page. There was a space for Everett to sign, as well. The top of the stationary was wrinkled and tattered. With both hands, she smoothed the paper—and swayed.

Leaning against the desk, she barely managed to keep herself from falling. She choked on a sob and pressed her trembling hands to her mouth.

She was going to cry, but not there.

After placing the parchment in the ledger, she clutched the leather bound volume to her breast and fled the study.

Ware stood in the foyer. "My lady, are you all right?"

"It is nothing serious." She lied. "Please, tell the marchioness and Lady Celia that I am unwell." Grasping the newel post, she ascended the grand staircase.

"Perhaps a pot of tea will help?" the butler offered from below.

Bitterness rose in her throat. "No, thank you," she replied without looking back. "I do not wish to be disturbed."

Her heart was heavy in her chest, and tears welled in her eyes. Pain was too pale a word to describe the agony investing her body. Breaking into a run, Sabrina sailed down the hall and through her sitting room.

In her bedchamber, she dropped the ledger to the floor. At her washstand, she convulsed over the basin and was violently ill. It seemed forever before the vicious paroxysm passed, leaving her weak.

She slid to the floor and crawled to the ledger. Closing her eyes, she felt for the crisp parchment that had turned her world on end. With a death grip on the offensive document, she prayed she was wrong, prayed she had somehow misinterpreted the words at the top of the page.

Inhaling deeply, steeling herself for the worst, she focused her stare and read aloud, "Petition for dissolution of marriage."

And she swooned.

CHAPTER NINETEEN

*W*ell, for good or ill, Sabrina had the answer to her quandary. It was too bad it was not the explanation for which she had long hoped. Rolling on her side, she propped herself on one elbow. The floor of her bedchamber seemed to pitch violently, or perhaps it was her stomach, she was not sure.

After a few minutes, she sat upright.

The paper lying on the floor seemed to mock her, and a hideous laugh teased her ears. She was certain it was no less than she deserved. What had she thought? She actually believed Everett had fallen in love with her. That she had gained a measure of his trust and respect. In reality, he had grown distant, separating himself from her. Preparing for the end.

Sabrina vented a self-deprecatory sound.

In hindsight, it all made sense.

While her husband had consented to join her for love-making—no, sex—he wanted nothing to do with her outside the bedchamber. There were no more companion-able rides throughout the countryside, no more romantic walks in the gardens, and no more evenings spent in conversation before the fire in his study. Their relationship had devolved into a series of illicit trysts, not unlike that of a gentleman and his mistress.

In fact, Everett no longer slept in the same bed with her. He only shared her four-poster while they performed the act. There was the coupling of their bodies for what?

Gratification?

Sabrina shuddered.

She could not do it again, could not let him touch her, could not let him enter her body. Not now, not when she knew the horrible truth.

Clutching the stationary to her breast, Sabrina walked to her vanity and sat. Smoothing the crinkled edges, she read and reread the document.

Hours had passed when she roused from voices emanating from her husband's suite. At the door leading to his room, she listened with renewed intent. She covered her mouth to smother a gasp when she overheard Everett dismissing his manservant.

That meant one thing.

He undressed himself and would shortly thereafter come to her.

In frenzy she tugged at her laces, but it was no use. There was no way she could disrobe and gain her bed before her husband entered her quarters.

After pulling the pins from her hair, she dashed about the chamber and blew out the candles. In the dark, she kicked off her slippers and slid, fully clothed, between the sheets. Remembering the document she had left in plain view on her vanity, she bolted upright.

With a flick of her wrist, she flung the covers aside, dragged herself from the mattress, and ran to the vanity.

Sabrina had just whisked the paper into her grasp when a familiar creak pierced the silence of her chamber. In a rush, she ran to her bed, tucked the parchment beneath her pillow, slid, quick as a wink, between the covers, and tugged them to her chin.

Though she rested on her side, facing away from the corridor, the soft light from a candle signaled the arrival of her husband. She closed her eyes, breathed deep and steady, and prayed Everett would not hear her heart beating in her chest.

"Sabrina, are you awake?" Through the layers of bedclothes, his hand settled on her shoulder, and he shook her gently.

Feigning sleep, she hoped her incoherent mumble lent credibility to her ruse. From behind he sighed, and it struck her as an anchor about her neck, conveying her to a watery grave. His fingers speared through her hair, and she tried not to flinch.

Behind her, the mattress dipped. She bit her lip, and then she realized he only sat on the bed. Again and again, he stroked her hair, and on occasion he scratched her scalp.

It felt so good.

Tension drained from her body, and she sank further into the down mattress. Her appreciative moan was genuine. Sabrina knew not why Everett was there, but at the moment, she cared not.

Ere long, she truly slept.

When she woke, hours later, her legs throbbed, and her body ached. It was as though she was covered by lead weights, and Sabrina struggled to sit upright.

She squirmed left, then right. Still she could not move. Then she remembered why. She had spent the entire night fully clothed in bed. When a few strategic tugs failed to set her free, she resorted to kicking herself out of the tangled bedclothes.

Bent forward, she unfastened her garters and rolled the stockings to her ankles, before slipping them from her feet. Then she reached behind and yanked the laces of her gown to loosen the bodice. Inching her hips from side to side, she managed to extricate herself from the wrinkled dress.

Clad only in her chemise, she tossed her legs over the side of the bed and stood. In an instant, her legs buckled beneath her, and she grasped the edge of the bedside table to steady herself. Gnawing her lip, Sabrina turned and reached under her pillow.

The divorce petition still rested in its hiding place.

As she withdrew the document from beneath the down, she slumped her shoulders. For a scarce moment, she thought she might have dreamed the events of the previous night. But the proof in her hand told her she had not imagined anything.

And, at that instant, her heart broke.

She supposed she could cry, and she would produce a river of tears if it would make the paper disappear, but Sabrina knew it would not. She wondered when Everett was planning to tell her he no longer wished to be married to her. That he sought a divorce. Had he intended to confront her when his parents departed? Would he do the deed once they were alone?

Well, she was not going to wait and find out.

Shrugging at no one, she walked to her escritoire and sketched a missive to the lone person she could trust to help her. After sealing and addressing the envelope, she folded the petition and hid it amid her stationary, where she hoped no one would find it.

A leisurely soak in a hot bath went a long way toward

soothing her many aches and pains but had done nothing to ease her heartache. Sabrina tarried in her chamber to avoid meeting anyone at breakfast. As a consequence, it was almost noon when she ventured forth. She was halfway down the stairs when Everett strolled into the foyer. Halting mid-stride, she held her breath in the hope that he would not notice her.

To her misfortune, he stopped at the foot of the grand staircase, stared in her direction, and frowned when he met her gaze. "You look a bit peaked, my dear. Are you unwell?"

My dear? She managed to bite back an impolite snort. Instead, she smiled. "I am sure it is nothing." As would a Douglas, which she considered herself, given the petition, she marched forward until she stood before him.

Surely that was not concern in his expression? Damn fool man. He would not have to divorce her if she were dead. He would be rid of his countess without any taint of scandal. No doubt, he would garner plenty of attention as the grieving widower.

She wanted to cry—or hit him.

"My lord, I have a letter." She held out the envelope. "Would you frank it for me?"

"I shall do it now and put it in the post, myself." As he accepted her summons for assistance, he furrowed his brow. "I need to check the north fields. Would you care to join me for a ride?"

Under normal circumstances—normal being a marriage in which one party was not seeking a divorce—Sabrina would have accepted his offer. As she was aware of his intent to end their union, she could not bear to be alone with her soon-to-be-ex-husband.

"I must review the still room ledger." She clutched the

leather bound account book to her bosom. "And I should calculate the gardener's budget."

"But I can help you with that later." Everett took her hand in his. "The fresh air will do you good, and it has been some time since we enjoyed a ride."

How strange it was that only yesterday their positions had been reversed. She begged for a ride, and he rejected her. Cursed with the knowledge of their impending divorce, she could understand why he had no interest in her pursuits. And yet it physically hurt her to deny him. Why act nice? The situation would be so much easier if he were cruel and if he would admit the truth.

"Ah, there you are, my boy." The marquess entered the foyer. "Thought I would accompany you on the survey of the north fields."

"Go with your father." Relieved, Sabrina mustered another smile. "I shall see you this evening."

As she retreated, Everett tipped her chin, bent his head, and gifted her an impossibly tender kiss. "Until this evening." He pressed his lips to her forehead. "Do not over-tire yourself."

Her knees weakened, and she leaned against the newel post for support. Everett and the marquess stepped outside, and Sabrina summoned the strength to walk to the study, where she plopped behind the desk and buried herself in her task.

When next she looked up from her figures, the setting sun filtered through the windows, bathing the room in gold light and warmth. Resolved to leave the grand estate in better working order than she found it, and that was not saying much, she continued to fulfill her duties as chate-laine. She totaled numbers, made new entries, and composed a list of necessary purchases.

Her stomach growled, and she pressed a hand to her belly. She had not eaten, because she feared she would revisit whatever she consumed. Raking a hand through her hair, which she was certain stood on end; she set down her pen and sighed in frustration.

An amber sparkle caught her eye.

Sunlight shone through a crystal decanter of brandy. Sabrina pushed from the desk and stood. A few brisk steps brought her to the side table bearing a silver tray laden with brandy balloons and a full decanter.

Whenever her mother was upset, her father always handed her a glass of the strong smelling intoxicant to settle her nerves. She wondered if it would work for her and poured herself a glass. A high-back chair before the fireplace seemed the perfect place to take her ease. Settling herself, she raised the glass to her lips and sipped. Warmth pervaded her flesh, trailed a comforting path down her throat, silenced her protesting belly, and quelled her jittery nerves.

As she emptied her second refill, and sank further into her seat, the door to the study opened.

"Are you hiding from us?" Celia cast her a pout.

"Sabrina, are you feeling well?"

Inclining her head, Sabrina glanced at the marchioness. "I feel quite well, thank you."

Celia's eyes grew wide as saucers. "Are you drinking?"

Sabrina stared at the empty crystal. "Not anymore."

In an instant, her mother-in-law snatched the balloon from her grip, raised it to her nose, and sniffed. "You have been drinking brandy."

"I might have had a small portion." Sabrina hiccuped. "Would you care to join me?"

With a hand to her chest, Celia peered at Lady Elizabeth and asked, "Do we dare?"

"We do." With an imperious nod of approval, the marchioness said, "After all, the men are out. What harm is there in partaking of refreshments before dinner?"

While Celia dragged a third chair before the fireplace, Lady Elizabeth retrieved the decanter and two additional glasses.

Sabrina accepted her refilled balloon with a clumsy salute and an appreciative moan, which soon bubbled into nervous giggles.

Her mother-in-law held her glass high. "To what shall we drink?"

"How about men?" Celia offered with a shy grin.

Sabrina had not wanted to toast the opposite sex but drank anyway.

"And to my marvelous daughter-in-law," the marchioness added.

Sabrina snorted before surrendering to another fit of giggles. For some strange reason she could not fathom, she felt compelled to air the truth. "You did not think me so marvelous when first we wed, my lady."

Celia gasped.

Lady Elizabeth, in the process of sipping her brandy, choked violently.

As her soon-to-be-ex-relation leaned forward, Sabrina reached out and slapped her on the back. "You know, you are quite pleasant when you are not nagging me to death."

That time Celia choked.

"Great heavens." Nonplussed, Lady Elizabeth pressed her hand to her temple. "My dear, please allow an old woman the benefit of making a mistake."

One corner of her mouth lifted, Sabrina gave vent to an exceedingly skeptical sound. "A mistake?"

"Indeed." Lady Elizabeth peered at her from over the rim of her glass. "You must understand, I have always looked on marriage as duty. There were agreements made, and that was all I considered."

"But what of love?" Celia inclined her head.

The marchioness shrugged. "Love never entered into the equation."

Despite the pleasant fog in her brain, Sabrina remained coherent. "Do you not love the marquess?"

"Our marriage was arranged. I hardly knew him when we wed but, over the years, we have become something akin to old friends." Her mother-in-law sipped her brandy. "Our relationship is one of mutual comfort, nothing more."

Sabrina gazed on her with pity. "How sad."

"Oh, do not waste your sympathy on me, my dear." Lady Elizabeth patted Sabrina's arm. "It is what I was raised to expect, and I have no regrets. My position is compensation enough." After a moment, Everett's mother added with a wistful air, "I do wonder what it is like to fall in love. My son said you met while Lord Lockwood courted his wife. Tell me, is there such a thing as love at first sight?"

Sabrina considered her now empty glass. She held the brandy balloon as the marchioness refilled it. "The truth is that was not the first time we had been introduced."

"The devil you say." Kicking off her slippers, Celia tucked her feet beneath her skirts.

As she swallowed a sip of brandy, Sabrina noted it no longer burned her throat. "No." She shook her head with a vengeance. "We had met before, though I am certain he does not recall when."

With her elbow propped on the arm of her chair, Celia rested her chin on her hand. "Do tell."

Sinking deeper into her seat, Sabrina stared unseeing into the fireplace. Since her husband was divorcing her, the tale dancing on the tip of her tongue seemed innocuous. "Well, it began with my come-out..."

"Sabrina, stop fidgeting," Cara admonished her for the umpteenth time that evening. "You look lovely."

"I look ridiculous," Sabrina complained. "And this blasted knot is too tight. It pulls the corners of my eyes." She patted the taut knob of black hair atop her head.

Behind her, several young ladies giggled.

"What do you want to wager she does not make it through the night without falling on her face?" one said.

"Sabrina Douglas? In a dress?"

"Do you suppose she knows how to dance?" snorted another.

"First she has to find a partner."

Sabrina tried to ignore the criticism but was too self-conscious to disregard it. At the ripe old age of eighteen, she found the idea of a come-out the height of humiliation. All trussed up like a Christmas goose, she was intensely aware that if this were the feast, she was the main course. Why on earth had ladies ventured to Almack's, just to beg a bunch of old crows for permission to waltz?

She would rather fish trout.

The strings of a waltz sounded. Dashing rakes and beautiful ladies paired and headed for the dance floor. A tap on her shoulder had her turning around.

Countess Lieven smiled. But it was the tall handsome man standing next to her who commanded Sabrina's attention.

How sad was it that her first partner was far lovelier than she? Actually, if truth be told—and she considered herself a brutally honest sort—the man was a veritable god.

With unruly brown hair, amber eyes that danced with amusement and naughty thoughts, naughty like the time she ate the last of the cherry compote, and a boyish smile, he was fascinating and frightening at once.

Fascinating because he set her heart pounding.

Frightening because he set her heart pounding.

Were they outside, Sabrina would have sworn she had been struck by a thunderbolt. The thought seemed unlikely. But he was a vast deal more exciting than a large trout dangling from the end of her line. And if she had to marry, it was certainly desirable to wed someone she found more interesting than trout.

"My dear, may I present Lord Everett Markham." Countess Lieven turned to Everett. "Lord Markham, may I present Miss—"

"—Smyth," Sabrina interjected. "Miss Smyth." She extended a hand and engaged him in a vigorous shake.

"You told him your name was Smyth?" Celia laughed and took another gulp of brandy.

"I did." Sabrina nodded with a mischievous grin.

"And Countess Lieven did nothing?" asked Lady Elizabeth.

Sabrina wrinkled her nose. "I think she was too stunned."

"But, why did you not tell Everett your real name?"

Sabrina glanced at her mother-in-law. "Because I set my cap for him right then and there. The only problem was I did not know how to attract a man. I was a terrible dancer, a bit gawky, and feared my reputation would scare him." She shrugged and considered her glass. "Thereafter, I stayed out of sight, avoiding him whenever he was present. Trouble was, I never seemed to improve. I was always tripping, stepping on toes, and speaking out of turn. I almost fainted dead away when Trevor introduced us. I kept waiting for him to recognize me, but he never did. Later, my awkwardness did not seem to matter. Everett married me in spite of myself."

"How romantic." Celia sighed.

"If you only knew." On a hiccup, Sabrina swilled the last of her brandy and waved her hand in front of her face. "Ish it hot in here or ish it jush me?"

EVERETT and his father rode into the forecourt and around to the stables. The marquess prattled about agricultural management, but Everett ignored him.

Because something was wrong with Sabrina.

Lately, she had seemed pale and almost fragile. His wife was a lot of things, but he would never describe her as such. Worse, his usually ebullient bride had withdrawn from her favorite activities. She had never turned down an offer of a ride, yet she had that day. It was only yesterday when she had sought to join him on his evening ride, yet he had spurned her offer because he suspected he would be tempted to rush a declaration. And he wanted to wait until they were alone to broach the tender subject. But her delicate nature concerned him enough that he considered postponing his trip, which meant delaying his declaration.

Of course, if something were amiss with Sabrina, it would take precedence over his pledge of love. He had the rest of his life to proclaim his undying devotion. And he required no journey to an outlying estate in preparation for an oath. It just seemed a golden opportunity to get himself in order, gather his thoughts, and compose a suitable affirmation adequate to the occasion. At the moment, he drifted at sea.

"*Everett!*"

"What?" He glanced left and realized his sire no longer rode alongside him but had, in fact, dismounted, and an undergroom had secured his horse. Everett shifted in his saddle.

"Well, are you going to sit there all night, or are you going to come down so we can have dinner?" The marquess stood, hands on hips, one brow arched. "I am starved."

"Er, yes, sir." He descended his mount.

In silence, they crossed the yard and entered the house through the back parlor. They walked the length of the hall, past the library, the dining room, and the drawing room.

Ware stood in the foyer and collected Everett's hat and gloves. "Good evening, your lordship."

Everett scanned the staircase, expecting his wife to coming running at any minute. "Where is her ladyship?"

"The study, I believe," Ware replied with a strange expression Everett could not decipher.

"What is she doing in there?" the marquess inquired.

Everett was already in the hall. "I had better check on Sabrina before I dress for dinner."

"And I shall come with you." His father cleared his throat. "Could use a brandy."

The marquess in tow, Everett turned the knob, set the door wide, and entered his domain. Three chairs sat before the fireplace, their backs to the door. From where he stood, it appeared the room was empty.

Until someone hiccuped.

"Sabrina?" He arched a brow.

His most unlikely lady appeared at one side of the middle chair. With eyes half open, she smiled and hiccuped. "*Hhhhiiiii!*"

"Good heavens," the marquess exclaimed. "The girl is drunk."

"She ish not drunk," his mother insisted as she leaned on the armrest of her chair, her head bobbling like that of a newborn babe. "Ladies do not get drunk. We get tipsy."

The marquess glared at his wife. "Lizzy, what is the meaning of this?"

"Oh, shut up." When her elbow slipped from the armrest, his mother slumped.

Everett stomped forward and discovered Celia, passed out, in the third chair. He scratched the back of his head. "Bloody hell. Sabrina, what have you to say for yourself?"

"*Hiccup.*"

CHAPTER TWENTY

*H*er head ached. If for no other reason, she truly wanted to die.

"My dear Sabrina." Lady Elizabeth hugged her daughter-in-law and pressed a motherly kiss to her cheek. "I shall forever rue the time we wasted at odds."

She managed a smile for her mother-in-law. After all, she was no longer the thorn in Lady Elizabeth's side. "Do not dwell on it, my lady."

"Oh, but you must call me Elizabeth." Everett's mother cupped Sabrina's chin. "We are family, you know."

How ironic. Her marriage ended just as her mother-in-law finally gave Sabrina use of her name. One more shock of that measure, and Sabrina thought she might throw herself from the roof of the estate house.

"As you wish, Elizabeth." She inclined her head. "Safe journey."

Celia approached. "Dearest friend, I owe you a debt I fear I shall never be able to repay. My parents will laud you until they pass from this life for saving me."

"Nonsense." Sabrina chucked her shoulder in play.

"There is no debt. We are friends, and that is what friends do."

"Dearest girl." The marquess stepped up and held her in a fatherly embrace. "Take care of my son."

At his words, she forced the slightest grin. So Everett had not confided in his parents his plans for a divorce, because the marquess was not a cruel man. She nodded once. "I will do my best by him, my lord." She comforted herself in the knowledge that she had not lied.

As a dutiful wife, Sabrina stood beside her husband, enduring the weight of his arm about her waist, and waved as the sumptuous traveling coach, bearing his parents and Celia, bobbled down the graveled drive.

The chilly September morning mirrored her husband's mood. Everett had scarcely spoken to her at breakfast, preferring instead to glare at her across the long dining room table.

Since all three women still suffered the effects of their indulgence, or perhaps drunken foray was a better description, their last meal together had been a conservative affair. To her amazement, she dreaded the departure of her mother-in-law, because she relished not the idea of being alone with her husband. But he would soon depart for Osterly.

And tonight, she, too, would embark on a journey.

"Shall we?" Everett nudged her.

Sabrina blinked. "What?"

"Let us go inside." Everett turned her toward the house. "Perhaps you will tell me what you have been about these past few days."

"Oh?" She stumbled, and his arm tightened at her waist. "I do not know what you mean."

"I would like an explanation for your behavior, of late."
He steered her in the direction of his study.

"But—are you not departing for Osterly?"   As she
returned to the scene of the crime, fear nipped at her heels.
"Surely you want to make the journey in the light of day."

"I have decided to postpone my trip." He frowned.

She halted in the doorway to the study. "Why?"

He ushered her into his domain.   "Because I am
concerned for your welfare."

"My lord, I assure you, such concern is unfounded."
Sabrina faced him and rested her palm to his chest, ever
aware that her display of affection exacted a high price in
the coin of self-control. "I am quite well."

"Of course you are." Everett rolled his eyes and shook
his head.   "My dear, you have not been yourself for a
sennight. Are you going to tell me that getting foxed is
normal fare for you?   I have seen you commit some
outlandish acts, but yesterday you surpassed yourself."

"It could not be helped." She bit her lip. "I enjoyed
amiable conversation with your mother, and she kept
refilling my glass. It was unintentional."

"You are pale." He narrowed his stare. "And you seem a
tad out of sorts."

Her mind raced in search of an adequate excuse. She
had to convince him his worry was unwarranted, or he
might not make his journey. Worse, he could use the opportunity to broach the subject of divorce. While she was
willing to grant such request, she doubted she could do so
without embarrassing herself.

Divorce was mortifying enough.

"My lord, I have spent most of my time entertaining our
guests and working on the household accounts. I have had
little opportunity to venture into the sunshine."   She

managed a brittle smile. "Now that we are alone, I hope to resume my outdoor activities."

He cupped her cheek and caressed her skin with his thumb. "Fishing, I presume?"

"I have always found it relaxing." Placing her hand over his, she ceased his maddening massage. "Go to Osterly."

"It is only for one night." Everett inclined his head and grinned. "If you are sure you are all right."

"I am fine." She wrung her fingers and curled her toes in her slippers.

"There is something we should discuss, but I suppose it can wait." How earnest he appeared.

Oh, why could he not just confess his plans? Even as she stifled a shudder, her knees buckled, her ears rang with alarm, and she shivered with dread.

That discussion will never happen.

"Go." As she had on so many occasions, she pressed her lips to his palm. "See to your property."

And only a half an hour later, for the second time that day, Sabrina stood in the forecourt and waved at another departing carriage. Her husband leaned out the window, pressed a hand to his lips, and blew her a kiss. She smiled, made a show of catching the imaginary buss and held it to her cheek. When he disappeared inside the carriage, her smile faded to a frown.

SABRINA SPENT her last day in the grand structure she had come to think of as home, wandering through the cavernous halls and chambers. She walked the gardens, at times closing her eyes and committing to memory the sights, smells, and sounds unique to the estate.

She searched out each servant, inventing one excuse after another, to say goodbye. Though none knew it was goodbye.

Late in the afternoon, she donned her riding habit and toured the fields once more as mistress of Beaumaris. She rode hell bent for leather through the meadow and jumped the fence at the north end of the property.

That night, wearing her best gown, Sabrina ate dinner in the formal dining room, using the finest china and silverware. Crisp white damask linens trimmed in old gold blanketed the long table. And she sat at the head, presiding over her final meal as the countess of Woverton. As she stared at the empty chairs on either side, the future she had thought she would enjoy played before her.

Memories she would never make.

There were children she would never know, save the one she carried, celebrations of which she would never partake, and family traditions she would never begin. She would never know how it would be to grow old with Everett and raise their babes. To stand together as their offspring went to school, to watch in pride as they married, to rejoice when they had young ones of their own. To spend lazy afternoons strolling arm in arm through the gardens, to snuggle in bed on cold winter nights. There was so much.

So much Sabrina had looked forward to experiencing with her beloved husband.

Subconsciously, her hand fell to her belly. It was too soon for her to evidence any hint of her condition, but she knew of the life growing within her. Somehow, she would shield her child from the mistakes she made, and, more importantly, her shame.

Afterward, she met the butler in the foyer. "Our guests

joined us so soon that I never had the opportunity to thank you, Ware."

"Your ladyship does me great honor." The very proper manservant blushed. "I know not to what I owe such approbation."

"You have always been so kind to me." She studied the elegant entrance of Beaumaris. "I was not to the peerage born. In fact, I am the daughter of an admiral, and the rank has been difficult to negotiate."

"If I may be so bold, my lady." Ware compressed his lips. "You are a fine countess."

"Praise, indeed." Tears beckoned, and she swallowed hard. "I shall always remember you."

"I beg your pardon, your ladyship." Ware clasped his hands behind his back. "But are you unwell? Should I summon a doctor?"

"I am sorry, Ware." Sabrina rubbed the nape her neck. "I am tired. And given the number of guests we have hosted, the staff has earned an early rest. Send everyone to bed, as any lingering chores will keep till the morn."

"Yes, my lady." He lowered his chin. "Shall I escort your ladyship to your quarters?"

"That is not necessary." Her plan progressed as she hoped. "Goodnight, Ware."

He bowed, and she turned on a heel and marched into the breach.

As the night grew old, she paced the floor of her bedchamber. It was just past midnight when Sabrina emerged from her dressing room, garbed in what was known as her fencing attire—breeches and boots.

She walked to her escritoire and completed the letter she wrote, so Everett would know she was fine with his decision. She detailed her appreciation for all he had done and explained that she understood his reasons for seeking a divorce. And never would she speak or think ill of him. After folding the slip of stationary in half, she tucked it inside a matching envelope, which she sealed, and then she wrote his name on the front.

Her gaze lit upon the parchment she wished she had never found. She convinced herself it was much easier that way. There would be no begging, no pleading, no crying, and no more humiliation than necessary. Without hesitation, she signed on the line just above her printed name.

"Well, I suppose it is official." She slumped.

With the note and the petition in hand, Sabrina charged through the tiny corridor leading to her soon-to-be former husband's bedchamber. Because he was not in residence, no fire burned in the hearth. The room was dark, but the smell of sandalwood hung in the air and evoked his image in an instant. Haphazardly, she wiped the moisture forming at the corners of her eyes. There would be time enough for tears later.

With newfound resolve, she trod to his bed, tried not to think of all that had occurred there, and placed her correspondence and the petition on his pillow.

In mere seconds, she navigated the hall leading to the back stairs. She wanted to run but fought the urge. She wanted to be gone from that place before she lost her nerve.

Sabrina was thankful no one had discovered the horse she saddled just after dinner. He munched some hay and nuzzled her as soon as she entered his stall. That was her first break. She would need several more were she to succeed.

In the dark, she mounted the hunter she had chosen for the journey and, conscious of the noise, nudged him into a walk. Once they were beyond the main house, she would give the impressive steed his head.   Undetected, she cantered across the forecourt, down the drive beneath the formidable oaks, and reined in at the main gate. Only then had she turned to gaze once more on the house that had become her home and so much more. It was a part of her she was reluctant to relinquish.

Because Sabrina loved her husband, she had to set him free. She had learned a lot since she married Everett. Had grown a lot, too. Loving someone meant putting them first, which meant placing Everett's needs before her own, regardless how much it hurt.

Everett deserved better for a wife and, however late, it was obvious he had realized it. Though she tried, she was not angry with him. Their child manifested a lifelong connection for which she was grateful.

And Sabrina resolved that part of her would remain at Beaumaris.

She would leave behind the best of her, the optimist and the fanciful dreamer. The brash spirit of the girl who never cried, who believed anything was possible. The fearless female who slid down banisters, out-fished any boy, and swore a blue streak that could make the crustiest sailor blush.

The carefree sprite that ran through fields and climbed trees would inhabit Beaumaris, to mingle with the spirit of a little girl yet born, with new hopes, new dreams. And perhaps, with a bit of luck, her dreams would come true.

The sounds of children laughing and playing came to Sabrina on the wind. They called to her so strongly she could almost picture their smiling faces.

Mama, swing me!

But as the breeze subsided the voices died, as had her vision.

Tears coursed her cheeks, and she allowed herself one gut-wrenching sob of misery. With unfailing determination, Sabrina raked her sleeve across her face and heeled hard the flanks of the mighty hunter.

THE BUTLER who answered the door of the fashionable London residence early the next morning had not recognized her. He stared down his nose, barely masking his disgust. When Sabrina handed him her card, his eyes narrowed. He looked skeptical and ordered a footman to watch her.

If she were not so tired, she would have laughed. Instead, she yawned. It had been a long night, and the ride had passed with no fanfare. She had stayed on the verge, afraid that if she rode on the lane she would confront more highwaymen. Since she had already survived one robbery, she thought it best not to tempt fate any further.

"Brie?" Caroline appeared in the hall to the left. "Is that you?"

With a shivery sigh, Sabrina nodded. She tried to be strong, tried to remain complaisant. But in the end, she succumbed to her grief. Bursting into tears, she fell into Caroline's waiting arms.

"Tea, in the back parlor," Caroline said.

"At once, my lady."

Sabrina followed her dearest friend down the hall to a warm comfortable parlor. She had been there many times since Caroline married Trevor. Of course, those had been happy occasions.

Now, she was miserable as the reality of her situation dawned. She was a woman without a home, without a husband, and with a child on the way. On the thought, another deluge poured forth.

"Sit." Caroline pushed her into an overstuffed chair in a scene that was all too familiar. "Now, tell me what this is about. Your letter explained nothing. I gather things are not going smoothly between you and Everett?" Reclining on a daybed, Caroline settled her skirts. "And what on earth are you doing in fencing clothes? You know I cannot partake of the sport as long as I am increasing. Trevor would kill me. Well, he would wait until the child was born, and then he would kill me."

Sabrina wiped her face and yawned. Just as she was going to speak, a servant entered with a tray. She greedily eyed the squares of shortbread stacked neatly on a plate. As the maid exited, she reached forward, swiped a square, and stuffed it into her mouth.

As she poured two cups of tea, Caroline laughed. "Goodness, Brie, did you not eat breakfast?"

"I came straight here." She glanced at the door. "Is Trevor home?"

"No, he is down at the docks."

"What time will he be back?"

"Brie, what have you done?" Caroline selected a scone from the plate. "Are you in some sort of trouble?"

"I must hurry." Sabrina chewed her lip. "I do not want Everett to know where I have gone."

Preparing to sip her tea, Caroline lowered her cup. "I do not understand. Did he not journey to London with you?"

"I am alone."

Her brow a mass of furrows, Caroline returned her cup to the tray. "Sabrina, start from the beginning."

Her eyes had grown wider by the minute, but Caroline had not interrupted as Sabrina recounted her discovery of the divorce petition and the midnight ride to freedom. In an attempt to avoid any persuasion contrary to her plan, Sabrina explained she had left Everett and had no intention of returning to him.

"My marriage is over," Sabrina said with an air of finality.

"I do not believe it. He threw you out? No carriage? No money? No food?" Her anger obvious, Caroline stood. "The blackguard ought to be horsewhipped."

"No." Sabrina leapt from her chair and swayed. The room seemed to spin out of control, and she splayed her arms to balance herself. At once, her friend gave her support.

"Are you ill?" Caroline asked.

"No," Sabrina insisted. "I am just tired. It was a long journey by horseback."

"I can imagine." Caroline humphed. "The man should be shot."

Sabrina inhaled in an effort to calm her nerves and was overcome with nausea. Tea and shortbread rebelled in her belly. In the excitement, she had forgotten the morning malaise that assailed her every day without fail.

With a hand to her mouth, she spied a large decorative bowl, filled with fruit, on a side table. Quickly, she grasped the bowl, dumped the fruit on her chair, and disgorged the contents of her stomach into the dish.

Caroline held her until the shudders passed. Afterward, she wet a napkin and pressed it to Sabrina's forehead.

"Better?"

"Yes." With Caroline's assistance, she eased to the daybed.

"How far along are you?"

Sabrina feigned ignorance. "What do you mean?"

"Brie, I have spent too many mornings on the other side of that green face not to know what is going on. When are you due?"

"I am not sure." On a sigh, Sabrina accepted the fact that she had no suitable excuse for her condition. "I have never been pregnant before."

Caroline's eyes flared. "And he is still divorcing you?"

"I did not tell him." How she wished she had prepared for that discussion. For some reason, Sabrina had thought her childhood friend would help her without questioning her motives. In that moment, she revisited her heartbreak.

"He does not know?" Her shock was palpable as Caroline opened and then closed her mouth.

"I will not use this child to hold him to me. It is not fair to Everett, it is not fair to me, but more importantly, it is not fair to our child." And despite efforts to the contrary, Sabrina burst into tears.

"There, there, Brie." Caroline wet another napkin and pressed it to the nape of Sabrina's neck. Then Caroline held Sabrina, offering a shoulder on which to cry, without complaint. "What of your parents?"

"They are in the country." Again, she sobbed. Her failure compounded by the second, and she forced herself not to think of her family or their disappointment. She would have the rest of her life to atone for her epic founder. "I will tell them soon enough. Right now, I need some time to myself to ponder the situation. Surely nine months will provide ample opportunity."

"Sabrina, I cannot help but think you are making a grave mistake." Caroline patted Brie's back.

Sabrina sat upright and hiccuped. She stared at her hands and her white knuckles. "In my letter, I asked for your help."

"You will have whatever you require."

"I need a place to stay." Sabrina marveled that she had not choked on the statement.

"You are always welcome here," Caroline replied in monotone.

"Thank you, but that was not what I had in mind." She looked Caroline in the eye. "Do you and Trevor still have that cottage on the beach? The one in Sussex?"

"Yes, but it is very small, only two bedchambers." Caroline tapped a finger to her chin. "And there are no quarters for servants."

"It sounds perfect." She pressed forward, her goal in sight. "It will only be me, so I will not require servants."

Disbelief evident in her expression, Caroline held a hand to her throat. "But you cannot stay there alone—not with a baby coming."

"I will not be there that long. By the time the baby comes, I will probably be installed at my parent's estate in Kent." Where she would live out the remainder of her days.

Hands clasped in front of her, Caroline stood. She paced the floor, mumbling to herself. Occasionally, she checked off an imaginary list on her fingers. Sabrina was about to interrupt her silent deliberation when Caroline whirled about.

"Here is what we will do." Caroline set her jaw. "First, you are going to soak in a hot bath. Afterward, you shall have a light meal and some chamomile tea, which will settle your stomach. Then, you will nap in my bed."

"I cannot." Alert in an instant, Sabrina flinched. "I must be on my way. What if Trevor comes home and finds me here? He is a friend of my husband—I mean, my former husband."

"Rubbish." Caroline waved dismissively. "When I tell Trevor how Everett has treated you—"

"No, please do not," Sabrina cried. "It is not his fault. His mother was right, I never should have married him." She choked on a sob. "Promise me you will not say a word."

"Shh, I will not tell a soul." Caroline hugged Sabrina. "Now, as I was saying. While you rest, I will have our carriage packed with supplies to convey you to Sussex. I will also send a footman and a maid to see you comfortably situated. They will return tonight with the carriage, and Trevor shall be none the wiser."

"Thank you, for everything." A glimmer of hope for her future and that of her child flickered in her heart. Sabrina knew she had made the right decision.

"Cheer up, Brie." In an affectation as familiar as their friendship, Caroline chucked Sabrina's chin. "You are a survivor."

THE SUN WAS high in the sky when Sabrina departed London for Sussex. Tucked snug and warm in Caroline and Trevor's luxurious traveling carriage, gowned in one of Caroline's dresses, and her belly full and quiet, she sank into the squabs and stared out the window.

A black pall chilled her to the bone.

In the seat across from her, a maid sat, as the city passed in a blur. Every now and then, she glanced at Sabrina and smiled. Sabrina returned the gesture. Grateful for the company, she was certain she could fill a chalk stream with her tears were she alone.

In the peaceful solitude, her thoughts turned to Everett. She wondered at his reaction when he returned to find the divorce petition signed and her gone. Would he rejoice in her absence, be glad to be rid of her? Would he be angry? Would he be sad?

She hoped not.

Well, she would not mind if he were a bit sad. It would be nice to think he cared for her a little.

Beyond the windows, the buildings became fewer and fewer, signaling they departed London proper. And in her heart and mind, Sabrina closed the door on her brief marriage.

CHAPTER TWENTY-ONE

*H*is heart was light. It was as if the weight of the world had been lifted from his shoulders. Swaying softly with the movement of the carriage, Everett could not suppress a sigh of content as he passed through the main gates of his estate. The sun was low on the horizon, well below the yardarm. Gold light flickered between the thick trunks of the mighty oaks.

For the first time since his wedding, his properties were in order, demands on his time were few, and he was, at long last, becoming accustomed to his new title. The one thing he had yet to accomplish he would set right immediately upon his arrival home.

For good or ill, he would tell Sabrina he loved her.

It was time she knew it, time she accepted it. He shook his head and chuckled. He was going to lock her in his bedchamber and make love to her until she declared herself, in kind. With any luck, his bride would be stubborn, and he would be at her a sennight. He smiled at the prospect.

Being in love made him want to conquer the world, made him believe he could. If only to place the spoils at the feet of the woman who held his heart and hear her utter those three most precious words ever spoken.

I love you.

So simple a phrase, yet so powerful.

He understood now why the poets wrote in praise of it.

Why women lived for it. Why men killed for it.

Love was comforting and frightening at once.

Comforting because it could consume a man and make him forget everything else in the world.

Frightening because it could abandon the same man and deliver him to the gates of hell the following day.

In the forecourt, the carriage slowed to a halt. Everett stepped down, and gravel crunched beneath his booted feet. He skipped up the entrance stairs, and the doors swung wide to admit him.

Anticipation shimmered, lust roared through his veins and pooled in his loins. In a moment, he would be in his lady's arms. He scanned the foyer and glanced at the landing. He sought her thick locks, black as a crow's feather. His ears trained for the lively pitter-patter of her feet on the marble floor.

When he caught sight of his butler, Everett knew something was wrong.

Ware bowed. "Welcome home, my lord."

"What is it?" He stopped in the doorway and had not bothered to doff his hat or gloves. "What is wrong? Where is her ladyship?"

"Gone, sir." Ware's tone bespoke ire. "Her ladyship left a note in your bedchamber."

The words echoed in his ears.

Ware had to be mistaken. Shielded by denial, Everett charged the stairs and ran to Sabrina's quarters, with the butler in his wake. Upon realizing his wife's chambers were empty, he strode down the connecting hallway and entered his suite. Everett spied the envelope and crumpled sheet of parchment on his pillow the moment he burst through the door.

His hands shook as he digested her note.

Blast his miserable hide, she had discovered the petition in his desk while searching for the still room ledger. Why had he not burned the deuced thing? Sabrina thought she had done him a kindness. "You do not deserve to be burdened with me," he read aloud and snorted. "I damn well do deserve her. I earned her with every trounced toe!"

He scanned the written correspondence, scoured the page for clues to where she had gone. "I shall always look on our time together fondly." The weight of the world seemed to settle on his shoulders, and he sighed as his heart sank in his chest. "I count myself fortunate...to have had the opportunity...to know...t-true love." His voice cracked as pain welled in his throat and choked him.

Why had he not shared his love with her sooner? Why had he insisted on formulating a pledge more akin to a lethal rake seeking access to his favorite skirt? Why had he not recognized his wife's distress?

Instead, Everett had wrapped himself in a cold façade and kept Sabrina at a distance. He had ceased sharing his bed with her and had ended their evening walks, because he was terrified of enduring rejection. And in his ignorance, he had rejected her. Since Sabrina had accepted the petition without complaint, it was a safe wager she would not have believed him or his declaration.

Everett had to compose himself.

"Best wishes for your continued happiness?" he said sarcastically. "How the devil am I supposed to be happy without her?"

And then it hit him.

He read and reread the passage.

When reality sank in, he almost swooned.

Sabrina truly loved him.

Since he was a little boy, Everett had thought a title equated said emotion, that rank determined one's worthiness in regard to devotion. And no second son, however wealthy, however accomplished, could win such a prize.

What a fool he had been.

His wife had loved him from the first. She had seen in him the characteristics she deemed deserving of her heart and gifted him her most precious treasure. And as proof of her regard, she placed his needs before hers and signed a petition she mistakenly thought he sought. She had surrendered her place as his countess, if only to secure his happiness.

Everett was not a failure.

He had claimed the most priceless gem of all—Sabrina's love.

A feeling of acceptance, of overwhelming comfort and something he could not describe invested his body—and was quickly replaced with sheer panic. "*Bloody hell, she has left me!*"

"I beg your pardon, your lordship?"

Everett flinched. He forgot that Ware had accompanied him to his bedchamber.

"When did she leave?" Everett smacked a fist to a palm.

"Presumably, at night, my lord." The butler clasped his

hands, lowered his eyes, and raised his chin. "While the household was abed."

"How did she travel?" That made no sense, and he narrowed his stare. "I had the coach."

"By horse, sir," Ware replied dryly.

Everett hurled a slew of inventive curses on her imaginary head. "Are you telling me my wife journeyed to God knows where, alone, at night, on horseback?"

Ware remained unfazed. "It would seem so, my lord."

"When I find her, I swear I am going to put her over my knee and beat some sense into her. Of all the half-brained, ridiculous, careless—" He reminded himself of whom he spoke and cut short his tirade. What Sabrina had done was foolish, but with her, under such circumstances, foolishness was a given.

He could only wonder—no, not wonder, because he knew exactly how she must have felt upon discovering the petition.

Betrayed. Abandoned. Unwanted. Unloved.

And nothing could have been further from the truth.

Everett trembled with anger, not directed at her, but at himself. He had been so involved in managing his estates that he forgot to take care of the one thing without which he could not live.

Sabrina.

It was a grave mistake, one he would not repeat.

In his other hand, he clutched the petition. Her delicate signature mocked him. Emitting a primal growl, he stomped to the fireplace, wadded the legal document into a ball, and hurled it into the flames.

"I should have done that in the first place," he mumbled.

There would be no divorce.

How many times must he say that?

The *ton* was littered with men who wished for nothing more than to be rid of their wives. Yet there he was, truly happy with his chosen mate, and he was afforded endless opportunities to be free of her. Now she was gone, and he would not rest until he got her back. "Ware, have my horse saddled."

"But, my lord, it is after dark." The butler waned. "There could be highwaymen on the roads. It is dangerous."

Everett arched a brow. "If my wife did it, so too can I."

As his butler rushed to relay his orders, Everett walked to the washstand. After filling the basin with water, he set the ewer aside. Then he stood still and gazed, unseeing, into the water.

Where had Sabrina gone? Where would he look? Her letter gave him no hint of her whereabouts. It was obvious she had not expected him to search for her.

That could only happen to him.

Leaning forward, he plunged his hands into the cool water and splashed his face. The refreshing chill jarred his memory. He raised his head, stared at his reflection in the mirror, and smiled. Everett might not know where his errant wife had ended up, but he knew where to commence the hunt.

THE BUTLER who answered the door of the fashionable London residence appeared not to recognize him. The servant blinked several times, as if in shock. Had weary travelers landed on the steps of the townhouse every day? Everett glanced down and checked his attire. For a man who had ridden all night, he had not thought he looked half bad. He handed the butler his card and was shown to the drawing room.

"Everett?" Trevor strode forth, a hand outstretched, and they exchanged the customary pleasantries. "What brings you to London? I did not think you were coming in for the Little Season." His relaxed expression mutated to one of shock. "Good God, what the devil have you been about? I have seen better dragged in with the tide."

With a cluck of his tongue, Everett rocked on his heels. "I daresay you would appear the same had you spent last night in a saddle."

Trevor inclined his head. "What has happened?"

"I seem to have misplaced my wife." As his friend sputtered, Everett explained, "Sabrina left me."

"You cannot be serious." Trevor's brows nearly reached his hairline. After a moment of silence, he sighed and shook his head. "Commiserations. I gather you did not heed my advice. So what can I do?"

"Indeed, I have made a mess of my marriage, and I should have listened to you, but that is blood under the bridge, old friend." Bone-weary despair chilled him to the marrow. "Right now, I need to find my bride."

"You think I have knowledge to that effect?" Trevor shifted his weight. "Were I in possession of that information, you would have it, posthaste."

"It is evident she did not disclose her whereabouts to you." Everett folded his arms. "But I would wager Sabrina confided in Caroline, as the two are thick as thieves."

THEY LOOMED AT AN IMPASSE.

Amid the leather wall coverings and the faint smell of

cigar smoke, in the impressive, potently masculine study, Trevor and Everett, once known as two of the Royal Navy's most cunning seamen, stood on either side of a wing-backed chair. In said chair, Caroline sat, with her jaw set in firm defiance, hands fisted in her lap, pointedly ignoring them both.

"I do not believe it." Standing with legs spread and knees locked, Trevor gazed toward the heavens. "You did not tell me she was here? What else have you kept from me?"

"Do not take that tone with me, Trevor Reed Marshall." Her chin inched to dangerous heights. "I will not tolerate such behavior."

For some reason he could not begin to fathom, Everett had assumed his friend's wife would be happy to aid his cause. That when he showed up at her doorstep and made his intentions known, Caroline would burst into tears and confess the location of his most unlikely lady, thrilled at the aspect of furthering their reunion. Had all women not existed for such sappy endeavors?

He had been grossly in error.

And he now understood why Sabrina had chosen Caroline in which to confide. Strong, determined, she was every bit as willful as his wife. And his wife had not buckled under pressure, nor had she appreciated it.

"*Caroline!*" Trevor raked a hand through his hair and groaned. "Go to your room."

With a distinct air of supremacy, the young countess smirked. "It would be my pleasure."

"Wait." Desperate circumstances necessitated desperate measures. And right then, Everett was a desperate man. "A moment, please."

In a move he knew he would never hear the end of, but

would never regret, Everett knelt beside the chair. He reached for her hand, covered it with his own, and prayed in silence that he could sway her. He had one chance, and he knew if he failed, she would shut him out and end all possibility of finding his saucy Sabrina.

There was only one thing he could think of to melt her cold façade. It was something he should have told his wife but, if he could not, he would declare himself to her best friend and confidante.

"Caroline, I love Sabrina." He squeezed her fingers in emphasis. "Do you hear me? I love her."

In an instant, Caroline faced him. "Then why do you want a divorce?" It was an accusation, not a question.

Quelling the urge to shout from the rooftops, Everett growled. "I do not want a divorce—"

"But the petition—"

"—Was my mother's idea." He paused in anticipation of another interruption.

Instead, Caroline looked her query.

"I put the petition in a drawer in my desk, intending to destroy it," he explained. "But there was so much work to be done, and the demands on my time have been great. I forgot about it. And as for my mother, I daresay, hers now rivals my devotion to Sabrina. I do not want a divorce. Indeed, there will be no divorce. I burned the blasted paper before departing Beaumaris."

Caroline bowed her head but said nothing.

"Please, I beg you. Tell me where I may find my wife." Sensing he advanced some measure of success, he pressed his suit. "I know she suffers, but only because she does not know the truth. She has to know I did not abandon her. She has to know I love her. And she has to hear it from me."

"The woman who came to my door was a mere shadow

of the friend I once knew." With an icy stare, Caroline silenced him. "Sabrina was devastated."

"I can make her happy again." Her words struck a blow to his heart, and Everett swallowed hard. "Help me set it right."

"Help you?" She snorted. "I blame you. I hold you entirely responsible for what happened. You did not just make her sad, but you broke her spirit. You destroyed her joyous, carefree, beautiful spirit. Why did you not stand up for her with your mother?"

"I did." He compressed his lips. "And I tried to speak with her after the incident in the dining room, but she refused to see me."

"Oh, dear." Her expression softened. "I suppose she was too angry to think clearly."

In a gesture for which he would be eternally grateful, Everett was struck speechless when Trevor dropped to his knees before his wife.

"I love you, my sweet Caroline." Trevor framed her face with his hands. "If you recall, those words did not come easy for us either, dear one. In our courtship, I made mistakes, which almost cost me your precious life, and subsequently, my whole world. I shudder to think how difficult it would have been had I not been able to talk to you, had I not been able to tell you how I felt. We are none of us perfect, my cherished wife. Give Everett and Sabrina the same chance."

She pouted. "But I promised Brie."

"When she discovers Everett had no intention of divorcing her, she will thank you." Trevor leaned forward and kissed her. "Where is Sabrina?"

Caroline turned to Everett, and the tension in his shoulders abated. He knew that look. It was the same dreamy expression Sabrina wore whenever he managed to touch her without touching her.

She bit her lip and hesitated. It was a pleasantly familiar affectation his wife often mimicked, and he fought the urge to influence her further. Let her consider her next move. Just as he thought he had reached the end of his tether, she spoke.

"Sabrina is in Sussex, at our beach house, where she has food, supplies, and the comforts of home." She inhaled a shaky breath. "Your horse is in the mews. I had her driven to the cottage in our traveling coach."

Everett smiled, took her hand in his, and brought it to his lips. "Thank you." He stood.

"One more thing." Caroline halted him. "If you journey to Sussex, I insist you take the coach. Sabrina is exhausted, and I am concerned for her health. She is fragile, and Sabrina is the last person I would ever describe as such."

"I understand." Everett gulped. What had he done to his bride?

Trevor sent his butler to have the coach brought around and then walked Everett to the door. "My friend, I am more sorry than I can say for your present difficulties."

"It is of my own making, and I should be keelhauled for allowing this to happen." Everett shuddered. "My staff are en route to the city as we speak, and my equipage will be at your disposal until we return. If Sabrina is well enough, I intend to bring her to London tomorrow."

"Take your time." Trevor shook Everett's hand. "And tell her how you feel."

"I will, in no uncertain terms." And somehow the prospect no longer seemed daunting. "Wish me luck."

Grinning from ear to ear, Trevor chuckled. "You will not need it." He glanced over his shoulder, where his wife stood in the doorway of their home. "I daresay Caroline is the one who requires your luck. If she were not with child, I would heat her posterior. Damn willful woman."

"Rubbish." Everett stepped up, took a seat inside the Lockwood traveling coach, and smiled. "You would not have her any other way."

A brow arched, Trevor inclined his head. "Since when are you an expert on wives?"

"Since I married one just like her." He snorted. "By the by, if Caroline is anything like my wife, which we both know she is, you would do better giving her a good tumble."

Trevor waggled his brows. "Perhaps you are right." He closed the coach door and stepped back. "Safe journey." Sketching a mock salute, he shouted, "Drive on."

Everett rocked as the coach lurched forward. He dipped his hand into his waistcoat pocket, retrieved his timepiece, marked the moment, and re-pocketed it.

Settling back for the journey, he gazed outside. With a bit of good fortune, he would be in Sussex before sunset. That was the easy part.

Getting his wife back—he was not so sure about that.

In the quiet solitude of the coach, he let himself consider, for the first time, that Sabrina might not want to be his wife. She never aspired to the peerage and made it clear she did not fancy the title.

The idea that she might have welcomed the petition she inadvertently discovered had come to him during the dark, lonely ride to London. Worry and fear danced a merry jig over his heart. He shuddered to think it.

Closing his eyes, he inhaled a deep, calming breath.

What if he journeyed to Sussex only to be rejected?

Everett withdrew her letter from his breast pocket and unfolded the paper. The pain behind her words was evident as he read. No, his worry was unfounded. Immediately, he ceased the self-torment.

Sabrina loved him as he loved her.

He would tell her of his devotion and somehow secure her declaration.

He would get her back.

CHAPTER TWENTY-TWO

*T*he traffic on the roads had been mild, and they made good time. As a consequence, the sun had not yet touched the horizon when he arrived in Sussex.

Everett stared at the beachfront cottage and waited until the coach disappeared over the hill before entering the yard. He had sent the driver and footman to stay the night in a roadside inn they had passed a few miles back, with instructions to return late the following morning.

Made of grey stone, the small structure had a thatched roof and a door painted bright red. A white picket fence bordered the yard, and a cobblestone walkway led to the front door. At present, the yard was filled with chrysanthemums in fall colors.

He unlatched the gate and strolled to the entrance. When his knocks went unanswered, he tried the knob. To his surprise, the bolt was not secure, and he let himself inside.

"Sabrina, are you there?" Everett called out to her.

There was no response.

A quick survey found him in a large room. On the left was a makeshift kitchen with a fireplace and a small table. In front of him was a welcoming living area, with overstuffed, slightly worn furniture. Fluffy pillows engulfed a huge sofa. Thick rugs covered the wood floors. Small comforts hinted at a woman's touch, and a large bay window looked over the ocean.

It was a lover's hideaway, the perfect place for a weekend tryst.

Everett grinned. Trevor was a sly one. He imagined his friend had brought his wife there on many occasions. No doubt to escape her rather odd extended family—the same one that came with marriage to Sabrina.

He passed through a small doorway on the right and discovered two bedchambers. The first contained an old wooden rocking horse, a table, and a crib. Various toys filled a basket in the corner.

He stepped into the other room, which was considerably larger, and discovered a massive bed, sound and sturdy, which brought a smile to his face. At the foot of the bed was a nightgown and matching robe. He had the filmy silk gown in his hand, raising it to his face, before he knew he had moved. He inhaled, and Sabrina's scent wreathed him. Ensorcelled him.

His body reacted as it always had. Thousands of tiny fires ignited beneath his skin. Everett closed his eyes and held the soft fabric to his cheek.

At the sound of feminine giggles, he jolted alert.

Like the one in the great room, the window in the bedchamber offered a spectacular view of the ocean. On the beach he spied Sabrina.

Her raven hair flowed down her back in lustrous waves. Dressed in ivory muslin sprigged with tiny rose clusters, she frolicked on the sandy beach. Barefooted, she danced in the tide, kicking playfully in the water.

What struck him was she had not appeared sad, had not appeared heartbroken, or even lonely. He held his breath when she raised her face to the sun, a glorious smile on her lips. No, she was not dispirited, as Caroline had suggested. Nor was she melancholy as her letter had implied. She looked happy.

She looked like Sabrina, the woman with whom he had fallen in love.

Though Everett had not wanted to do it, he asked himself if he had a right to steal her from that simple existence? If she was truly satisfied with her life as it was then —without him—was he justified in insisting she return to him? An action that brought a title, social strictures she abhorred, and numerous responsibilities she had never agreed to assume when they married.

He stared at her nightgown, still in his grasp.

Because he loved her, he had to consider her best interests. He had to set aside every inclination of his own and put her needs first. And right then, at that very moment, she appeared happier on her own.

Everett sighed with resignation and shook his head. He lifted his chin and gazed once more at his wife. After several minutes passed, he swore violently, tossed her gown on the bed, and strode from the room.

SHE WAS FREE.

Sabrina hiked the skirt of her dress, the first one she wore in months that was not black, and romped in the sand. The minuscule granules, warm from the sun, sifted between her toes. As evening approached, the incoming tide crashed ever closer ashore. She chased the water toward the sea, and then retreated, giggling with unabashed cheer as it encroached once more.

She stopped on a dune and wrapped her arms about herself. Thrusting her chin in the air, she sighed as the sun's rays kissed her face. Everything had worked according to her plan. And after spending the previous night mulling her situation, she knew what she would do next.

If Trevor and Caroline allowed it, she would stay at the beach house until her divorce was final. She would send word to her parents that all was well and take full responsibility for the failure of her marriage.

She would write Everett and ask for a small house, a cottage not unlike the one she occupied at present, and retire there. Never again would she journey to London, because she could not bear the thought of seeing her former husband with his new wife.

His new wife.

On the thought, she shivered. Covering her face with her hands, Sabrina sank to the sand. She had not allowed herself to cry since she arrived at the beach house, because she feared she would not be able to stop. Since there was no one to hear her mourn, she opened the door to her heart and let grief flow like a rushing river. In seconds, she was overcome, drowning in sorrow and loss.

She tucked her legs close, wrapped her arms around her shins, and rested her forehead on her knees. Her body shook as she sobbed without restraint. Her agony seemed inconsolable. Just when she thought her misery at an end, another spate of tears overtook her, and she wiped her face on her sleeve.

"Darling, use my handkerchief, else you will spoil your lovely dress."

Sabrina gasped and then closed her eyes. "You are not here."

Everett stared at his wife and frowned when her entire form quavered. "Look at me, and you will see I most certainly am here."

"I am hearing things. I am just out of sorts." Though she raised her head, her eyes remained clamped shut. "It will pass." The last was said slowly, as if she tried to reassure herself.

He reached down and tapped her shoulder. "Sabrina, look at me."

She lifted her lids, and her tear spangled lashes glittered in the sunlight. "You are not here. I have imagined you." Scooting backward on her bottom, she inched away. "I have finally lost my mind."

"Stop saying that." He took two steps, bent, and hauled her into his arms.

"What do you want?" she asked between choking sobs, which made his heart ache.

With her arms braced against his chest, she squirmed, and he tightened his hold. "Stop pushing me away."

"How did you find me?" She continued to struggle. "What do you want?"

"Caroline told me—"

"Caroline?" She stilled. "She disclosed my confidence? This is about the baby, is it not? She insisted I tell you. You are here for your heir. You do not want me."

"Baby?" He blinked. "You are pregnant?"

It was her turn to blink. "You did not know?"

Eyes wide, mouth agape, Everett just stood there. Finally, he shut his mouth and gathered his wits. "We are having a baby?"

She winced. "I only just discovered it."

The tension investing his frame balled into a fierce mass in his belly and then rushed forth. "You rode on horseback, overnight—alone—through the country, endangering not only yourself, but also our child? Good God, woman, *are you mad!*"

"Yes, I am mad." With clenched fists, she pounded his chest. "I must have been insane when I married you!" She burst into tears and buried her face in his coat.

Everett stared at the heavens and prayed for patience. "Sabrina, what am I going to do with you?"

"You are divorcing me," she mumbled before sobbing in woeful gasps.

He groaned. "I am not divorcing you."

"But the petition—"

"—Was my mother's idea." Had he not already participated in that conversation?

She shifted in his arms, raised her head, and glared accusingly at him. "I found it in your desk."

"I put the bloody document there after a quarrel with my mother and forgot it," he explained.

His wife appeared skeptical. "Are you positive you were not having second thoughts?"

"Second thoughts?" He searched his mind and tried to make sense of her words. "What in the devil are you talking about?"

"You did not consummate our vows after our wedding." Sabrina fidgeted. "You waited."

Everett realized he had erred once again. For some

strange reason he had thought his wife would be glad to see him. He had imagined she would come at him with all the enthusiasm he recalled in more pleasant times.

"That was because I did not want to make love to you at Tantallon Hall," he expounded. "I hate that place. It has never been my home. And my brother had just died. I wanted us to begin our marriage on a happier note—in our house."

"Then why did you not tell me?" How he wished he had.

"Because the time never seemed to lend itself to the conversation." And he had been terrified of dismissal.

"It does not matter. Your mother is right. I am not good enough for you." Sabrina bit her lip. "You should divorce me. I signed the petition and promised not to fight you."

If he wanted his lady, it was time to make his stand. "You are wrong."

A tear slid down her cheek. "About what?"

"Everything." Spearing his fingers through her hair, Everett forced her to face him. "In light of recent events, my mother adores you. And in regard to a divorce, you have got it backward. If you want this marriage dissolved, you will have to divorce me, and I will not allow it."

"But—"

Everett silenced Sabrina the best way he knew how.

By kissing her.

He only meant to quell her protest but, as usual, got carried away. And neither had her appreciative hum helped the situation. So he ravished his wife right there on the beach. The better to show her how he felt.

How he felt...

He retreated from their kiss.

"What is it?" she asked in a small voice.

"There is something I need to tell you." He stiffened his back. "I should have said it long ago."

She skimmed his arms with her hands, which came to rest at the nape of his neck. "Yes?"

"I love you." It seemed as though ages had passed while he waited for a sign, some hint she might share his regard. "Sabrina Francis Douglas Markham, I am so in love with you."

"Oh, Everett." Sabrina burst into tears. "I do not know what is wrong with me. I swear I am not a water pot."

"I know, darling." He licked away her tears. "And I did not intend my declaration to make you cry."

She wailed louder.

Finally, Everett relented and hugged her close. "Must be the pregnancy."

"Oh, no." Sabrina struggled and withdrew. "This is wrong. I promised myself I would not do this, and you should not be here."

"Doing what?" He scratched his head. "We are married, and I belong at your side."

"You must go." A sorrowful river coursed her cheeks. "If you love me, then take another wife. Someone you can be proud of, a perfect chatelaine. A real lady."

His fears had come to fruition. "But—I love you."

"You will learn to love another." She sniffed.

"And what of our child?" He tightened his hold, as he would not surrender her without a fight. "I am its father. I have rights."

"You would take my baby?" Sabrina stood her ground.

"I want you and our child," Everett replied with absolute finality.

"Cannot you see, it will not work." She shuddered on a

sob. "I would only do something else to embarrass you. You must take another wife."

"You want me to choose another?" His ears rang with panic. "Truly?"

"Truly." And still she wept.

"You would condemn me to a life without love? Without happiness?" The world teetered perilously, a vortex of desolation and despair opened beneath his feet, and he shifted to keep from falling on his bum. "Do you care so little for me?"

"No." She held him at arm's length. "It is because I love you that I am doing this. You will be happier without me. You will love again."

Stripped of his defenses, Everett stared at the ground. "But how can I love again without my heart?"

"I do not understand." Sabrina choked on another sob.

"Do you not?" He grasped her wrists. "You are everything to me, Sabrina. You are my life, my only love. Long before I inherited the title, you wanted me for who I am. Was that a lie? Am I a fool?"

Faced with losing his anchor, the center of his universe, he searched in desperation for an argument to persuade her to stay. Pain seared a knot in his throat. Inside him, something shattered. A chill of dread shivered over his skin, his legs weakened, and Everett knelt in the sand as a broken man. With tears welling in his eyes, he gazed at his elusive bride. "I beg you, do not leave me, because the man you claim to love will cease to exist. If you care for me in the least, please, do not abandon me."

"Oh, Everett, I only left because I thought it was what you wanted." Sabrina dropped to her knees before him. "I do love you. And if you truly want me, I will be your wife." That time, his most unlikely lady cried not as a child, or a brash young debutante, but as the woman and countess she had become.

Relief cascaded through him, and he closed his arms about her. "Darling, I said I would have no other, and I meant it. Do not cry." When she trembled, he nuzzled her temple. "Sabrina, please, I can bear anything but your tears."

Recalling his earlier tactic, and subsequent success, Everett tipped her chin and set his lips to hers. And true to form, Sabrina softened, her sobs transformed into the moans of a well-pleasured woman. Were he unaware of her delicate condition, he would push her to the sand and take her on the beach. Because the sun danced on the horizon, the wind coming off the ocean was cool, and his wife shivered.

He slipped out of his coat and draped it over her shoulders. "Where are your slippers?"

"In the house." She clutched the lapels.

"You walked down here without—" He bit his tongue and reminded himself to whom he spoke. No doubt one day he would have to smile patiently as she explained she had forgotten where she put their child. "Never mind."

Settling on the sandy dune, he patted the space between his bent legs. With a somewhat shaky smile, his countess plopped down. In an instant, he turned her to the side and pulled her to his lap. Her knees draped over his thigh, and he rubbed her toes in an effort to warm them.

In mere seconds, she fell asleep in his embrace, and he recalled Caroline's warning in regard to Sabrina's health. For a while, he studied her features, sublime in repose, and he counted himself a most fortunate man, as his countess was the most beautiful creature of his existence. Every now and then, he gave her a gentle squeeze and kissed her.

When only a thread of glittering gold lit the sky, and twilight encroached, Sabrina started.

With nary a word, she touched his face. "You are here? I did not dream it?"

"I am here, darling." He chuckled. "And I may never let you out of my sight, again."

"Do you really love me?" She sniffed.

"Are you going to collapse in a fit of tears at my response?" Since Sabrina appeared to be holding her breath, and he feared for her and their babe, he said, "Yes, I love you. I believe I have loved you from when we first met. Though I was too young and randy to recognize it. Of course, I had no opportunity to explore the theory, seeing as how you disappeared. By the by, what happened to you then?"

"I recall no absence." With a finger pressed to her chin, she furrowed her brow. "As always, I retired to the country for the summer."

"That is not what I was referring to, *Miss Smyth*."

She winced and smacked his chest. "You knew."

Now he laughed, and it felt so good. "Of course."

She wrinkled her nose. "But—what gave me away?"

He snickered. "A waltz."

"A waltz?" Sabrina clucked her tongue and frowned. "Which one?"

"Does it matter?" He snorted. "My dear, on the dance floor, yours is a singular talent unmatched by any woman."

Now she pouted. "That is not a very nice thing to say."

"Perhaps, but it is true." Everett nipped her cute little nose. "Why did not you tell me your real name?"

"Because I set my cap for you that very night." She rested her head on his shoulder. "I had hoped I would improve with age. I am sorry I did not."

"What is this?" He nudged her. "Does my saucy Sabrina lack confidence?"

"Do not tease me." She hid her face in his coat. "I am an awful countess."

Would her self-doubt never cease?

"God, grant me patience." He tried to pull back, but she clung like a wet blanket. "Sabrina." He wedged a hand between them in an attempt to capture her chin, but she resisted. In light of her condition, Everett hated to be rough, but she left him no choice. Fisting his fingers in her hair, he brought her gaze to his. "Darling, you have succeeded as my countess beyond my highest expectations. You command the hearts of everyone with which you come in contact. You have my staff hanging on your every word, prepared to defend you at the slightest hint of trouble. They were ready to string me up from the nearest tree when they thought I sought a divorce. I do not dare go home alone. And that house was nothing more than mortar and stone until you arrived. But now, Beaumaris is a warm, loving environment to rear our children, to live out our years—together. And as for me, I cannot imagine my life without you. You are my only triumph." He grimaced. "As an earl, I fear I am not much an improvement on my brother."

"You cannot be serious." Sabrina framed his face. "You —a failure?"

"Not a failure, but certainly no smashing success." And it killed him to admit it.

"I do not believe it." With brows arched, she shook her head. "My fearless lord lacks confidence?"

She mocked him with his own words, and Everett compressed his lips. "You do not understand, I have the earldom to manage. It is new to me, and I am not doing very well."

"Balderdash." She slipped an arm about his shoulder. "You are a wonderful earl. Everyone says so, and I should know because I talk to everyone. The farmers think you generous and wise, their wives think you the most thoughtful lord. And as for the staff, they worship the ground beneath your feet."

For a moment, Everett stared at his wife. When the reality of their situation hit, he succumbed to gales of laughter. "Sabrina, we are a fine pair."

"Indeed, we are." The joy in her expression melted his heart.

Slowly. Determinedly. He kissed her.

And kept kissing her.

After a few breathless, desperately sweet minutes, he lifted his head. "Is it true? Do you really love me? Or do you say so because you think it will make me happy?"

"You cannot be serious. Would I have left you if I did not love you?" Sabrina nestled close. "My shameless lord, I love you so much it hurts."

Trevor had been right. Her declaration was a priceless treasure. "Surely that is a piece of logic I dare not question."

"What is to question? I love you. I thought you wanted a divorce, so I left you." She shrugged. "It makes perfect sense."

To wit, Everett could only sigh. "My dear, I submit that you and I, our marriage, our future, is a *fait accompli*. There is no use fighting or denying it."

"My lord, I have to agree." She traced the crest of his ear with her nose. "And I have decided I want enough children to fill the dining room at Beaumaris."

Everett choked. "Darling, that table seats twenty-two."

"Oh, I have faith in you." She giggled, and again he laughed.

For a while, they sat in silence, as the incoming surf swirled and foamed. To the east, night blanketed the earth, and the sky boasted rich indigo speckled with stars twinkling like countless diamonds.

Sabrina shuddered, and her teeth chattered.

"What the devil am I thinking?" Everett stood and carried her with him. "Let us get you to the house before you catch a chill."

Hand in hand, they turned toward the beach house.

"Are we journeying to London tonight?" She whisked a stray lock of hair from her face.

"No. The coach will come for us in the morning." He brought her knuckles to his lips. "But I believe I shall send them to the city with orders to return at week's end."

"Oh? There is not much to do here." Her countenance was one of innocence. "Will you not be bored?"

"I can think of something we can do—many times, in fact. Given that my countess desires such a large family, practice makes perfect." With wide eyes, Sabrina appeared shocked by his salacious inference, but he knew better and smiled. "So I intend to keep you quite busy, my beloved wife."

"My lord." She gasped, before bubbling with flirty giggles. "How scandalous you are, but that is one reason I love you." Clutching his hand, she dragged him over the dunes.

"Slow down." He planted his feet firm, stopping her flight. In a flash, he scooped her up and transported her along the gentle slope to the house, kissing her all the way. "God, it feels good to have you in my arms again," he murmured against her lips.

Juggling her in his embrace, Everett flipped the latch and swept her through the gate entrance. He repeated the maneuver with the front door and kicked it shut behind him. Nothing, not even a sudden attack by the entire French Army would coax him to surrender his wife.

A peaceful calm fell over the charming cottage, broken only by the keening gulls in the distance and the roar of waves crashing ashore. A gentle breeze rustled the tall grass.

Approximately thirty minutes later, a breathless "Holy Mother" and a lusty howl shattered the tranquil serenity.

And then there was laughter.

Joyous, heartfelt laughter.

EPILOGUE

"*E*verett, darling." Sabrina shook his shoulder. "Wake up."

"Hmm? What is wrong?" He rubbed his tired eyes. "What is it, sweet? Are you ill?"

They had retired late the previous night, because they hosted their first weekend house party as husband and wife. Earl and countess. Beaumaris was alive with boisterous mirth and the occasional mischievous prank. The Brethren of the Coast were in full attendance. And whenever the Brethren gathered, rollicking celebrations erupted.

"Ho-hum," she yawned and patted her hand to her mouth. She stretched long in his warm comfortable bed before sitting. Leaning forward, she kissed him. "I am fine, but we must not dally. Now, get up."

"Mmm, I am already up." He took her hand and drew it down to show her exactly what he meant.

"My lord, that feels lovely, but we have to go." She shimmied out of reach and leapt from the bed. "Hurry, and dress for a ride."

Everett rolled to his side and frowned. "We usually ride naked."

"Get out of that bed." Sabrina gathered the garments she had laid out the previous night. "And are you ever going to tell me what happened to the four-poster in my chambers? It quite startled Caroline when I showed her the blue gown you purchased for me."

"My dear, I already explained my position." Everett punched his pillow. "This is your bed. I want you with me. And in the event you forget your place, the empty spot in your suite shall serve as an excellent reminder."

"And what of our London accommodations?" She could not resist teasing her husband, even though his heavy-handed possessiveness thrilled her. "May I presume you have removed the furniture there, too?"

"You may." At last, he slid from the mattress. "A month ago, I hired a builder to tear down the wall between our chambers, and, henceforth, we shall share a larger space."

"Will you not grow weary of me?" She cast him a pout that never failed to rouse him, as she stepped into her wool riding habit. "Women require a vast deal more than men, just think of my toilette."

"But I consider your bath a treat not to be missed, love. And I warned you in November, after your midnight ride to freedom, that I wished never to be parted from you again." He rubbed the small of his back and grimaced. "My arse still smarts from my pursuit."

"Should I soothe it with a kiss?" She presented herself, so that he could tie her laces. "I am yours to command."

"Darling, I will oblige you wherever you wish, but we do not need clothes to—" She smacked him with a pair of buckskin breeches.

"Hurry, we do not want to be late," she said over her shoulder.

"Late for what?" He snorted. "It is still dark."

Ten minutes later, they strode into the stable.

"Should you be riding in your condition?" Everett lifted her to the saddle.

"Caroline says it is all right, but in a few month's time, it is ill-advised." Sabrina drew rein. "And I do love you for caring."

"Of course, I care. And I love you, too. Are you cold, dearest?" He mounted his horse and nudged him to a canter. "I can fetch you a heavier wrap."

"I am quite comfortable, my lord." With a smile, she heeled hard and set a blazing pace, leaving him in her wake.

They rode through the meadow, toward the north fields. Sabrina knew exactly where she led her husband.

High on a hill, eleven cloaked figures stood, wrapped ethereally in the mist. Behind, the sun embarked on its usual journey, bathing them in gold brilliance.

When Everett caught sight of the mysterious silhouettes, he shot her a quizzical glance.

Sabrina winked and urged her mount faster.

The Brethren of the Coast were not only her friends, but also they were her family.

Long ago, on a moonlit night, they had taken an oath.

Promised their love, honor, and devotion.

In the distance, they waited to vow the same to their newest brother—her husband. Happiness filled her heart, lit her soul. Mentally, she replayed the words in her head. It was an ancient covenant first pledged by warriors long dead but not forgotten. Their spirit, their honor survived. It beat in the heart of every Nautionnier Knight.

For love and comradeship we live.

And how they lived.

~~~~~~~~~~~~~~~~~

If you would like to read the story of Admiral Mark and Lady Amanda Douglas, download *Loving Lieutenant Douglas* for free at all major book retailers.

ABOUT BARBARA DEVLIN

A proud Latina, USA Today bestselling author Barbara Devlin was born a storyteller, but it was a weeklong vacation to Bethany Beach, Delaware that forever changed her life. The little house her parents rented had a collection of books by Kathleen Woodiwiss, which exposed Barbara to the world of romance, and *Shanna* remains a personal favorite.

Barbara writes heartfelt historical romances that feature not so perfect heroes who may know how to seduce a woman but know nothing of marriage. And she prefers feisty but smart heroines who sometimes save the hero before they find their happily ever after.

Barbara is a disabled-in-the-line-of-duty retired police officer, and she earned an MA in English and continued a course of study for a Doctorate in Literature and Rhetoric. She happily considered herself an exceedingly eccentric English professor, until success in Indie publishing lured her into writing, full-time, featuring her fictional knighthood, the Brethren of the Coast.

Connect with Barbara Devlin at BarbaraDevlin.com, where you can sign up for her newsletter, The Knightly News.

ALSO BY BARBARA DEVLIN

The Iron Corsair

The Buccaneer

The Stablemaster's Daughter

The Marooner

Once Upon a Christmas Knight

The Reaper

WORLD OF DE WOLFE PACK

Lone Wolfe

The Big Bad De Wolfe

Tall, Dark & De Wolfe

MAGICK TRILOGY

Magick, Straight Up

A Taste of Magick

Magick in the Air

PIRATES OF BRITANNIA

The Blood Reaver

THE MAD MATCHMAKING MEN OF WATERLOO

The Accidental Duke

The Accidental Groom